Sam Binnie has written for the *Guardian, Vice* magazine, and Google's Creative Lab, among others, and was the 2005 winner of the Harper's/Orange Prize Short Story Competition. *The Kindness Project* is her fourth novel.

The Kindness Project

The right of Sam Binnie to be identified as the Author of
the Work has been asserted by her in accordance with the
Copyright, Designs and Patents Act 1988.

First published in Great Britain in 2021 by
HEADLINE REVIEW
an imprint of HEADLINE PUBLISHING GROUP

1

Cataloguing in Publication Data is available from the British Library

ISBN 978 1 4722 7015 3

Typeset in 12.5/14.75 pt Adobe Garamond by Jouve (UK), Milton Keynes

Printed and bound in Great Britain by Clays Ltd, Elcograf S.p.A.

HEADLINE PUBLISHING GROUP
An Hachette UK Company
Carmelite House
50 Victoria Embankment
London EC4 0DZ

www.headline.co.uk
www.hachette.co.uk

The Kindness Project

Sam Binnie

H

REVIEW

For the river women
and
For JEM – witty, wise and welcoming
Legal carer organises warmth? No lie. (6-2-3)

Prologue

She sits at the kitchen table, a table worn smooth with years of teacups and plates of biscuits, balls of wool, tears and paint and linseed oil and birthday cakes.

Her pen is poised over the note-paper, but she takes a moment to put the pen down and flex her fingers — writing for even this long has made her hands tired — before taking it up again and finishing her note.

She pauses for a moment, looking at what she has written, then signs off,

Forever, always, and above all,

Your mother
x x x

She folds up the paper, slides it into an envelope, addresses it and adds it to the small pile. Small, but more there than she'd dared hope, and she looks at them with a smile. It's time now, she thinks.

Chapter One

The sky has got bigger on this journey, Alice thought to herself with purposeful calm.

From the muddy skies of Cambridge in the last days of April, all cranes and yellow spires and corners of grey light, the train had carried her away from office blocks and reading schedules and into huge, blooming landscapes of hills and clouds.

'Next stop, Polperran,' called the guard at the end of the carriage. 'Polperran, laaast stop.'

I didn't even know they still had guards, she thought again, in the same rigidly bright internal voice. Anything to keep herself distracted on the journey.

It was one Alice had taken every year through her childhood and twenties, bagging up her books and clothes to travel down to Bea on her annual visit to the tiny fishing village. She had never consciously intended it to be only once a year; as a child, other friends spent summers in Cornwall with their parents and siblings, revelling in the sun and sea air, and as an adult Alice knew her colleagues would love the idea of a coastal bolt-hole, but of course that bolt-hole was owned by Alice's mother, and between one thing and another through her thirties the trips had become further and further apart, more than a year, eighteen months, the gap growing each time, and the phone calls had become more sporadic, shorter, with Alice always snipping short each call, massaging her temples and thinking afterwards, *Next week, I'll speak to her properly next week*. But next week never came, then it had been almost seven years since Alice had last visited Bea in Polperran.

Bea had been the most beautiful person little Alice had ever seen. She sported bright, wild clothes and occasional dashes of blue-green eyeliner, and sometimes when Alice brought a friend home Bea would have made a huge multi-coloured jelly just because it was a Tuesday. She let Alice wear whatever she wanted to birthday parties, offering her feathered hats and silk scarves and nail polishes and pixie boots with socks stuffed in the toes to fit her. Alice had always just worn her own clothes, though, uncomfortable in her mother's rainbow outfits. But it had always felt so exciting to go into Bea's wardrobe and press her face into the clothes, feeling their satins and soft wools on her skin and smelling her mother's paint and perfume soaked into it all.

Her father, Maurice, was more like the other fathers she knew – maybe even less visible than them, if that was possible – but when Bea seemed cross with him, for being too quiet, being too like those other dads, for talking too softly or always choosing the same thing from the same takeaway place, Alice hadn't worried: she knew that they loved each other, because Bea had always told Alice how much she loved her, and how much she loved their small family. Alice hadn't worried even when Bea got angry more often, and then stopped getting angry, and just became quiet, even quieter than Maurice, because Bea had always promised Alice that everything would be OK. Looking

4

back, those years seemed so perfect, though Alice knew that was impossible.

Now, on the train, on proper leave from her grown-up perfect life (perfect little house inherited from Maurice, perfect job in the History Department, perfect control over what she ate, where she went, who she saw, no messy spontancity, no time for this trip), leave taken properly from Morag, her Head of Faculty, so she shouldn't need to worry about what she was missing or who would be teaching her classes. In fact, after Alice's last seminar – her final seminar? – Morag had taken Alice to her big Head of Faculty office, windows glinting with sharpened spring light, and they had talked, in a way, about the letter Alice had received. Morag said, 'Do you want to go?' and Alice hadn't been sure how to take it, not really, wasn't sure of anything right at that moment. But Morag was her friend and said to her more gently, 'Do you want to go down to Cornwall, get all this –' she swirled her hand around, looking at Alice as she did so ' – sorted out?' Alice had felt slightly better then, for a moment, and Morag had said a few others things to her in her reassuring, capable tone. After that, she had all but pushed Alice out of the door, saying, 'Take your book, work on your book, don't rush back.'

Alice looked down at her 'book'. Its latest incarnation was three notebooks and a two-inch-thick pile of papers, printouts from all the various iterations Alice had produced of *Scapegoats and Buboes: the Growth of Persecution during the Black Death*. She had been drawn to the Black Death as her topic after reading about the side-effects of such a massive plague, how something so deadly had changed the very fabric of society. Like all historians, she loved to feel she was discovering something hidden, some part of human nature that no one else had ever noticed before from the privileged position of surviving it all. She had understood even at school, when history was still mostly taught as if it was a tight, straight line joining one event to another, that history was not just three-dimensional but worked in four, five, infinite dimensions, of time and money, biology, chemistry, lust, trees grown to make ships, and the eye of a king on a girl, a tinder-spark at a meeting, death and travel and love and luck. As she grew to understand this more she wanted to find something new not for the glory – glory in historian circles was bloody and viciously won – but to feel that she was treading upon un-ruined ground, unspoilt by other historians ploughing it up to inspect it better, or putting modern clothes on old bodies so they'd look empathetic and sexy to students and colleagues. The Black Death was hardly un-studied, but Alice felt there was still something worth uncovering in the persecutions that had taken place across the whole of Europe; what protections those pointing their fingers felt the accusations gave them; what consequences there were for those pointing. But Alice knew that the idea of this book becoming anything other than a distraction was almost laughable. Not that she felt like laughing these days.

Alice looked down at the letter tucked into the top of her bag, and unfolded it again. It still said the same thing.

Dear Ms Kimbrel,

I am writing from the firm Blandford & Sons in Polperran, Cornwall, to pass on my most sincere condolences on the death

of your mother, Beatrice Kimbrel. More than a client, she
was a friend for many years and we all will mourn her loss.

As her legal representatives, we have details of the legacy to
be passed on to you, her sole heir. There are some details
around Mrs Kimbrel's will which merit a little discussion; if
you would be able to attend my office at your earliest possible
convenience, I can more fully explain your mother's legal
wishes.

Might I suggest for your ease staying in your mother's house
while you are down here? Any travel costs will of course be
paid from Mrs Kimbrel's estate.

With warmest regards,
Peter Blandford

Alice hadn't even known her mother was ill when she received the letter. During a phone call with Mr Blandford, it emerged that Bea had discovered her cancer three months before, had learnt it was incurable, widespread and swiftly growing, and had chosen not to pass word on to her daughter.

Alice was so shocked by the letter and the subsequent phone call she'd made – stunned and guilt-ridden and lost – that her last seminar had suffered, somewhat. And afterwards, Alice had called Mr Blandford and told him she would be down the day after next.

She had tried not to think about her mother, dying alone in that house. All the years her mother had had no one, because Alice was too busy to visit and Maurice had almost nothing to do with Bea, once Alice was old enough to manage the trips without his intervention. By that time, when she had stopped wearing headphones for her rare visits, there was so much silence between her and Bea, and the habit of not going out while she was there had gone on for so long that Alice didn't know if she could leave the house even if Bea had suggested it, which she had long since stopped doing. Alice was used to sitting in the cottage with her homework and then her college work, counting down the minutes and hours until the visit was over, and she could forget about it all until the next time. On one visit, Bea had said to her, 'You know, you can bring anyone here with you. Anyone . . . special you might want?' and Alice had looked at her with the blank face she didn't have to practise any more and Bea had never mentioned it again.

Whenever Alice visited Bea, it was clear that the cottage in Polperran was Bea's true home. Alice wondered how many people found their true home: both a building and its contents, perfectly matched to who they were. Even the light seemed to suit Bea. The blue Cornwall glow Alice watched from her window spoke somehow to her of Bea's silk scarves and capable hands, even though she never saw the paintings that Bea worked on in her studio at the back of the house, hiding as she did each visit in her attic room, from both the paintings and from Bea.

How many people matched their homes so closely? Alice thought of the Cambridge flats in which she had lived, all similarly neat and functional. Their small gestures at decorative notion (an art print, a cushion, new curtains) always made Alice feel that she was living in a catalogue, not the world that was in her own head; even in Maurice's house, when it became hers. Instead, it had been Bea's gift to make the world in her own head appear around her.

And then Bea had died alone and all Alice had now was a pile of notes on the societal side-effects of the Black Death and an empty house to empty even further. She felt something rising in her chest, steel-cold and suffocating. Something worse than grief, something tiresomely familiar. Alice closed her eyes, breathing in through her nose, out through her mouth. *Slow and even. Ignore the panic. Slow and even.*

'End of the line,' called the guard. *'Everybody off.* End of the line!'

Alice opened her eyes, took one more slow, practised breath, slowly flexed and curled her fingers, mindfully packed up her letter, notes and luggage, and stepped off the train into Polperran.

The station platform led directly on to the road, where two dusty-looking taxis sat in the late spring sun, their drivers sitting with the windows down and their radios up. The driver of the first taxi was fanning herself, head tilted back on the headrest, mouthing silently along to a tinny Madonna song as Alice approached. Only when Alice was actually blocking the sun did she look up, squinting at Alice's dazzling silhouette.

''Ello love! Wanting a lift? 'Op in the back, you can tell me where you want to go dreckly we've got a breeze goin'.'

Alice opened the back door and hefted her luggage onto the seat, then slid in beside it and piled her papers and handbag onto her lap. The driver looked confused for a moment, turned around to look at her, then said, 'Oh, all right. There we go, then,' turned back and started the car, pulling out into the lane before Alice could give directions.

After a moment or two when Alice told herself to enjoy the scenery – sweeping fields and wind-bent trees, distant pastel houses and coves with white-flecked waves – and tried not to think about how she must look after her journey, she leant forwards and shouted over the radio the driver had turned up, 'Do you know where Blandford & Sons are? The solicitors? Or you can just drop me in the high street and I'll find it.'

Alice felt herself being scrutinised in the rear-view mirror, but busied herself pretending to look for the address. After several moments of further examination, the driver spoke again. 'Yup, I know it. I'll take you all the way there.' Somehow the goodwill from her pickup at the station had drained away, but Alice couldn't understand where or why. They sat in silence until they drew up at a black and white, beam-fronted building that looked older than much of the rest of the street.

'Thank you,' Alice said to the driver, as she hauled her bags from the car and handed over a ten-pound note, hovering uncertainly by the driver's door as she waited to see whether there'd be any change. The driver held the note up to the light, nodded again, revved the engine and sped down the street, leaving Alice even dustier than before.

Looking at her watch self-consciously, knowing half of Polperran must be watching her through their curtains now, Alice saw she had nearly an hour until her meeting with Mr Blandford. She glanced around the high street and felt the foolishness of never having got to know the village before. Even as a sullen child, why hadn't she been dragged out by Bea for a single ice cream on her visits? She noticed a café opposite, looking as tired as she felt, and headed across.

Opening the door and stepping into the gloom, she saw battered tables and old, odd chairs spread about. The sole staff member, a stocky woman in her fifties wearing a bobbled yellow cardigan that had seen better days, was sitting on a tall stool behind the counter, auburn hair pinned up with a clothes peg. She was engrossed in a book.

'Hello?' Alice said eventually.

The older woman slowly held up one forefinger and began to stand, still reading her book. After almost a minute, when she was fully upright, she raised her head, and looked distantly over Alice's shoulder. Then her eyes came into focus, and she gave a small jump.

'Hello?' Alice said again, wondering how soon she could get the train home.

The woman squinted more closely at her, then let her shoulders drop.

'Oh, I *am* sorry, I just . . . Sorry, love.' She sighed and shook her head, then smiled at Alice warmly. 'Can I get you anything to eat?'

Alice looked around at the bare walls, the counter empty of any menu. 'What have you got?'

The café owner looked puzzled. 'We're a café, love. Tea, coffee, sandwiches, cake. You know. The usual.'

Alice felt like crying. She tried to think of what she'd had for lunch yesterday. 'Um. Tea? And a sandwich?'

'Right you are,' the woman said, scribbling on her pad without hesitation. 'Take a seat, love.'

Thrown that she wasn't asked for any further details about her order, Alice dragged her things to the table nearest the window. She lost herself in watching the street outside. A slender, nervous-looking woman scuttled past, peeking out through the fringe of her bright-ginger hair as if for wild animals; an elderly grey-haired man hurrying by, bow-legged, scowling at passing cars; a mother with thick, bowl-cut hair dragged two young children along the street behind her, dark circles under her eyes.

An arm reached across her view, the yellow cardigan pulled up to the elbow, and when Alice looked down her table was filled with a tray containing an enormous, buttery sandwich, crispy bacon poking out of each side with creamy avocado chunks, a huge blue teapot, silver milk jug, fine white china cup and saucer, and a small bowl of orange-blush apricots on the side.

Alice blinked, first at the woman, then at the feast before her. 'Thank you!' She remembered that she had eaten nothing but a stale, cold station pasty since her early morning start.

The café owner smiled at her. 'S'all right, my love! Thought you might need a bit of a feed if you've been travelling,' she said, nodding down at the luggage. 'Come for a holiday?'

Alice touched her finger to the top of the sandwich, focusing on the bounce of the bread and the scent of the tea. 'Not exactly.' She pointed briefly to the old timbered building opposite. 'Just visiting the solicitor over there.' She couldn't resist any longer, and took a sizeable bite of bread, bacon and avocado. She closed her eyes as she chewed.

'Good, isn't it?' the owner asked. 'My son's chutney. Apples from my own garden, that is, but he makes it. The apricots, though, they're grown by him. Glad you're enjoying it.' She walked back behind the counter, and sat back

12

on the stool with her book, while Alice made short work of the sandwich and stared out of the window again.

A plate with a square of cake appeared on the table, as the sandwich plate was whisked away. Alice looked up again.

'Hevva cake. You'll be needing that too if you've got business over there, I imagine.' She gave Alice one more smile and returned once again to her book behind the counter.

With a sandwich inside her, plus two cups of tea and most of the cake, Alice started to look at the café more closely. It was even more tired-looking than at first glance. Every table had scratched tops and wonky legs; there were cracked chair backs or padding puffed out of every seat; drooping window-nets hung sadly each side of the window. Nothing on the walls, either – who knew what the colour had once been, but now it was simply murk. On the other hand, the view on to the street was ideal for watching the world go by, and the food was excellent. She would perhaps come here again if she had time, despite its air of being forgotten by the world.

Pulling the letter from her bag for the hundredth time, Alice looked at the words without reading them. Now she was here, in her mother's village, to hear her will, she felt even worse. Had her mother even been in this café? Ordered a pot of tea, had a slice of Hevva cake? Alice didn't know anything about her life. Every time she'd visited Bea she had only ever gone straight from the station to Bea's house, stayed there for the requisite few days, then travelled straight to the station in time for her train, seeing no one, and seeing no one talk to Bea. Alice looked at the café worker, disappearing into the kitchen again. She wondered how the woman would react if she shouted, 'My mother just died! And I don't know what to do!' But Alice had never – *hardly ever*, she thought nauseously – shouted anything in her life, and she wasn't about to start here. Particularly when her impulsive sentences were so ludicrously woolly. And particularly when her sandwich had been so good.

As she turned to go, she noticed someone was now sitting at the corner table, furthest from the window, the nearest table to the till. It was the slim copper-haired woman Alice had seen from the window; she seemed to be about Alice's age, but it was hard to tell as she had so much hair hanging down and covering her face, not just her fringe. She must have slipped in while Alice was eating. She said something, but so quietly that Alice couldn't hear what it was, or even if it was directed at her. She looked around the café, and seeing no one else there, said, 'Sorry?'

The woman stayed sitting but tilted her face up slightly, her green-blue eyes mildly concerned. 'Are you all right?'

Instinctively, Alice reached up and touched her face – it felt fine. No tears. 'Yes? Fine, thanks.'

The woman looked at her again. 'Are you here for a holiday?'

'No, actually,' Alice said. 'To hear my mother's will.' She astonished herself, telling the unknown woman that, but the woman just nodded.

'I'd say I'm sorry, but people just assume, don't they, that when someone dies it's bad.' She shrugged, and softly brushed her hair out of her face. 'I don't know how you're feeling about it.' She stood up, and drew closer to Alice.

'Sometimes, when people die, at first it's mostly just a bit . . . *crap*.' She smiled gently at her, her face softening. 'I hope things get better for you.'

Alice didn't know what to say to this. But she suddenly saw the clock on the wall, checked the time on her watch with a gasp, and leaving money on the till, hurried across to Blandford & Sons. As she stepped off the kerb, the strap of her bag snapped and sent it tumbling into the road, but she was walking so fast that she'd taken a further step or two before her brain realised what had happened. As she bent down to pick it up, there was a scream of brakes fol-lowed by a deafening horn blast – a car had stopped only a foot from her crouching body, but it reversed and sped around her and away. She heard a voice calling from the rapidly disappearing window, 'What the *hell* are you doing?'

By the time she arrived at the door of Blandford & Sons, she was too busy shaking to wonder at how the speeding driver had echoed her thoughts precisely.

Chapter Two

Peter Blandford was a bittersweet reminder of her father, and his presence calmed her. He had the same musty, academic air, as if he lived off nibbles of paperwork and Garibaldis and cups of cold tea. But he also had her father's kind eyes, and if that hadn't reassured her that she wasn't about to be exploited by some shark-eyed legal embezzler, his untameable nose hair and the biscuit crumbs dusting his tie finished the job.

'Ms Kimbrel! A delight in such a time of sadness,' he pronounced, with a voice of warm solemnity, shaking her hand and leading her to the chair in his office, before sitting down behind his huge dark desk. 'Alice Lowena Kimbrel. That's right, isn't it? And my goodness, you really are the picture of her, aren't you?'

'Oh, er – thank you?' she replied. 'I don't know how long you were my mother's solicitor, but I appreciate you getting in touch so . . . promptly.'

He looked shocked. 'Ms Kimbrel! I may reassure you that your mother was a great deal more to us here than simply a client. She has – excuse me.' He paused. 'She *had* been with us for more than twenty years, and she had become a good friend to all of us.'

A good friend and steady money, Alice thought, cynically.

'Mr Blandford, you said in your letter that I needed to come here to discuss things.'

'Ah yes,' he said, shadows appearing beneath his eyes. 'The letter I wrote you – it would never have been my intention for you to have found out about your mother's passing that way, Ms Kimbrel. We had never had a cross word between us, but I argued quite forcefully to Bea – to your mother – that it wasn't the right thing to do. But she had made her decision, and I do believe that she thought she was doing the right thing for you.'

Alice watched him shuffling his papers with shame, and gave a soft, neutral cough. 'Mr Blandford, may I ask if the will is complicated? Do I need to take care of anything other than getting her house on the market?' She saw his face looking shocked once more. 'I'm sorry if this seems . . . impatient of me. I'm not after her money, I don't even know if she had any – but this distraction . . . I mean, I work, and my college has given me just a little time off –'

'Ah yes!' he said, clearly back on more cheering territory. 'Wickham College, isn't it?' It was Alice's turn to look surprised, which made Blandford smile. 'Your mother talked about you a great deal, you know. Her daughter, at Cambridge! In fact, we've all read your doctoral dissertation, from all those years ago. She made enough copies for everyone. "*Was the Black Death a Good Thing for Europe?*", yes?' He chortled again. 'Got quite the debate raging in the outer office, I can tell you!'

Alice felt her mouth dropping open, unable to find a reply. She'd sent her mother a copy of her dissertation, at her father's suggestion, but she'd imagined her mother had simply filed it away with Alice's photocopied school reports.

The thought of Bea having it copied, and encouraging people to read it? Alice's brow creased.

Blandford spoke again, more gently. 'As I said, Ms Kimbrel, your mother was very much a part of our lives here. We were very fond of her. We'll do everything we can to help you with her instructions.' He tapped a file on his desk.

'Instructions? So it *is* complicated?' Alice felt her stomach sink a little. She had hoped she could be done and dusted here within a few days: hire a house-clearing company, sign what she needed to sign, and be back at Wickham in her little house and her office in time for next week's lectures. She *would* be ready to get back to lectures, she told herself.

'Ms Kimbrel –'

'Alice, please.'

Blandford smiled, and indicated himself. 'And Peter. Please. Alice, your mother was an ambitious woman.' He noted her wry smile. 'And I mean that in the best of ways.' He straightened his papers. 'Many people, when they move somewhere like this from . . . anywhere else – they tend to have a strong *holiday* spirit. The houses are for summer breaks, the shops are for buckets and spades, the pavements are for them and their families. Local people are a backdrop to their wonderful photos. That kind of thing. Some people learn gradually that if they are living here, that doesn't really work. Some people never learn at all.' He sighed. 'Forty-five years ago I was fortunate enough after only a few months here to meet the woman who would become my wife, and I swiftly understood that I was lucky enough to have found my home and I should make awfully sure that I was welcome in Polperran. Your mother –' He stopped for a moment, and cleared his throat. 'Your mother seemed to arrive already knowing that she wanted to stay here for the rest of her life, and she would do anything she could to show her gratitude. She quickly learnt everyone's names, joined all the clubs, visited those who needed visitors, became very good friends with my wife, for the short time –' He broke off again, his voice disappearing.

'Mr Blandford?'

He coughed, drew a handkerchief from his pocket, and dabbed at his eyes. 'Please, *Peter*. I'm sorry, my dear.' He folded up the handkerchief and looked down at it, stroking its pattern. 'When my wife was dying, it was your mother who visited every day. She organised the rota of meals brought to us, ensured our sons were kept up to date with everything. She would sit for hours reading to Margaret.' He smiled at Alice, his eyes still wet. 'She was immensely kind to all of us.'

Alice swallowed. 'I'm glad,' she said. 'I didn't know if she had anyone down here.'

Peter gave a short bark of laughter. 'Had anyone!' He seemed immensely tickled at this. 'My dear! Oh, my dear!' He chuckled again, unable to contain his amusement. Alice wasn't used to these storm-and-sun emotions – her father had barely displayed more than a short chuckle at *Monty Python* on the television, and even his own mother's death had prompted little more from him than a long evening spent silently watching the fire in their hearth. Peter reached into the drawer beside him, took out a small bunch of keys and reached across the desk to press them into Alice's hand. 'My dear Alice. The keys to your mother's house. Besides a few odds and ends, the items inside the house, and a little money of which you are also the lone beneficiary – the details are in the file here – it is the sole piece of her estate.'

Alice took the keys and the plain brown folder, comparing the dull gold and shiny silver of the keys, old and new.

'But I mentioned your mother's ambition. By the time of Beatrice's death, she was someone at the heart of our village. She had become something of an "agony aunt", as we would say in my day, and she had quite a knack for helping people out. Sometimes,' he coughed politely, 'even when they didn't quite know what help they needed.'

Alice stared at him for a moment. 'Do you mean my mother was a busybody?'

'Oh no, goodness me, no, not at all. A busybody! No no no, not at all, nothing like that.' He smoothed his hair down, which had become ruffled in his agitation. 'No no. People would come to her. People from all over the village, of all ages. As I say, she just . . . had a knack. People liked to talk to her. And whatever their problem, no matter how small or large, she would *listen* to them. Often that's all they wanted – much of the human race, my dear, just wants a listening ear occasionally, don't you find? But *sometimes* they actually wanted to change something, and your mother had a most remarkable talent for recognising what it is they wanted – or should I say needed – and helping them work out how to achieve it.'

'So not a busybody, but a fairy godmother,' Alice said.

Peter chuckled again. 'I suspect you're having some fun with me, Alice, but she helped a lot of people. She was incredibly well-loved around Polperran.' He smiled fondly at her. 'And however long you're here, I'm sure you will be too.'

'Oh no, thank you, er – Peter, I'm just here to sort out anything that needs . . . tying up. And then I have to get back.' She smiled back at him tightly, feeling a wave coming, her pulse rising, hoping this would soon be over, trying to ignore her sweating palms, her speeding heart. 'I *need* to get back. *Soon.*'

'I see. Well. Let's get to business then. The other legacy your mother left you.' He opened the file on his desk, checked something in it, then started rummaging in his desk drawer again.

'But I thought the house was the only piece of her estate?'

After a moment, he pulled an envelope triumphantly from the drawer and placed it on top of the file in the centre of his desk. 'Ah, and her car, let's not forget.'

'The old Fiesta?'

'Still as reliable as ever – although perhaps you're not a driver?'

Alice wove her fingers together and squeezed her fingers tightly. 'No, no, I can drive. I just prefer not to.'

'Good, good,' the solicitor said, reassured. 'But! There is one other item in her will.' He slid the envelope towards her, but kept his hand on top of it. Alice unwove her whitening knuckles and tucked her sweating hands under her thighs to stop herself grabbing the envelope. 'Shortly before your mother died, she developed an idea. It was something she called "The Kindness Project", something she had been working on quietly for some time. Of course, she only called it that when we discussed her will in these offices.

But she wanted it to have a certain . . . optimism. And she wanted you to complete it.' He held out the envelope.

Alice let her head drop forwards, and took a deep breath. *Just send whatever emails this requires or donate whatever donations, and go home*, she thought, lifting her head, taking the proffered envelope and recognising her mother's hand on the front. *To my daughter Alice*, it said. She traced her finger over the letters, watching her own hand as if from a great distance.

'That's to get you going,' Blandford said, in a soft voice.

Alice looked up, puzzled.

He smiled gently. 'Oh yes, Alice. Your mother knew you'd be able to face a challenge. This is the first in a series.' He stood up, walked around the desk and held out his hand. 'Until we meet again? And please,' he added, shaking hands, too polite to react to the state of hers, 'I am always at your service.'

As Alice stepped out into the bright spring sunlight, the envelope pressed between the pages of her notes, she realised that she needed three things: a hot shower, something a little stronger than tea, and a shortcut back to her real life.

Chapter Three

The garden gate had been tricky to open, but the shiny new latch key slid easily into the front door. As it swung open, the house-scent Alice hadn't even known she knew filled the late-afternoon air around her: her mother's paints, herbs and perfume, mixed together with the salt air to make a clean, warm smell that left Alice exhausted. She dropped her bags on the hall floor. She hadn't felt this tired since – well, since after her last seminar, perhaps. She'd slept for a whole day after that. But before that, not for years. That was how it went, mostly.

The time before that was when her last relationship ended, seven years ago: a fine-boned Geographer from Canada, who she had been seeing for eight months, on and off. It worked well for a while because he was often out of the country, until he was given a position at a neighbouring college and it became clear that Alice saw no future for them, as she barely saw a present. She tried to be grateful that he would be around more, his presence guaranteed at least for the next twelve months, and she was grateful for the sex, which was more physical contact than she'd had for many years. But there was no space in her life for him; in her mind, she was a precise spinster, living as if she was a preserved figure in history already, set in her ways despite being then only in her early thirties.

She had lived so long with her own schedule, her own manner of getting things done, that the idea of having someone else in her space was unimaginable – someone chewing, choosing what was on television, their underwear in her drawers, toothbrush on the sink, more and more of herself being dissolved away as her carefully shaped life bent and warped around someone else.

So they had broken up. Although Alice had been thinking of it more as a *thank you so much, but no* on her part, the Geographer clearly had seen them being together a long time. His hurt made him whine, revealing then that he had gone for the college position only because of her, that he had thought they were on the same page, that he'd met her friends (*colleagues*, Alice internally corrected) and he was serious about her. When Alice didn't soften and match his own tone, her apologetic politeness seemed to enrage him, and he had furiously broken down all the reasons their relationship would never have worked anyway, mostly revolving around his need to be with someone actually living and her inability to fulfil that particular need.

She hadn't cried even then, nor when he had tried to storm out of her house and knocked a picture off the hall shelf, breaking it – something which was clearly accidental because he had stopped immediately and turned to her, horrified, an apology forming with his mouth and his hands, and if they had any kind of chance together it was the perfect icebreaker to pause the moment and bring them back into coupledom again – but when she had let him out, swept up the glass and turned the frame to face the wall, she was overtaken by the most overwhelming exhaustion, and she had stayed in bed for two days. Not sadness, she knew, probing around her mind for any bruises or sore spots, just being completely drained, and then on the third day she woke as if nothing had happened, and she wondered if it had just been some kind of bug, picked up at exactly the wrong moment. But she found herself more panicky afterwards. More nervous, even though she hadn't felt that way in the moment of the Geographer's anger. And soon that panic melted in with all the rest and became normal too.

Bea's house was old – ancient, really – a fisherman's cottage that from the outside looked in danger of falling down at any moment, but from within was cosy, full of snug rooms like ship cabins. The tiny room nearest the sea, the one where Bea's ancient television lived beneath art books and brightly coloured plant pots, actually had a little round window in it, a real brass porthole taken from a wrecked ship many years ago, Bea had told her.

Without her mother there, without having to hide herself in textbooks, Alice felt free to examine the house almost completely. Bea had collected sea-polished glass from the beach and lined them up on particular windowsills, so the afternoon light now sent rays of blue and green across the walls. Trinkets that Alice remembered playing with as a child at their home in Cambridge – a long, dark-blue sausage dog, a solid-silver rooster, a ceramic scalloped bowl, a mechanical wooden angel – were placed around the house, on mantelpieces, bookcases, cabinets and kitchen shelves. She picked up the bird and held it in her hands for a moment, turning it over and over. Alice didn't want to go into her mother's room yet.

She had taken after her father from her earliest years, a fact which used to make her mother laugh when Alice was very little, but had made her laugh less as the years went on until, just after Alice's eleventh birthday, Bea had told her that she was moving to Cornwall and Alice could come with her if she'd like. Even if that was something she had wanted – which it absolutely wasn't, leaving her school and friends behind for a house full of sand and paint fumes and canned sardines for tea when her mother had been too *creative* to remember that they needed to eat, at the age of eleven who wanted that? – the sight of Maurice over Bea's shoulder, quiet and slumped on the sofa, looking at his hands while Bea talked, was enough to make Alice say no.

'Well.' Bea knelt down in front of her, so her face was just below Alice's. 'You can visit whenever you like, I'll always keep your room ready. And you can bring a friend, too!' Bea smiled at Alice, but behind her face she was already sliding away, perhaps thinking about the little cottage she'd found in Cornwall, crashing waves audible in every room, sea salt frosting the garden plants. Bea laughed again, a different kind of laugh to normal, almost like she was laughing at herself, but she was gone within a day, picked up in a van Alice didn't recognise when she watched from the window in the pre-dawn light, before she could say goodbye.

So Alice had stayed with her father, in the safe and sensible house in Cambridge she'd grown up in, two up, two down, just Alice and Maurice, crouched over their books every evening in silence, reading and making notes. For a long time, Alice and Maurice didn't mention Bea, and had no contact with her. They ate two meals a day together during the week, Alice doing the breakfast eggs and Maurice some kind of shepherd's pie or hotpot for tea from colourless supermarket mince and packets in the cupboard.

At the weekend they would add a sandwich at lunchtime, made in the kitchen together while Radio 4 played on the battered kitchen radio. Their routine was unchanging, perfect. No surprises, no impulsiveness, just the same meals and homework at the same table, day after day. Roast turkey at Christmas, swimming for her birthday, a trip to the library every Saturday morning.

If Alice ever felt anything, perhaps that something inside her head was forming crystals when it should be growing buds, no one noticed. She could hide things well enough; without anyone there to look closely at her any more, she could control it. A pattern developed: as each school holiday approached, Maurice would say, 'Shall I book you a train ticket?' and Alice would tense up and put on a calm voice to explain why she couldn't go this time: a school project, plans to reorganise her bedroom. All that chaos, all that change. So at Christmas and Easter and half-terms, she would stay in Cambridge. But at the start of each summer holiday, Alice would hear her mother's voice on the phone while Maurice just said, 'Mmm, mmm, I see, well I – yes, I see,' until eventually he would say to Alice that he had to go to a conference for his work and would she mind going down to her mother's for just a week or so?

Alice would pack her bags full of books and her three favourite outfits, making a list in her notebook of exactly what she'd packed (purple t-shirt with the stars on left shoulder, grey socks with thin blue stripes, shorts with red elastic, shorts with green elastic), and read all the way down on the train with her Walkman headphones clamped to her ears. She would keep the headphones on for as much of the trip as she could get away with. She wouldn't go out. She wouldn't visit the village, or the beach, even when her attic room grew hot and stuffy and she was desperate for the sea breezes.

For the first visit or two Bea would call her to the table in the garden and serve her Stargazy Pie, fish heads poking up, desperate for Alice's attention, or homemade bread and local prawns, dripping with lemon and butter. Bea would try to talk to her about why she had left so quickly, how she had thought it was the right thing to do, in order to hurt Alice and Maurice less, how she saw now it had been the wrong thing to do, absolutely, and Alice would eat half of the food before asking if she could get down to carry on with her holiday homework, and Bea would smile and say, 'Of course, darling.' And Alice would go back to her attic room under the low roof there, and think for only a little while about how much Bea had loved her and Maurice, and how much her mother must be suffering having her here now when she no longer loved them, and then she would get back to her headphones and her reading and not think about it any more, until her next brief visit the following year.

When visits were very bad – the attic suffocating, Bea's attention torturous, some unintentional reminder of something they used to do as a family – she would turn her music up louder and stare up at the ceiling to see how long she could lie there without moving, as if she were a dead body.

So she had barely looked around this place previously, travelling mainly between the front door and her bedroom, as she arrived and left. Downstairs, the dark hallway led in one direction to the porthole television room with two small sofas squeezed in, and through that was the biggest room where Alice had been only once, on her first visit: white-walled, filled with Bea's easel and paintings, a spattered trestle table laden with brushes and paints, a box of rags, a dark dresser filling one wall. Canvases lay in piles against the wall, Bea's work over the decades.

The other side of the hall led to the kitchen, blue-tiled and full of pots and pans, striped pots of wooden spoons, a large pine table, scrubbed and smooth. The far wall was decorated with notes and cards spanning decades, all pinned with pegs to lengths of string across the wall's full width. Alice looked at a few.

Dear Bea,

Thank you so much for the advice. John has finally talked to me about what's been bothering him . . .

Dear Mrs Kimbrel,

Just a quick note to say thanks for the kick up the backside. I'm off tomorrow but wanted to leave this message for you . . .

Mrs Kimbrel,

Thank you for our jam. My mam says it's the best she's ever had . . .

So Bea was still the woman Alice remembered, moulding the world around her into the shape she wanted. Why on earth would she care about leaving her own child behind when she had all these adoring fans here? Leaving envelopes for Alice about kindness and facing a challenge, when she couldn't even face the challenge of raising her daughter. *How dare she.* The guilt Alice had felt at her mother being alone! *Ugh*, Alice thought, half-heartedly pulling down one strand of the string, and then remembering that Bea was dead and there was no point to Alice's disapproval any more. Her tiredness flooded back, drowning the energising anger.

Opening the fridge to distract herself, Alice found it immaculate, with only a bottle of milk, a packet of butter and some eggs inside. She sniffed the milk. *Fresh*. Perhaps Peter Blandford had arranged for someone to leave it there for her. She put in the gin and bottle of tonic she'd just bought from the village shop, on the way here from the solicitor's office, then tried the enamel bread bin and found a round loaf there, fresh too, from its warm doughy smell. Pulling out the breadboard and bread knife, Alice cut off two thick slices and scraped the cold butter on to them while the kettle boiled. Tea first, gin later.

Her mother had made quite the home for herself here, she thought as she waited for the kettle to boil, only having her daughter over for visits few and far between while she cultivated her devoted public in Polperran. Alice found a bottle of cooking brandy in one cupboard and slugged some into her tea, swigged it, and tried to breathe slowly, *in for five, out for six, in for five, out for six.* Brandy first, then gin? *Shouldn't drink, that's what the GP recommended, wasn't it?* She just needed to get the house cleared, do whatever this ridiculous errand was, then she could get on the train and be back in the warm embrace of the Black Death in a few days. Everything could get back to normal.

As the tea cooled, she noticed a large piece of driftwood propped up in one corner by the back door, its branches serving as a coatrack. Bea's yellow waterproof was still hanging from one offshoot. Alice hung up her own jacket on a spare branch, touching the sleeve of the waterproof, feeling its rough fabric, blasted from years of walking in high salt winds. A small wooden trunk sat just below; inside, a treasure trove of hats. Of course! Bea had always loved her hats – part of the excitement at the end of school would be seeing which hat her mother had chosen that day. Alice crouched down and lifted them out one by one: berets, bonnets, cricket caps; a handsome trilby with a tiny feather; a half-hat with a delicate plum-coloured veil; boaters, flat caps, sun hats, in every colour with every trim.

She lifted out an emerald green turban: one of young Alice's very favourites – Bea would invite her to borrow it when they drank cups of tea and ate crumpets in front of the fire on grey Sunday Cambridge afternoons. Alice put the turban on and stood to look into the mirror on the wall beside the driftwood. Her mother seemed to look back at her, the velvet's green deepening her eyes and emphasising Alice's paleness, a look that had always given Bea something of a Pre-Raphaelite air. She looked this way and that, turning in front of the mirror, amazed at how she had always assumed she'd taken after Maurice physically, a fact she had taken for granted since they were so similar in their temperaments. *Can I keep the hat if I don't finish whatever her ridiculous project was?* The envelope from Peter Blandford remained unopened in her bag.

A movement made her turn suddenly to the window, where she saw a wide-eyed face filling the view. She shrieked, just as the face did the same, before abruptly disappearing. Her heart was pounding. What was this place? *Obviously not haunted*, Alice said to herself as firmly as she could through the deafening roar of adrenaline.

She pulled open the front door and rushed outside, hoping to catch a glimpse of whatever had been watching her, but as she hurried around the corner she had to stop herself inches away from a tall man in a raggedy blue jumper, with a wild beard and boots splitting on one toe. She let out a slight shocked cough.

'I – it – DO YOU WANT SOMETHING?' Alice asked him loudly, trying to disguise her terror with calm, loud questions. 'THIS IS MY MOTHER'S HOUSE.' She clenched her shaking fists at her sides.

The man gave her a strange look.

She tried again. 'ARE YOU LOST?' She tried to think. Where was Bea's phone in the house? Where was hers? Could she get to it in time?

He looked puzzled.

'DO YOU WANT ME TO CALL SOMEONE?'

He rubbed his beard. 'I'm not sure, do you *want* to call someone?' His voice was gentle and precise, though amused. 'You made me jump a bit, there. And no, I'm not lost.'

'Oh.' Alice took in a long breath, feeling something spiking in her. Not just her racing heart, but that *thing* being pumped into her nervous system, accelerating beyond her control. *Slow down*, a tiny voice inside said, but it was too late. 'What the hell are you doing? WHAT are you *DOING*? Is this your garden? This is my MOTHER'S house, and I don't think *ANY . . . WEIRD STRANGER* is supposed to be here but *ME*!' She was shouting now, her voice cracking. *Too fast*, the voice said, distantly.

The man backed away, holding his hands up. 'It's all right,' he said softly, 'I'm just doing Bea's garden. I promised I'd look after it. For your mother. You know?'

'Well . . . I . . .' She tried to take a deep breath. *In through the nose, out through the mouth.* Not a ghoul or a wandering lost spirit, just her mother's green-fingered helper. She stretched out her fingers, watched as she clenched and loosened them. Almost to herself, she added, 'All right. You're just the gardener.'

'Luke Penrose.' He kept both hands up, showed her the front and backs. 'I won't shake, I'm a little too muddy for such a fine scholar as yourself, Miss Kimbrel. *Just a gardener* like me won't get in your way.'

'Thanks, I – look, I didn't –'

He picked up his garden fork and disappeared behind a small black door in the side of the house that Alice didn't remember even noticing before. 'Find your milk and things?' he called.

'Yes. Yes! Was that you?' Alice called back, weakly.

'Aye,' he said, his voice muffled. 'Peter said you'd be here today.' He came back out a moment later, pulling a moss-dusted old woollen hat over his sandy hair. He nodded at her, then walked towards the garden gate.

'Wait, thank you, you –'

'Pleasure to meet you at last, Miss Kimbrel,' he added over his shoulder. 'Come!'

Alice leapt again as a glossy red setter appeared from under a bush behind her and trotted after the gardener. Someone knew their way around this place.

Her vision slowly calmed as she heard an engine start up and drive away beyond the gate. She squeezed her fists one more time as she marched back inside.

I'll call Peter Blandford tomorrow and offer to give up this house, she thought, pacing the dark hallway back and forth, *if I can just go home and get things back to normal.*

33

Chapter Four

The tea helped, but the gin and tonic helped more, whatever the doctor had advised. Alice took her things upstairs, hurrying past her mother's bedroom with the large window, the tiny bathroom with plants hanging everywhere, and up an extra half-flight, to her own tiny little attic room, the window in the roof showing the sea if Alice stood on tiptoe on the bed. She didn't go in her mother's room – wasn't ready yet, didn't want to see the fading light in there or her clothes, or the bed Bea had died in, she assumed. Instead, she laid her things out in the attic room, drawers waiting for her, old oak shelves ready for her books and notes. It was the same familiar blanket on the bed, a fisherman's-blue quilt on top of old green sheets, sheets that must be almost as old as Alice and grown soft as seaweed, one of Bea's landscapes above the drawers. A few nights here, then she would go home. She'd managed it before.

Taking herself back downstairs, Alice settled into the armchair in the porthole snug, ice cranking in her gin glass, and took out her phone. *No signal.* She remembered her mother mentioning this before, but she'd hoped things had improved on that front in recent years. At least with Bea's car, Alice could potentially drive somewhere to keep in touch with Morag and the college.

Taking another sip, she took out the envelope from her

mother. *To my daughter Alice.* She remembered the writing well, because even though Bea hadn't been around to sign school forms or write sick notes, Alice suddenly remembered that she had written postcards to Alice frequently. She didn't know where they all were now; she had fuzzy memories of reading each one quickly, when it arrived, and then trying very hard to forget about it. She couldn't even say whether they had been heartfelt declarations of maternal affections or brief monologues on the weather, but she remembered the writing, warm and curved, swooping tails and dots like commas in the air. Alice remembered the distant pang each time, that Bea somehow continued to exist, even all those miles away from her.

She opened the envelope before she could talk herself out of it.

My dear Alice,

How are you? I hope Peter Blandford has made it clear that my home is your home, now — it always was, and now you own it entirely. I cannot give you the sea and the sky and the hills here, but remember they are there, if you wish to enjoy them, for as long as you stay. And I am sorry if this is all a shock — why don't we all plan our afterlives a little better for our loved ones? — though there will be plenty of people to take care of you.

I have tidied my studio but it will all be left pretty much untouched until you come here. Everything in it is also yours, so keep whatever you choose and dispose of the rest.

My darling, this is sounding like mere practical instructions but I so much hope you will find more than that here, if you continue this project. I asked so much of you when I left, when you were still a little girl, and there is more asking here – but will you have a little faith in me? Or if you can't, will you enjoy the break from Cambridge?

Hopefully you have already met a few people in Polperran. They've been so kind to me in the years I've been here, and I know they will all love you immediately. I've made my peace with not being around for much longer, but it does bother me greatly all the things I haven't yet managed to achieve while I've been here. Please, Alice – will you try to finish those few jobs still left hanging? Peter has all the details you need for each task.

First of all, would you go and see Joy Garland at Pilot's Cottage, my darling? She used to run the bakery (it's now the vet's, three down from the village shop) but she doesn't really leave the house any more. Will you give her a visit and see if she needs anything? It shouldn't take long, and it may just be what she needs to bring her out of herself.

Love you the most,
Your Mum

Alice sighed and tipped her head against the back of the armchair. Neighbourhood errands. Visiting, cheerfully knocking, pointless, frustrating, boring small-talk. *Just like college*, she thought, and breathed out sharply. But here: 'Love you the most', as if Bea was just leaving a quick note for Alice when she got back from school, while Bea popped out for extra milk. Bea hadn't earned the title of Mum since Alice was eleven, yet here she was, requesting Alice run errands for her as if everything was unchanged from her happy childhood and Bea needed a little help from her loving daughter to go and check in on their elderly neighbour. And *my darling*. Bea had no right to make claims with words as weighty as *my darling*.

She thought: *It's just another day or two. Morag did tell me to take a couple of weeks off, and I can get some reading and revisions done here on the book. I'll see this woman, get her milk and bread or whatever, and that's it. Work on the book. Get some sleep. Sleep will help.*

Alice read the letter again, and wondered for the first time how many 'projects' her mother had planned. Would she need to stay more than a few days? Packing up the house would take that long, even if it was just about hiring people in to do it for her, so she might be able to cram in a few of these jobs before she went back to Cambridge. And at least Peter Blandford knew about Alice's work, which would make things easier when she explained about a work emergency at the college that she had to return for.

The rest of it could be smoothed over, she thought, and then she would never have to see Polperran again. It had been years since Alice had done anything apart from college work – even her holidays were formed around conferences and planning for her seminars, and her weekends were filled mostly with reading and marking. A break would be good for her work. Just a few more days here, some reading time, and then everything would be back to normal again. It wasn't like she actually had to do these tasks, or sit around having sing-songs and organising village fêtes with the locals. Just keep her head down, and she'd be back in Cambridge before she knew it . . .

When she opened her eyes, it was getting darker. Dusk had settled into the windows, and Alice realised after a day that had seemed to last for weeks, she was starving and bread wasn't going to be enough. She wiped her mouth, put Bea's green turban back on to cover her train-flattened hair, locked up the house and headed towards the pub she had passed earlier, following the lights and the faint scent of spilled pints and microwaved meat.

The Dolphin looked even older than Bea's cottage, with a thatch frowning so low Alice had to duck her head to enter. There was a brief lull in the low conversation while the pub's clientele gave her a quick once-over, then backs were turned again as she headed to the bar.

A woman stood behind it, spiky purple hair and matching eye-liner, mopping up in a harassed manner.

'Yes, love?'

Alice looked at the sticky bottles behind the bar. 'Just a lemonade, please.'

The woman narrowed her eyes at Alice and her turban for a moment, then nodded, still watching her. She poured her drink and put it on the bar, but held on to the glass. 'You visitin', my love?'

Alice missed the college bar so much at that moment, where you could drink every day if you chose, and never speak a word to anyone. 'Just sorting some things out. A short visit. Are you still serving food?'

The woman nodded and released the glass, passing her a battered leatherette menu from under the bar. 'Janet, if you need anything while you're here.'

Alice held out a five-pound note. 'Thanks.'

Janet tutted and held her hands up. 'No, you have that on me. Tell your friends about our wonderful atmosphere,' she said, and gave her an amused smile. Alice smiled back, caught off guard, and took her glass and menu to a table in the corner. The menu must have been mass-printed for pubs like this across the country: lasagne; battered cod; bangers and mash; some kind of beef; *all served with a basket of chips and a depressed salad,* she thought. As she debated her options (she was sure they'd all taste the same) she felt a sharp kick to her chair leg. Looking up, she saw a tall, broad-shouldered figure in a dusty-looking hooded jumper, with dark hair and a charming grin.

'I know you,' the figure said. 'I very nearly ran you over earlier. Santo,' he added, offering his hand.

Shocked, Alice reached her own out instinctively. She felt it disappearing into his.

Behind the bar, Janet looked over. 'You ordering, love? Kitchen closin' soon.'

'Oh, I – excuse me –' Alice stood up and edged past the man's thick body to the bar, but by the time she'd paid for her lasagne the man was sitting at another table, thank god, his back to her, apparently having his ear chewed by a sharp-faced elderly woman in Danvers black who shot vicious glances at Alice while the man sat sheepishly fiddling with his empty pint glass.

Alice had forgotten to bring a book or her notes to the pub, and there was no sign of any newspaper or magazines, so she spent her wait looking at the other customers. They sat in ones or twos, mostly looking into their pints or occasionally muttering to one another like a distantly dripping tap. The lasagne came suspiciously fast, lava-hot around the edges and counter-top warm in the middle; she ate it all, leaving only the saddest of the salad leaves. By the time she'd finished and brought her plate and glass to the bar to pay, thanking Janet, the place was almost empty. No one else had spoken to her, including the broad-shouldered man who had left the pub without looking at her again. The old woman he'd been with had watched him go with something like satisfaction, and continued glaring at Alice before shuffling out herself.

As Alice bid Janet good night, she stopped, wanting to ask about the old bakery. 'Is there a . . .' She suddenly lost her nerve. '. . . a phone box here? I don't get a signal . . .' she finished lamely.

'There's one up there on the right, near the shop, but I can't guarantee what state it'll be in,' Janet said. She frowned and threw her towel over her shoulder. 'I think your mum had a landline, didn't she? That's your best bet.'

So Janet knew exactly who Alice was. At least she had the grace to look a touch embarrassed. But someone was calling for her at the other end of the bar; she threw Alice a wink and a grin, and was gone.

Outside, beyond the pool of the pub's lights, it was dark. A few feet out, Alice tried to calculate where Bea's cottage would be in relation to the moon – the road was pitch-black in shadows, though the sky was lit up. She followed her instincts as far as possible, before she recognised a large bush that ran along the side of Bea's garden, and up to the gate. She could hear the sea, in the still of the village night, the murmur of water on pebbles across the quiet air.

Unlatching the gate and unlocking the front door in pitch darkness wasn't easy or enjoyable, and once inside Alice rushed to lock the door behind her and climbed upstairs. She brushed her teeth, wrapped herself in bed-sheets, and lay awake for hours wondering what awaited her tomorrow.

Chapter Five

She finally dropped off around three a.m., and woke again at 4.15, 4.32, 5.04 and 5.20 before she abandoned her bed and her attempts to sleep. It wasn't the gin from the day before – she'd had only one after the brandy in her tea – but she hadn't slept well in years. As a child, she'd had a vague sense of something soothing carrying her under every night, the muffled hum of Bea and Maurice watching the television together downstairs, before waking up warm to the morning radio sounds of her parents in the kitchen, but Alice could never tell if the memory was just a misremembered fairy story. She couldn't imagine sleeping like that now. Alice also knew that she'd likely fall asleep somewhere during the day: she did it with enough frequency that she had been to a sleep clinic to investigate the possibility of narcolepsy. Eventually the doctors had just offered the same thing they always did: pills, pills, pills. Pointless. Besides, she could get through her days at college; she might have the odd cat nap in her office, but who didn't? Students were exhausting and their essays weren't always the most riveting stuff. Exercise, vitamins, turkey, bananas, sleep hygiene, yoga, bedtime stories: she'd tried them all, and nothing seemed to move her brain to shut down for an entire night. Maybe she should accept the ancient way of sleeping, and accept that her working day had two parts, a day shift and a night shift, and her sleep did too. Or maybe she should try going fully nocturnal here, while she had no major daytime commitments. She might finally get her eight hours, even if they were in bright sunlight.

The Canadian Geographer had asked her once if she thought her insomnia was related to Bea sneaking away in the middle of the night; maybe Alice was worried she might miss something equally important if she was sleeping regular hours, he said. The question was so stupid Alice genuinely hadn't known how to respond, something which the Geographer had taken as an emotional breakthrough. He had insisted on holding Alice until she couldn't bear it and had to feign a coughing fit as an excuse to fetch a glass of water from the kitchen.

Getting dressed now, Alice decided to explore her surroundings a little. It wasn't the bakery she really needed to find anyway, she realised, but Pilot's Cottage. Perhaps she could find it now, before anyone else was about, and tick visiting Joy off by mid-morning at the latest.

The garden had a clinging green brightness to it, freckled with dew that was rapidly disappearing in the coastal early morning heat. Alice unlatched the garden gate and turned away from the pub and the high street, heading instead along the path which ran towards the sea front. It switched downwards, between a high brick wall and Bea's hedge, before eventually splitting in two: towards a sea path and a semi-rotted handrail leading down some stone steps to the beach, and a cobbled path which ran inland slightly, in the direction of roofs Alice could glimpse over the high wall. She turned towards the sea.

Alice could see the distant blur of a young woman towards the water, pulling her thin anorak around her, huddling against the cool sea winds rolling steadily inland. As Alice got closer on the sea path, the young woman continued to stare out across the waves, apparently unaware of the tide pulling in, the spray gradually soaking her shoes. She folded a little deeper into her faded purple anorak, and before Alice could get near enough to speak to her – not that Alice would have, or wanted to, or would have known what to say even if she could or did – the young woman turned back up the beach and crunched away rapidly to the far set of steps, vanishing up one of the many little alleys and pathways that seemed to fork in every direction from that end of the beach, trying vainly to escape from the reach of the sea winds. Alice watched the sea for a while, the height of the waves and the lack of swimmers, then looped back, taking the cobbled path towards the roofs she had glimpsed over the wall.

Slate-roofed rather than thatched here, the houses had romantic names: Pentrig and Wave's View and The Nest. But their paths were overgrown and the house fronts with their tiny windows looked storm-worn and fatigued, rusting bikes lying on dried-out patches of grass, bins overflowing. These were not glossily painted, bunting-strewn holiday homes; these were houses where people lived when they faced the financial realities of holiday spots – unreliable, seasonal jobs, unaffordable homes, uncertain economies.

Tucked on one corner she found Pilot's Cottage, paint flakes from the front door sprinkling the pathway. If the other houses looked worn, this one looked positively beaten. The front curtain twitched and Alice realised other people might already be stirring, but before she could step away the door opened. From the shadows, a low voice said, 'Can I help?'

Alice peered into the gloom. 'Joy? Garland? I'm Alice. Bea's daughter. Bea Kimbrel?'

'She died,' the voice said flatly.

'I know,' said Alice. 'She was my mother.'

A ruddy-faced woman with thin mousy hair growing in a grown-out bob stepped out onto the front mat, in a dress that might once have been red, but had been washed into a lank pink that almost matched her complexion. 'But you weren't at her funeral.'

Alice looked at her. She had been expecting someone elderly, for some reason, who had run a bakery all her life before taking retirement and seeing the business close in her absence, but this woman could only have been a touch older than Alice. She also couldn't resemble her name less: Alice had pictured Joy Garland as a fresh-faced figure with sparkling eyes, not a washed-out, faded creature, fingers bunched grimly in the pocket of the apron around her waist.

'I wasn't invited,' Alice said simply. The woman nodded. 'But Bea asked me to come and see you. To see if you wanted anything?'

The woman gave a small smirk that disappeared again immediately. She turned her back and walked inside. Over her shoulder, just as Alice was wondering what to do, she said quietly from the gloom, 'You can come in, then.'

The house was dark inside, and Alice sat on a sagging sofa while Joy moved around in the kitchen at the back. Alice wanted to apologise for coming so early, for disturbing her at such an ungodly hour, but before she could Joy brought

44

a tray through, placed it on the table between the sofa and a high-backed armchair, and poured out two cups of tea as if this was the middle of the afternoon and Alice had been long expected. Then she passed an astonished Alice a small plate, with several small flat cakes with raisins glistening at the edges. 'Welsh cakes,' she said in her flat voice. 'Made them this morning.'

'Oh,' Alice hesitated, checking her watch, 'no, thank you, 6.30 is a bit early for me,' Alice said as warmly as she could in this strange dark house. But she saw how Joy's eyes stayed on the plate, so said, 'Go on then, I am on holiday, I suppose.' She bit into one, displaying a polite, tight smile at Joy, but then her face changed and her eyes closed as she felt the flavours of the Welsh cake burst in her mouth – buttery salt, fat raisin, sweet crunch of granulated sugar. 'You made these? Today? Already?'

Joy allowed herself a tiny smile. 'Good, are they?' She picked at her own, taking tiny crumbs at a time. 'I bake most mornings. I don't know what to do with them, though. I end up binning most of them.'

'You *bin* these?' Alice said, stopping chewing. 'Why?'

Joy pursed her lips, but couldn't hide her pleasure. 'You should try my pavlovas. And I always heard good things about my custard tarts.'

Alice paused for a moment before her last bite of Welsh cake. 'You had a bakery in the village, didn't you?'

Joy's smile vanished, and she put her plate down on the tray. 'We did. But my husband left me.' She lifted her hands up slightly before letting them fall back into her lap. 'No bakery.'

Alice put her own plate on her knees. 'I'm sorry. I didn't

know. Bea didn't tell me.' Joy looked sceptically at her. 'But these are wonderful,' Alice said quietly. 'Is there nowhere else you can sell them?'

Joy stood up. 'I thought we'd had enough of your mother instructing people what to do with themselves.' Anger was suddenly making her flat voice louder.

Alice put her plate and cup down, and stood up too. 'I'm sorry, Joy –'

'Don't you Joy me – you don't know me. I've never met you in my life and you come into my home and tell me how to live my life –'

'I'm sorry, I'm sorry –'

Joy looked at Alice. She seemed to be thinking. Then she said blandly, 'If your own mother didn't even want to see you, in her dying days, why on earth should I?'

Alice took in a sharp breath, and felt it starting – the hard build in her chest, rushing, pushing upwards, her heart speeding up, her pulse quickening, and she rushed to the door, pulling it open with a bang, hurrying, hurrying up the cobbled lane, past the sea steps, past the old woman in black from the pub watching her from a bench, stone-faced, as Alice raced by, along her mother's hedge, racing to overtake that feeling, to get back to safety before it over-whelmed her. *It's true,* she thought, *she hadn't even cared enough to say goodbye, no no no no no,* then Alice was in the garden, in the house, up the stairs and into her room, under the blanket which she wrapped tightly around herself, pull-ing it closer and closer to try and stop this terror in her lungs, freezing her gut and spreading ice through her veins. *Her mother hadn't cared about her, and even that strange, washed-out woman knew it.* She remembered the taxi driver yesterday, how her manner had cooled – was Polperran full of people who recognised Alice, and wanted to know why she had left her mother to die alone?

Alice lay frozen, unable to move, humiliated, drowning in nothing at all, unable to manage like a normal person, always just waiting for this pathetic, pointless, paralysing animal to take control of her body again.

When Alice had first received Peter Blandford's letter and called his office, she had asked when her mother's funeral would be. His voice had caught, and he explained to her that the funeral had been a few days before, that Bea had not intended for Alice to have to attend. 'She thought it would be fairest to you,' he had said.

As Alice had hidden back in bed, blanket wound close around her, she'd thought of the distance at which Bea must have held her, to have deliberately planned for her own daughter not to attend her funeral. Not an oversight, not crossed wires, but a calculation made to keep Alice as far as possible from the life Bea had built. She didn't even know what the funeral had been: a cremation? A service at the church near the village green? Had it been empty? Or had everyone attended but her?

She had put a pillow over her head, eventually, to try and better hear her own breathing, and had fallen asleep. She woke mid-morning, starving, her breath no longer hitching but still with the ghost-ache of her panicked lungs, with the faded taste of Joy's Welsh cakes souring on her tongue. Why had Bea not mentioned Joy's husband? Was every task going to be like this, booby-trapped to turn all of Polperran against her? Was Bea just trying to ensure even now that she and Alice remained blasted apart, the life she had carved out here separate from the dragging needs of her unwanted daughter?

As she disentangled her legs from the blankets, there was a knock at the door. She toyed with the idea of staying in her room, still and silent until whoever it was went away, but she thought it could be Peter Blandford checking on her progress, and she could truthfully tell him she had done what she could.

When she opened the door, it wasn't Mr Blandford, but the gardener.

'I borrowed your mother's fork,' he said, 'or your fork, I should say.' He held up the item. 'I'm just popping it back in the shed, the door round the back, didn't want you to be alarmed if you heard me clattering about in there.'

'That's – that's fine,' Alice said, trying to smooth her wild hair down. 'Clatter away.'

She looked around the garden in the mid-morning light, and saw how fresh it was still. No fairy lights and plastic garden carpets, no identikit chairs like the ones in her tiny courtyard garden at home. This was a place where things *grew*: everywhere, and in every shape, busting out in blossom and fruit.

He looked at her. 'If you don't mind me asking – are you all right?'

She waved his look away by pretending to do a button up on her shirt. 'Fine. Fine, thank you. Just . . . busy.' Between her broken night's sleep and her panicked, shutdown nap after visiting Joy, she couldn't work out how much rest she'd had in the last twenty-four hours. She knew she wasn't making a good second impression.

After a moment, he nodded and began walking to the built-in shed. He turned back after a few steps, and added, 'Bit weird being here? Without Bea?'

'No, it's fine, honestly,' Alice replied. 'Really, come and go as you please; you know this place better than I do. Have you got a key, if I'm – when I go?'

'I do. If that's still all right?' He smiled. 'No, I meant, are you finding it weird being here without her?' He stuck the fork in the ground, came back and held his hand out. 'And it's Luke, again.'

Alice gave her own, and they shook hands, his cool hand wrapping around hers. 'Yes. Sorry. Luke. Alice, again.'

'Yes, hello Alice,' he repeated with mock-formality. 'And I believe you've met Belle?' At the mention of her name, the red setter appeared from under one of the bushes to sniff Alice's hand, tail wagging, before curling up at Luke's feet.

She sighed and gave a weak smile back. 'Sorry. About yesterday. Sorry about all that stuff, it's just all so odd, and she's set me this odd stuff to do – my mother – Bea – good turns, or something – and I didn't know anything –'

Luke opened his hand gently. 'Alice, your mother just died. You can behave however you want. It's just nice to meet you at last.'

Rather than meet his eye, she took her hand back and gazed over his shoulder. 'Can I ask you a question?' He looked at her. 'Did you go to Bea's funeral?'

He shifted, looking down at the dog. 'I did.'

'Can you tell me what it was like?'

'It was good, Alice. A nice service,' he said. 'At the church. It was full.'

49

Alice looked down at the dog too now, so Luke couldn't see her face. 'And did anyone wonder where her daughter was?'

'Mum told me that Bea hadn't wanted you to be told until after the funeral. I think she thought she would be doing you a favour.'

Something in his voice made her look at him. 'But?'

Luke scratched his beard briefly, his blue eyes growing darker. 'When my dad died, my sister and I were just kids. Some people said we shouldn't be at the funeral, that it was too upsetting for us, but Mum said the funeral was for us more than anybody. And I'm glad we went. I cried even more than Mel, but we agreed it was worth it to hear people talking about Dad like that.' Belle stood and nuzzled his hand. 'Bea was a good woman, in lots of ways. But I don't know that I'd have made the same decision as her about that. If you don't mind me saying.'

Alice closed her eyes, and let out a deep breath. When she opened them, she could just make out the sea sparkling through leaves at the edge of the garden. 'Is that an apple tree?'

Luke turned, and followed her gaze. 'Which one? I mean – there are four apple trees you've inherited, plus a pear tree, a quince tree that's shaping up nicely, and a lot of soft fruit in the beds around the side.'

'Soft fruit?'

'Raspberries, strawberries, gooseberries, blackcurrants, and we were experimenting with some goji plants last summer that seem to have done OK through the frosts.'

Alice looked around her. 'And can you tell me about them? If you're not too busy?'

Luke seemed to watch her, trying to establish if he had

50

overstepped some line and this was sarcasm, but Alice appeared sincere. So he took her clockwise around the cottage in the warming, late-morning sun, Belle occasionally trotting over to review the growth in case any of it was for her. He showed her the soft fruit beds and the vegetable beds, both already full of canes and twine for the growing plants; the immaculately kept compost – 'Fish guts,' Luke said, when Alice asked how it looked so good, and she didn't know if he was joking – the hydrangea plants that seemed so often to greet visitors to Cornish houses, plate-sized clusters of blooms colour-changing from an almost neon pink to a cornflower blue all on one plant; bristling bushes of sea pinks and fleabane, and huge ferns either side of the garden gate. He took her to the fruit trees and explained when each fruit would be ripe, as well as the best thing to do with each, jellies and tarts and side dishes.

He turned to her by the apple trees, and said, 'But whatever you do, don't get a Cornishman started on which apples are best for cider.'

Alice laughed.

He didn't smile. 'I'm serious.' He clapped his hands together and scanned around the garden. 'Right, is that everything? Next time, I'll show you what you need to do to take care of it all.'

She watched him walk away, then called, 'Luke?' *I should be paying him for his time*, she thought. *I'll make sure Peter takes it out of the estate once I go.* 'Do you know Joy Garland? She was the first task Bea set me. To go and visit her.'

'Joy's a task?' Luke leant on the fork. 'And it didn't go well, I take it?'

Alice shook her head. She couldn't tell this stranger,

51

however friendly, how truly disastrously it had gone. 'I think my mother made a mistake, leaving this to me. I don't think I'm who she thought I was.'

He watched her silently again. 'Give it another go, I think. Maybe . . . come at it from a different angle. She never wanted to talk to your mother – which might be why Bea left Joy to you – but you might be able to find something else she needs.' Luke hoiked the fork out of the ground and turned once more to the shed. 'Tell you what though,' he called over his shoulder, 'her custard tarts were to die for.'

Alice remembered the Welsh cakes, and thought for a moment. Slowly, she began to smile.

Chapter Six

Bea had always been a great shopper, possessing the gift of making every trip to the market or supermarket into both a social occasion and an adventure. The market stall holders all knew her – of course they did, Alice thought now sardonically, Bea who had time for everyone – and so did all the cashiers at the little beige and orange supermarket near the house in Cambridge. Bea would let Alice choose the fruit and vegetables, praising her skill in selecting exactly the right ones, and in the pasta aisle Alice would be encouraged to pick a pasta shape they hadn't had for a while, or was brand new to them both. If they spotted a jar or tin they didn't recognise, they would buy it, and Bea would sit with her cookbooks to try and work out what to do with the new ingredient. When Alice got tall enough, Bea finally let her carry the wicker shopping basket all the way to the shop, but Bea would take the full basket and fold her arm through it for the walk home, giving Alice an apple from the top of it, like a witch in a fairy tale. And like a fairy tale, Alice thought if she could just complete the tasks the witch had left, as quickly and painlessly as possible, and without thinking at all about the witch's opinions on how Alice was managing these tasks, she would be free to return to her normal life.

In the cottage, Bea had helpfully left the shopping basket on a shelf in the kitchen, looking no older than it had when Alice was a little girl. At lunchtime, after Luke's tour of the garden, Alice filled it with everything she needed from the village shop where she had been only the afternoon before for the gin and tonic; which was staffed again today by the woman with the thick bowl-cut hairdo whom she had seen from the window of the café, yesterday, pulling a child or two behind her. Heading back down the cobbled lane, Alice carried the basket in the crook of her elbow and enjoyed the peaceful midday light.

At Pilot's Cottage, she left the basket in the doorway – eggs, milk, sugar; nutmeg, butter and flour; everything necessary, according to the cookbook she'd found on another of Bea's shelves. Not that Joy would be lacking any of it, but Alice didn't want to offer her an excuse. She stopped for a moment as she laid the basket down, wondering if she would mind possibly losing this basket, carried for decades by Bea in both her lives, before shaking herself and walking back up the path. *You can't miss what you already thought was lost*, she thought. As she looked back to check the door again, she saw the curtains move in the front window, but didn't wait to see Joy. She didn't know if her idea would work; and she simply couldn't face any more of Joy's particular kind of hospitality.

She walked further along the beach, curious to see if she could find a route to the high street from the other direction. Around the end of the bay the cliffs curled back into a second bay, containing a small harbour and a minor flotilla of boats. The smells of the harbour were strong, the scent of fuel and fish guts, but the wind carried them past her so swiftly they never had the chance to sour and sharpen. She found an empty wooden crate and sat on it, enjoying her peaceful invisibility against the sea wall behind her, watching for a while the boats jostling on the water, the breeze clattering metallic lines against boat masts. The men and women here worked busily dragging ropes and crates, loading and unloading in the warm sun.

Eventually the sun grew too warm, and she lost her nerve about finding a new route, creeping back instead along the beach and taking the known path to Blandford & Sons. As she walked, she realised she had no idea how long her mother's project would take. There was no point trying to calculate how many hours per day she could apply herself to it, as if it were any normal piece of work. She tried not to feel too anxious about all that uncertainty, about not knowing how many tasks there were, or how intricate each one was . . . Still, if she could maintain her current rate, she could potentially be done here in a matter of days. And if they became harder or more involving, she would be happy to walk away: her real life was in Cambridge, and needed dealing with far more pressingly.

At the office, Alice didn't have to go inside. As she arrived, Peter Blandford was just approaching from over the road, clutching a brown paper bag.

'Alice! What a pleasure. And what fine weather you've brought with you to enjoy our wonderful village.' He beamed at her. 'I've just been out for my lunch – while I miss my wife's sandwiches, the prawn rolls that Gwen makes are very nearly as good.' He indicated the café that Alice had visited only the day before.

Alice nodded. 'Yes, I had her . . . Hevva cake? Is that right?'

Peter Blandford clasped his paper bag to his chest in delight. 'Ah! A true local delicacy. And while the decor may have become a little – what shall we say – *loved*, Gwen's food is quite without compare. But I'm sure you haven't come to discuss culinary forays with me – if it is me you have come to see, that is?'

Alice almost smiled at his fusty manner. 'It is you, yes. I've come to get my next envelope.'

'Already!' He looked delighted. 'Goodness me, after only a day! Perhaps you take after your mother even more than you may have thought.'

'No – I mean, I think I need the next one. I've . . . done what the first one said, but at the moment it's more letter of the law rather than spirit of the law, if you see what I mean?'

He nodded, thoughtful. 'Very well, that is of no matter. If you feel ready for the next envelope, I shall go and fetch it for you.'

'Peter?' Alice stopped him. 'Where's Bea now? I mean . . . since the funeral. Her funeral. I don't even know – does she have a gravestone?'

Peter Blandford swallowed hard, and touched his tie a few times, before saying in a voice caught with emotion, 'Oh, Alice. Yes. Your mother was cremated, as she'd requested, and the ashes are waiting for you, should you wish to keep them, or dispose of them.' He coughed, trying to clear his voice. 'As we've discussed before, I did suggest to Bea that she might give you a little more . . . warning, or choice, but your mother . . .'

My mother what? Alice thought. *You knew her longer*

than I did, really. And she realised that if one believed that Alice had stopped knowing Bea the day she walked out on her and Maurice, that was actually true.

He folded over the top of the paper bag and scored it with his thumbnail while she watched. 'And yes, we can organise a memorial headstone for the cemetery, if you'd like Bea to have a place there. Just let me know and I can begin making the arrangements.'

They stood in silence together for a moment, before Alice shifted and squinted in the sun, then said, 'There's one other thing: how many envelopes are there?'

'Ah,' he said, slightly relieved to be on to a different topic, 'I'm unable to tell you that – it's one of the few conditions your mother had on this whole enterprise. Is that a problem?'

'No, it's not a problem. But . . . is it *many*? Because . . . you know, I have a life, in Cambridge . . . and . . .'

The solicitor smiled. 'While of course I couldn't tell you a number, I can reassure you that there is an end in sight for even the greatest task. Now, let me pop inside and fetch your envelope – unless you care to stay and share my luncheon?'

Alice demurred and waited in the sunshine. She saw again the copper-haired woman from yesterday, timid, peeking out from beneath her fringe as she left the café, walking down the street like a mouse scuttling from shelter to shelter. She watched her until, before much longer, Peter Blandford returned with an envelope.

To my dearest Alice, it said, and this time had a curlicued *No 2* in the right-hand corner.

'Are you all right, my dear?'

Alice realised she had been rubbing the writing again. She remembered this hand so well, which seemed impossible when she knew her mother so little.

She nodded again at his anxious face. 'Yes. Of course.' She held the envelope up like a trophy. 'Onwards and upwards.'

Along the sunny street, there was almost nobody about. Alice found it baffling how quiet everywhere seemed to be – the pub, the high street, the beach; everywhere, it seemed, but the small harbour. The only person she saw was the old woman in black from the pub the night before, shuffling slowly down the street and glowering at Alice the whole time. Despite the notes to Bea that filled her kitchen, the population of Polperran seemed to Alice to keep themselves to themselves, outside of fishing; a quiet, apparently unconnected group washed up on this stretch of coast like so much tidewrack. But Peter's sandwich had made her hungry, and her thoughts turned from the silent streets to the café opposite.

Unfortunately, the auburn-haired woman behind the till showed no signs of being lost in her book today. Rather, she greeted Alice as if she was a beloved regular, sitting her at her table in the window, bringing her a pot of tea and a bowl of bursting purple grapes while Alice decided what to order – from her own imagination, of course. She wondered what would happen if she ordered something fantastical, half-believing it would, regardless, still appear from the kitchen. Alice chose a cheese and onion toastie, thinking this was challenge enough for the menu-free café; when it was ready the older woman brought it over, loitering by the table with an empty cup until Alice looked up again.

'By the way, love, I'm Gwen.'

'Oh. Thank you. Alice.'

Gwen smiled. 'I know that, spit of your mother, you are.' She indicated the other chair at Alice's table. 'May I?' She sat down, leaning backwards while she poured herself a cup of tea and pulled some grapes from the stalk. 'I know it can't be easy for you, love. Coming to a new place –'

'I'm not staying,' Alice explained politely, puzzled at this woman joining her table and apparently having knowledge of her. 'I mean, not that there's anything wrong with Polperran, it's just that I've got to get back to college. My mother – she's left this list of *things* I have to do, this project, and once all that's been sorted out –'

'Sorted? Things in the cottage?'

Alice concentrated on cutting up her toastie. What was this interrogation? 'No. Things . . . in the village. People.'

Gwen laughed, crossing her arms over her ample chest. 'I'll just bet she has! People, I can well believe it.' She narrowed her eyes. 'Who's on there? The list?'

'I don't know,' Alice said, 'I've only opened one envelope so far. Do you know Joy Garland?'

'Oooh, I do,' Gwen said, curling her hands around her cup. 'Bit tricky, is our Joy. She's had a hard time over the last couple of years. Not that she was the warmest child even in the playground – same age as my boy, you see – but it takes all sorts, doesn't it? Maybe her gift is her baking, not her way with people.'

Alice took a few bites and looked back out of the window.

'But we're not all so bad here! You know Melder, my daughter.'

Alice hesitated. 'No, I don't think –'

'Yesterday, in here! I saw you two talking just before you left. You just missed her, in fact.'

'Oh! Your daughter?' She wondered why she hadn't made the connection between the two women, one just a heavier-set, older version of the other. 'Imelda?'

Gwen smiled. 'Melder. Means honey sweet.' She took another sip of tea. 'And her little brother Luke you know, of course – it's him who makes our chutney, you know.'

'Luke? Bea's gardener?' It took Alice another moment to connect tall, sandy-haired Luke with the woman behind the counter.

'Gardener, coastguard, all sorts is our Luke. But now that's three of us, and Peter over there, so you'll know already that we're not all like Joy. Not that Joy's even that bad. Honestly,' she said, looking around the empty café, 'if I could get my hands on some of her recipes – and some of her skill, to be fair – this place would be raking it in.'

'There's an older woman, too – the one in black? I've seen her a few times and she's given me some very –' Alice paused, and tried to think of a polite way of saying *Wicker Man vibes*, but Gwen interrupted her anyway.

'Ena?' She paused for a moment, looking at Alice, but then carried on, 'Oh, if Joy's had bad luck, Ena's had it even harder. A hard war when she was a little girl, my mother told me about that. Her parents died soon after and she was left on her own, still only a young thing, and no one to marry her – shortage of men, of course – so she sold their farm and worked her way up to postmistress, knew everyone's business of course, but never gossiped bad news, never celebrated good, my mother said. Just a hard shell, she had, and no one looking after her except the few people who knew her as a girl, and of them, there's really only Tressa that still counts. Have you met Tressa yet?'

Alice shook her head.

'You will,' Gwen laughed. 'Anyway, I'm not saying just ignore Ena, but it can help to remember there's a person in that bag of crow feathers. You don't have to be terrified of her, much as she'd love you to think so.'

Alice thought for a moment. 'Did she know my mother?'

'Ena and Bea?' Gwen took a sip of tea and paused again. 'Oh *yes*. By the time your mother died, she and Ena were thick as thieves. Ena might even have been the last person to see her. It took those two a while, but perhaps it just takes her a while to warm up to anybody.'

Well, if I have a spare few decades, Alice thought.

Gwen drained her cup, and stood up from the table. 'Give her time. Plus, if not her, you've got everyone else in Polperran watching out for you.' She picked up the pot. 'Another? It's on me, since I drank most of it.'

'No, thank you – I've got to get back to the cottage,' Alice said, trying to pile up her crockery as Gwen's hands kept getting there first. 'Another note from my mother that I need to get started on.'

Gwen stopped with the teapot and plates in her hands. 'Is it strange? Getting letters from her even though . . . she's passed? How are you feeling, love?'

Alice hadn't thought of them in terms of a potential source of grief: they were a To Do list, posted to her via the hands of a legal professional. Were Peter and Gwen waiting

61

for her to break down in front of them? 'I'm fine. It's just . . . what she wanted, I suppose. Not my style, but my mother and I were very different people.'

Gwen gave a short sceptical hum, but took the rest of the dishes away as Alice packed herself up and left money on the table.

Outside, on the warming pavement in the white glaze of the sun, the streets were empty. As she turned onto the green, a horn beeped lightly and the dark-haired, grinning man from the pub waved at her from the window of his passing mud-streaked truck.

Chapter Seven

She didn't open the envelope once she got home. She had promised herself (and Morag, of course; she would show Morag her new material when she returned to the History department) that part of this trip was to do work, her own work, not just act out her mother's fairy stories, so when she got back to the cottage after the café she stuffed the envelope deeper in her bag, and laid out her notes and books on the kitchen table.

She worked successfully for the rest of day and all evening, only stopping once it showed dark through Bea's windows and her rumbling stomach was louder than her scribbling pen. More bread, still delicious a few days old when toasted, and some eggs, a bright scrambled yellow in the pan. In bed by eleven, but as ever Alice found that sleep didn't come. She got out of bed and started working again at the kitchen table at one a.m., finally starting to doze over her books around three and crawling back up the flight and a half of stairs to catch an hour or two of sleep before fully waking just after dawn.

Cracking the attic window a few inches, Alice could hear the sea. She wondered again if today would be her day for swimming while here: it was one of the few pleasures she had besides reading. She loved the silence of underwater, the world reduced to muffled thuds while the colours grew denser, no teammates, no conversation, just weightless movement. A long time ago, she and Bea had often swum together, both with their long hair streaming behind them below the silver surface. One of the greatest shocks Alice had on her first visit to Polperran was discovering Bea had cut off her mermaid hair and replaced it with the shaggy bob she had kept for the rest of her life. Alice had felt that Bea, despite moving closer to the water, had cut off her swimming tail and left Alice behind in new, unexpected ways.

Alice had kept swimming as she grew up, but never again with Bea. One visit to Polperran, Bea had bought her a new swimming costume, but Alice never even tried it on. It had stayed in the drawer for two visits, then when it was clear Alice had outgrown it, it vanished and remained unreplaced. In Cambridge, Alice had stuck to early-morning lengths at the college pool, before a chance encounter had introduced her to a stretch of river favoured by swimmers, uncovered, unbleached, un-guarded. Early on in her career, a History colleague from Edinburgh with whom she'd only previously had email contact, albeit warm enough, dropped her a note to say he would be visiting Cambridge for a meeting, and would she mind taking him to a stretch of river he'd heard about? He knew she swam (it had come up in a conversation about a Trade Routes talk, absurdly) and had assumed she would have taken advantage of the countless lidos and river bends around Cambridge, and she hadn't wanted to reveal her tame, secure-locker-and-public-showers habits to someone who felt exciting and foreign to her college-shrunken mind.

She had found out details of the swimming point from someone down the hall from her office, who had looked surprised that Alice was engaging her in conversation. It made Alice realise how little she talked to people in the department, when they weren't travelling to a conference together, or planning lecture schedules. (But she couldn't remember if she'd ever talked to this woman again.) The morning after her visitor arrived, Alice and he had met early at a corner between the two of them, and walked together to the swimming spot, in quiet but continual conversation almost until they were in the water, and Alice had wondered how they would swim and keep up their talk. But when they had stripped and got in, warm at the surface still in late September, they hadn't spoken any further. They'd both let out low sounds as the cooler, deeper water was kicked up – they seemed to be the first swimmers in that morning – but they had swum up and down, with and against the gentle current, for three-quarters of an hour before he'd said, 'Enough?' and Alice wondered if he'd been waiting for her. But she didn't care because she had found something more important in that river.

Perhaps because she'd been so distracted by the thoughts of the water, she'd brought him back to her flat, and they'd had sex, and she had never seen him again, their emails diluted down to shallow wading and then silence. It had been a frictionless pleasure Alice hadn't known for many years, but she was too nervous to explore whether she could ever have it again with him; soon it wasn't even the sex she remembered, only the discovery of the water.

Staying in the house to work today wouldn't succeed, Alice realised. She had to get out, find a new table or desk where she could spread out. She needed fresh air, if only metaphorically, and without Bea's shadow over her. As Alice packed up her book, notebook and pens into her tote bag, she noticed how Bea's painting here in the bedroom captured the exact colours she could currently see from her windows. Was Bea also awake at dawn on May Days?

But once outside the garden gate, she didn't know where to go. In Cambridge there was her office, the library, the college library – sometimes the place seemed to be made *only* of desks – but if she wanted to leave the confines and memories, or lack of memories, of Bea's cottage and have anything to show for it, she would have to explore a little further than the pub or beach or Blandford & Sons.

She knew the right-hand fork took her to the sea and Joy's house, and although she hadn't explored fully, that didn't seem a promising direction. She turned left, towards the pub and Blandford's. She *could* spend the morning in the café belonging to the talkative woman, Gwen, although she'd rather not have to make small-talk when she could be analysing recently unearthed tax documents from 1360s northern France. It was unlikely, anyway, that the café would even be open at this hour. She wished, for a moment, that she still had the Walkman of her childhood now that she had returned to these familiarly unfamiliar shores. She suspected she would still enjoy those circles of foam connected by a thin wire strip to music that would protect her from having to talk to the outside world. But she'd grown out of the Walkman habit at college; there were too many people wanting to grab her for a word, too many chances there might be someone she needed to talk to. Now it somehow seemed like a distant behaviour belonging to someone else entirely. She didn't have a long commute or noisy household or crowds around her to justify headphones: she lived a quiet life, deliberately so, inside and outside her home. And she remained just as isolated as all those busy, sociable people around her with their eyes on their phones and their ears full of noise.

Studying history hadn't made Alice stuck in the past. Instead it was a useful tool for viewing the present, and imagining the future: if most times people did *this* and then *that* happened, what could you do to make *the other* occur instead? She'd read over and over about isolationism in various forms, tribalism, division, civil wars; what she didn't know was how to *want* to join in with anyone when it seemed easier to keep yourself in a tribe of one. Why would one want to press oneself against the heaving masses?

But was solitude its own tribe? The thing was, Alice thought sometimes, that isolationism at least meant banding together with a *few* people, even if it was against the rest of the world. These days, everyone was becoming like her: individuals, too weak to sacrifice their self-care routines of alone-time and submerge themselves in a club, a team, a community, even a classroom with any commitment or regularity. Alice understood, although she didn't want to, that individualism and isolationism, historically speaking, didn't tend to result in a rich palette of colour. It ultimately veered somewhat towards the grey end of things, at the very best. She was also beginning to understand that she cared less and less about how things were tending in the near-to-medium future. And she didn't know what to do about it.

*

As Alice walked through the village, she saw only a few gardens that looked cared for, like Bea's. One stood out among all the rest, with two huge hydrangeas at the end of a low stone wall, one blue, one a lilac pink, fat waxy blooms dotting each bush. There were enormous ferns, as in Bea's garden, lining the wall of the house, and multi-coloured flowers poked their heads above the low wall along the road. Instead of a lawn, there were pots of every height on an immaculately kept patio, and a garden table covered in gardening tools and old plant pots. As Alice drew closer, an impeccably groomed white-haired woman in khaki trousers and bright pink jumper stood up and leant against the wall.

'Hello!' she said. 'I'm Frances. Isn't it a beautiful morning?'

Alice blinked at her, torn from her pitiful thoughts. 'Yes, it is. Alice,' she added, reflexively. She looked over the wall again. 'What a nice garden.'

'Thank you! Would you like to come in and have a tour?' The woman looked at her expectantly, but the last thing Alice wanted was to get drawn into more mindless chitchat.

'Oh, I can't right now, but thank you. Perhaps another time?' Alice ignored the disappointment in the woman's face as she continued along the road. *Touring a stranger's garden.* Alice was perfectly fine walking on her own, thank you.

Shortly afterwards she reached the green, her stroll having become something of a march, but was pulled up short when she walked straight into someone coming from behind one of the trees around the edge. Alice let out an *ooof* sound, and looked accusingly at the solid form she'd run into.

It was the man from the pub again – Santo. He was smiling that same infuriating smile.

'We must stop running into each other like this,' he said.

She shook her head, used to tiresome students with their exhausting confidence. 'If I get concussion after this –'

'Ach, it wasn't your head, it was your body. And I can't say I didn't enjoy the experience.' He kept his eyes on hers, but Alice had the strong sense he'd taken a good account of exactly what was going on under her clothes. She blushed, furious at herself for it.

'Good for you,' she replied, taking her eyes off his thick-lashed, hazel ones and looking around to see if the green offered any clues of where she could work.

'Sorry,' Santo said, his tone changing to one of genuine apology. 'Alice, right? I wasn't looking where I was going, it wasn't your fault.' He saw her looking around. 'Are you after something? The least I can do is show you round, you being new and everything. Didn't your mum leave you a map or anything?' His tone was teasing, but he was smiling at her again, and she didn't have the time to wonder how exactly he knew who she was. 'Come on, what do you need?'

She had no better ideas, so told him: a quiet place, shaded, out of the breeze, where she could sit and work in peace and quiet. He thought for a moment, then said, 'Oh right. I know. Come on, then.'

Their initial impact had knocked the bag from her shoulder, so Santo waited while she finished collecting everything together and packing it back inside. 'You seem to make a habit of that,' he smiled. He nodded to the opposite corner to where they stood, away from the high street, Blandford's and the café, and they started walking towards it, keeping in the shade of the oaks that ran along one edge of the green.

As the green met the far path, running along a moss-furred

low slate wall, the bowl-cut woman who had served Alice in the shop on her two visits was coming up with one of her children. Distracted, it was only when Alice raised a hand in greeting that she looked up from her tired reprimanding and gave Alice a smile, which froze and fixed when she noticed Santo with her. The woman hurried off.

'She's . . . nice?' Alice said, after the woman half-hauled her young son across the green and left them taking the path. She thought she was going to have a break from grown adults openly freezing one another in the street when she left Cambridge. Some of the most senior members of her college had maintained decades-long silences between themselves and their closest colleagues.

Santo looked amused. He scuffed his feet slightly on the dried-out path as they walked, and said, 'Sally is, actually. I wouldn't fancy being stuck in that shop, living over it with her two young 'uns, and her dad the way he is, not well. Hard for her.'

If that was all true then he was right, she knew, as well as charitable, especially after Sally had seemed to greet him so oddly. When she was little, her mother had always joked to Alice and her father that the colleges were run like little villages, with their gossips and outcasts, rivalries and local news, and Alice was seeing it play out here: Santo was like those scholars who 'just didn't have the right face', in one Senior Fellow's skin-crawling phrase. *Although to be fair, his face was perfectly all right from where she was standing,* she found herself thinking, and shook her head quickly.

Eventually, at the end of the path, there was a wrought iron gate, and Santo held it open for her.

'The cemetery?' Alice asked.

70

'You said it was for history. Nothing more historical than a cemetery,' he replied.

Alice thought, *Religious sites? Parliaments? Palaces? A library?* but he looked so pleased with himself that she thanked him and mentally kicked herself. It had been too long since she'd spent time with anyone who wasn't a colleague or a student. He kept walking through the grounds, picking his way on the thin path between graves, and gestured for her to follow him.

Further through the cemetery, there was a large weeping willow. He held a section of leaves aside. Beneath the branches, there was a single bench, long and sheltered, in a cool, green shell of willow branches. Alice looked quickly at Santo.

'Good, eh?'

She stepped inside, where the May breeze was just a soothing sound and her papers could sit on the bench undisturbed.

'This is lovely. How did you know about this?'

Santo smirked at her, and let the willow fronds fall back behind them, closing them in from passers-by. 'Growing up in Polperran, there's not a lot to do but explore places you probably shouldn't be. Had my fair amount of hanging about and getting into trouble.'

Alice sat down and started taking out her things. 'But now you're a fine upstanding member of the community?' she asked.

Santo watched her making neat piles, lining up her pens across the bench seat. 'I do all right. You going to get straight to it?'

She nodded. 'But I forgot to bring anything to eat or

drink. I'll go to the café on the high street later . . . ?' Alice didn't know entirely what she was offering.

He looked at her, as if trying to judge the same thing. 'No, you're all right. I've got some things to be doing at the harbour.'

His tone had changed, and Alice wondered briefly what she'd done wrong. 'OK. Thanks for . . . this,' she said, indicating the bench, the spot. He ran his eyes again over the books and pens, and over Alice, gave her one more dazzling smile, and was gone.

The willow-hidden bench turned out to be the perfect place to work. It was quiet and cool, and when Alice heard someone moving about the cemetery they couldn't or didn't see her. She was entirely uninterrupted.

When she checked her watch for the first time and realised it was already mid-afternoon, she began packing everything back up. She found in one pocket of her bag the second envelope from Bea, and nearly laughed aloud at her task.

My dearest Alice,

Would you go and see Sally Hobson, at the village shop? She took over the shop single-handed when her father developed dementia – he may outlive me yet, but it's her who runs the whole thing now, and she's only in her twenties still, raising Tom and Iris all on her own. She's such an incredibly sweet girl, but one can tell that her heart is not in the shop at all, not like her father. It's clear she has some other path ahead of her, and it's too soon for her to give up on it; do you think you might uncover what makes her tick?

When I arrived here, someone was kind enough to put me up until I found the cottage and was able to buy it with the money your grandparents had left me (your father refused to take a penny of it, and wouldn't ever take any money from me to raise you). But the bills still needed paying each month, and it was Sally's father George who gave me a job at the shop to ensure I could keep living at the cottage. Soon I worked wherever anyone needed me, and between that I painted. For his sixtieth birthday, I gave George a painting of his favourite view from Polperran, and Sally told me he still has it in his room, that he still talks about it. It was the very least I could do for him after what he had done for me.

I don't know if you remember your grandparents (not your father's parents) as you were so little when we lost them. Your grandmother died when you were only six, but my father lived long enough to suffer from dementia too. Do you remember visiting him? It was so upsetting for all of us, seeing him like that, and for him when he would be struck by those brief moments of clarity. The last time we went, just before your tenth birthday, your father said you shouldn't come along for future visits, but your grandfather barely lasted a month more so we didn't need to decide one way or another. Can you remember that?

Your father was so good to both of my parents. It was one of the reasons I married him. He was such a strange figure when I met him at that party, the only person there in a suit and tie, everyone else in cheesecloth and corduroy. He looked so out of place, and I couldn't help but go and talk to him — partly curiosity, partly pity. But I could see immediately how kind he was, and I loved that what I'd taken for discomfort was actually fascination: he loved watching the colour and habits of our art school world, so different to his own. We thought we were making a fair deal when we married, bringing our very different selves to balance one another out. But life is unbalancing, with high and low tides – we are given things we didn't know we wanted, and we grow to want things we thought we didn't need – and eventually the imbalance wasn't fair to any of us in that house. He was always kind, to everyone, and although we had never planned to have children I was so delighted that you had such a good man to be your father.

My mother did everything she could for me, and I vowed to try and always be the mother you deserved. I am very afraid that I failed us both. But I never failed for a single moment in loving you completely.

Yours ever,
Mum

Alice did remember both of Bea's parents, both so old to her young self; they'd had Bea late just as Bea had Alice comparatively late for the times, waiting until their forties were looming. By the time his wife had died, Bea's father looked ancient, a hunched figure in a stiff-backed chair, politely asking who Bea was over and over again, looking for a tin of sweets to offer Alice, while Maurice chatted loudly and cheerfully to him with little response. Alice felt now that she and her grandfather were almost from the same generation, age compounding into one dilapidating blur after thirty-five, but at nine, Alice had thought he was a different species, something frightening and unrecognisable. She didn't remember Bea's grief for either parent.

Maurice had once told Alice, before Bea had left, that Bea's mother had been a good woman, but had been ill much of Bea's childhood. She had been closer to her father, and had wanted him to stay with her and Maurice and Alice after his wife's death, but after a few days it was clear they couldn't provide all the care he needed. He lived in a home for his final few years, and while both of them would visit much more frequently, they would bring Alice to visit him once a month. Alice did remember.

And what Santo had said was true: if Sally was running the shop, coping with two children and looking after her father with dementia, she was certainly in need of help, or at least sympathy. But Alice wondered at the letter, wondered if Bea had written her letters like this before but never sent them because Alice had made it clear that she didn't want Bea in her life. She knew so little about Bea's life before her, or even about her marriage to Maurice, and questioned for the very first time if there was another parallel life where Bea had stayed in Cambridge, had re-found her happiness and the pleasure of sharing afternoon crumpets with her daughter on rainy days. What would it have been like if she had stayed all the way through Alice's teens, and Alice thus knew all about Bea's childhood, and her engagement to Maurice, and the thousands of other tiny details that peppered most adult children's mental terrains, to be absorbed or avoided? She realised the huge gaps that instead made her up now, at the age of almost forty.

And Bea didn't even say please, Alice thought absurdly. But she had at least been in the village shop already and seen Sally twice, plus on the way here today. And yes, her mother was right, Sally didn't seem to be fond of the job she did with a sort of drudging Dickensian duty. And not even thirty! Alice had pegged her as much older than that, with her strange, ageing haircut, despite the young children. But Alice, a perfect stranger to this village who needed to return to her normal life – or at least escape this one – was meant to not only get to know this woman, but also uncover her deepest heart's desires? Alice felt exhaustion creeping back in, her heart beating with a sludgy lethargy.

After the cemetery Alice went to the café, but asked Gwen to bag her sandwich so Alice could take it with her, past the cottage, to the light of the beach in the softening sun. The young woman was there again on the pebbled shore, in the same faded thin anorak. Alice, now thinking deeply of the overlap of medicine and witchcraft during the Black Death, was already almost parallel with her on the railed-off sea path when she turned, and they made eye contact over the railing.

Alice raised one hand. 'Hello,' she called, muting her voice at the last minute so the second syllable came out as a whisper in the late afternoon stillness.

The girl looked down at her shoes, then scuffed one toe through the pebbles, before looking back up and raising her own hand in reply, just to hip-height. She turned away quickly before Alice could say anything else, hurrying along the beach to the furthest steps, disappearing again into some unseen path.

Chapter Eight

The basket had not been taken into Pilot's Cottage when Alice went to check the next morning. She took it back to Bea's house, threw away the runny day-old butter, and the spoiled eggs and milk, and headed back to the village shop for fresh supplies. She would also, she decided, take another look at the forlorn figure Bea had selected to be Alice's next project, keeper of shops and dragger of children, unknowing victim of a dead woman's best intentions.

When she handed over the items to the woman behind the till, there appeared no recognition at all from her that Alice had bought the same exact things the day before.

Eventually, Alice said, 'Hello.'

The woman blinked, and seemed to come to. 'Sorry, love, what was that?'

Alice smiled, and said, 'Been busy in here this morning?'

They paused and both looked around the completely silent, empty shop.

Sally looked at her. 'No, not today.' She handed Alice her shopping, which Alice stowed back in Bea's basket. 'Is that Bea's? Did you know Bea?' She looked in disbelief at Alice, then again more carefully at Alice's face. 'I saw you yesterday, didn't I? With Santo Hammett.'

Alice didn't know how to answer the latter question, so she ignored it. 'I'm Bea's daughter. Alice.'

Sally gave her a sympathetic smile, and put a hand upon her chest to indicate herself. 'Of course. Sally. I'm sorry about your mum; she was a lovely woman. In here all the time, letting me chat to her about her garden, she was.' Sally looked somehow as if she never had a moment for herself – just as Bea had surmised. She wore a sort of housecoat over her real clothes, which included grey joggers and a nondescript sweater, the greyish-green poking above the scoop-neck of the housecoat, emphasising Sally's exhaustion and seemingly doubling her age.

'Well.' Alice's instinct was to escape this small-talk as soon as possible, but she had to know *something* about Sally before she could even pretend to do something about this task. *It's just research*, she thought. *You're just dealing with a primary source.* 'It's certainly nice. Much nicer than mine at home.'

Sally settled herself against the cash register to make herself more comfortable, picking up a steaming mug from beneath the till and holding it to her chest as if to warm herself. 'Where's home for you again, love?'

Alice thought with a throb of her small, tidy house, and its tiny bare paved courtyard garden, wilting pots in the corners.

'Cambridge.'

'Oh, that's a way from here, isn't it? How is it having your mum's garden there? Will you stay for long?'

Alice shrugged in response to all three questions, then picked the middle question again. Sally seemed to want to talk gardens. 'It *is* a nice garden.'

78

'Isn't it just! Bea used to bring me in cuttings all the time, such a treat that was. Those greens, and the colours in the springtime – it's a paradise, really.' She looked wistful, and suddenly so much younger and more alive. 'Imagine having all those flowers,' she added, staring at something invisible near the bread rack.

'It's a very nice garden, but it's not fair for Bea to take all the credit,' Alice said, 'since I get the impression that it's Luke that does all the work.'

'Luke?' Sally raised one eyebrow. 'You've been chatting much to him too?'

Alice didn't feel that this talk with Sally had been enough of a conversation yet to count as *much chatting*, and wondered if she was talking about some other heart-to-heart Alice had forgotten about. Or maybe, she thought, Sally had a crush on Luke – maybe they had some kind of history? 'Well,' she said finally, 'I can't imagine Bea out there in all weathers slicing off branches and digging up roots, all covered in soil. I suspect it's Luke's hand there.' She smiled, but realised as she did so that she had absolutely no idea what Bea was like – had been like – in recent years. And now she thought about it, she could imagine Bea in her garden, in bright, battered gardening clothes and some enormous old straw hat, pottering about and probably growing enough soft fruit for the entire population of Polperran.

Sally blinked at her, still lost in some floral reverie, so Alice thanked her again and left with her shopping. As she walked, not really taking in her location, Alice thought of the difference between Bea's garden here, and the garden in Cambridge.

It had felt bigger then, because Alice was smaller, and sat tucked between their little terraced house and the brick wall that separated them from the identical garden behind. Both gardens had then had a herb bed, some flowering bushes, and a few climbing roses – identical plants, because Bea and the neighbour behind swapped cuttings with greater or lesser success, depending on the light and their soil. After her hours as a receptionist in a GP's surgery around the corner, Bea would almost always be in the kitchen, cooking for them all, or in the poky front room, reading and painting and making notes and little sketches, illustrating what she would like her garden to be, when she had more time, when she had more space. The garden Bea managed was in small pots, a sink she had picked up, larger terracotta pots she had found in a junk shop, and the main feeling in their garden was one of bricks and walls, illuminated with greenery and free without being overgrown.

The back-wall neighbour had a daughter, Alice's friend, whom Alice had known from birth, since Bea and her mother became friends when both heavily pregnant at an antenatal group at the community centre. Alice and the daughter had gone to the same nursery school, and the same primary, and were due to join the local secondary school together when her friend had come to Alice's door in tears, telling Alice that they were moving away for her mother's job. The whole family had packed up and left within two weeks, and although Alice and her friend exchanged addresses and promises to write, Alice's three letters had been answered only by a single postcard, and then nothing. The family hadn't responded to a Christmas card from Bea, either, because by that time Bea wasn't there to *send*

Christmas cards any more. When Bea had left, there had been no one to tend the garden either, and it had gradually died, leaving Maurice and Alice with the empty pots and blank walls that they had ignored for years and which these days Alice tried to brighten with plastic rugs and solar-powered fairy lights.

Alice thought she had forgotten all about the neighbour's daughter, her friend, Safina, but all of a sudden in the blue of the Cornish sun she could remember everything about her – her plait and her lisp, sleepovers in Safina's bunk bed, and the way she had refused all sweets but fizzy cola bottles; and the small but vicious grief that came each day with no word from her.

Alice looked around her and blinked, gradually registering where she was. Too late. She had stopped absent-mindedly next to Frances's house.

Frances popped up from behind the wall. 'Ah, Alice! Time for your tour?' Alice looked both ways, hoping for some inspiration.

'Not today, I'm afraid.' She indicated the basket vaguely. 'Just off to the house to do some work,' she lied, lifting the full basket.

'Oh?' Frances said cheerfully, her neat white hair almost glowing in the sun.

'Next time, I hope,' Alice said, quickening her steps and turning to give a small wave as she left the house behind.

After returning the whole basket to Joy's doorway, Alice arrived back at Bea's, looking forward to quiet again, but thinking still about Joy. Why redeliver the basket? Peter Blandford seemed content with Alice's word that she had done what she could, and completed that particular task. And Joy clearly had access to ingredients from somewhere other than Alice. Perhaps it was a soft-heartedness Alice had never admitted to, the need to bring comfort to someone who had also been hurt and shaped by abandonment. Or perhaps it was Alice's sheer bloody-mindedness, that she would succeed with this single task where Bea had so clearly failed.

As she opened the garden gate, she found Luke beside the hedge, standing very still and looking pensively in what Alice thought was the direction of the sea.

Remembering how Bea would ask her the same thing, she said, 'Penny for them?'

Luke turned to her, bending down just in time to stop his dog leaping forwards, paws up to Alice's waist. 'Whoa! Calm down, Belle, show some dignity.'

'Dognity,' corrected Alice.

Luke laughed, a short bark, and bent down to stroke Belle's velvet ears, watching the dog's delight. 'Sorry I keep turning up. I've put your mum's table out – I didn't know if you might want to work out here in the sun, but I've put it under the apple trees so it's not too bright. I can move it if you want, it was just – just a thought.' He pushed his hat back. 'There's just a few more jobs that need doing – I'll be out of your hair soon enough.'

Alice shrugged. 'Don't worry. I won't be here much longer.' It sounded colder than she intended, so she added, 'And it's good to have the garden being looked after. Somewhere to look wistfully at the horizon.'

He looked up at her, confused for a moment, then laughed again. 'Oh! No, it's that terrace, next to the ferns.'

Alice looked at where he was indicating, but could only see a huge wall of tangled brambles and what looked like more hedge, the only part of the garden which didn't appear to have been carefully tended. 'Honestly. I know it doesn't look like it, but there's a terrace under there. You can see it better from down on the beach – it looks directly over it. I was just wondering whether to get started on it while the weather's good. Your mum and I debated for years about clearing it, but it just seemed such a huge job that she always had us working on something else instead.'

'Us?' Alice repeated.

Luke looked at Alice, amused. 'Bea and I.' He smiled. 'Do you think she just watched me from the windows while I slogged in her garden?'

Alice imagined her mother in the role of older woman ogling the handsome gardener and felt herself blush: for the picture of Bea ogling anyone, and for thinking of Luke as handsome, as if he could hear the thought.

Luke hurried on, seeing her face and realising how his question had sounded, suddenly finding something in the branches of the quince tree which needed his attention. 'We did most of the gardening together, her planning and planting, me lifting and digging. It was so easy to work with her, after a while it didn't feel right to be charging her for it, but she'd refuse to not pay me. To be honest with you, most of my clients don't need me at all, even for lifting and digging, but they're just paying someone to be with them for a cup of tea and a chat a couple of times a week.' Alice must have looked shocked at this mercenary business model, because Luke hastily added, 'Don't worry. I barely cover my petrol costs with what I charge them. I save the big invoices for the holidaymakers and their totally essential overnight tropical garden transformations.' He smiled.

'Does that mean I don't count as a holidaymaker?'

'Depends how long you're staying.'

Alice looked again at the mass of brambles. 'So that's a terrace?'

He paused for a moment, scratching his beard. 'Like I said, you can see it from the beach, if you go round the rocks a bit. It'd be in terrible condition, though – might need repaving, ironwork's probably gone, and that's after you've cleared it. We always said we'd do it the next year. You'd have amazing stargazing from there, though, all that sky in front of you.'

Alice looked into the sky, just beginning to blaze for the day. 'It's good round here?'

Luke gave a mock-gasp. 'Alice Kimbrel, don't tell me your mother never took you stargazing when you visited.' He saw her face, and immediately changed tack. 'Don't get skies like this round where you're from, I bet – I've got to take you, it's the clearest skies at the moment, tomorrow's going to be perfect for it –'

'Oh. OK. OK,' Alice said, just as Luke said, 'I mean, it doesn't have to be with me,' and they were tumbling over each other trying to extricate themselves from the tangle before Luke cut in and said, 'Tomorrow. Pick you up at ten? And wear something warm.'

Alice didn't have time to refuse before his red setter escaped Luke's grasp and launched herself at Alice again. 'Belle! Down, girl. She never does this, do you, girl? What're you doing? What're you doing, girl?' Belle's tail waved wildly at this attention, Luke scratching the back of her

84

neck, Alice tentatively reaching out to stroke the dog's ears. Belle let out a soft whine of delight, then leapt away to canter around Bea's garden and back to them, overcome by some inner canine happiness.

'You know what they say about dogs?' Luke asked. 'They're either happy, or waiting to be happy. Not a bad life, eh?' He looked at Alice. 'Listen, have a think about the terrace. It'll be a good size, once clear, enough for a few chairs or whatever. You never know, the next owners of this place might pay a good price for a garden feature like that, if they're in the market . . .'

Alice suddenly remembered. 'Oh – that reminds me – do you know Sally in the shop?'

'Sally Hobson? Is everything all right?' Luke looked concerned.

'Yes, fine, but I was wondering – do you ever need another pair of hands? Someone to help on any of your jobs?'

Luke's concern turned to puzzlement. 'Sometimes. I just ask one of the coastguard lads, normally. Why, does she know someone looking for work?'

Alice felt abject nausea asking this, for someone she'd barely met to someone she hardly knew. 'No! It's her . . .' She tailed off, then took a deep breath. 'I think – I *think* – that she wants to be a gardener, not stuck in the shop all day, and I was just hoping you might be able to give her a bit of . . . work experience, I suppose. Or at least a break from the shop. It's one of Bea's tasks . . . Is that possible? Do you do that here?'

Luke reached under his hat to scratch his head. 'It's not the strangest thing a customer has asked me to do . . .' He smiled again. 'But if that's what you think she wants, I'm happy to help out, I suppose. Monday, I've got a big job – I could do with someone then?'

Alice clenched her fists triumphantly, then laughed in surprise at her own gesture. 'Sorry. Am I getting too invested?'

'Ooh, careful,' Luke raised his hands in pretend-fear. 'You don't want to get *invested* in us.' He turned away and whistled for Belle. 'You don't want to actually get attached to us.' He looked back and smiled as he left.

Alice screwed her face up at his back, then as he closed the gate called out, 'I'll let Sally know then. Monday!'

Belle gave a bark of agreement over the wall.

At the pub that evening, Alice sat at the bar with her gin and tonic and shepherd's pie, watching as Janet tidied and cleaned endlessly around the bottles and pumps.

'Is it always like this?' Alice asked.

'What's that, my dove?'

Alice suppressed a smile at this casual endearment. 'Is it always . . . this quiet?'

Janet looked around. 'Quiet? This is one of our busiest nights.'

They both looked around at the near-silent room, packed with tables of one or two, flecked with occasional mutters. It reminded Alice of Sally's shop or most of the village itself, like the rooms and grounds of Sleeping Beauty's castle, everyone half-asleep or vanished, whole crowds reduced to footprints and dirtied pint glasses.

'It used to be loud in here,' Janet said. 'I remember when I was a kid not being able to make myself heard, but that was a long time ago. Used to have music in here too, all the time. In fact –' she started whispering, 'see that fellow in the corner? With the hat? Bert. He's one of the best accordion players you'll ever hear.'

Alice looked at the figure in question, a crumple-faced old man in a fraying fishing jumper, his mouth a perfect straight-line match for the line across his forehead and the flat cap on his head. 'But he doesn't play any more?'

Janet held up one finger, then indicated the opposite end of the pub. Another old man sat there, striped jumper and old trousers, a cheerfully blank expression on his turtle-like face, his head shining but for small puffs of white above each ear. 'Him in the jumper? That's Clemmo. *He's* one of the best fiddlers you'll ever hear.' Janet smiled at Alice's bafflement. 'They used to play *together*. Fill this place with people from miles around, it would. Singing, dancing, all sorts, when those two were at it. Sometimes they'd pretend on a Friday night that they'd forgotten their instruments or they weren't in the mood, just to hear people plead, but they'd always have 'em, always played.' Janet looked between them. 'Cor, I'd forgotten about that. Seems like a different time.' She shook her head.

'Did my mother – did Bea see them play?'

Janet laughed. '*Oh* yes. I remember her from when I was a much younger woman, kicking up her heels with the best of them, always one of the first dancing, right up until those two stopped. She tried to get them playing again, but no luck, as you can see.'

Alice felt a small jab of pleasure at Bea's defeat. But she also remembered Bea dancing; when Alice was a much younger girl too, in the kitchen, in the lounge, even in

Alice's bedroom when she was supposed to be going to bed, to cheer Alice up after a bad day at school or to make her laugh after a good one. When one of her favourite songs would come on the radio, Bea would grab Maurice and try to dance with him, but he would stand stiff and embarrassed, eventually muttering could she ask Alice instead? And Bea would stand away from him, her own face growing stiff too for a moment before she would see Alice and seize her, dancing her around to Whitney Houston and Elton John, both of them collapsing against the worktop when a twirl became too ambitious, Maurice watching them, delighted. Of course, once Bea left, no one danced with Alice; any friends she had at school were not the type to dance in their rooms with her, so while Bea danced here, Alice had stopped altogether.

Janet nodded over Alice's shoulder. 'Ooh, hang on.' In the mirrored backing behind the optics, Alice saw Clemmo, the ex-fiddler, shamble over to the bar, ask for another cider, and take it with just a nod of thanks to Janet. 'Clemmo?'

He waved a hand over his shoulder. *Not now*.

Alice looked at Janet, who shrugged wearily. Alice said, 'So . . . what happened between them?'

Janet sighed, and started wiping the bar down once she'd checked Clemmo was fully out of earshot. 'Well,' she said, voice back to a whisper. 'They had a fallin' out, of course, despite them being the oldest friends in the village. Best friends since they were born, their mothers best friends themselves. Had an argument that no one could get to the bottom of an' neither of them would ever speak of. Just put their instruments away one day and no amount of begging could get them to bring them out again, or even talk to each other.' She sighed again. 'Silly bloody fools.'

Alice thought about her own friendships. Morag would probably be one of the few people to notice Alice had left Cambridge, beyond a few of her seminar students. Alice had never been one of the most popular children at school, but she'd been sociable, and been to parties, and had friends over – friends who always loved Bea, naturally. As her teenage years progressed, Alice's friendship circle had grown smaller, but not tighter; it had thinned out rather than contracted. Coupling-up had contributed to that, where friends had got crushes or partners and Alice hadn't. Or rather, she had, but always held them in orbit around her, centring her studies instead, letting her success with her marks and the clear-headed focus it gave her carry her from one rung to the next.

After a while, friendships seemed to be something she left behind at school. Why wouldn't she rather enjoy her steady rise, with a small handful of sex or short relationships over the years? Familiarity had brought her and Morag close, as they climbed those rungs together and Morag remained present, showed that she had no expectations of Alice. Alice hadn't even minded when Morag was promoted over her, advancing all the way to Head of Department, because Alice didn't care for the politics Morag was so skilled at; her attention was always, always on her papers, her reading, with a small slice spared for those rare students who showed real understanding and intelligence, not just knowledge and rhetoric, and beneath that the whole of her mind was bedded in water, the multiple swims she required through each week, every week, to paddle against panic and maintain enough calm and cohesion that she could function in the frenetic life of her department. She never wished for more friends, but she also never allowed herself to think about how lonely her life might look, from the outside.

Alice looked at the two men, sitting in such similar poses, sharing such a solitary air as they sat and looked into their pints in the still, quiet room.

In the doorway of the Dolphin, just as Alice was setting off for Bea's, a soft voice caught her.

'Alice?' It was the slight, red-haired woman from Gwen's café, Luke's sister – Melder? – just coming from the path past the pub, her green eyes glowing in the light of the pub's solitary front porch lamp. 'Do you want some company on the walk?' Alice heard a snuffling sound, and saw Melder was holding Belle on the end of a leash.

She nodded, then said, 'Yes,' when she thought Melder might not have seen. Then added, 'Please,' to be polite, and felt miserable at how weak she sounded.

Melder took her arm, easily, without a word, and they went together towards Bea's cottage, Belle snuffling the ground ahead of them, her collar jingling softly. Alice became aware that Melder was looking around the surrounding darkness as they walked, and was about to say something, but Melder spoke first.

'How are you finding it?'

Alice shrugged in the dark. 'Polperran?'

Melder was quiet.

'Well, it looks lovely. But I don't know it at all, yet. And on the beach in the mornings it feels like no one lives here at all, sometimes. I don't think I'm used to somewhere so quiet.'

'You'll come to know it soon enough, I hope.' They waited while Belle investigated a telephone pole. 'And you've been visiting Joy?'

Alice huffed. 'I've seen her. I wouldn't say we're best friends yet.'

Melder laughed softly. 'She is who she is. You can only be disappointed if you expect something different to what you're being offered. But Bea's – how is it, being in the cottage?'

'Well,' Alice mused. 'It's a very nice cottage.'

'Hmm,' Melder hummed. They walked further in silence.

'Is Belle yours too?' Alice asked eventually.

'Oh god, no,' Melder said. 'Belle is a one-owner dog. I'm just taking her as Luke's out tonight.'

'Oh, right,' Alice said, feeling a slight clumping somewhere in her ribcage.

'Have to keep her on the lead, though,' Melder went on, 'Otherwise she'll run all the way to the station. Done it before, haven't you, you silly beautiful dog!' Melder bent down and ruffled Belle's ears, but Belle turned away, too noble to be patronised even though her wagging tail betrayed her. 'He's on a coastguard shift,' Melder explained. 'And Belle always gets so spoiled there she gets furious when she can't go with him. I don't think she's speaking to me at the moment.'

'Oh! Right,' Alice replied, almost laughing, glad of the night hiding her face.

They arrived at Bea's garden gate.

'Listen, Alice,' Melder said softly. 'I know you won't be here for long, but – if you want a walk, or a coffee, or something . . . I'll get Luke to give you my number, and we can do something. Or nothing. Whatever.' There was a pause. 'Are you still there? Christ, it's dark.'

Alice laughed and said, 'Yes, I'm still here. Sorry, I forget you can't see me. I'm nodding.'

Melder called to Belle who was snuffling at Alice and stepping on her feet, said, 'Night, then,' and let Alice slip away back into Bea's cottage.

Chapter Nine

She didn't know if she had slept at all the night before, but she had watched the light gradually grow brighter across her room until she'd surrendered and got up at five. She still hadn't swum. She'd gone down in her costume, certainly, with layers on top to warm her up afterwards should the water warrant it, but despite having the whole pebbled beach to herself Alice had only dipped her toes in the cold sea to try and shock her tiredness out. She was nervous. Rivers and lakes, although possessed of their own hazards, felt leagues away from the infinite sea, but the inevitability of an eventual swim was enough to keep everything else quenched for now as she felt the cool water around her feet.

Back at Bea's, she had worked for a while at the kitchen table, but her mind was distracted again, and her stomach empty. She realised she couldn't keep on relying on occasional pub food, Gwen's café and the magical bread bin, so she made a list of basic groceries, plus a few other items – soap, washing powder, a new lightbulb for the flickering lamp on the landing – before she found herself wandering around the house to check for anything else. She still couldn't go into Bea's room. Although the door was open, Alice realised she hadn't even turned her eyes in that direction, speeding by just as she had the spooky under-stairs door in her childhood home.

In Bea's studio, however, the walls were so bright that no phantoms could remain. Some of the oils were still tacky on their palettes, though the brushes had been cleaned meticulously. Did Bea stop painting when she knew she couldn't clear up any more? Or had someone else helped her to keep painting until the very end, ensuring her small income remained to the last? *Until* her *very end*, Alice corrected herself. *It wasn't the end for anyone else.*

She lifted one of the canvases from the floor, onto one of the tables. A sea view. *Coming to Cornwall and painting the sea*, Alice thought. *Gosh. How original.* The next one was different: abstract, with a great dark mass on one side and two different coloured shapes, one large, one smaller – moving towards one another? Joining? Pulling apart? – on the other. The background looked muddy, angry, but although the mood was entirely different, the brushstrokes were recognisable from the sea view painting.

The third canvas Alice picked up was a landscape again, but distorted, and Bea had been facing inland, this time. A tiddlywinks game of green, tinsel clusters of bushes and hedgerows between them, the sky a dizzying pink above. The colours were fantastical, but Alice still felt like she understood the feeling of this picture. Maybe she would take this one back with her. She wondered why she had never looked at the paintings before – had Bea discouraged Alice from coming in here? She knew that Bea would never have done such a thing, would have welcomed Alice in with open arms, would have set her up with her own easel and paints, but Alice had only ever once stood in this doorway, on her very first visit here. Otherwise, it was in her room, at the table, in the car. That was it. The fathomless ache in her chest.

Alice would have to drive to get any meaningful supplies, although she hadn't driven for years. She had passed her test six months after turning seventeen, her usual effort and application meriting the usual success; since then it had been only a handful of times. Her first time on the motorway had resulted in a three-day panicked exhaustion, her muscles steel as she had driven home on what she had been reassured was the simpler route. She had told Maurice it was flu, when she arrived at his house and stayed in her old room for days, and the thought that he suspected it wasn't flu made her feel even worse. Behind the wheel, in a metal death box planing towards other metal death boxes, all heading towards death one way or the other, her only thought was of twisted limbs, torn flesh, hideous wounds and terrible, life-changing injuries. So she'd avoided driving, suiting her life to a city of bicycles and public transport, doing the very minimum to ensure she could still drive a car if her life depended on it.

Did this count as one of those occasions? She packed her bag, and headed outside to the car.

It had taken fifteen minutes of sitting in the car, starting it up then turning it off again, before Alice had found the courage – or rather, talked herself into just doing it, just do it, just do it, do it now, *do it* – to get out onto the road. Bea's car was steady enough, but so old it drove with a slight whine whichever gear was selected. Alice drove under the speed limit the whole way to the nearest town, with frustrated drivers hooting on the narrow, steep country lanes and overtaking on the straight, and when she parked she realised she was covered with a fine oily sweat. The supermarket had been easy to find, though, and when Alice was loading the car afterwards she realised that her phone had a signal, as well as several messages from Morag checking up on her.

'Alice?'

'I'm here, I'm sorry, there's no signal in my mother's village, she doesn't even have wifi in the cottage, it's like being back in the nineties –'

'Oh thank god! How are you? How are the locals?'

'Not sure yet,' Alice said. 'Not actively hostile. Although I'm trying not to think about why my mother hired such a suspiciously handsome gardener.'

'A handsome Cornish gardener, you say? Maybe I will come and visit. How's the book?'

'Good! I've done some good work here, some really interesting things with the Sayers document.' Alice felt pleased. 'Do you want me to send anything over?'

There was a brief pause. 'I'm glad you're well, Alice. What's the weather like down there?'

Alice looked around. The sky was a blue-gold, fresh with sea air, and she could see flocks of birds wheeling over the boats, wing-tips dipped in dashes of sun. 'Fine.'

'Alice?' Morag waited. 'Just enjoy being away from all this! Keep up with your work – I'm happy to read anything you want me to, when you think it's ready. But just try to . . . take it easy, OK?'

'I haven't checked my emails yet – if there's anything

urgent, I can give you Bea's landline number, if I can find it . . .'

'Just take it easy,' Morag repeated. 'That's an order. There's nothing urgent, we can handle everything. But if you ever need to call, Alice, you know that I'm here. God, where else would I be?'

Alice laughed. 'My students –'

'We'll talk when you're back, OK? Just . . . go and have some fish and chips, or something.'

'It's eight o'clock in the morning, Morag.'

'Well. A pasty, then.'

Alice was glad to have spoken to Morag – she'd been so insistent on Alice's break from the History Faculty that Alice didn't know whether Morag would take her call. But Morag had been her friend long before any of this difficulty, even when they were both humble research assistants, and Alice should have trusted her more. Maybe Morag really was looking after Alice's best interests, and maybe Alice shouldn't be thinking about any return to marking or planning while she was down here; the book, that's what she'd focus on, some factual death and destruction and paranoia and persecution, and then when she was back at college after a week or so, she'd have had a bit of space to get everything settled in her mind. Her reading was a technicolour of browns, blacks and reds at the moment: rivers full of corpses, families destroyed between sunrise and sunset, villages blighted by fear, division and death. Old documents had somehow survived to record the lives of those who hadn't – which was all of them, of course – and seven hundred years later here she was poring over them, someone who had never even come close to the extremes of creeping death infecting every corner.

She couldn't remember the last time she'd had a break from Cambridge, when her daily life wasn't shaped around the Faculty's daily, monthly, annual schedules. Even between terms she'd be there, researching and submitting, applying for funding and conferences. Those conferences were generally her only holidays: a hotel room for one in another student city, a chain restaurant meal for one, a train journey back to Cambridge, occasionally a flight if her topic was deemed sexy enough that year. She *should* make the most of this Cornish trip. It was what Morag seemed to want for her, and as long as Alice could get back to the History Faculty before her absence was really taken seriously, she'd be able maybe to one day look back on this trip fondly. Perhaps.

With phone signal at last, Alice wondered if there was anyone else she should be contacting while she could. She still, even twelve years on, had the impulse to call Maurice, his phone number unchanged from her childhood, tripping off her brain like a jingle. But Maurice, like Bea, was gone. At least, Alice thought, she had given Bea the courtesy of being invited to Maurice's funeral. Bea had come, with her shaggy bob and her black funeral outfit, her ears ticking with huge green chandelier earrings, kissing Alice's temple as Alice tipped her face away. Alice had been out of her mind with grief, after Maurice had died suddenly from a heart attack just after his sixty-fourth birthday, and Alice had needed to do all the brutal necessary paperwork completely alone, entirely rudderless and constantly wanting to call Maurice to tell him about it all, even though she never would have bothered him with something so tragic when he had been alive.

Some of Maurice's friends had given Bea the cold shoulder at the wake, literally turned their backs on her, and Alice, in her early twenties and feeling like she should know how to behave like a grown-up, was shocked through her grief, even as she knew she would have asked them to do it if she could, to shun this woman who had broken Maurice's heart and had little to do with him after the day she had walked out on them both.

Looking back now, she wondered at how much she had loved those people that day for that, although in Maurice's life they had never demonstrated such fierce loyalty and strength of feeling. Even the word friends felt too strong. They were simply long-standing acquaintances from bell-ringing, allotments, church rotas, volunteer groups. They had always spoken together with friendly small-talk, about the issues in their immediate vicinity – the new compost bin, the fundraising quiz night – polite and gentle with easy laughter, and she couldn't imagine Maurice even mentioning his wife leaving him and his daughter, let alone breaking down and revealing how deeply it might have affected him. She remembered the hard-eyed, black-clad crowd, their eyes flicking to and from Bea, and she queried for the first time what they had loved more: quiet, reliable Maurice, or the juicy disapproving of this woman who had abandoned her family.

At the time, she had also wanted to go to Bea and stand by her side, smell her familiar perfume, while Bea was mostly ignored by the people she had warmly hosted countless times over the years at coffee mornings and dinner parties. But as Alice watched, some of her father's colleagues – who perhaps knew less of his home life – greeted her and fell into easy conversation with this charming woman. Alice kept watching as Bea began to talk, moving her hands, her earrings glittering, and the group dissolved into gentle but genuine laughter.

Alice had gone to the kitchen, had buttered sandwiches and plated biscuits, with a fury disguised in an almost zombie-like grief. As people began to leave, she said goodbye politely to her father's colleagues, their faces aglow after their fascinating afternoon with the dead man's ex-wife, and let Maurice's friends hug her as they dabbed their eyes, *You will get in touch with us if you need anything, Yes of course, Anything at all, Yes I will.*

Bea had hung around, piling up plates and cups, and Alice had gone out of the back doors of the building and squeezed through a hedge, a bedraggled young woman in mourning clothes, and had fled to Maurice's house, her house now. She hadn't answered Bea's phone calls for the next few hours. Two days later, she received a letter from Bea, the familiar handwriting on the envelope, and Alice had folded it neatly and dropped it into the wastepaper basket, then shortly afterwards had taken it out again, torn it methodically into twelve pieces, then walked with the pieces to the corner of her street and dropped them into the bin by the bus stop. Then she ran a deep bath, and lay in it until it was colder than blood temperature, submerged with only her nostrils above the surface.

Bea hadn't tried to call her again for a couple of weeks, by which time Alice was sufficiently in control again that they could return to their former telephone calls, Alice disengaged and brief, Bea conversational and breezy.

And now there was no Maurice, no Bea. Morag had all but warned her off contacting anyone else in the department while she was away, and Alice realised she had no one else to call. She thought of the colleague with whom she'd swum in the ponds, and wondered whether he'd remember her now, or the Geographer, or the countless name-badges she'd met over the years, never taking anyone in for more than a day or two. Her phone sat full of numbers, but there was no one she could call.

At Bea's, the shopping was swiftly unloaded, and Alice set herself up again at the kitchen table; knowing Morag was waiting to see this was what Alice needed. The uncertainty brought about by working away from all her colleagues and rivals was gone, replaced by the laser focus she had perfected from her early teens. Anything that could shut the world out was a positive. Besides, she wanted very much to not be thinking about tonight, going stargazing with a man she barely knew in a place she definitely didn't.

The work went well, when she could forget about the stargazing. Luke hadn't reminded her of his offer as he'd left the day before, nor she him. It was unlikely to happen so should be forgotten. Her shopping allowed a sandwich for lunch – her meal-time habits with Maurice had barely changed, even in his long absence – and then more work, an early evening brisk walk around the village – still so quiet, where does everyone go? – after which she sat and felt her body grow heavier in the armchair in the snug.

She was at a party in one of the college rooms. It was busy, guests chatting happily, someone playing piano in another

101

room, trays of bright food on every flat surface that she could only see out of the corner of her eye. And something else: Bea, or rather the back of her head and her shoulder, disappearing through the doorway towards what Alice could now see was the staircase of Alice's childhood home. Eventually Alice followed her, but there was now no one there, or no one Alice could notice, but through another doorway was Bea again, or her back and one foot, a sliver of her slipping though again. Again Alice slowly followed, with no urgency, only curiosity, wondering if she could ask Bea about these tasks, hoping she could have Bea take the tasks from her so Alice would be free to go home. But instead through the other door was —

She woke with a snort, her heart pounding, dizzily fogged over where she was and what the time was. She looked at her watch. Not late yet.

Alice didn't know what one wore for stargazing, besides something warm, so settled on her warmest jumper, jeans, and Bea's green turban, clothes she could legitimately have been wearing around the cottage anyway. When she heard Luke's van outside, her pulse quickened, not in her stomach, but in her shoulders — something lighter, not the usual concrete ooze of anxiety. She left the house and pulled the garden gate closed, and when she turned to the van it wasn't Luke she saw first, but Melder.

'Hello again!' Alice said, with genuine pleasure. She realised she had quite liked the gentle honesty of that calm, strange woman from the brief walk with Belle last night. 'I didn't know you were coming too.'

'I hope you don't mind,' Melder said, looking uncomfortable. 'Luke told me I had to, I'm so sorry. I hope it's OK.'

102

'Of course!' Alice said, trying to think of something to reassure Melder. 'It's . . . family, isn't it?'

'Mel doesn't like to spread it around; it ruins her reputation to have such an uncool brother,' Luke said, opening the door for Alice but smiling at Melder too. 'Hope you don't mind a bit of a squeeze here.' He offered his arm, for Alice to boost herself into the high bench seat of the van.

They drove in peaceful silence, Melder quietly pointing out landmarks to Alice, until they turned down a small single-track road which quickly became little more than a dirt track. It came out on a tiny beach, where they parked and climbed out, Luke leaping around first to offer the same arm down to both of them. The beach itself was dimly lit by a fingernail new moon, and the stars outshone it. This far from large towns and busy streets, the sky was filled with them, impossibly many jewelled fistfuls sparkling on a velvet bed. 'I feel like I could touch them,' Alice found herself saying, and Luke and Melder hummed agreement.

Luke said, 'Hold on,' and dashed to his van, pulling out three sun lounger cushions that Belle had been lying on in the back, plus a thermos flask and two plastic cups. He laid the lounger cushions on the beach while the dog made herself comfortable at his feet, gestured for them to take a seat, then poured out the contents of the thermos into the lid and cups. 'Tea,' he said, passing them around. The cushions were comfortable, and once Alice had drunk the tea and let it warm her, she lay back and watched the sky.

On a night this clear, shooting stars came every minute or more, as well as satellites and occasional planes at high altitude. The three of them lay still for a long time, and

Alice was glad that Melder had come. She'd been pleased to see her, of course, but now she was also glad that with her there, there was no weird awkwardness between her and Luke, out on what would be a remarkably romantic date if Alice was inclined that way; instead there was the comfortable peace that comes with close adult siblings. Melder asked Alice if she wanted to know any of the constellations, which of course she did; Melder showed her Aquila and Cygnus and the Dragon, distant Ursa Minor and swooping Ursa Major. Luke added a few others, and Alice was just about to ask what a steady twinkling green light was when they heard the noise of an approaching vehicle.

Immediately Melder was up on her feet, alert as prey, with Luke calmly but swiftly raising himself up to stand beside her, a look passing between them. *Is this place dangerous?* Alice thought. *They look like we're about to be attacked.*

But when the car appeared at the end of the dirt track, both Penroses relaxed, and Melder even seemed to recognise the people in the car. 'Back in a second,' she said, giving a laugh that was part-amusement, part-relief, and left Luke and Alice together.

'Melder's come out of a tough relationship recently,' Luke said after a moment.

'Oh. I'm so sorry. Did they come here a lot?'

Luke chuckled bitterly. 'No. But her ex has a habit of turning up coincidentally at the same place, despite that very much not being the deal.'

'Oh. Shit.'

'Yup,' Luke replied. 'He is.' He shook out his thermos lid

and screwed it back on the flask. 'Sorry. But he followed her earlier today, and it shook her up. That's why I asked her out with us tonight.' He looked at Alice, and held out his hand. 'If that really was OK?'

'It really was, honestly.' Alice paused and swallowed and before she could think twice put her hand in his proffered one. Luke's eyes sprang wide just as Melder returned.

There was a single moment when all of them seemed to be frozen. 'I – sorry – did I . . . ?' Melder looked mortified.

Alice pulled her hand away. 'No, no, it's –' She got up, and started dusting herself off, horrified and humiliated by Luke's reaction to her touch, feeling the pressure of where they had touched like a burn.

Melder helped fold the cushions away as Alice stood uselessly to one side, and Luke said quietly, 'Mel, your cup?' holding his hand out in exactly the same way as he had reached out to Alice. Suddenly she realised – she saw what had happened – her mistake, his repulsion, another person to be clipped out of her life before they could clip her. She thought she might be sick, right there and then, into her own lap. If she could just keep her lips clamped tight and keep swallowing the bitter taste in her mouth, she could get home, shut down, and be apart from everyone once more.

The drive home was quiet again, but this time it was a tense silence. Alice felt like steel rope, stretched to its limits, that snapping could be fatal. Something pulsed in the front of her skull. Melder tried once to ask a question about a farm they drove past, but Alice didn't know the answer and Luke just grunted. When Luke's van pulled up at Bea's, Alice all but leapt out, twisting her ankle and waving to them both without making eye contact as she tried to hide her limp up to the front door.

She unlocked the door and, inside, tore off the turban and made it to her room and the heavy blankets, before she collapsed, humiliated, miserable and alone.

By 4.30, Alice knew she wouldn't be sleeping. The attic was stuffier than ever, even with the window open, and the burning shame of her interaction with Luke was too strong. *Idiot idiot idiot idiot idiot.*

Downstairs was a notion cooler. Opening the back door, Alice could hear the sea, which brought down the wild fizzing in her head slightly, the rough voices babbling at her and about her. In the garden, the night was balmy, with the hangover of yesterday's hot day still in the dawn air, and a golden shadow looming on the horizon. She heard the splash of the water on the breeze, and closed her eyes. The cold waves were what she wanted.

In her room, she found her swimming costume. She got changed, her heart thumping with the delight of solitude, and put on a dress over it, plus sandals and a jumper for the walk home. On the landing outside Bea's room she paused and remembered: looked at the dresser on the landing, filling the space between Bea's bedroom and the stairway to her own attic room. It was a large, oak thing, six drawers and four shelves, heavy and solid, older than Bea, older than Alice, and likely to outlive her too. She opened the drawer closest to her, and found Bea's swimming costume and a bright, floral swimming cap, the type models wore in 1950s sunny cigarette ads. She tugged the hat on, tucking her hair underneath, and looked at herself in the landing

106

mirror, the silvered surface spotted and aged by salt air. *You shall go to the ball*, she thought, her mouth quirking at her absurd reflection. By the time she was ready, the light was warming, a glow tinting the sky, but at the shore the cliffs were all shadow.

Down by the sea, sandals off, dress off, Alice bundled everything into a neat parcel on the pebbles and walked straight into the water. Her toes felt the cool-bath warm of it, and she walked on, thinking only of getting braced for the cold that never came, the pebbles softening to sand after a few paces. There were tiny shards everywhere, wood and leaves, bits of creature and non-creature, and she waded on, knee-deep, up to her thighs, waist-deep, rising up her chest. Then her feet were lifting behind her and she was swimming, kicking gently in breast-stroke, hands joining in front before spreading and drawing deep ovals each side of her, joining and circling, joining and circling, forwards and through, onwards, making no noise at all in the noise-less waves, just the sound of birds on the clifftops around her and the water's arrival on the shore. Something in her unwound and opened up.

She turned onto her back and floated there, paddling hard in her mind not to notice what could have been Cupid nor to think about lovers, trying to find the few constella-tions the Penroses had shown her that she could remember. The Plough – no, Ursa Major, the Great Bear. And beside the bear lay Boötes the Ploughman, relaxing after his long day. Was that Hercules, with the dragon beneath his feet? That cluster looked familiar, but the sky had wheeled in the night and she had never seen them look as clear as they looked out here, even in the growing dawn, so the whole sky could be new above these waters and Alice wouldn't be surprised. Was that green twinkling light there again, so bright in the sky?

Out here it was just Alice and the rapidly dimming stars, water lifting her up and along. Did Bea do this too – night swims? Dawn dips? Did she swim regularly? Did she come with friends? *Or lovers*, Alice thought again, before she could stop herself, and dipped her face beneath the salty dark blue to stop the thought returning.

The sky warmed and the waves rumbled on, and Alice turned parallel to the beach, swimming back and forth along it, half an eye on her belongings for bearings, the other half turned to the roaring expanse in the other direction, limitless death and open space. She didn't feel anything would come from beneath – her fears were never so tame and practical – but the infinity to one side gave her swim a soothing thrill. Every single swim was the same, weightless serotonin-lapping waves across her brain, and each swim was different: lobster-red skin in the winter, the first dawn chorus each spring, the tilting light, the midges, the rain, so different in February and in August, hisses and murmurs on the surface of the water.

No one took the beach path while she swam. Early or late, people in Polperran seemed to keep at home, hidden, busy, doing who knows what; even on these beautiful days, no one appeared to come to the beach or sit on the green, even the younger members of the village who must, despite little evidence, exist here in a meaningful number. She remembered in Cambridge how the mere presence of young people seemed to terrify large swathes of the community, as if it were not sixteen-year-olds roosting on the benches but a flock of bloodthirsty Harpies.

She kicked back to shore, standing up only when both knees were stroking the sandy bed, and found her clothes and dressed, walking back up the path to the cottage with a delicious sleepiness upon her: not exhaustion, but a warm-milk-and-clean-bed feeling, a child being carried from the car in spangled night, home again at dawn's rosy fingers.

At the still-dimmed cottage, Alice didn't turn on any lights. She didn't want to wake herself, so simply stripped off clothes and bathing cap and slid between her tangled, cooled sheets, asleep before she knew it. She dreamt of waves, carrying her, somewhere dark and cold.

Chapter Ten

Alice slept in until nearly noon, and woke up in high confusion, the white sun hot on her roof. That was usually the advantage to her insomnia, when she visited Bea: she was very rarely still in bed when the day, and the room, had grown too warm, instead having got up early to sit in the shadiest corner with her books and pens.

Her mouth now was dry, and her body was dusted, brushed with sea salt where she hadn't washed last night. Pulling herself upright, she looked at Bea's painting again on her wall. How cool and blue it looked through her semiconscious heat-haze.

She washed quickly, dressing in her only remaining clean dress – *I need to do some laundry today*, she thought, *and I can take whatever's still clean back with me to Cambridge* – and realised in the kitchen that for all her grocery-shopping yesterday, she still needed milk. Putting on a large pair of sunglasses she found in one of Bea's drawers by the front door, Alice stumbled outside and past the green, to the village shop.

Sally wasn't there, which reminded Alice that she hadn't yet given her the news about working with Luke – Alice winced behind her glasses – but an older lady was behind the till, who jumped as she walked in.

'Good lord, my love, you'd give a statue a heart attack!'

Alice looked over her shoulder, wondering who she was talking to.

'Yes, you, dear, looking the spit of your mother, and in her glasses too!' Alice pulled the glasses off, squinting in the neon strip-lighting of the shop, her own heart pounding now. 'Alice, isn't it?'

Alice stepped forwards a little, letting the door close fully with a little *ding* of the shop bell. 'Yes.' She tried to draw her breath in as slowly and silently as she could, focusing on the slowness, and on not letting this woman see her heart at frantic work.

The woman tilted her head to the side, and smiled, her eyes watching Alice closely. She was impeccably dressed in what looked like a butter-soft twinset, neat cropped trousers and suede loafers, which made Sally's housecoat, worn over the top of her outfit, look even more forlorn than before. She came out from behind the till, and came close to Alice. 'I'm sorry, love,' she said gently, 'it was just such a shock. I'm Tressa. I knew your mother,' she said. 'A *long* time. She was all right in the end, you know.'

Alice just nodded, confused at the phrasing.

'I'm sorry, Alice.' She backed off a little, adjusting her horn-rim glasses. 'If you need anything, I'm always about.' Ah, so this was Tressa, who Gwen had predicted she would meet. Or warned that she would meet? But Tressa hadn't sounded an alarming prospect, not like Ena, the old woman in black.

Tressa turned and stepped back behind the till, busying herself with unseen boxes, which allowed Alice to gather herself. She found the milk and a fresh loaf, and returned to the front of the shop.

'I heard you were out last night,' Tressa said, touching her immaculate grey-blonde hair with one hand and scanning the milk and bread with the other, 'with Luke and Melder Penrose.'

Alice gave her a polite and non-committal *Mmm*. Gossip happened plenty in Cambridge, but usually it was decent enough to stay behind your back.

'It was a beautiful night for it, I must say. Nowhere else like the peninsula for seeing a sky like that. And those two know it well. Their father used to take the pair of them when they were too small to see over this counter.'

'Did you . . . ?' Alice cleared her dry throat, and thought of Bea working here when she'd first arrived. 'Did you work here back then?'

Tressa laughed, sincerely and with great amusement. 'Oh no, dear, Sally's father wouldn't have had that, not with my lot. My two eldest got the whole family barred here for a month when they were young 'uns. Not that you could tell now –' Her voice dropped into conspiratorial tones. 'They're the most boring grown ups you could imagine, nowadays.' She grinned, then grew solemn. 'No, I'm just helping Sally out here and there while she visits her father. He didn't have a good night last night so she's dropped the children with a friend up the road while she sees him.' She looked at Alice again. 'But if you're looking to work here, I can certainly have a word with her – I know she'd appreciate having someone else she can trust when she needs to deal with other things?'

The meaningful quality of this last suggestion made Alice wonder if Tressa already knew about the work Alice had got for Sally, and threw her completely from the real question Tressa was asking her. She gave another *Mmm*.

Tressa looked pleased. 'Lovely! Oh, and Alice, before you go – can I ask you something? About Melder?' Alice felt her face closing down even further. 'I want to know if she's all right. With that . . . ex of hers still kicking around. How did she seem last night?'

Alice shrugged. 'I don't really know anything – I mean, I know she had a bad break-up.'

'Bad break-up?' Tressa scoffed. 'Is that what she said?'

'No, Luke said. And that the ex . . . follows her?'

'*Hmph*,' Tressa snorted, and took off her glasses to polish them. 'A bad break-up is a bit of an understatement. Alice, that man put Melder in the hospital *four times* before she eventually left him. And I don't know if you can say she really left him – it was something of an intervention, from what I hear. A communal understanding from those around her that it would save *both* of their lives if he let her go. But it doesn't seem like he's playing by the rules.' Tressa shook her head, her voice hard. 'It'd be a cold day in hell before I was seen talking to that man, I'll tell you.' She looked meaningfully at Alice.

'I didn't . . . I didn't realise.' Alice felt the prickling of sweat on her palms. 'No wonder she was so frightened when she thought he'd followed us. Why wasn't he arrested? Why . . . how . . .' Her voice tailed off.

'Yes. Exactly,' Tressa said. 'But any number of arrests doesn't stop a man like that tormenting a woman like that, do you understand? Warnings don't change him, they just make him punish her more.' She passed Alice her bread and milk, as her tone changed completely. 'Anyway, my dear, like I say: anything you need, you'll find me about. Ah, there you are, Sally!' She broke off, and stepped out

113

from behind the till as Sally came in the door, pale under her wilting mop of hair.

'Morning . . .' Sally said, waving vaguely and stepping around the shop, mindlessly moving things on each shelf. 'Oh, Alice, hello.'

Alice drew a little towards her down one tiny aisle, and spoke quietly. 'Sally! Um . . . do you remember we were talking about my mother's garden, her cuttings and things?' Was it more humiliating to have people know she was doing this strange morbid quest of her mother's, or to let them believe she had simply inherited Bea's busybody gene?

Sally looked over at Tressa, who was trying her very hardest not to appear like she was listening to every muttered word. 'Were we?' She smiled, clearly exhausted.

'Yes – the other day – remember? Anyway . . . I hope you won't mind, but I had a chat with Luke. He said he's happy to take you on for a day, to see if you really like it . . .' Alice petered out, embarrassed.

Sally stopped for a moment and looked at Alice for the first time. 'Like what?'

'Gardening . . . If you like the gardening work.' Alice's voice faltered. 'He said he can take you with him on Monday, and you can get a feel for things.' Her voice had almost completely disappeared. *Did you check this was what Sally wanted?* she thought. *No. No thought. Just a mess. Why get involved at all?*

'And don't worry about the shop – Alice has volunteered to help here as well!' Tressa called, before appearing at the end of the aisle. 'If you show her how this all works,' she added, waving her hand loosely at the till, the tobacco and alcohol, the stock room, and the shelves filling the rest of the shop, 'I'm happy to keep an eye on her.'

114

Sally looked at Alice, her face lightening. 'You volunteered, Alice?' She put her hand on Alice's arm, and Alice fought the instinct to shake it off, nodding slowly instead.

'There you go!' said Tressa. 'See: it's all worked out perfectly. You'll have a grand time with our Luke. And who knows – maybe we'll need to find someone else to run the shop long-term?'

Sally looked slightly panicked. 'Monday . . . ?' she said faintly.

'And if the children need picking up, I'll let Gina know,' Tressa added, comfortingly. Alice was glad – none of that had crossed her mind.

'OK,' Sally said, her pale cheeks pinking. She shook her head, and looked quizzically at Alice. 'Luke agreed to have me?'

'Not just agreed – he was eager,' Tressa cut in, looking to Alice for agreement. 'You'll be fine, Sally. Now: what time do you need Alice here?'

Sally looked at Alice, who had stood mute and still through most of this. 'Do you really think you'll be OK with the shop? It's an early start, here at 5.30 for the deliveries. And the post office – I'll just have to put a sign up that we're not doing the post office on Monday. Oh god. Do you really think it'll be OK?'

Alice looked at Tressa and found herself nodding, a nervous pit opening up in her stomach.

Tressa shook her head at them. 'It'll do both of you the world of good – get out of your heads for a bit.'

Sally rubbed her face with her hands. 'All right. OK, why not? Once won't hurt, will it!' She looked excited. 'Thank you, Alice, if you're sure –'

There was a *ding*, as the shop door opened, and the old woman in black shuffled in with her shopping trolley, looking around her as the door swung closed again.

She narrowed her eyes at Alice. 'Ah,' she sighed theatrically. 'The great Alice Kimbrel.'

'Ena,' Tressa called warningly from between the shelves.

Ena let out a slight *Ha*, a puff of air dismissing her friend's caution, and turned her back on Alice. Alice didn't know what she could possibly have done for this woman to have taken against her this way, besides being Bea's daughter, and another outsider.

Sally stepped up to her till, and said sweetly, 'Ena, shall I get your shopping for you?' and took the proffered list. They all stood in silence while Sally collected everything, Ena staring fixedly at Tressa, Tressa watching her in return, just as closely. Sally handed the full basket to Tressa, who began scanning, while Sally then carefully packed everything into Ena's wheeled shopper. Tressa narrowed her eyes as she scanned the final item.

'Ena Penhaligon, I'm watching you. What are you up to?'

Ena sniffed. 'Absolutely nothing that would interest you, I'm sure.'

Tressa lowered her glasses. 'That means trouble.'

'*Tsk*. You don't know what you're talking about, you old fool.' She seized the shopper handle from Sally, and turned back to the door.

'Still on for a coffee this afternoon?' Tressa asked.

'Four o'clock,' Ena muttered as she slowly pulled the door open. 'And don't be late.'

They all waited until the door had dinged behind her once more.

116

'She all right?' Tressa asked Alice. 'Not really causing you any trouble, is she?'

Sally looked at Alice too. 'I don't know why she can't just say hello – I'd have thought she knows better than that.'

Alice noticed for the first time the bottle of milk sweating in her arms, the condensation soaking through her one remaining clean dress. 'At her age,' she said, 'I understand it's always difficult when new people come into the place you've lived. And she probably had enough of my mother poking her nose in. I don't know I'd want another one of Bea around.'

'At her age – I'll give you *at her age*. She might be older than me but not by a lot, you young cheek. And as if her having lived longer was a licence for anything!' Tressa polished her glasses again. 'Anyway, you just need to stand up to people like Ena. I learnt that a long time ago.'

'And she will,' Sally said, with something like hope. 'Won't you, Alice? I'm sure you'll be firm friends any day now.'

Alice snorted, surprising herself.

'Maybe so,' Tressa said, looking again at Alice, scrutinising her. '*Tsk*. I've not got all day to waste standing about with you chatterboxes. Now you're back, Sally, *I've* got things to do.'

Sally took this as her cue to explain everything about the shop to Alice – who followed her around the shelves for the next half-hour, listening in panicky near-silence.

On the way back from the shop, Alice was thinking about what post-plague witch hunts might have looked like in Polperran when she heard someone fall into casual step beside her. She was distracted enough that her face gave nothing away when she realised it was Luke, although her heart sank. He was carrying a large potted chrysanthemum in the direction of Bea's cottage, Belle padding beside him, and she worried that he was heading to Bea's garden to work there all morning, unmissable and unavoidable.

'How are you finding things?' he asked, as if last night's humiliating misunderstanding had never happened.

She squinted over his shoulder in the noon sun, exaggerating the brightness so she would not have to look directly at him. 'Well.' Her voice wobbled, and she coughed to clear her throat. 'My body clock isn't managing too well.'

'Jet lag?' he suggested.

'Exactly,' she agreed, grateful for the words filling the silence. 'All those time zones between here and Cambridge.' Luke stopped for a moment to put down the large pot, and she stopped with him. 'Um. I think I should say sorry, for yesterday, I didn't mean to put you in an awkward situation, you and Melder had been . . . so kind –'

'Hello!'

Alice heard a voice from over the wall. 'Oh no.' She sank down slightly, trying to hide behind one of the large ferns overhanging the pavement.

'What's wrong?' Luke said.

Alice's voice dropped to a whisper. 'We've stopped at just the wrong place.'

'No, we haven't,' Luke whispered back. 'Come on.'

Frances appeared from behind her low garden wall. 'Good morning, Luke! And Alice, too! What a treat.'

'And as always, a treat to see you too, Frances. Shall we get started?'

118

'Absolutely, I'll get the kettle on. Alice, will you be joining us today?'

'She will indeed,' Luke said cheerfully. 'She hasn't had your tour yet, has she?'

As Frances headed indoors, Alice turned to Luke desperately. 'The tour?' She looked down at the milk and bread in her arms, but he took them from her and put them on Frances's table, covering them with a large cool terracotta pot.

'It's worth it,' he said. 'And she always likes the company.' Alice realised Frances must be one of Luke's clients who needed conversation more than gardening help, and when she came back out shortly with a tray laden with cups and biscuits and a teapot, Alice accepted hers and tried to ask polite questions as Frances began showing her around.

It turned out that while the front garden was pretty enough, and ingeniously designed, the back garden was utterly staggering. Alice had been lucky enough to visit several of the world's great gardens during her travels, but the pocket-size of this, handmade and yet somehow limitless, and made purely for one woman's pleasure was, in this moment, beyond all the Alhambras and Majorelles. The front garden had violet-tipped ferns and multi-coloured hydrangea bushes, dilute-ink blue through mauve to salmon-pink, which Alice madly felt she'd almost seen enough of, but it continued through a side gate into something like a paradise.

Behind the house there was a huge space, divided by pathways and walkways, with compact benches, small pools with slow-swimming koi carp, trickling fountains, statues, fruit trees, banks of succulents and more ferns. A cluster of giant gunnera formed an archway into an area bursting with colour, and Frances named all the plants for Alice: swaying lavender, purple-blue agapanthus, buds flowering into tiny trumpets, bright orange California poppies like crêpe paper decorations, and low pink and white Erigeron daisy-bushes lining the path. Through a wooden pergola, under which was placed some wrought-iron chairs and matching table with a pile of books on it, yellow-gold honeysuckle climbing up and collapsing back to scent the air; beyond this a tiny rose garden, with blooms of every colour and a hundred different perfumes. Further along the path were trees and bushes, thick with flowers: magnolias, rhododendrons, and camellias, the blooms of the latter like immaculate, delicate wrapping around a hidden, precious gift.

As Frances took her onwards through the whole garden, showing her a new feature with each turn of the path, Alice grew speechless. Luke followed, amused, occasionally joining in to point out something else Frances had chosen or created. 'Frances made most of these statues herself, didn't you, Frances?' he said, indicating a pair of statues momentarily adorned with a matching pair of landing butterflies.

'I did – one of my many careers, a long time ago,' she answered happily.

Towards the back of the garden was a wooden bench, hidden under the tallest trees: palms reaching up to worship the sky, ginkgo biloba with their musically elegant fan-leaves, and copper beeches, whose leaves turned the sunlight a soft lilac as it shone through onto the bench. Past the trees, they ended on a terrace with a curved bench, the terrace surrounded by an iron circle propped up in the air on four iron stems, all wrapped about with flamingo-coloured roses, and with a view that looked out uninterrupted to the sparkling sea beneath a bright cobalt sky.

Alice's pulse was so slow she felt almost underwater. She turned to them both, unsure if she could speak. 'This is . . . *heaven.*'

Frances laughed, delighted. The three of them sat for a while, Luke and Frances discussing what they might do with various beds at the end of the summer, while Alice remained still, half-listening and half-watching, breathing. The smells and colours were hypnotising, not in amount or strength but in how different they were to Alice's normal interior life. Harmony, greenery, stillness, calm. A wild-flower bed thick with bees. Alice had never been anywhere like this in her whole life. The closest may have been the swimming pool that Maurice and Bea would take her to when she was young, where she and Bea would compete to see how long they could swim underwater. She remembered the quiet of those long lengths, her mother beside her, two mermaids smiling at each other, bubbles pearling from their lips, distant flashes of coloured swimsuits far above them at the surface. But this was living, and fixed, and Alice felt drugged with it all.

Then it was time to leave, and Frances took Alice's arm to walk her back out and handed back her bread and milk. Alice managed some kind of farewell, before Luke guided her back to the road and they walked in silence in the direction of his van parked at Bea's.

'Worth it?' Luke asked eventually.

Alice shook her head, although she meant the opposite. 'I just don't understand why people don't spend their lives doing that more . . . I mean . . .' Belle snuffled at her palm sympathetically.

'I know,' Luke said. 'She's one of the most creative people I've ever met. I did a lot of the grunt work there, but she knows her stuff – the number of arguments we had about plants that I said would never work, but they always did. She really knows what she's doing. If I've got green fingers, she's got green blood.'

'Something so beautiful . . . imagine that being your legacy? People could enjoy that for *years*.'

Luke turned his gaze on her, his blue eyes warm but serious. 'Alice, nothing lasts forever. Even Frances knows that the point of a garden is change. Who knows if it will even exist in five years? In one? We just have to enjoy it now. That's the beauty of it.'

Alice still felt too full of the garden to reply. They returned to Bea's cottage without speaking more.

Luke packed his tools back in the van. 'See you next time?' he said, slapping his thigh to summon a curious Belle from beneath the hedge. Alice raised a hand in farewell, still delighted, still dazed.

Chapter Eleven

She had to admit, when Monday came the shop was fun to begin with. Alice had already been up long before she was needed there, rising before dawn to swim while the sky was warming up, lengths up and down the shore in the growing light, slapping back up to Bea's cottage in her mother's old leather sandals, washing off the salt for her day ahead. She had taken in everything Sally had shown her previously, even through her panic: till, float, keys, stock, orders, and if all else failed, a notebook and pen where Alice could write down anything that went dramatically wrong and Sally could deal with it when she returned.

Sally had appeared both nervous and excited about her own day. She had dressed up in soft linen trousers and a matching tunic top when Alice had waved her off at six, like the costume of a gentlewoman gardener from the Sunday supplements, but seemed to have no concerns about Alice's performance, only her own. She left Alice restocking the dairy cabinets and the bakery aisle, and by the time Alice had flipped the sign to Open, the shop was in full readiness.

But the customers. The *customers*. The bread was too large for one person, or instead was far too small to feed another man. And two loaves was ridiculous – he wasn't going to pay double just to get a sensible amount of bread. The ice cream wasn't the right flavour – could they not try getting some salted caramel in? – and they shouldn't have the crisps so close to where children might pass and then demand some. Alice wondered where, in the small, low-ceilinged shop, the woman would like them to suspend or bury the crisp rack, but didn't ask. Someone was furious that they not only didn't have a full leg of lamb in for roasting, but that it couldn't be ordered to arrive later that day either. Someone was looking for birthday cards for a 22nd birthday, and yes, the numbers did have to be on the card; someone else wanted the paper from two days ago, and wouldn't believe Alice that the previous day's papers were taken away when the latest ones were delivered. Mustard but not that mustard; orange squash but not that orange squash; teabags but not those teabags; did they have any Christmas wrapping paper in, perhaps left over from last year? All of them muttering that *This is what you get when you holiday in the arse-end of nowhere.*

More than the absurd questions, it was the humour in which they were asked which rendered Alice utterly exhausted by closing time. Rarely a please, almost never a thank you, and not once did Alice hear, *Yes, I can make do with that!* Disappointment, mealy-mouthed and spluttering from each customer, made Alice marvel that Sally had kept the shop for this long. And all of them tourists like Alice. She felt embarrassed, as well as angry at their behaviour, and tried not to think of how she might have seemed, through her carapace of anxiety and anger, to the locals of Polperran. She understood Ena a little better, at least.

The only pleasant interaction Alice had all day was with the young woman from the beach. She'd spotted her familiar faded purple jacket disappearing around the bakery shelves, and waited until she came to the till, the young woman concentrating hard on the few items she carried.

'Hello,' Alice said.

The young woman jumped.

'Sorry – it's me, from the beach? Sorry. I've . . . seen you in the morning, early, on the beach?' Alice realised this had been a mistake. She added faintly as she scanned the products, 'We waved to each other the other day.'

The woman nodded, hesitantly.

'Yes? I'm Alice.' She held out her hand. The young woman looked at her hand, and at Alice, for long enough that Alice wondered if she'd made some terrible Cornish faux pas. Then the girl reached up and shook it gently. She gave a shy smile.

'Radka. My name . . . is Radka.'

'Radka! What a lovely name. Is that another Cornish one?'

Radka watched Alice's face, and gestured to herself. 'Romanian.' Suddenly her accent was much clearer.

Alice's face screwed up, and the young woman drew away, hurrying to pack her shopping into her bag. '*Bună! Ce mai faci?*' Alice finally said. 'Is that right?'

Radka gave a gasp, dropped her shopping back on the counter and leant across to pull Alice into a hug, her face alight. She started talking, fast and faster, in what must have been fluent Romanian until Alice laughed and said, 'Wait, wait, that's just about the limit of my Romanian, I'm afraid.'

The young woman switched to English. 'But that is amazing! I haven't heard my language here for . . . a long time! And not when I come to Polperran. But now you!'

'I had a Romanian student last year, and she managed to teach me that. I'm only sorry I don't have more to offer.'

Radka beamed, and said, 'Now we say good mornings when I see you and you see me on the beach, yes? Me in English, you in Romanian.'

Alice nodded, and said, 'And you're up so early, like me. Is that work getting you up?'

Radka frowned and shook her head, her face closing in as rapidly as the embrace had appeared. 'Thank you.' She took her things. 'Thank you, Alice.' She gave her a momentary smile, then left the shop solemn-faced again, without another word, her head down, hurrying along the pavement.

Sally wasn't back in time to close up the shop, but had left Alice instructions on turning everything off and locking everything up. As requested, Alice posted the keys through the letter box in the side door (the entrance to the flat Sally and her children lived in, over the shop), and headed home for the night. She had hoped to see either Sally or Luke to ask them how their day had gone, but for once there was no one in her garden when she got home.

She scrambled some eggs and ate them with bread from the shop, and was only half-way through a post-dinner cup of tea before she realised she was nodding over the kitchen table. She tumbled into bed, barely readying herself, and fell fast asleep. *It wasn't being on my feet for all those hours,* she thought as she drifted down. *It was having to face all those people.*

The next morning was perfect: golden-blue sky again with a cool damp that was already burning off. Working at the kitchen table, Alice had half an eye on the clock as it crept towards eight, at which point she hurried to the hall and picked up Bea's house phone, tapping in the numbers from her own phone.

'Hello?'

'Morag?'

'Speaking.'

'It's me!' Alice said. 'Alice. This is my mother's phone – I realised last night that with such an unreliable signal here, you had no way to contact me. I remembered about her landline, so . . . if you need to get in touch or anything, *for* anything, then, you know, you can call me here.' She felt herself beginning to ramble.

Morag let a second of silence hang in the air between them, then said, 'Alice! It's good to hear you. Is it glorious sunshine down there?'

'It's OK,' Alice answered. 'What's it like with you?'

She heard Morag pause. 'Hang on . . . ooh, it looks grey out there. What happened to spring? Or is it summer now?'

'I know,' Alice said mindlessly. 'Morag, how *is* everything there?'

If Morag knew what Alice was really asking, she didn't show it for a second. 'Oh, you know – panic around exams.' She paused again. 'How's stuff with your mum? I mean, sorting everything out?'

'It's fine. She left me . . . she's asked me to complete this project for her. Around the village.'

'Local history?' Morag asked.

'Not exactly. More like . . . errands. Like . . . helping people out.'

'Oh,' Morag said. 'Right.'

'I know. I haven't seen her for years and suddenly I'm meant to be finishing all her odd-jobs in a place I don't even know.'

'Are you enjoying it?'

Alice looked out of the window at Bea's fruit trees. 'It's a nicer view,' she said, just as Belle leapt across the lawn, followed by Luke in his fraying wool hat. *In this weather?* she thought. 'But the book – I've done some good stuff on it! Shall I send the latest chapters –'

'Alice. Just . . . go and sit in the sunshine. Help your gardener. Do you need a hand clearing the house? I've got a cousin just up the coast who can probably recommend someone.'

'No, I want to get on to the plague spreader myths before I get back –'

'OK, OK. Have you checked out the monk's records from the abbey near . . . *tsk* – Thingummy, in northern France? What is it?'

'The one with the illuminated dogs?'

'Yes! That would be perfect for any plague spreading stuff, unless – oh christ, that's someone at my door,' Morag sighed. 'I'd better go. And Alice?' Alice waited. 'Thanks for this number. I'll call whenever we need you.'

Alice opened the back door and poured coffee into two mugs, put on Bea's sandals and largest sun hat, and headed off down the path to the beach with the drinks. She wouldn't stay inside any longer. The shop's tourists yesterday had brought back memories of beach holidays with Bea and Maurice: Bea bringing them all ice creams which would melt and drip all over their hands; Maurice and Alice in rock pools with a fishing net, trouser legs rolled up; fish and chips, bucket and spades, all the tourist clichés. Sand in her bed. Seagulls waking her every morning. Bea and Maurice talking quietly every evening while Alice drifted to sleep in a small room at the top of the stairs. She remembered that Bea would always end those holidays saying, 'Just *imagine* having a house here! Being able to see the sea whenever you wanted!' And Maurice would hum and say, 'Bit of a commute every morning, though,' and Alice would laugh and they would return to their little house in Cambridge.

After Bea left, she and Maurice didn't take holidays. They did day trips, explored local areas, but Alice didn't have a holiday until she was in her late teens, and went away with a friend's family for a weekend. In Alice's mind, despite knowing how much she loved Maurice, there was something so fundamentally unlovable about them both that to travel away, to take their unlovability somewhere new, rather than couched in their comfortable routines at home, would be to make it unignorable.

As she had half-hoped, Radka was there again, wearing her purple anorak even in this beautiful early morning sun. The young woman raised her hand, again only a hip-height wave, and squinted at Alice through the clear light as she came to stand beside her. They both watched the waves for a moment.

'Good morning,' Alice said quietly. She offered Radka one of the mugs, to which Radka shook her head. 'I haven't drunk from it, you won't get my germs,' Alice joked. Radka looked at her, squinting again, then gave her a small smile, and took the cup. She took a grateful sip, sighed with pleasure, saying, 'It's a nice coffee.'

'Thank you very much,' Alice said. 'The best Sally's shop sells.'

Radka laughed. 'It's a good shop, too.'

Alice smiled. 'Do you like shops?' *Idiocy*, thought Alice. *This is why I don't talk to people.*

But Radka said, 'It's not the same as my mother's,' with an apologetic, shy look. 'Of course, all children like more the things of their mother. But . . .'

'Your mother has a shop?' Alice asked. 'Near here?'

Radka took another sip. 'No. Back home, in Romania, she has a shop, a very good shop full of food and drink.' She turned back to the waves.

Alice blew on her coffee. They both watched the sea. 'Do you get to see your mother much? Do you miss the shop?'

Radka shrugged. 'I see them both if I can. It is like that.' She shrugged, but kept her eyes on the water.

'Do you like your work here? Can your mother come –' but before Alice had finished her question, Radka thrust her mug at her, gave her a muttered goodbye and headed back up the beach, hurrying to the far steps before Alice could even return the goodbye.

Alice sat down on the pebbles, clutching the mugs in hands that suddenly felt weak. What is it now? She could pretend with every fibre of her being that she could contribute something to the world, in conversation or action or spirit, but what was she really? A dusty shadow of a bookworm with no one to miss her if she dissolved in the sea right now. They'd find her clothes and books at Bea's eventually, but they wouldn't *look* for them. They would assume that she had had enough and fled back to Cambridge, and they would never think of her again. And only Morag missed her in Cambridge, and she was actively telling Alice to stay away. She didn't even move her feet as the water came in, and it was only the sound of a dog-walker heading in her direction that made her finally stand up, her trainers soaking. She climbed the steps and turned to the high street. The sooner she could finish this task and get the whole thing over with, the better.

When the shop door dinged for Alice, Sally greeted her with enthusiasm.

'Alice! Good morning, love, how're you? How did you get on the other day? Everything was lovely and clean when I got in!'

'Fine. Fine,' Alice murmured. 'Good.'

Sally looked down at the coffee cups Alice was still carrying, puzzled, but Alice was too exhausted to speak more, to make her sentences fit together into sense.

'Ah,' said Sally slowly. 'Good. I mean, I know the tourists aren't always the easiest, but their money does a lot to keep Polperran going, and they bring a bit of life to the village –' Alice let out a dull *mmm* ' – when we're lacking a person to herd us out of our shells a bit, if I can mix my metaphors.'

'Mix away,' Alice said. It was so hard to get the words out.

Sally glowed, her usually dimmed eyes beneath her heavy hair now sparking with energy. 'It was wonderful on Monday, though. In fact . . . I don't suppose there's any chance you might be able to cover Friday too, is there?' She saw Alice's face. 'No, no, sorry, that's too much –'

Alice sighed. 'I don't know how long I'll be here for. I mean, if you're happy, I might be off . . .'

Sally looked confused again. 'No, that's fine, you need to go, sorry. I'll see if I can move that other work . . . to another day . . .' Sally's voice trailed off.

'No you don't!' called a voice from behind the shelves. Alice and Sally both jumped, as Tressa appeared in front of them from a side aisle. 'Listen to me, young lady, your father thought he was leaving this shop in safe hands, giving it to you. But if you can't keep it open when it needs to be open, then maybe you need to start looking for other people to get involved.'

'No,' said Sally. 'I wasn't going to close it –'

'Good. Then while you're working on this other . . . thing, between us, Alice and I can take care of the shop, can't we?' She looked at Alice. '*While she's here*,' Tressa added heavily.

'Tressa, that's very kind, but we can't afford to pay proper staff – certainly not to run the shop for more than a few hours.' She looked hastily at Alice. 'No offence, Alice.'

'Sally Hobson, as if I'm making offers like this to line my pocket. You should be ashamed of yourself.' Sally, appropriately, did look ashamed, although Alice couldn't see what she was meant to have done wrong. 'I'm doing it because all those old people in the village *need* this shop, and if you're not here then *I'm* doing them all a favour.'

Sally's mouth twitched slightly. 'Besides, young things like me need keeping out of trouble.' Tressa looked challengingly at Alice, but Alice saw a twinkle deep in her eye.

'If you're sure –'

'Fine,' she said. 'I'll have this lot now, and Alice and I will sort out Friday between us. Won't we, dear?' Tressa's attitude and energy were astounding, and her white silk shirt, oversized pearls and bright green wide-legged trousers painted a picture of snowdrop springtime positivity. Alice wondered why she couldn't match Tressa's high spirits, even a little.

Sally scanned Tressa's shopping and took her ten-pound note, gave her change. 'All done for you, Tressa. If you're sure, then?' Tressa only rolled her eyes in reply, before leaving the shop.

When Tressa was well out of earshot, Sally let out a big sigh of relief, glowing again. 'She's ever so kind, is Tressa. Heart of gold, looks after her great-grandchildren most of the time and half the other children in the village, pops in here to give me a little break every now and then. Can't be anyone living here who hasn't had Tressa read them bedtime stories or give them ice cream in the summer.'

'Good,' said Alice, unhearingly. 'Great.'

Chapter Twelve

She didn't know how much she had slept, if at all, but Alice opened her eyes that morning with the strongest urge to walk. It couldn't even have been five by the time she left Bea's cottage with a travel cup of coffee, and a small backpack of necessities; not knowing how long she might be, she tried to guess at what would be useful for an early-summer dawn walk in the Cornish hills. Instead of turning towards the village or the beach, she took a third route, the public footpath sign she'd noticed the other day half-hidden by ferns, which took her up a steep track behind Bea's garden.

It was a hard hike, harder than she had expected, and her legs were shaking by the time she got to the top, her body warm with exertion. It had repeatedly levelled off, turned behind a hedge, and become even steeper, and Alice stood breathing heavily when she could finally see only gently undulating fields ahead of her. When she turned, she could see all of Polperran, tiny doll houses on the mossy, distant landscape, sea an impenetrable, milky green-blue, miniature clanking, bobbing boats in the small harbour. A Lilliputian white house stood alone on a hill of fields, the clouds sliding behind it in a white dappled sheet – and she suddenly remembered Bea making dens with her, old white quilts draped over dining chairs and drying racks, and they would have picnics and read underneath for hours, their feet getting tangled in blankets and bath towels, until Maurice came home and, in trying to join them, would pull much of it down around their giggling fabric-swathed forms.

She walked on, following the signs, almost marching again, across muddy tractor lanes and through archways of blossoming hawthorn, occasionally snagging her t-shirt or skin on hedgerows, marching on, enjoying the sweat and the ache in her legs. She remembered too that she would walk like this when she was only ten, getting a bus out of Cambridge and walking alone for hours over fields and through villages, or sometimes in the town itself, looping around and around the backstreets and colleges, her eyes and ears open to things of interest, things to tell Bea and Maurice when she got home: funny animals, funny arguments, new clothes or cars or trees she'd never seen before.

Alice thought how small her life had become at Cambridge; there never seemed time to walk like that now, and even when she travelled, her schedule was precise and the margins for free time were carefully allotted and scheduled. She hadn't walked like this for years. As she continued on, and minutes became one hour, then two, she felt her shoulders dropping, her breathing deepen, her eyes opening and absorbing all the light and movement around her. She heard the seagulls and liquid song of the curlews above her, and as the path turned again and pitched downwards, towards Polperran and the sea, Alice remembered how, when she was young, Bea had always taught her to go to running water when she was in trouble.

'Running water is magic,' Bea had said. 'And the birds there will look after you, if you can get there. Rivers are good, but a bath will do at a pinch. Your rubber duck will keep an eye out, if I can't.' Alice had laughed, but she'd thought of Bea when she'd had that first swim in the river with the man she barely knew, and thought now of whether the sea would count as running water in Bea's eyes. Of course, it moved, but from this descending path it looked too large, too solid to run anywhere; it just *was*, a massive bulk of shifting depths that shrugged and waved but never ran.

As she got to the end of the path, she saw she was at the other end of the beach to Bea's cottage, and noticed Radka close to her on the shore, alone again. Crunching towards her, Alice thought how small Radka looked, how slight against the sea.

Alice dropped her rucksack down and pulled out her coffee, still – just – warm. They stood together in silence and watched the water.

'Hold on,' Alice said. She thought for a moment. '*Bună dimineața*'

Radka gave her a gentle smile, then immediately burst into tears, tears that didn't slow but bloomed into full sobs, racking sobs that she couldn't speak through, as she clutched her hands to her chest.

Alice put a hand on Radka's shoulder and Radka's body seemed to collapse, curling up into a ball around her hands and sobbing face. Alice sat beside her, and let her hand stay on Radka's shoulder, keeping it still while the young woman wept. She knew she had a reputation within the college of not caring about her students, but she also knew that her male colleagues behaved exactly as she did and were loved for it: she cared about their marks, and their studies, and she didn't try hard to disguise the fact that she didn't find their break-ups and their falling-outs remotely relevant. But here, seeing Radka like this made Alice wish that she had a little more experience in giving comfort. Her life had been shaped always around managing; never, she began to think, about connecting.

Eventually, her sobs slowed, and with a great shuddering breath, Radka sat upright.

'I'm sorry,' she said. 'Thank you for the greeting.'

Alice laughed, despite herself. 'I can tell how much you enjoyed it,' she said, and Radka smiled. 'Did I say it wrong? I was *trying* to say good morning.'

Radka gave a little hiccup, and a weak smile. 'It was very good, yes. Good morning. *Bună dimineața.*' She started crying again, softer now. 'I miss my mother very much, and it is so nice to hear this. I am sorry. This,' she gestured at Alice, 'this is very good for me. Thank you.'

Alice gave her shoulder a squeeze before pulling her hand away, and felt a rush of maternal affection for this younger woman, trying so hard to feel better when she clearly felt terrible. 'Is it missing your mother that's so sad? Or is it my Romanian accent?'

Radka gave another smile. 'It is not your accent, although perhaps it is not quite ready for you to learn more words yet?' She looked down at her cup, then spoke quickly, almost in a rush. 'I came with a job, to England, and now the job is gone and I have no job and no money and I don't know how to tell my mother –' and she broke into Romanian, clearly berating herself or her lost job or bad luck, but it was clear she was desperately unhappy.

'Radka, is it going to be OK? Are you –'

'I don't know, Alice, what is going to be OK. I know at the moment that plenty of places do not have jobs to give Romanian people.'

Alice looked steadily at her. 'And you feel like that here? In Polperran?'

'All of Cornwall does not have so many jobs right now.' Radka gave a shrug. 'No one in this village talks to me. I am a stranger here. We would not behave this way to visitors where I was a girl.'

'If it's any help,' Alice eventually said, 'where I live no one really talks to me either, if they don't have to. And my mother lived here since I was just a girl, and it took years for *everyone* to welcome her.' She thought of Ena. The sea shushed softly at them both, and Alice took another sip of coffee. Before she could think about it, and keeping her face in her cup, she said, 'The two of us could talk . . . to each other?'

'You and me?' asked Radka.

Alice moved her toes so they delved among the pebbles, and ran her free hand through the comforting shapes. 'You meet me for a walk occasionally, so I can practise my Romanian. And I'll . . . help you find a job, if you want.' She thought. 'I can at least help you with a CV.'

'Really?' said Radka. 'I don't think it will be easy but I think it is very kind of you to try.'

Radka stood first, and helped Alice to her feet.

At Blandford & Sons, Peter Blandford was standing in the main office talking to his secretary when Alice came in for her third task.

'Alice! My dear, do come in. Shall I put the kettle on?' he asked, semi-rhetorically. His secretary stood up to make the drinks. 'A pot of tea, please, Sean,' Peter requested, opening his office door and shuffling Alice through.

He settled behind his desk, and dug around in his drawers until he found a packet of Garibaldi biscuits, which he shook out onto a clean folder and offered to Alice. She shook her head and he took a biscuit, nibbling at one corner.

'Now my dear, what can we do for you today?'

Alice sat up on her chair. She didn't know how to explain to Peter about the conversation with Radka. How it had made her feel, just at the moment she was wanting to call Morag and ask if she could come back yet, please; that perhaps just being present here could offer something worthwhile. 'The . . . project. I'm wondering if I could have the next one? Please.'

Peter looked at her over the top of his glasses. 'Number three? Already? My my, this really is very remarkable. Do you feel the first two have now been completed to your satisfaction?'

She slumped a little. 'How completed do they have to be? Will someone . . . evaluate if they're done or not? Do I have to wait for the previous ones to have been approved to get the next envelope?'

Peter chortled at the idea. 'Good lord, no, no no! Your mother was very clear that the envelopes could be given to you at any point you requested them. By which I mean: you are the sole judge of the project. If you request an envelope, I am bound to pass that envelope on to you.'

Feeling guilty for a moment, wondering how complete either task truly was so far, with Joy still apparently locked in isolated antipathy to the entire village – Alice hadn't got Bea's basket back, nor seen Joy kicking her heels up at the Dolphin recently – and neither Sally nor Luke reporting on Sally's gardening progress, Alice thought, *Could I ask for all of them now? Get them over with, and be done with this whole thing?* It was only Peter's face, so like her father's with its lifelong optimism in Alice, that stopped her.

She tried to turn her huffed sigh into a controlled breath, while Peter found the envelope.

'Here we are,' he said. 'Number three.'

Out on the high street, Alice suddenly missed the caffeine hit of her favourite café in a little passage in Cambridge, and was just about to turn to Gwen's when she heard someone calling her.

'Alice!' Tressa came jogging up to her. 'Alice, I've been meaning to catch you – to discuss Friday at the shop. Does that still suit?'

After only a moment of standing still, Tressa's breath had returned entirely to normal. Alice's own level of fitness suddenly seemed embarrassing. 'Yes – well, I mean –'

'Excellent, thank you so much. Now, do you want to do another full day there? Or would you rather we half-and-half it; it's completely up to you, I've got nothing on in the afternoon, so I'm happy to take over from you then, if you've work to do.'

Alice leapt at that chance. 'Yes! Yes, work, that would be great, Tressa. But . . . will Sally be . . . doing this long?'

Tressa pushed her hair back into its smart bob, and gave Alice a calm look. 'Why? Wasn't it your idea in the first place?'

Alice opened her mouth but found she had no answer. Obviously it was her idea, but was Tressa expecting her to give up her Cambridge life for the foreseeable future so Sally could continue dead-heading a few rose bushes?

Tressa flapped her hands. 'Never mind, never mind. How are you getting on with everything? I heard you were down at the beach with someone this morning?'

Conversation with Tressa could be dizzying, Alice realised. She closed her mouth with a snap, then opened it again to say, 'Yes. Radka. Do you know her?'

'Radka?' Tressa said thoughtfully. 'It doesn't ring a bell. Is she Romanian, though, with a name like that?'

'Yes!' Alice was surprised.

'And here on her own, or with family?'

'On her own – she lost her job –'

'Any plans to go back?'

'No, it's partly money and partly not wanting to let her family down –'

'And living in the village?'

'Yes, but I don't know where exactly –'

'Do you know which area of Romania she's from?'

Alice squinted, trying to remember if Radka had said.

'Never mind. Let's leave that for now. Just an old woman's nosiness. Off to Gwen's?' Tressa smiled at her, and patted her on the arm. 'Good for you. Have a nice time!' She bustled away down the street, occasionally calling out to people as Alice stood speechless, blinded by the hanging sun over the high street.

Alice hadn't opened the envelope that day. She'd gone into the café, once she'd found her voice again, and Gwen had

141

miraculously been able to provide both the latte and the cheese scones she had been missing from her regular café back at college. While she'd been eating and drinking, Melder had come in too, and Alice had invited her to join her, and they'd spent a pleasant hour playing a board game Alice had forgotten from her childhood that Gwen had dug out from under the till, with a hand-drawn spinner and pencil in place of the missing die. For that hour they had all laughed a great deal, and Alice could almost forget the animal terror Melder had shown that stargazing night. In Gwen's café, there was only the board game, the laughter and an endless parade of scones.

All of which meant that when she returned to Bea's cottage and found Luke working there, again, Alice didn't rush into the house after the minimum possible small-talk. She stayed outside, and told Luke about the third envelope, and the game she and Melder had played, and if part of the pleasure of telling him everything in the lengthening, cooling shadows of Bea's garden, still smelling greenly of cut stems and turned earth, still laughing at the game, was that she couldn't also be opening Bea's letter at the same time, then so be it.

Chapter Thirteen

She'd worked through the night again, although 3.30 was hardly the end of the night. Alice pulled at the light shirt she'd worn for the last eighteen hours, letting the air flap beneath it and smelling her stale skin, feeling the closeness in this airless pre-dawn, and went to find her swimming costume.

Minutes later, she was padding down the garden to the sea path, faded towel in one hand, swimming costume and Bea's swimming hat on, her shirt thrown over the top, sandals flapping gently where she hadn't done the buckles up. At the beach, the air was warm, blowing gently over the waves which summoned her softly in the undisturbed dissolving night. She was completely alone – at this hour, even the most hardy of holidaymakers would be tucked up in their rented house, sleeping off their rosé and dreaming of Polperran's clear skies.

Idiot, she thought. *As if I'm so very different.* She kicked off her sandals and folded her shirt carefully on top, followed by the towel, trying her best to keep it off the sandy ground, suddenly feeling self-conscious, as if on a busy afternoon beach, and hurrying to the edge of the water to hide. There was something she was missing, that she had been thinking of earlier, but it had gone for a moment. She'd remember later.

Alice dressed afterwards in the warm hint of dawn, scrunching her damp hair briefly and wrapping the towel around her waist, her shirt over her damp costume. As she walked back up the path, she pulled the towel off, and let the air dry her legs and feet, dusty now but not sandy. Back at the house, she made a fresh coffee, changed into a dress, brought her books to the kitchen table and began work. She became so absorbed so quickly that she didn't even have time to realise that the thing she was missing was her usual feeling of dread.

At lunchtime on a self-imposed break from work, Alice set off on a quick walk around the village. If she was going to spend the rest of today working, as well as possibly dealing with the third envelope, she needed air and perhaps something more sustaining than old bread crust. But from outside the village shop, she could hear shouting: Tressa, shouting. 'No! No, no!' Alice heard. 'No, no you don't!' She rushed inside, banging the door open to rescue Tressa.

She found Tressa standing calmly behind the counter, with Radka in her purple anorak the other side of it, turned away from Alice.

'What's going on?' Alice called, looking between them, only now feeling her heart hurrying.

'This young lady,' Tressa said, 'is having the best luck I've ever seen in my life.'

On the till counter, Alice saw a pile of playing cards, and both Radka and Tressa holding a hand of cards. Radka was grinning. 'If you grow up playing Durak, you win the game.'

Tressa frowned at her. 'I've played Durak longer than you've been alive, I'll have you know.'

Radka said, 'She knows Romania!' and Alice looked quizzically at Tressa.

'My father was there in the Second World War, helping some of the resistance groups. He stayed in touch with his friends there, so we went a few times, before he died. One of the most beautiful places in Europe, I think.' Radka looked like she might actually burst, and when Tressa said something to her in Romanian, she had to close her eyes with joy. 'My accent's not brilliant and it's really only small-talk I can do, but it's nice to use it. Keeps the old noggin sharp,' Tressa added, tapping her head. 'I recognised the accent the second she asked me where the porridge was – if you'd ever spoken up when you came in here, I would have spotted it months ago.'

Radka blushed. 'Oh, you are very, very good accent,' Radka insisted, then looked at Alice and added quickly, 'And you, Alice, yours is good too.'

Alice narrowed her eyes. 'Yes, my five words of another language are a marvellous feat, thank you.'

'Feet?' Radka said, lifting a shoe off the ground.

'No, a –' Alice realised her self-effacement was foolish, but explaining would have been difficult. 'My five words aren't very good, but Tressa's is . . .' Alice tailed off and just made a smiling face. 'Much better.'

Radka looked slightly embarrassed for her, but Tressa put the cards down and exclaimed, 'Anyway! Alice,' she said, lifting a bag onto the counter from the till, 'when you've got what you need, would you mind dropping a few things at Ena's. I've bagged them all up here, they just need taking over.'

145

Alice had work to do, along with the new envelope, and didn't like visiting people at the best of times. Certainly not Ena, who still hadn't spoken a single word to her. 'I . . .'

Alice didn't have time to refuse before Tressa added in a low voice, despite no one else being in the shop, 'And if she offers you a cup of tea, you *will* take it, won't you? She's an old woman on her own and she won't ever say that she needs company, but when she can't get out . . .'

'Is she ill?' Alice asked.

'No, love, but she's ninety-two, and sometimes that can feel like ill.'

As Alice paid for her own items, Tressa handed her Ena's bag with a few things in – milk and biscuits, some tomatoes, a box of teabags – and a little pencil-drawn map of the village with a large X to one side of the green, with a number 3 beside it. 'All right?' she added, with bright cheerfulness.

Following the map, the house was easy to find, a slumping cottage behind three unlikely palm trees, the rest of the garden tidy but uninspiring. Alice wondered if Ena was one of Luke's 'gardening' clients. After her second knock, the door creaked open: Ena, in a shapeless black dress, and rainbow striped fluffy slippers, as incongruous as the palm trees.

Alice lifted up the bag she'd brought. 'Ena? Tressa asked me to bring you these.' The old woman looked surprised to see Alice – more than surprised, shocked – and stared at her for a moment. 'I'm Alice?'

Ena's face shrank from surprise into something like anger, waspish and diminishing. She grunted. 'Fine. You'll be wanting a cup of tea then, I expect.' She said it like an accusation, and was already turning away, so Alice could do nothing but follow her in with her shopping, closing the door behind her and copying Ena's slow shuffle to her kitchen. There, Ena slowly filled the kettle, put it slowly back on the base and set it to boil, reached up slowly to the cupboard for cups.

'I can help, Ena, if you want to sit down.' Alice reached past her to try and get the cups down.

'I'll thank you not to touch my things. I'm perfectly capable,' Ena snapped.

Alice backed away. 'Sorry, yes, I'll . . . sit down . . . here,' she said, looking around and finally edging herself towards the two armchairs near the unlit fireplace.

Ena grunted again, and moved around the kitchen until she brought Alice a mug of perfect tea, creamy tan and steaming. She sat down in the other chair with her mug, and from the pack beside her, shook out a biscuit which she dunked in. Alice waited to be offered one.

'I've heard you've been getting around the village a bit,' Ena said, putting the pack down the side of her chair instead and stirring her tea noisily with a teaspoon.

'What a lovely way to say I've been meeting some of Polperran,' Alice replied. There was that feeling again – her anxiety lessening, in the face of something so ridiculously hostile: not an imagined foe, a potential danger, but a silly rudeness that Alice could more than cope with.

'Luke Penrose? And Santo Hammett?' Ena asked slyly.

Not just anxiety-lessening: Ena was so openly hostile that Alice felt free to actually say what she was thinking. 'Oh, so you *were* implying something,' she said. 'I was just *meeting* them, as I said, Ena. And believe me, I wouldn't be doing any of this it if it wasn't for my mother's . . . project.'

'Stuck in her cottage all on your own, is it then? Bored, are we?'

'I shouldn't even be here, Ena. I should be back at my college, all of this just a distant, one-day memory from when I put her cottage up for sale and went back to work, unencumbered by the petty politics of a little seaside village.' She was almost enjoying herself.

Ena slurped her tea loudly. 'Sounds to me like you've been rather lucky, then. Stuck here rather than in those dusty libraries.'

Alice narrowed her eyes at her. 'I don't know what you think life in Cambridge is like, that Polperran is so much better.'

'Oh, I know, all this *fresh air* and *sea* and no pollution and no noise. It must be hideous for you.' She slurped again, then added pointedly, 'Maybe it's nice for you to have a change.'

'And to meet all these lovely people,' Alice said dryly.

Ena scoffed, and pulled a blanket onto her lap. 'If meeting's what you want to call it,' she said in dark tones.

'Right,' Alice said cheerfully. 'That's my limit for today! I'll be off now.'

Ena looked suddenly smaller, older. 'You'll be coming back, then?'

Her teacup in the sink, pot back by the kettle, Alice looked at Ena in the chair, fussing with the blanket on her lap, lining up the crochet squares exactly.

'I'll be back, Ena,' she said. 'I've missed being critiqued by people from history.'

Ena grunted again, and pulled her blanket a little higher. 'Mmm. You should be so lucky to be as historical as me. The things I've seen, Alice. Mines closing. Floods like you'd never believe. The Second World War.'

'Not my era, I'm afraid. I'm a bit before all that. I'm sure you could find someone from my department who'd relish your first-hand accounts.' She wiped the counters down and looked back at Ena, who had woven her fingers into the crochet and was staring at them distractedly.

'Go on, get out,' Ena said quietly. 'I'll see you next time.'

Chapter Fourteen

Bea's room still loomed somewhat in the corner of Alice's eye whenever she went to and from her own, but she had started exploring more of the things Bea had left behind. In the bathroom, still crowded with lavish plants hanging and resting and balancing on every surface – somehow since she'd been here, the plants hadn't died – Alice found her mother's make-up bag in a drawer beneath the sink. For a moment, she felt she was intruding, then remembered that Bea had had time enough to choose what was left and what was taken from the house, so anything remaining was something for Alice. But she hadn't expected this: a pill packet, with a printed label saying *Citalopram 10mg, Beatrice Kimbrel, Take once a day.*

Alice knew what this was. She'd been prescribed it herself several times, among other things, but she'd never taken any of them. Never even gone to get a prescription filled, had just kept the slips in her handbag until eventually they went out of date. But Bea had the same prescription, the same dose, and going by the number of pills missing from the packet had taken them more than once. Citalopram? For depression and panic attacks? Alice kept staring at the pack, then put it back, zipped up the bag, and put the bag back in the drawer. But before she could even leave the bathroom, Alice wanted to check again – yes, it was the same medication, yes, Bea's name was on it, yes, this prescription was recent, not a relic from years ago. She didn't understand. Or she did, but it didn't make any sense.

She zipped everything back up, made a cup of tea and took it to the porthole snug where she rarely went, and pulled one of Bea's blankets over her knees as she sat huddled around her mug. This was always the coolest room, but her discovery of Bea's medicine had made her feel completely icy. It was, in fact, the exact wrong moment to take a closer look at the photos on the coffee table beside the sofa, photos no bigger than the palm of her hand. One of Alice, one of Bea with some friends, among them Tressa and Gwen, one of Bea holding the hand of a toddling Alice, the photograph fuzzy and worn – and one of Bea and Maurice. But it wasn't the presence of her father than surprised her; Bea's chosen photos clearly tended towards the sentimental. It was how they looked in the photograph. Maurice had just turned fifty when Bea left, and she wasn't far behind, but they had both always looked good for their ages. In this photo, however, Maurice's hair was thin and almost white, and Bea wore a sea-blue scarf wound around her shaggy bob. And in the background, there was unmistakably a young Janet, pulling a pint behind the bar. This was taken in the Dolphin. Maurice had been here. With Bea. At the Dolphin. But – Bea had *left* Maurice. And he had never recovered. And yet there they were, together, in Polperran.

None of this made any sense.

She walked out of the house, heading straight for the shop, the nearest of the three places she knew there would be someone to answer her questions.

As the door dinged, Tressa, Radka and Sally all turned to her.

'Good morning, Alice!' called Radka, leaning back against the main counter. Tressa seemed to have taken Radka under her wing, and Alice noted vaguely through her confusion that Radka seemed to be blooming in her care. Alice lifted a weak hand in greeting to them all.

'Tressa, could I –' she began, quietly.

'Alice, you should hear how Sally's been getting on. The whole thing is working out marvellously!'

'Oh . . . yes . . . right . . . with Luke.'

Sally looked coy for a moment. 'Oh, the gardening –' she shot a look at Tressa. 'It's going really well, thank you. Really, thank *you*, Alice – it wouldn't have happened at all without you.'

'Good,' Alice said dimly, feeling Tressa's eyes on her even as Sally's slid away, 'Good, I'm glad. Tressa –' She saw Radka looking at them all, perplexed.

'And do you know what else?' Tressa said. 'That delivery of flour this morning – it reminded me,' she said. 'The first Saturday in June was always Polperran's Cake Competition, wasn't it? Long as I can remember.'

Sally clapped her hands together. 'Ooh, Tressa. How could I have forgotten that? My mum didn't speak to her sister for three years because she said Auntie Elaine had cheated her out of a prize for her apple tart.'

Radka put down a newspaper she had been looking through at the till. 'Anyone can be in competition?'

'Well, that's only two weeks away. It's not been done for a few years – we'd need a few helpers with a bit of spare time,' Tressa said, then turned to Alice. 'Alice, how's that book of yours coming along?'

'*Tressa*,' Alice said again.

Tressa finally stopped and looked at her, slightly taken aback.

'Please could I talk to you for a moment? Outside?'

She didn't wait, didn't want to see the three of them looking at each other and maybe making concerned faces over her, but she let herself out and waited for the *ding* to sound as Tressa joined her in her warm breeze by the bike rail.

'Alice?'

When Alice looked down, she realised she was still holding the framed photograph of her father and Bea. She passed it to Tressa.

'Ah.' Tressa looked at it for a moment. 'He was a lovely man, your father. I only met him a few times, but I understand completely what Bea saw in him.'

Alice stared at her, then eventually said, 'A *few times*?'

Tressa passed the photograph back to Alice. 'Why do you think you didn't know he visited here?'

'Excuse me?'

Tressa spoke gently. 'Why is it, do you think, that neither he nor Bea told you that he came to Polperran sometimes?'

'I have absolutely no idea.'

'Of course you do. You're a smart girl.'

Alice looked at the photograph again, at Bea and Maurice's smiling faces as they drank together at Polperran's pub. She didn't look up when she said, 'But my father hated Bea. She broke his heart.'

'No, love,' Tressa said. 'Or at least, it wasn't so broken that it couldn't keep working again. After a bit.' Tressa stepped back to sit on the bike railing, and Alice, after a moment, joined her. 'They always kept in touch, because of you, of course. And things were hard: Bea's heart was torn out when she left you, left both of you, and every time you came it took her weeks to put herself back together again. And he had lost Bea, and struggled every day to give you the life he thought you should have, to try and keep you safe. But eventually the reasons they had been close before became a reason for them to still be friends.

'After you left home, he came a few times, stayed in a room over the pub. He and Bea would go on these long, long walks, up behind her house and over the whole county, it seemed like, and she would be painting like mad and said he'd sit there, content as anything, just reading in the room next to the studio, making them both lunch and cooking for them both in the evening before he went back to his room at the Dolphin.

'She made a lot of mistakes, your mother, and she didn't always make the choices I'd have done, but she did well with your father. They'd gone through a lot together, and if you can get through what they did while still being kind to each other, that's worth holding on to.'

They sat side by side for a long time. Then Alice said, 'They went through a lot – was that why Bea was on anti-depressants?' She saw Tressa look at her. 'I found them in her bathroom drawer. I wasn't snooping,' she added hastily.

Tressa laughed gently. 'I know, love, it's your house now, and Bea left everything in it to you. Yes, she'd been on

154

those for as long as I knew her, more or less. Those or something like them. She'd struggled with anxiety for years, a long time before she met your father or had you. It was a part of her.' Alice thought suddenly of that abstract painting in Bea's studio, of the great dark mass overwhelming two shapes, and realised it was precisely how her own anxiety felt, muddying up her mind and body. As Tressa began speaking again she also suddenly wondered if one of the two shapes was Bea. And if the other one might be her. 'That's part of why she came down here. She wanted to try and get better. I think she thought that one day she'd come back to you, once she was better, but sometimes things don't work out the way we want.' Tressa reached over and squeezed Alice's hand, and Alice let her but counted the seconds in her head until Tressa let go again.

'Why didn't either of them tell me any of this? Why does it all have to be so . . . buried?' Alice asked.

Tressa sighed. 'Sometimes we can't tell the things we'd like to. Sometimes we have to just let people come to things themselves. I imagine both of them thought they'd be around long enough for you to get there.' She stood up, and Alice looked at her. The older woman was smiling sadly. 'We never know when we're going to go, Alice. Bea thought she did and I still don't think she was completely ready. Why else would she have left you this project?' She watched her for a moment, then, content Alice wasn't about to collapse, she touched her on the shoulder and went back into the shop with a soft *ding*.

Alice tucked the photo frame into her pocket, and took the sea path down to the beach. The day now was grey, the wind colder and clouds fuzzing up the sun, so both the pebbles and the water looked flat and painted-on. She followed the path along the shore and realised she was heading towards Joy's house in the cluster of cottages behind the sea wall, and remembered that Bea's basket was still there.

Another thing, lost; and Tressa asking that Alice give more of herself to Polperran when Polperran kept on revealing more things it had kept from her; no word from Morag; and Bea had still left her. Alice thought she should be used to it by now, one way or another. She felt misery and frustration soaking into her bones, hardening into something featureless and grey-red. She let it saturate her and walked up the path to the door and knocked. This *woman*. These *people*. This *place*. *Why* did she leave her college and come here, *why* had she responded to Peter Blandford's letter, *why* had she got involved with this *project* –

The door opened. Joy stood there, tea towel over her shoulder, looking down at Alice's white face. 'You'd better come in then,' she said dully, heading back down her hallway. Alice followed, her limbs heavy, her mind soggy. She turned into the living room, but Joy called out, 'No, back here.'

She trailed after the voice and found herself in a cramped kitchen, filled not only with plates on the wall and pots and pans hanging from hooks on every surface, but with the most beautiful smells – honeyed notes of baked pastry and whispers of spice. She watched as Joy cleared a small section of table, put down a cup of tea that seemed to come from nowhere, and indicated that Alice should sit down. Once she had done so, Joy added a small side plate, with a glistening, wobbling slice of rich yellow custard tart.

Joy saw her looking at it. 'Don't worry, I got fresh ingredients. Go on,' she insisted, putting a fork beside the plate.

Alice picked up the fork, her hand feeling heavy and disconnected. She lifted it to the plate, prodding the custard. She felt Joy watching her. Eventually, she speared off a small section, put it in her mouth, and allowed the silky custard and short pastry to dissolve on her tongue. She took a sip of tea, and another forkful of the tart.

'All right?' Joy asked.

Alice closed her eyes for a moment, opened them, and gave her a small nod.

Joy in turn nodded back to Alice's plate, and Alice, in small forkfuls, finished the slice. She savoured each mouthful, the contrast of filling and pastry, the light nutmeg, the smooth custard.

When she was done, she had another mouthful of tea.

Joy was still watching her. Eventually she said, 'Better?' Alice nodded. 'Mm,' Joy said, almost to herself. She took Alice's plate and put it beside the sink, went out of the kitchen and came back with Bea's basket, leaving it where the plate had been moments before. 'There you go.'

Alice took the basket without standing up. 'Joy, can I get you anything? I mean . . . if you don't want to leave the house, I could . . .'

Joy took a sip of her own tea. 'Don't want to leave the house?'

'Since your husband . . . left. My mother said –'

'Marco. That was his name.'

'Marco.' Alice nodded. 'Marco. Sorry. My mother said that since Marco left you weren't leaving your house any more –'

157

'Yes, you're quite right, I don't leave the house, I just wait for the bakery pixies to bring me anything I might need. Flour, eggs, cake decorations, that's all I live on now, whatever the pixies bring me.' Joy's voice was sharpening.

'But . . .' Alice was confused.

'I do leave the house, Alice. Whatever your mother may have said to you.'

'No, she didn't say . . . it was in her will –'

Joy gave a croak of laughter. 'In her will? Ooh, I am flattered. So she never actually talked to you about me. You never had a conversation, just . . . a legal document?' Alice nodded again, and Joy looked at her, thin-lipped. 'I do *get out*. See the car outside?' She pointed over her shoulder at the window behind her, and Alice saw that these houses backed on to a road she hadn't seen before. 'I don't keep it for its looks. I just don't care to do my business in Polperran any more. Have them poking around in my life. I told your mother. I thought *she'd* have spread the word.' She finished her tea, then added spitefully, 'Can't abide gossips.'

Alice stared out of the window in silence, looking at the battered old car that sat there, Joy's escape from all of this. She thought of Tressa's attempt to revive the cake competition, another thing that had withered and died over the years. Eventually, she spoke. 'No one cares.'

Joy looked up from examining the dregs of her tea. 'What's that?'

Alice cleared her throat. 'No one cares, Joy. Out there. Most people. It's just mindless small-talk. If that. You should see the pub. It's bloody *dead*. And I'm amazed the shop is still open. Barely anyone on the green, on the benches, on the beach. No one out. Is everyone hiding, like you?' She looked steadily at Joy. 'Generally speaking, no one cares. About any of us. That's how the world keeps turning, OK? We just have to look after ourselves. And mostly, they probably don't even notice that neither of us are there.'

'But your mother did,' Joy said. 'Is that your point?' Alice raised her eyebrows and shrugged. 'And because you've lost her, you understand what I've gone through, don't you?' Joy went on, her voice growing sharp with sarcasm. 'You've lost your partner, you've lost your shop and your livelihood, the dream you and he had together, you've seen that future crash away from you while everyone's watching, and you could do nothing to stop him, and now you've been left with nothing but a collapsing cottage on the south coast of Nowhere –'

'We've established how I'm a terrible daughter, a terrible person, this isn't a competition. And your situation is something I can't even imagine, I know –'

'And yet you're still here, pretending that you can.' Joy was almost panting, her fury betrayed only by her breathlessness, before her face suddenly cleared. 'Oh my god. Do you think I need your *sympathy*?' she asked incredulously.

Alice felt rather than thought *waves of sympathy, everyone watching, everyone watching*, and her terror came back, her panic rising and claustrophobia swelling to fill the room, crushing the air from her lungs as she rushed from the kitchen, from the house, down the sea path, down to the beach, sweating, gasping, her muscles aching as she ran to the empty sea and let her feet disappear into the cold, cold waters once more.

Chapter Fifteen

It was a noisy meeting in the village shop. Ena was there, scowling in her customary black beside the drinks cabinet, and Radka was piling up boxes of fish paste on to the shelves, box after box, filling the shelves across whole aisles. Peter Bland-ford was also present, putting the fish paste into his shopping basket, while other people were just milling around and talk-ing. Sally served cocktails from behind the till, and Alice saw Morag sitting in a deckchair near the front door, making a mark in the book in her lap every time the shop bell dinged and a new person joined them.

At the edge of the bread section, a familiar figure. Bea was bending down over the rolls, tongs in hand, selecting two rolls to bag up for her wicker basket. Alice watched as Bea put one roll back, then the other, choosing instead a small loaf. She paused for a moment, and just as Alice was about to speak, Bea looked up –

Alice was stiff and sore. She had stayed on the beach until dusk, no one coming near her even if they had been on the cobbled way above the beach, then when the tide had fallen away and risen back up towards Alice's knees, she had stumbled up to the sea path. There, she'd heard someone call her name, 'Alice?' and when she'd peered through the gloom she'd seen Melder there, half-hidden in the shadow of a big fern.

'Alice?' she said again, her green eyes anxious. 'Are you OK?' Melder had taken her arm and walked back with her to Bea's cottage, and when Alice made no motion to get rid of her, Melder had come in and found a can of soup in the cupboard and heated it up. While it was heating Alice had wandered over to the cupboard and taken out the cooking brandy, but Melder had rolled her eyes at her and given her a cup of peppermint tea instead, leaves from the herb bed outside, sweetened with honey. When the soup was finished, Melder sat with Alice in the snug, reading one of Bea's books while Alice stared at the photos on the coffee table, then the scudding clouds through the porthole, and when Alice woke up at four a.m. Melder was gone, having left Alice covered with the patchwork quilt from the armchair. Dawn was pinking the sky, and she groaned as she sat up, wiping around her lips and feeling her furred tongue chafing in her sour mouth.

After a shower, Alice knew she wouldn't fall back to sleep again, so she sat in an armchair with her reading, notebook and pen on the side table. *The torture methods involved in the witch hunts throughout England and Western Europe echoed exactly those methods employed by those interrogating 'plague-spreaders' in the fourteenth century.* Did panic attacks exist in the fourteenth century?

Around six a.m., she was wondering how graphically she should describe the interrogation methods when she heard a noise in the garden. When she rose to the window she saw Luke, turning over the compost heap with a fork. He saw her movement at the window and turned, smiling and raising one hand in greeting, before continuing with his work. He obviously wanted conversation as little as she did, but she felt spooky standing and watching him; she'd had enough of her own work for a moment, though, and wandered instead into Bea's studio.

The canvases remained piled up – finding and calling whichever gallery sold Bea's work was one of the items on Alice's mental To Do list – and the smell of paints and oils remained in the air, no matter how much time had passed since Bea last worked here. Alice wondered if her own work would have any legacy, or if, when she published this book, *if* she ever published the book, it would disappear gradually from shelves and libraries until nothing remained. What was she bringing into the world, for all her efforts?

Bea's paintings glowed in the morning light, and although Alice didn't have much sense of the visual medium – witness her aggressively bland home, filled with the same minutely varied items owned by 95 per cent of the country, styled with the eye of the terminally unstylish – these paintings had something to them that had only a few times spoken out to Alice in art. She wanted to watch them, to read them somehow; but even the abstract one that had spoken to her so clearly and suddenly as she talked with Tressa now seemed to be in a language Alice did not understand, could not even begin to translate.

In the shop, Sally was out again, Tressa behind the till, and as Alice gathered her own few pieces of shopping she watched Radka looking at the shelves for a long time. She didn't pick anything up, but would occasionally nudge things on their shelf, or move things over from one place to another.

'Radka?' Alice spoke gently. 'Are you OK?'

Radka smiled at her. 'I always do this. Tressa does not mind. This shop makes me think of my mother's shop, and I think maybe I do a better job of making a shop look nice.' She looked amused at Alice's small breath of laughter. 'It is true – maybe I know what works, since I grow up in shop.'

'Don't say that to Sally, she grew up in a shop too.'

'In this shop? Here?' Radka was baffled. 'No, it is not possible.' She thought for a moment. 'Perhaps it is because Sally does not want to be running a shop, that she does not do it well. A shop needs . . .' She said something in Romanian, just as Alice had the brief thought that she hadn't seen Sally with Luke in the garden this morning. Or for a while. Then Radka remembered the word she needed: 'To *fit* the people using it, to make them happy. But I liked my mother's shop very much, and always hoped I would keep it after her.'

'Radka, I'm sure Sally and Tressa are happy that you're tidying the shop, but . . . it's not fair for you to work for nothing. We'll look at your CV, yes, and have a look at what's available?'

Radka swapped two bags of sugar around. 'Yes. But I think, this will not be easy to find work. At the summer, all the local people want jobs with all the tourists. Their children come back here and are waiters and cleaners and lifeguards. It will not be so easy for me.'

Alice looked around, hoping for some inspiration to

163

comfort Radka, and saw Tressa watching them both with a look of concentration on her face.

Tressa said, 'Oh, that reminds me you two, remember the cake competition we were talking about –'

And Alice was about to say, *Were we?* when the shop bell went, and Ena entered, shopping-trolley-first, her face going from harried to hard as she noticed Alice.

'Ena . . .' Tressa said, warningly.

'Honestly, from March to October, you can't ever escape the tourists, can you?' Ena said, still looking at Alice. Alice smiled warmly back. Ena looked away.

'What can I get you, Ena?' Tressa spoke again.

Ena finally turned to her. 'How long are you going to be working here?' she snapped.

'As long as I'm needed,' Tressa said calmly. 'Now what is it you're wanting today? Give me your list and Radka here will help me get your things.'

'More staff! Sally Hobson has clearly won some money, then, to be employing all these . . . *people*. And I'm not *dead*, Tressa,' Ena huffed, parking her trolley by the till and picking up a shopping basket. Regardless, when Radka came forwards Ena handed her the list with a head nod which was part patrician and part humble, transforming somewhere in the middle as Radka took it from her hand. With great solemnity, Radka began checking the list against the items, walking backwards and forwards to deposit them in a pile at the till, while Tressa began scanning and packing up. One item Tressa picked up and examined for a moment, and the next time Radka came with a few items Alice heard Tressa say softly, 'Not this one, love, get the one next to it with the yellow label, that's

164

the one she wants.' When Radka hurried back with the right one, Tressa said, 'Perfect, thank you, love.' Something was happening here that Alice didn't quite understand.

When Tressa had scanned everything, Radka gently loaded it all into Ena's shopping trolley while Ena paid. Only once that had been completed did she look at Alice again.

'Well?' Ena said. 'Can I help you?'

Alice smiled again. 'No, I don't think so.'

'Good,' Ena growled. 'Off soon?'

'I'd have thought so,' Alice said. Ena's face hardened, and she swept out of the shop with much banging of the trolley against doorframes and newspaper stands.

'Is she angry?' Radka asked.

Tressa sighed. 'No love, she's not angry. And you did wonderfully, thank you.'

Radka beamed, and only Alice seemed to notice that when Tressa had answered Radka's question, she had, for just a moment, looked directly at Alice.

'Now, Alice,' she said, returning to her previous thought, 'the cake competition –'

'Tressa –'

'I promise you, it's not a big job, but the more people who can help out, the more the community will have the occasion they deserve. Radka, I'll tell you what I need from you in a minute; now –'

'Do I count as the community? I mean . . . do people want me poking my nose into a community event like this? I can't imagine Ena's the only person who feels that way about tourists like me.'

'Don't be so ridiculous,' Tressa said, with some impatience. 'Community isn't some . . . *thing* we sign up for

165

with our parish magazine and our council tax, where we're all dancing together on the village green every day. Community is made up of people – and it doesn't mean you have to know everyone, inside and out. It just means you have to know someone, and that person might know two others, and so on. I know it doesn't always seem it from the streets of Polperran sometimes, but if we can make connections happen through little events like this, well,' she sighed, throwing her hands up, 'maybe we can make even Ena part of things.'

Outside, the day was still cool; the sun might burn off the cloud haze later, but morning left a faint mist over everything. With her supplies from the shop, Alice could spend the day working again, back at the cemetery under Santo's willow tree, away from gardeners and shops and her mother's paintings and secrets, with her notes and books and the most recent envelope from Peter Blandford. The envelope lay heavy in her bag, awaiting a decision either way: every day she didn't open it meant another day in Polperran, but opening and reading another note from her mother would be committing herself to continue Bea's legacy in a way she never would have chosen, had a living Bea asked.

As she approached Frances's cottage she heard voices in the usually silent Polperran, and in Frances's front garden she could see two figures standing, bent around the garden table, talking quietly together as they moved busily.

As she got to the low wall, Alice recognised the other figure working. 'Sally?' Alice said.

Sally and Frances turned around, and Sally gave a shy smile. 'Alice!'

Alice blinked at her. 'Aren't you with Luke today? I just saw Tressa at the shop . . .' She tailed off.

Sally looked at Frances, who was smiling back at her.

'Oh, no, Tressa knows where I am, don't worry. I'm afraid I haven't seen Luke for a while now,' Sally said.

Frances interjected, 'Not since his apprentice is so much better at flowers than he is.' She looked at Alice. 'No offence to Luke, of course, but Sally's an absolute natural. Never seen such instant skill with the blooms.'

'But – I thought you were working with Luke? When you've been off from the shop?' Alice didn't understand why no one had told her about the change of plans.

Sally looked worried. 'I did start off working with him, Alice, but it just seemed like there'd been some kind of misunderstanding about my . . . interests – that I wanted to be a gardener –'

'But . . . didn't you?' Alice asked, remembering her own hesitation at the too-swiftly made plans. 'I thought . . . the conversation we had in the shop. About my mother's plants –'

'It was her flowers,' Sally cut in, apologetically. 'She'd bring me cuttings that I'd grow in our window boxes out the back of the flat, or she'd bring me her spare flowers for me to dry. I've been wanting to work with flowers forever, really, but then on that first day with Luke it turned out that Frances used to be a florist –'

'Long before your day, of course,' Frances chipped in, 'And unlikely anyone would remember, but I have talked to Luke about it when he's been helping me.'

'So Luke asked Frances if I might help her with her flowers, and since then she's been training me in flower arranging, and cutting, and all sorts.'

167

Alice looked at them both. 'So every time you've been out of the shop, you've been here?'

'Oh no, not every time, and not all day! Luke's given me a few of his clients, where I can start learning about their flowers, and they've been paying me in flowers for me to practise with. They seem pleased, though, Alice,' she said, hopefully. 'It seems there's a few rose bushes even Luke hasn't been able to get blooming.'

Alice shook her head and looked at Sally and Frances. 'But . . . why didn't anyone tell me?'

Sally's smile faltered. 'Well, I do still see Luke –'

Oh, Alice thought sombrely.

'And this is still the gardening that you'd come up with, Alice – it didn't seem like there was anything to tell you. Then I did more arranging than gardening, often as not, and I didn't want you to think that I was ungrateful, or that I didn't appreciate what you'd done, and then it got so it suddenly seemed ridiculous that I hadn't told you, so I thought I'd show you, then I just . . .'

'She kept losing her nerve,' Frances said. 'Ridiculous, I told her, Alice of all people would know about learning as an adult, about research and new sources of knowledge and all that. Remembering names and details. I told her to just tell you, I said she was being a silly thing about the whole arrangement, over-worrying.' Frances's words were stern but her face was not; she looked at Sally with great fondness, while Sally's face grew lower and lower as she watched Alice.

Alice remembered that she wasn't local here. Unlike Radka, she wasn't finding a place in the village, no matter how small; unlike Tressa, she didn't know what was really going on, with anything or anyone. She hadn't even helped

168

Sally: Frances had, and Luke, and Tressa too, she supposed, but all Alice had done was barrel in with misinterpreted sources and decide it was enough information. No one owed her an apology, because nobody here owed Alice anything.

She looked away from them both, embarrassed, and hitched her bag higher on her shoulder where it had slipped down. 'It's fine, Sally,' she said, pulling her facial muscles into a smile. She floundered for a moment. 'Well done.'

Alice scuffed her foot briefly on the ground again before she turned away, lifting one impossibly heavy arm to wave over her shoulder as she walked down the road, away from Frances's garden. The embarrassment of her own presumption – *Here I am, saving the day* – soaked through her, bleaching the colour from her eyes, leaving a black and white misery that exhausted her beyond words.

At the cemetery, Alice could see only a distant figure mowing in the far corner, and slipped unseen beneath the willow before anyone else arrived. The dewy dampness in the air left her books almost wilting against the wood of the bench, and she caught herself repeatedly thinking not of the forced migrations of certain groups in fourteenth-century Europe, but of the envelope in her handbag, and how quickly it could be done so she could finally be away again.

Before she had the chance to take the envelope out, though, the willows parted and a figure came through.

'Mornin',' Santo said cheerfully. 'Mind if I join you?'

Startled, Alice drew her notes together slowly, marking her pages and piling the books beside her. Santo sat down, and pulled out a large, waxed parcel.

'Cake?' he said, pulling off a handful and offering the rest to her. Hesitantly, she took a wedge, and ate it gratefully, nodding her approval.

'That's good!' she said quietly. 'Yours?'

'Ena's,' he replied, then, when he saw her face, added, 'Don't ask, don't ask. Anyway, I thought someone better look after you. Hard work, all that thinking. S'why I try to avoid it.'

She laughed, surprising herself. 'And what *do* you do?' She was interested to hear her voice change, become more coquettish – this happened, sometimes, with particular people, and it always made her feel like she was watching herself from outside, curious about what that Alice thought she might be doing.

'This and that,' he said. 'Mostly fishin'. Got my own boat. I ought to take you out, while you're still here.'

'At the harbour? Round the bay?'

He nodded.

'Do you like it? Fishing, I mean.' *Do you* like *it? Honestly.* But Alice also knew from her observations that when a man was like this, it didn't much matter what you said to him.

'Love it,' he grinned. 'It's what I'll die doing.'

Alice took another bite of cake and spoke through the crumbs, letting the embarrassment of the morning dissolve in the warmth of the willow's shelter. 'That doesn't sound like a recommendation,' she mumbled.

Santo laughed. 'It's true! Fishing's not for soft men. Plenty die out there, you know. Even now. Sea can't be argued with. Just needs a good eye, good judgement, and when you need it, a good bit of force.'

She watched him for a moment, his dark, wavy hair falling into his thick-lashed eyes, looking every inch the hard-handed sea hero. '*Is* it actually dangerous? Round here?'

He looked back at her, chewing another mouthful cheerfully. Then he shrugged and burst into laughter. 'Can't blame a man for trying to impress a beautiful woman!'

He kept laughing as he left her the rest of the cake – 'You need it for your work, someone better take care of you' – and waved goodbye, promising he'd see her again soon. Alice was astounded to discover that she was sad to see him go, someone who was kind to her purely for the goodness of it. She also knew the feeling was due partly to his company, and partly to the lurking envelope she knew she now must read.

Besides the number three in the corner, she saw one other tiny difference to the previous letters when she eventually drew this one from her bag: a tiny smudge of blue oil paint on the back flap. When Alice lifted it to her nose, she could smell Bea again – linseed oil and ultramarine.

Dear Alice,

I hope that by now someone will have taken you to the Dolphin, if you haven't found your own way there. Until around ten years ago, it was the hub of the village, where the children would play together outside while it got dark and their parents sang inside to Bert and Clemmo's music.

It was one of the first places I frequented when I came to Polperran. I assumed that the best place to get to know everyone would be the village pub, and I wasn't wrong, although it took a long time for everyone to let me know them well. But I answered all their questions: where I had come from, how long I was staying, whether I had anyone down here already, what I'd do while I was in Polperran. I tried to be as truthful as I could, although I discovered that often too much candidness can make people suspicious: I had to allow a little bit of mystery to remain around me, or the villagers would assume I was hiding something.

It was strange to be so open here, and made me wonder how much I had kept hidden in Cambridge. I had thought I was utterly myself in our wonderful home there, but there was so much I couldn't tell you and so much your father didn't want to hear, for all the love he gave both of us. Did you listen to much music after I left? I know you listened to it when you came down here, on your headphones, but I never knew what it was, never knew if it was a song I loved too, or a song I could have teased you for, being an elderly parent who'd know nothing about young people's music tastes. I always wanted to ask. Did you know that your father loved the Carpenters and would sing 'Only Yesterday' to you when you were still in the womb? The soppy fool. I loved him for it, and for his sentimental music taste that seemed to go perfectly hand in hand with his dry academia. Don't the greatest intellectuals always have the most dewy-eyed hidden dispositions?

That first visit to the Dolphin was for the first birthday I celebrated here. I missed you and your father terribly, and wanted so much to come back to Cambridge and see you both, but I knew neither of you would welcome me after what I'd done. I thought I was going to fall apart. So instead I stayed in Polperran, and asked the landlady (Mary, may she rest in peace) if I could have a party there. Of course I knew almost *no one, but I told her I'd put some money behind the bar, and I'd bought the cottage by then, so almost everyone was curious to come and see this 'party'. And somehow it turned out wonderfully: there were so many people, and free drinks for the first round, and Bert and Clemmo played, and I started to be welcomed after that, a thawing that took years to happen completely but began that night. So I have always, rightly or wrongly, credited Clemmo and Bert with a little of that welcome.*

If you've been there already, you might even have seen the two of them. Do you think you could find some way to get them talking again? They might never play together, but they might at least become friends before it's too late. I know what it is to leave things too late, Alice.

Thank you, thank you, my darling girl,
Mum

'Thank you, my darling'. Again, as if she was just asking Alice to pick her up a bottle of washing-up liquid the next time she was in the supermarket. Alice remembered those birthdays too, another one of the mantraps scattered through the year that she and Maurice would silently navigate, both of them taut with the knowing and neither one daring to voice it. Birthdays and Christmas, Bea and Maurice's wedding anniversary, school performances and Parents' Evening. Sometimes it felt that Bea was a black hole, sucking everything else into the place where her light had been. But now of course Alice couldn't rely on those memories either, since Maurice had probably been sending her birthday cards, corresponding behind Alice's back when Alice could barely even speak on those days for years after Bea had left.

So Alice well recalled Bea's birthdays, and wasn't comforted to know that Bea had used them to bolster her new life here, buying new friends and lassoing locals into the role she then developed for years; Frontline Polperran Villager. When tourists bought those paintings from whichever glowing coastal gallery handled Bea, did they know they were buying the work of someone just as much an outsider as they were? Were they sold with a Local Artist sticker, when Bea was anything but? And now Alice was left to embed that lie in everyone's heads, Bea reaching back from beyond the grave to ensure her place as holy woman of Polperran, treasured by all, Alice returning to the Dolphin to bring this heart-warming story to Clemmo and Bert, uniting them once more at last through the power of eternal Bea. She re-folded the letter, running her nails tightly along the seams again and again until the edges of the folded letter were like little blades.

She stuffed the letter to the bottom of her bag, sighed, and tipped her head up to see the light coming in through the willow's canopy. She was right: the haze was dissipating, and the sky showed blue through the tiny shapes between the leaves. She opened her notebook and wrote the heading for her next chapter. *Blame in a Time of Trauma*. She could think about Bea's task later.

Chapter Sixteen

By lunchtime the next day, it was already too hot to work, even at the shaded garden table, even in the cool of the cemetery's willow. The heat was in her head more than in her body, and Alice changed into her swimming costume and loose dress, padding down the path to the sea with Bea's umbrella for shade. On the beach, the tide was slowly rising, and Alice sank down into the water and floated for a long time before taking a single stroke. On her back, she closed her eyes and let the waves lap against her face, then swam slow breast-stroke up and down the shore, getting occasional whispers of the harbour, fish and diesel. As she swam, she saw someone on the sea path, a distant figure she could just make out as Tressa. Tressa gave her an exaggerated two-armed wave as if to a distant ship, and Alice raised one arm and waved back, watching Tressa walk up in the direction of the shop before she swam on.

By the time she got back to the cottage, her hair had stiffened into salted rat-tails and her forehead and nose felt tight with sunburn, and when Luke, who was working on the hydrangeas, saw her, he touched his nose and forehead and smiled at her.

'Were you going to tell me about Sally not working with you now?' Alice asked.

Luke shrugged and went back to clipping something in the bushes. 'She did work with me, the Monday you asked. Otherwise, it was an arrangement between the two of you, wasn't it?'

'I'd assumed since she kept not being in the shop – I didn't realise she was with Frances. I don't care, I just . . .'

He stopped and looked at her. 'Good swim today?'

Alice closed her eyes, and felt for a moment like she was still in the sea. 'It's so warm already. And it's so different from my swims in Cambridge.'

Luke pushed up the sleeves of his thin blue jumper, and rubbed at some of the scratches he'd received from Bea's bushes on his darkening forearms. 'Better?' he asked.

She blanked for a moment, temporarily distracted. 'Ah . . . different.' She shielded her eyes from the sun as she looked at him. 'More water.'

He laughed. 'Who'd have thought.'

'But quieter too, somehow. I mean, the waves and the wind are louder, but – the size of it makes me feel quieter. When it fills your ears it means you can't hear your thoughts any more.'

Luke looked at her musingly. 'You will be careful, won't you? I don't want to be fishing you out on one of our call-outs.'

'I promise to not try and make it to France unsupervised.'

'Good. Just –' he stopped himself. 'Just . . . look after yourself.'

Alice bristled slightly. 'I'm not a total tourist.'

'I know,' he said, not looking at her. 'That's why I want you to make sure you're all right. When you swim,' he added.

Something in his voice stopped Alice, something that caught in her chest. She nodded at him, not sure if he saw, and she went inside to change.

When she came out a little later, Luke had gone. She didn't see him anywhere on the way to the Dolphin, and inside the pub the only people there were Janet and, at the end of the bar, Bert, one of the very people Alice was after. This one's grey hair was slicked back from his face, slightly long at the neck – with the air of a nineteenth-century sea-dog, somehow, even in his worn slogan sweater and faded jeans.

Janet was pulling a pint, but saw Alice and nodded. 'All right, love, gin and tonic, is it? Let me just finish with Bert here and I'll be right with you.' As the old man turned to look at Alice, Janet nodded towards him and widened her eyes at Alice – *remember the one I was talking about?* – so Alice returned his look.

'Alice,' she said. 'Bea's daughter. Bea Kimbrel? I don't know if you knew her.'

He took the pint from Janet, an odd-looking sludgy concoction, and took a long gulp. 'Ah, I knowed your mother.' He wiped his hand on his thigh, then reached out to shake Alice's. 'Bert. I was a young man when your mother moved to Polperran.'

Alice looked at him, and smiled slightly. '*I* was young when my mother moved to Polperran.'

Bert broke into a dry cackle. 'Come and sit over here with me, my dear. I'll tell you all the Polperran stories *she's* too wary of losing a customer to tell you,' gesturing with his pint at Janet, who shook her head at him, smiling.

He led her to a table in the far corner, the same table she

had seen him at that first night. She wondered how many of the other drinkers in here had their own tables, separated by some invisible but impenetrable line that not even glances crossed.

He settled himself into his chair and took another appreciative sip of his strange drink. He saw her looking at it.

'Ale and milk,' he said, as Alice grimaced. 'Drank this since I were a boy. Keeps the bones strong.'

She tried not to wince, taking a taste of her own drink to take the thought of his out of her mouth, and trying to think of a way into her task. Just then, she felt a gentle tug on her hair, and turned around to see the salt-dashed figure of Santo, grinning at her, hiding his hand behind his back as if it would fool her.

'Oh – Santo –'

'Can't stop, you two, just came to pick this up,' he said, lifting a small flagon of cider on one finger. 'Late night work on the boat tonight.' He gave her a wink and nodded at Bert, who only grunted and buried his face in his drink as Santo made his exit.

Alice looked at Bert. 'Bert.' He looked up. 'Do you know Santo?'

The old man looked back into his pint for a moment, then grunted again. 'I know 'im. Fished with 'im a few times when 'e were younger.'

'Isn't he still a fisherman now?'

''e is. But I'm not. And he should be careful out there. It's a dangerous place for a man like that.'

'He goes out on his own?'

'No, no,' Bert replied. 'It's a two-man vessel he's got, there's a couple of men he calls on to help out. Not that he really needs to – one of the best fishermen I ever saw. That man could catch a sardine with an 'ula 'oop.' He gave another grunt. 'God doesn't always hand out his gifts fairly, if you know what I mean. That's what my mother always said, least.'

'What do you mean a man like that? What does he need to be careful of?' Alice asked.

Bert picked up his empty pipe and gave a thoughtful suck on it. 'Let's just say that Santo Hammett doesn't always fish *where* 'e should fish and *when* 'e should fish,' he said. 'And *what*. Some men think nothing can touch 'em. And if you're where you shouldn't be, doing what you shouldn't do, there's no guarantee that things won't go . . . a bit rum.'

Alice frowned at him. 'Do you mean . . . he's fishing illegally?'

Bert yanked his pipe from his mouth, and looked around the pub. 'All right, gal, don't need to declare it to the 'ole world. It's no one's business but 'is, if 'e wants to do something stupid and if 'is friends are stupid enough to 'elp 'ee.' He drained his glass. 'Didn't you say it were your round next, my dear?'

Up at the bar, while Janet poured the drinks, Clemmo shambled up beside Alice, pulling off his coat, slick with the evening's warm rain.

'Alice, isn't it? We spoke last time you were in here.' She smiled in return. 'How're you finding Polperran? Janet making you feel nice and welcome?' Janet turned around at her name, gave Clemmo a friendly grin, and put Alice's order down in front of her. Clemmo's gaze was drawn to the drinks, and whatever he was going to say died on his

179

tongue as he saw the unmistakable sight of Bert's stodgy pint. Without looking at his old friend, his body stiffened and his face hardened as he realised who Alice was drinking with that evening.

'Excuse me – Janet, I'll be back in a minute,' he said, and shambled away from the bar, to the table furthest away from where Bert sat.

Janet looked at Alice in complicity. 'Honestly, they're as bad as each other, those two. Like a couple of little children.'

'Let me take this over to Bert, and I'll be back,' Alice suggested.

But Janet nodded at Bert's table. 'Too late – he saw you talking to his worst enemy. He won't be drinking more Black Mackerels tonight.' Alice was mouthing *Black Mackerel?* as she looked over at the table she had been at with Bert, and saw now that it was empty, Bert having decamped to sit in near-silence with another old man, his back set against Alice and her disloyal ways.

Alice sighed, and Janet laughed. 'No use looking for reasonable behaviour from most of the men round here. Sea wind's blown all the good sense out of most of them.'

Alice thought of Santo, grinning, in dangerous seas at dangerous times, and silently agreed.

Chapter Seventeen

It became clear that the cake competition was not only going ahead, but that Tressa had taken Alice's silence as happy complicity. She saw Alice a few days later and caught her by the arm, saying, 'Alice, just the person I was after. Thank you so much for your help, we *are* going to get the Polperran Cake Competition up and running again.'

'I don't –'

'What would we do without you?'

'I didn't –'

'And I know you're busy, so it's very little work – a hand with the tables and tents and things on the day, just so we've got somewhere to put the entries, but we've got a few people on that already so you won't be on your own; Sally and Gwen are doing the drinks, and we've got Kath doing the posters and things, and her nephew Steven is lending us the urns from his Scout hut. You know Kath and Steven, don't you, you'll have seen Steven's brother at the Dolphin, I'm sure. Plus John is going to bring the hay bales, for seating – as long as it's good weather, of course, although you know what he's like about that! And Julia and Marge, from the salon and the vet, they've said they can help with the prizes –'

'Fine. Fine, Tressa.' Alice knew that Tressa knew that

Alice didn't know what Tressa was talking about, and they both knew it was easier to lie down in the waves of Tressa's intentions than to stand and be knocked down. 'I can help with the tables.'

'Oh, perfect, you are a lamb, Alice,' Tressa smiled. 'And one other tiny thing. Can I pass the posters on to you? You'll need to hang them around the village, lampposts and so on, on the noticeboards of the church and on the green, in all the shop windows, and see if you can't get people to put a few in their windows. All right?'

Alice took a deep slow breath in through her nose. 'I don't . . . I don't think – I mean, I'm quite busy at the moment, I need to get my latest chapters to my supervisor . . .'

Tressa looked immediately apologetic. 'Of course, dear! I'm so sorry, I'd completely forgotten – Yes,' she paused. 'Yes, I'm sure I can do those myself, if all else fails.'

'Well, I –'

'Right, but I can put you down for tents and tables, then?'

Alice nodded.

'Wonderful! Wonderful. I shall see you then, if not before.' And Tressa bustled away, leaving Alice needing a moment of touching her head, then her pockets, then her bag, to remember where it was she had just moments ago been going.

The very next afternoon, Gwen knocked at the door of the cottage, looking flustered and carrying various bags.

'Alice, you're here, thank goodness!'

'What's wrong? Do you want to come in?'

Gwen started searching through her own bags, then

paused. 'No, I won't, there's too much to do, but listen – could I ask you an enormous favour? It's Tressa.'

'Is she all right?'

Gwen looked serious. 'I'm sure she will be. I hope she will be. She's at home now, but – well, she is nearly eighty-seven. She shouldn't be rushing around the way she does. The doctor says she needs to rest.'

Alice felt terrible, remembering how busy Tressa had been only the day before.

'So, the thing is, Tressa's worked so hard having these posters made – would you be able to just put a few up? Even a few would be amazing,' Gwen said. 'You know, so people know about the cake competition; it'd be such a shame after all the work Tressa's done for no one to turn up, wouldn't it? I'll take one for the café, of course.'

Alice shook her head, and said, 'God, yes, of course – of course – just let me have some and I'll put a couple up, absolutely. Is everything else OK? The café?'

Gwen shot her a look of exhaustion, and put all her bags down for a moment.

'Oh Alice, you are kind for asking. I just don't know what to do with myself sometimes. I mean – I love the place, but . . . when I look at it, really look at it, like I'm a customer coming for the first time, I can't help wondering if it wouldn't be better to hand it over to someone else. Someone who knows what they're doing.'

Alice didn't know what to say. 'Do . . . do you want to close it down?' She was momentarily pleased that she could still discover genuine interest in something that didn't originate from the pen of her deceased mother.

'No!' Gwen insisted. 'Goodness, no. I don't know what

I'd do without it. But I just feel like I have . . . some kind of responsibility, to the customers, or to Polperran, or Luke and Melder, and I'm letting someone, somewhere, down.'

'Gwen,' Alice said. 'This is just between us, but there was a moment in time when I arrived here, and it was only your café keeping me in Polperran. Your Hevva cake, Gwen!'

'It is good,' Gwen admitted. 'I mean, maybe not up to Joy's standards, but it gets by.'

'Exactly. And Polperran people love it, don't they? Doesn't Peter Blandford still come in for his sandwiches every day?'

'He does, he does. And you should see him when someone else gets the last of the prawns,' Gwen giggled.

'And Melder's fine, isn't she? And –' Alice gulped, coughed briefly, 'Luke, also, fine.'

Gwen looked at her, then put her hands on Alice's shoulders. 'You're right,' she said. 'You're right, absolutely, and I need to stop inviting trouble in where, for one rare moment, there's none there. Right! Off I go. You'll be all right with the posters?'

Gwen looked so happy and relieved that Alice didn't look inside the bag she'd been given, noting vaguely how heavy it was. It was only the next morning, when Alice saw it still sitting by the door, that she felt hugely guilty again for not helping an unwell Tressa sooner and opened it to examine its contents. Rather than just a few posters, the bag contained an inch-thick pile, complete with staple gun and extra staples, a hand-held sellotape dispenser, and a handwritten list of all the locations Tressa had mentioned to Alice, plus a few more for good luck. But Alice had said she would help, and she couldn't help but think *What if this is the last thing I can do for her?* as she pictured the elderly figure; so she borrowed Bea's big sun hat again, loaded up her bag with the posters and fixings, and started trying to work her way down the list.

Her very first item was the church noticeboard. Alice peered around for a while, but seeing no one about she began unlatching the glass cover and swinging the heavy door open.

'Excuse me! *Excuse me!*' a voice called, growing in frantic urgency. Eventually Alice located the source: a distant figure in black and white robes hurrying through the churchyard towards her. 'Hold on!'

He drew closer, then stopped, panting a little after his exertions. 'I'm sorry, you can't just put anything on our noticeboards. It belongs to the *church*,' he said, his chest gently heaving.

Alice felt like a child again. 'I know, I'm sorry, I did try to find someone . . .'

'Well, it's not just about finding someone – anything that goes on the noticeboard has to be brought before the parish council for approval. We've had all sorts of inappropriate items, and we have a *system*.' He sniffed.

'I know, I'm sorry, it's for the cake competition?' she said, holding up a poster. 'I'm just trying to help someone, Tressa –'

The man froze. 'Tressa?' he said.

Alice nodded, relieved.

'*Tressa* gave you these?' he asked again, his eyes darting from side to side as if she might be lying in wait somewhere around the churchyard. There was something on his face

185

that Alice was amazed to see was close to fear, and she wondered what that story was, and if it was related to the behaviour of Tressa's children, years before, that she had hinted at in the shop. Either way, he was now hurrying to reopen the noticeboard he had previously latched shut, and was offering her pins, straightening the poster for her, offering to take another for the porch of the church, maybe a few more. He could put one in the window of the vicarage too, and see if the verger wanted one, giving Alice more and more suggestions without her having to say a word. Alice left the churchyard smiling somewhat, hoping all of the list might be this easy.

But of course, it wasn't. Not that people were uncooperative – quite the opposite, in fact. Everybody wanted to talk to Alice about the competition, to ask her questions, and then, when it was clear she couldn't answer them, tell her their memories and stories of previous competitions. Recipes were recited to her, as if she would memorise them and make them for the contest, and shop owners closed their doors with a small sign in the window saying 'Back in 10' to take Alice to the back of the shop, where she'd receive more questions and more stories (and occasionally a cup of tea and biscuit).

The only person who didn't welcome Alice's posters with open arms was Joy. When Alice knocked, Joy just shouted, 'No!' through the closed door. Alice took a minute to fold a poster into a paper airplane, and slid it through the letterbox into Joy's dark hallway. And when she'd seen Santo, sweeping a cloud of dust up at the end of someone's drive, he'd been remarkably reticent about the event too, insisting that although it was hard to turn Alice down, he wouldn't be able to make it.

Alice thought the whole job would take an hour at most, so when, nearly four hours later, she staggered into the shop to ask Sally to put up one of her last posters, and found Tressa behind the till merrily handing several sacks of potatoes to a customer, she was too exhausted to do more than stand and stare.

'Alice! How wonderful! You got the posters?'

Alice gaped at her, then eventually managed, 'You're fine.'

'Well,' Tressa said, gently polishing her glasses as the customer left, 'I wouldn't say fine, but I'll live to fight another day. You can't be too careful at my age,' she added, seeing the look on Alice's face. 'Everything go all right?'

Alice shut her mouth with a snap, and Tressa held up her hands in surrender.

'I know, I know, but I'm only an old woman, and things need to get done with whatever means available. Don't you know that yet, Alice?' She paused. 'I bet the vicar tried to stop you, didn't he? And did you tell him it was for me?'

Alice couldn't hide a tiny smile.

'I knew it!' Tressa grinned wickedly. 'He's got some terrible views about me,' she said. 'I don't know where he gets them from.'

'I'm beginning to get an idea,' Alice said.

'Alice,' Tressa said more seriously, then seemed to change her mind. 'Look, how will we get Joy to enter? God knows I've missed her custard tarts. And I'm an old woman! We don't know how many custard-tart-eating days I've still got ahead of me!'

'Yes, yes, we've established that,' Alice said. 'But *I'm* not making anything. I'm not a baker.'

'That's fine, my dove! You've done your part already.'

Alice nodded, taped a poster up beside the door, and went to leave.

'Ooh, one more thing – you will still be free for those tables and tents, won't you?'

Alice gave a *huh* of tired laughter. 'Of course, Tressa.'

Alice was exhausted that night, worse than the day she worked in the shop. Too many people, too much conversation. From now on, she would have to remain mostly in hiding: from Tressa, in particular, but also from the hordes who had seemed so excited by the posters. Most of all Alice was worried that, for all Tressa's wiliness, she would end up being disappointed on the day. It was easy to promise something – *Of course I'll come, I'll definitely bake* – but people tended not to live up to their promises. The sole glimpse of sunshine in the whole thing had been when Alice had seen Ena, slowly walking up the road ahead of her, stop to read one of the lampposts, turn to spot Alice then lift her hand to the poster and tear it off. It was so childish that Alice had to laugh.

Alice decided to stay in the cottage for a while, working on her book in the shade of the garden and at the night-time kitchen table. She escaped for occasional dawn swims, glimpsing only Luke as she came and went to the sea, Luke who would unaccountably always still be nearby when she returned from the sea, even though he vanished off to some other job shortly after.

Chapter Eighteen

The day before the competition, Tressa came to the cottage, and stood talking to Luke for a long time, while he did something to the soft fruit beds. Alice half-watched her through the leaves of the apple tree, until Tressa seemed to notice her and came over.

'Alice! Glad to see you – now, before I forget,' Tressa said, as if she hadn't deliberately come to Bea's cottage to find her. 'Are you still OK to help with things tomorrow?'

'Yes, Tressa, ten o'clock, I remember.'

'Good. Thought you might need a more practical task to be getting on with for now. And Melder may come over later, you can help with her job too.'

'Here?' Alice said.

'Yes, is that a problem?' She went on before Alice could answer. 'Good. And tomorrow –'

'Tomorrow morning,' Alice said. 'Ten o'clock.'

Alice worked for a little longer after Tressa left, then made coffee for herself and Luke, and was just packing up for the day when Melder appeared through the gate, keeping one hand on the gatepost as if to pull herself out of the garden at an instant's notice.

'Mel!' said Luke. 'You coming in?'

Melder looked at Alice. 'Do you mind . . . Tressa sent me over, but . . .'

Alice could hear in Melder's voice that she'd had a very similar experience of Tressa to her own. *And probably for a lot more years*, Alice thought. She stood up to bring her in and help her with the bag she'd brought, which Melder waved her away from until Luke reached over and took it from them both.

'Inside, Mel?' he asked.

Melder looked at Alice.

'Alice?'

She shrugged. 'I don't mind! I don't know what we're meant to be doing. Tea?'

'Yes please,' Melder said. 'Peppermint, please?'

Alice looked at Luke, who began packing up his tools. 'I've got to go, but thank you – another time. Mel, I'll see you at the café later?'

He waved to them both, whistled for Belle, and was gone. Melder sat down at the garden table, and pulled things out of her bag – lengths of white cotton ribbon, triangles of fabric, and the staple gun.

'Oh god,' said Alice.

'I know, I'm sorry, this is the job Tressa's given me.'

'It's –'

'It's bunting, I know.'

'It's bunting,' Alice echoed. '*Bunting.*'

Melder paused from making the triangles into piles. She looked at Alice, her mouth slightly open. 'I never realised.'

Alice narrowed her eyes. 'Realised what?' she asked.

'I'm sorry, I know that we haven't known each other that long, and perhaps there are things people want to keep private, but . . .'

190

'What?' Alice said, a little nervously now.

'I never realised,' Melder said slowly, 'that you think you are *too good* for *bunting*.'

Alice laughed. 'I'm not too good for it –'

Melder cut in. 'Tell the truth.'

'All right,' Alice said, 'I do think I'm too good for bunting. But I think you're too good for bunting too! It's not just me. I think maybe we're all too good for bunting.'

'So – is it all markers of celebration that you're against,' Melder said, 'or just those public ones involving happiness and enjoyment?'

'All,' Alice said. 'We tried to have them banned in Cambridge but had to settle for making balloons illegal in 80 per cent of the colleges.'

Melder handed her a pair of oddly bladed scissors, and a pile of triangles.

'Here,' she said. 'Pinking shears. You trim, I'll staple.'

She showed Alice how to use the scissors to get a zigzag edge on the triangles, then began folding the ribbon in half and stapling each triangle into place as she worked along.

'We're making good progress,' Melder said after a while. 'I might not even be late for Mum.'

Alice finished snipping her triangle. 'Is it a special occasion?' she asked. 'Sorry, sorry, that's none of my business.'

Melder looked at her, bemused. 'You can ask, that's OK. Not a special occasion – well, not technically. It's special for the café, I suppose – we're repainting it,' she explained. 'Mum says she'll do it every year, then every year it's tourist time, and when it's not tourist time she finds a hundred other reasons to not decorate. I mean, she doesn't do badly from visitors but I think she'd do a lot better if she took care of the place like she used to.' Melder shrugged. 'You know, when Dad was alive.'

'Oh,' Alice said, 'I'm sorry.'

'Thank you,' Melder said. She paused. 'It feels silly, sometimes, how much I still miss him.' She wrapped the ribbon around her fingers. 'You lost your dad a while ago, didn't you?'

Alice nodded. 'More than ten years now. I was a lot older than you were, though, when my father died.'

Melder unwrapped and rewrapped her fingers. 'Doesn't really matter how old you are, though, does it? If your dad's half-decent, it's always pretty rubbish.'

Alice nodded again, feeling her eyes prickle. Melder put her hand on Alice's arm. 'I'm sorry, Alice. About your dad *and* your mum.' Alice didn't shrug off Melder's hand or make an excuse to move her arm, just looked down at them, still nodding, and after a moment Melder went back to stapling.

'If you're free tonight, though, and you're a *really* big fan of matte white and boiler suits, have I got an invitation for you!' she said.

Alice laughed. 'Won't I be in the way?'

'If you can work a paint roller –' Melder replied, then stopped. 'Alice. You *can* work a paint roller, can't you?'

'It was a genuine toss-up for my degree between that and History.'

'Good. Then please come. Mum's *feeding us* . . .' Melder singsonged, and Alice laughed again.

'Fine, OK, I'll come.'

They finished the bunting and agreed to meet at the café in half an hour, giving Melder just time enough to drop it off at Tressa's and for Alice to find some clothes suitable for painting.

When Alice arrived, Luke looked unnerved to see her, while Gwen was delighted.

'Wonderful! More hands make less work, they say!' Gwen cried, tying her apron on over a paint-spattered pair of overalls that were rolled up at wrists and ankles.

'No, Mum, they definitely don't,' Luke said, looking for a moment like an embarrassed teenager, and Gwen gave him a fond cuff about the head.

'Now, Alice, I'm particularly glad you're here, since you were the one who inspired me to finally get on with it this year.'

Luke looked at Alice in surprise. 'Did she?' He laughed. 'Sorry, Alice, that wasn't meant to come out with quite so much disbelief.'

'She did, indeed, something you and your sister haven't managed in all this time. We were having a chat about the place and it just made me realise that it's something I want to hang on to. It's worth looking after. What else would I do with my time if I didn't have the café? Come and join the coastguard with you?' Luke's face of alarm made both Gwen and Alice laugh.

'Right then. Coffee before we get started, Alice?' she said, and when Alice accepted Gwen disappeared into the kitchen and came back seconds later with a laden tray, cafetière and jug of cream and plate of biscuits. 'That's just for now, while we get set up,' Gwen explained. 'And a proper feed once we're a coat down. What do you think?'

Alice and Luke agreed, and they were just laughingly struggling into paint-spattered boiler suits when Melder arrived, slightly out of breath and wide-eyed.

'You OK, Mel?' Luke said, suddenly serious.

'Melder?' Gwen said.

She shook her head, still breathless, and Gwen said again, 'Melder,' and Melder shook her head again and eventually said, 'It's fine, Mum, stop.' Alice saw Gwen and Luke exchange glances, and both of them seemed to be checking through the big windows of the café as the light outside dimmed.

But there was much to be done. Gwen had scrubbed the walls and skirting in advance, but Melder, Luke and Alice needed to take the tables and chairs out to the street and set them in two piles (those to be fixed and those that would last a little longer), to take down the curtains to be washed, and cover the remaining floor and fittings with swathes of dust sheets, Pollocked with previous paint jobs.

It all took longer than Alice had expected, even with all three of them at work and Gwen apologising constantly from the kitchen that she wasn't doing more.

'You are allowed to occasionally relax, Mum,' Luke said, then looked at Melder and mouthed *No I'm not* just as Gwen called the words through the hatch. Alice laughed.

Alice gradually realised, too, that Gwen had donned the jumpsuit more in solidarity than for practical reasons, as she spent much of the time in the kitchen while the three of them got on with painting; in the end, though, the painting took no time, with three people and three rollers, and the smell of Gwen's cooking wafting through to spur them on. As Alice and Melder checked for any gaps they might have left, Luke and Gwen righted a table and set of chairs outside on the pavement, and laid out a meal of fish-cakes held in soft white rolls, dripping in tartar sauce and served with peppery skin-on fries. There was a brief silence as they all ate.

'Mmm,' Alice mumbled. 'This is lovely.'

Gwen looked critically at her handful as she chewed, then swallowed and said, 'The rolls. Have to buy them in. Can't beat the rolls from the old bakery, so I don't even try.'

'The fishcakes are good, though,' Melder said.

Luke added, 'And the chips. Mum, be fair on yourself.'

And Alice said, 'Everything, Gwen. Everything is delicious,' and was proven right by the completely empty plates minutes later. They sat outside for an hour, waiting for the first coat to dry, spending the time playing cards from the same box under the counter that had contained the board game Alice and Melder played. They played Cheat, and Rummy, with Gwen so chronically bad and both Luke and Melder so determined to help her, that every game descended into hysterics. Gwen's eyes were streaming with laughter and her children fell weakly against her, unable to speak, slapping down cards so shoddily that they had to keep scooping them back off the pavement. Occasionally, Luke leant over to Alice, pretending to be spying on her cards to bring her into the silliness.

It was only later, when they had returned to painting, that Alice watched as Gwen came to hold a stepladder for Melder and rested against it, and Melder reached down to touch the top of Gwen's head and Gwen twisted to lean her head against Melder's leg. It was only then that Alice thought, *Oh*. And something in her heart cracked a little, and she hurried her section and asked if that was all, could she head off now?

All of them had looked worried; Gwen had asked her if she'd stay for a drink at the end, or if she needed anything else. Alice tried to reassure them that she was fine, just tired, *Long day*, she said, *And tomorrow will be busy too*, and eventually they let her go.

Chapter Nineteen

Pink and green, everywhere. It was a busy party, everyone mov-
ing swiftly from place to place whilst also remaining still, talking
impossibly slowly to their neighbours as they flitted by, stationary
beside Alice. But Alice knew there was someone else there, some-
one at the party she had to talk to, in the house that was also a
collection of abstract fields and seascapes. She just needed to get to
the door, to step out into the hallway under the trees, and she was
sure Bea would be just outside, she could smell her paint –

Alice woke in her attic room tangled in her sheets, sweating and confused, blank and hot. The sky had no shape or
colour at all through her slanting window – it was as if a
dirty blanket had been laid across the glass, flat and depth-
less. She lay in bed for a few minutes, underused muscles
stiff from last night's painting, wondering what dawn
silence was ahead of her. It was only the sound of someone
in the garden that made her check her watch.

With a lurch, she saw that it was already nearly ten, and
though she had intended only to fall asleep for a brief time
after working until the sun came up, she was now –

– the person in the garden was knocking at the door,
and Alice was so confused and befogged that she bashed
into doorways and banisters stumbling to get there before –
she didn't know. She didn't know who it was or why it

mattered, and she barely knew in that moment where and who she was.

She opened the door to the flat, blank day, and the light was smothering. It took a moment to recognise Luke there.

'Morning!' He looked cheerful, then concerned. 'Are you all right?'

Alice continued to blink at him, flinching from the brightness, raising one hand to see him better. 'Yeah – yes – I . . . ?'

Luke stepped towards her to look a little more closely at Alice's face. 'Alice, are you OK?' before recoiling a little. At his feet, Belle whimpered. Alice suddenly realised her breath and her body were giving off powerful waves of noxious sweat from her brief hours of hot, airless sleep. She backed away too, waving her hands in front of her mouth and her body.

'Sorry, I'm not – I think I'm still asleep, I only just woke up . . .' she finally managed.

She realised Luke was trying not to laugh. 'Do you need help?' he said, before pressing his lips together to steady his face. 'I mean, the competition is setting up, and they wondered if you were coming to help. Shall I tell them you're not well?' His voice softened with his final question, and Alice knew he would, if she said yes, and he'd do it convincingly too. But then she'd have people knocking with all sorts of nosiness, plus she didn't want to discover exactly why the vicar was so frightened of Tressa. Really it was easier to plunge herself under a cold shower and wash away both her foul miasma and this strange head of dreams.

'Give me a second. I mean, come in and make yourself a

tea. Or you can go back there and tell them I'm on my way. Whatever suits,' she muttered, shuffling back indoors.

'I'll take that tea, if that's all right. Do you want one, while I'm making?'

Alice raised an approving hand that was half thumbs-up and half pointing to the kitchen, a wobbly finger-gun, noticing that she still had flecks of paint on her arms and smudged around each fingernail, and stumbled back upstairs to the bathroom.

After an icy shower and five minutes of tooth-brushing, Alice dressed and went downstairs, where Luke was waiting with a pot of tea and two mugs, plus a large pile of toast.

'It's only just brewed – I waited until you were coming down,' he reassured.

Alice looked at him with mock-surprise. 'Oh, Luke! Hello! I didn't know you were coming over today.'

Luke laughed and said, 'I suppose I met your twin earlier?'

'She's a mess,' Alice said. 'I normally keep her locked in the attic.'

Luke poured the tea and they ate for a while in companionable silence, before Alice looked at her watch and jumped. 'It's half past! Tressa will be furious!' They looked at one another guiltily before leaving the house in a flurry, hurrying to the village green where two large camping tents had been pitched, facing one another, with a long trestle table between them, hay bales scattered in threes and fours around the edges. The table held urns for the hot drinks and jugs for the squash, and each tent was filled with borrowed tables, gathered from around Polperran.

199

The plan was to load them with any cakes and puddings entered into the competition. Already it looked like a thin but steady stream of villagers were building up into a small crowd, waiting to taste the entries.

Tressa caught sight of Alice, and crossed her arms over her chest. 'Afternoon,' she said, pointedly. Alice saw in her peripheral vision Luke making gestures to Tressa, and watched Tressa's face soften. 'Come on, love, see what you think.'

She led her into the slightly smaller of the two tents, where she'd put a huge tray of her profiteroles. 'I know they won't keep for long in the heat, but I doubt they'll last that long anyway – they're my grandchildren's favourites.' There was also an oversized Chelsea bun beside the tray, and two Victoria sponges, plus a number of fairy cakes decorated by children from the village. Alice was pleased there were a few entrants after all – her greatest concern about the event had been that only Tressa would enter – but Tressa said, 'Wait! Have a look at this,' and took her to the larger tent. There, the tables were already heaving: buns and tarts, cakes, sweet rolls, rolled puddings, cheesecakes and brownies and more.

Alice surveyed the tables. 'That's . . . a lot.'

'Everyone I know has been baking all night,' Luke said. 'That's my apple pie at the back, but I can't really take credit when it's Mum's recipe.'

'So really our problem is whether we can get any more tables, Alice,' Tressa said in a pleased tone. 'Or even another tent?'

'Your mum kept a pop-up gazebo in the shed,' Luke told Alice, before turning to Tressa. 'If that's any use?'

'Perfect – can I leave that with you two?' asked Tressa,

before turning her attention to more entrants, and one of her teenage grandchildren who she had also tasked with finding more tables.

'Come on, then,' Luke said. 'Give me a hand?'

As they walked back to the house, Alice didn't speak for a while.

'Still asleep?' asked Luke.

'No. But there's so many *entrants*,' Alice eventually said. 'I thought Tressa said this hadn't been on for years. I mean, everyone seemed interested when I put the posters up, but I didn't think they *meant* it. I thought people . . . wouldn't be bothered.'

Luke gave a quick shrug. 'People like doing things together. We can't all be bookworms.'

Alice looked sideways at him. 'Bookworms do serve a purpose, you know. We're not just dormant inside our cocoons until someone is charitable enough to pull us into the fresh air to carry gazebos.'

He laughed. 'I know – but look at lots of my clients. They just want to see someone, and be with someone, even for an hour. I'm sure you know what most people are like now with their phones; the first moment there's a signal or a silence they're on it. But maybe what we really all want is the chance to *be* with those people when we still can.' Alice rolled her eyes. 'Wait, I know, I'm a Cornish yokel who's frightened of the modern world. But Alice: would you rather have seen pictures of Frances's garden, or walked around it yourself? In real life?'

She gave a *don't be ridiculous* look, softened by her memories of the green paradise.

'Exactly. There are plenty of good things about being

able to chat to people anywhere in the world all day and all night, but there are some things – like cake competitions,' he said, gesturing with both hands back to the green, 'where people really like smelling those cakes, tasting them, making their own to join in.'

'*Join us* . . .' Alice intoned, stretching out zombie arms in front of her.

'You were the one who asked.'

'Perils of being a bookworm. Nosiness. And look what all that nosy asking gets us – electricity, clean water, medical advances . . .'

'I told you, I'm just an old Cornish yokel.'

'Younger than me, Melder says.'

'My sister is such a blabbermouth. How am I supposed to remain aloof and inscrutable if she's telling every attractive woman who comes to the village secrets like my *age*?'

Alice kept her head down, and walked on to the cottage. She felt a faint glow in her throat and tried to hide her smile from Luke as they went through the gate, but as Alice opened the door to the black shed behind the house, Luke seemed to realise what he'd said. Gruffly, he instructed, 'This one, and that bag at the back. I can take it.' As she passed the bags out to him, he hoisted them onto his shoulders, not looking at her. 'Oh, that small bag on the floor, too, that's the pegs.' Alice reached down for it and turned to go, but Luke's hand was still outstretched for it. She veered wide of his reach, offering the peg-bag by her very fingertips – it seemed imperative now that her hand didn't touch his – and said as casually as she could, 'It's fine, I can manage this one. Even with my puny bookworm muscles.' Luke gave a smile without looking at her – she snatched a glance at him – and they headed back to the green.

As they rounded the corner of Bea's hedge, within earshot of the tents, there was a man loading up the back of an old flatbed truck.

'Santo!' Alice said. 'Come to deliver your cakes to the competition?'

Santo looked up, smiling, but saw Luke at Alice's side and his face turned. 'I'm afraid not, thanks for asking. Just going to see Ena, then on my way out of Polperran.'

'Don't let us stop you,' Luke said. Alice could feel his whole body tensing up beside her, and Belle gave a soft growl in the back of her throat.

'Only for the afternoon,' Santo replied, with exaggerated cheerfulness.

'Shame,' Luke said.

'Well, this has been lovely,' Alice interrupted, 'but we do need to be getting back with this. Can't tempt you for a slice, Santo?'

He grinned at her. 'You could tempt me with anything, Alice.' She heard herself give a ridiculous giggle, as he slid into the driver's seat and revved the engine up. Luke just watched him steadily as Santo reversed and drove away.

'What was that?' Alice said.

Luke said nothing for a moment, then looked at her. 'He's been no good since school.' She was about to ask more questions but he just said, 'Come on. We're late enough already,' and walked ahead of her back to the green.

Alice didn't know why she was being punished, but she half-ran behind Luke as his long legs carried him ahead of her. By the time she'd caught up, he'd already emptied out his bags and was laying out the gazebo and poles to start putting it up.

'Right – shall I do the cross-poles?' Alice asked.

He took them gently from her hands, and put them back on the floor. 'No, you're fine, I can manage.' He still wouldn't look at her, but he no longer seemed to be angry. 'Just . . . does Tressa need any help?'

Alice understood needing to be left alone, and it looked like Tressa did need help: she was trying to set out several heavy-legged ancient folding tables while also babysitting a clutch of toddlers, all of them very fast, very unreliable on their feet, and in possession of a great number of trappable fingers. When Alice came over to ask if she wanted a hand, Tressa looked relieved. 'Yes, my love, can you do the tables for me? And get them under the gazebo once Luke's got it up – we've still got a few more people coming in with cakes and things, and I'm worried my lot'll have at them if we don't get them out of their line of sight.' Alice could see in the smaller tent that Tressa's tray of profiteroles was already severely diminished.

The tables were heavy but easily unfolded, once the toddlers had been removed, and a few other people came to help her carry them over to the gazebo which Luke and Melder had quickly built together.

The tables kept filling right up until the closing time for entries, at which point Tressa rang a handbell and brought Frances, Gwen and the vicar around, the three of them now wearing homemade judges' sashes, each of them taking teaspoons or slivers of every dessert as they went around the tables.

On the green, the crowd stood in silent clumps, occasionally muttering to one another in the sunlight. But the rising heat slowly thawed the silence: Alice saw one woman walk over to another to offer wipes for a bleeding child, and someone else said something that had the surrounding villagers laughing gently. By the time something went the wrong way down the vicar's windpipe and some wag called out, 'I'll give you the antidote if you let me win!', the crowd was warm enough for the comment to elicit the kind of over-generous laughter usually only witnessed at wedding speeches. Soon the people of the small village were chatting to one another, sharing recipes and old gossip, still watching the judges as they conferred, moved dishes around, carried plates from one area to another to look at them side by side, and re-tasted. Eventually, Tressa rang her handbell again and announced, 'We have our winners!'

Everyone drew a little closer as the judges lined up.

Gwen held up a plate of brownies. 'Our favourite chocolate dessert,' she said, 'has been made by –' She consulted the label on the edge of the plate, although one boy was already hopping up and down, tugging at his mother's shoulder, ' – Billy Keats. Billy?' He rushed forwards and stood eagerly in front of the judges, who each shook his hand formally before Gwen handed him a tiny golden plastic trophy.

The applause died down into an expectant silence. 'Oh, is it me?' The vicar looked down at the table through his spectacles. 'Our favourite pudding . . . is this Summer Pudding, made with real skill and flavour by Meg Mantle. Well done, Meg.' The crowd clapped politely again, as Meg came forwards, shook hands and took away another small plastic cup.

'And our overall winner,' announced Frances, her voice cracking as she tried to speak above the excited muttering, 'is this stunning summer cake, blueberry and peach with a wonderful lemon glaze, made by Joy Garland. Thank you so much for this, Joy, and I hope we are once more able to taste your wonderful cakes in the future.' Alice looked through the crowd. There was Joy, pale hair and pink face, trying to hide her pleasure at the applause and smiles. She stepped forwards and shook the judges' hands, taking a large glazed platter from Tressa as her prize.

'Now,' said Tressa, as the applause quietened, 'all of these lovely cakes and puddings are here to be eaten. Donations to the coastguard – you know they need a new roof before winter comes, so let's not see any short arms in your deep pockets, do you hear me?' There was good natured laughter before everyone surged towards the tables, manned by Tressa's experienced-looking relatives who displayed very clear opinions about the size of the villagers' optional donations. Alice caught Melder's eye. She was helping with serving, and gave a wave.

Letting the crowd move around her, Joy watched Alice approach. 'Are you going to take credit for this?' Joy asked.

'For your cake? My baking skills aren't that good. No one would believe me.'

'I meant getting me out of the house. Wasn't that what your mother wanted? Have me milling about with all the Normal People? Getting outside myself again?' This was so close to Bea's actual words that Alice blinked. Joy laughed. 'I thought so. Well I hope you and your mother, wherever she is, feel very pleased with yourselves.'

The words seemed weighted with unkindness, but Alice could see Joy didn't mean it. In the time she had hidden herself away from the people who knew her, she'd got out of the habit of massaging her thoughts into the niceties that oiled society, and Alice didn't blame her.

'I'm pleased you came. I didn't know you were entering,' Alice added.

'I didn't know myself before this morning. By ten it seemed a shame to waste this cake when this was happening just up the lane.'

'I was worried you wouldn't come.'

Joy laughed again, sharply. 'Do you think you're the only one who remembers poor Joy? I do have other visitors, you know, keeping me in touch with Polperran news when I can't be bothered to find it out myself. Very interesting stories I've heard too, you know.' Joy raised both eyebrows.

'Right. Well.' Alice took in and let out a slow breath. 'Congratulations on the prize. I might go and try some of your cake, while I still can.'

They looked over at the table with the winning cakes, and Joy smirked. Three of Tressa's smallest grandchildren were scraping the very last crumbs of Joy's cake from the plate, while others grabbed the last few fragments of the winning brownie and pudding from the other plates. Alice sighed.

'Right.'

Inside the smaller tent, there were a few things left – some of Radka's *cozonac*, some forlorn-looking beetroot fairy cakes, and a solitary profiterole miraculously remained. Alice ate the profiterole in one mouthful, and as no one else seemed to be coming for the rest, took a slice of the *cozonac* and a purple fairy cake on one of the mismatched plates someone had piled up on each table. She heard a noise outside, two voices talking crossly to one another. She stepped out.

'You're a sore loser, Ena Penhaligon, and you always have been.'

'I'm not, I just don't need everyone to love me all the time. It's pathetic.'

Ena was sliding a large tray of fresh profiteroles onto the drinks table, clearly having arrived too late to enter the competition.

'It's not pathetic, it's friendly. You should try it sometime.'

'I know what friendly is. The sheer volume of your children shows everyone just how *friendly* you've been in your lifetime.'

There was gasp from the crowd, as Ena and Tressa stood almost nose-to-nose.

'I'll have you know, you old bat,' Tressa purred, 'that having you as my children's godmother is one of the biggest mistakes I've ever made. I'm amazed they all made it past their sixteenth birthdays without pricking their finger on a spinning wheel and falling asleep for a hundred years.'

'You're just jealous,' Ena retorted. 'You stole my profiterole recipe and you still can't make them properly. They're just dried up little lumps of dough – *speaking* of your children . . .'

At this, Tressa picked up one of Ena's profiteroles from their glossy pyramid, examined it carefully, then pushed it slowly and carefully into Ena's forehead, before licking her fingers clean with relish.

Ena stared at her, letting the creamy bun roll down her

face and fall to the floor with a faint *fop*. She picked up her own profiterole from the pile, and without looking at it, raised it to Tressa's face. 'Maybe you need to remember what these are *supposed* to taste like.' She put the bun against Tressa's lips, then pushed it with the flat of her hand, squashing it against Tressa's closed mouth.

Without parting her lips, Tressa reached over and picked another one up, palming it onto Ena's hat. Ena retaliated by picking up a whole fistful and rubbing them all over Tressa's neck and chest.

Alice had never seen anything so decorous yet shocking in her life. She looked around, wondered who would put a stop to this – would none of the children or grandchildren step in and do something? – and locked eyes with Melder, as wide-eyed as Alice felt. But when she looked back, she saw that both Tressa and Ena were beginning to bend over, weak-kneed, both laughing so hard it was almost soundless, clutching one another as Tressa tried still to mash her bun into Ena's hat, and Ena tried valiantly to ensure the front of Tressa's dress was entirely smeared with ganache and fresh cream.

Frances rang the bell. 'If anyone still has their appetite after that, there's some very kindly donated sandwiches and drinks now being served along the road on my patio.'

Leaving the two older women in the care of Tressa's eldest daughter, who was giving them both a stern telling-off, Alice and Melder joined the rest of Polperran and headed towards Frances's beautiful garden.

She realised when she got to Frances's that she hadn't expected so many people. For the rest of the afternoon, Alice, Luke, Melder, and other helpers ran back and forth between the Dolphin and the garden, bringing top-ups of sandwiches and drinks, paid for by donations into a bucket Frances rattled occasionally. Other people brought garden chairs over, which filled up the front garden and spilt out onto the road, effectively closing it so a large crowd could sit in the sun, dozing and catching up.

When the time came to tidy, Alice dreaded seeing what damage had been done to Frances's paradise. But she watched one man gently grip his son's ear to direct his gaze to the can he'd left on the edge of the flower bed, and the boy pick it up with an apology to Frances, and she felt the edge blunt on her concern. Indeed, in the back garden – Alice had not made it there through the throng of people – it was immaculate, bar a few broken stems of the extra-large bushes where visitors had been forced to squeeze past.

'Those needed trimming a while ago,' Frances said, appearing beside Alice. 'But they seemed to like it, didn't they?' She was beaming, aglow with the rare chance to share her passion with so many.

'They did. Is everything else all right in here? Nothing broken?'

'No, no, nothing that didn't need fixing already.' Frances looked around. 'You know, it's funny. Your mother always said I should open the garden to the public. I thought she was joking, but it worked out rather well, didn't it? And plenty of people asking about the plants, gardening tips, all sorts. They spotted Sally's arrangement in the front there, too, plenty of comments.' She looked at Alice with delight. 'Rather a good day, I'd say.'

Alice had been leaving Frances's garden, arms full of cups and plates to return to the pub, when Tressa caught her.

'Oh, Alice, I was hoping I'd see you. When you've got rid of that stuff – in fact, hang on – Michael?' Her son, cheerful and large, took the crockery from Alice's arms and headed to the Dolphin with them. 'Right. Would you mind going to check on Ena again? Not a long one, she doesn't need tucking in for the night,' Tressa's eyes twinkled briefly, 'but maybe just a cup of tea? She couldn't make Frances's, and it'll set my mind at rest.'

Alice tried to turn her sigh into a slow breath. 'What happened today? Between you two?'

Tressa grinned at her. 'Well. The public always likes a show, doesn't it? Besides, no one insults my profiteroles and gets away with it.'

So there she was, in Ena's kitchen again, still not being offered a biscuit – not that she could possibly have fitted in any more that day anyway. Alice noticed some leftover profiteroles on Ena's table, those that perhaps hadn't made the cut for the competition. Ena saw her looking.

'I should have won that prize,' she snapped.

'You shouldn't have been late, then,' Alice said calmly.

Ena glared at her.

Alice tried to change the subject. 'Did you try any of the cakes? Besides the profiteroles Tressa served you, obviously.'

Ena continued to glare.

'Radka's cake was lovely, I'd never had anything like that –'

'*Ucht*,' Ena spat, waving her hand dismissively.

'It's a classic Romanian cake. It was actually very nice.'

'Why should she get to enter when I don't? She doesn't even live here.'

'I think you'll find she does, Ena.'

'Moved in with Tressa, I heard? And you know what I mean.'

'Yes, I think I do. Heaven forbid someone travel from one place to another in the hope of improving their life –'

'Don't give me that. I've got some idea, thank you very much, about people travelling in the hope of improving lives,' Ena said, in such a quiet vehement voice that it made Alice turn to look at her. Ena's eyes moved from her cup of tea to Alice's face, with such pain that Alice felt dizzy, and saw with shock that Ena's eyes were filled with tears. 'Ah, what would you know, you who never go anywhere or do anything?' Ena barked, swiping at her eyes and picking up her cup again in a hurry. 'You don't know what being a stranger really means.'

'I've come *here*,' Alice said indignantly.

'*After* you were invited, when everyone's already rolled the red carpet out for you and heard all about you and read your clever university work – oh yes, your mother gave me a copy, too,' Ena said, noticing Alice's surprise. 'Few escaped that pleasure.'

'Well, I'm sure you didn't have to read it,' Alice said. 'She was just being polite. Didn't want to see you entirely cut off from polite society.'

'You don't need to tell me about your mother, I knew her well enough, thank you.'

'Good for you.'

'And I don't need you telling me to be nice to that Radka, either. Looks like Tressa's adopted her, as if she doesn't have enough children filling up the village.'

'Good. Then we agree,' Alice said, gritting her teeth behind her smile.

'All I'm saying is, those judges were biased. And the clock was wrong. And the idea that Joy Garland's cakes are the best in the village – *come on*. Is that the consolation prize for her husband not being able to bear her any longer?'

'Ena!' Alice scolded.

'Well. From someone who knows, it looked a lot like that. It was ridiculous, giving a cake prize to someone who used to run a bakery. Why are we all tap-dancing around to give her a medal just because he had the good sense to leave?'

'Right, I'm off.' Alice drained her cup and headed out.

Ena made a *tsk*-ing noise. 'Have it your own way,' she said.

Alice pulled the door firmly closed behind her.

On the way home, she saw that the Dolphin was lit up with impromptu lanterns and lamps outside. The crowds from Frances's garden had travelled up the road to the pub, cele-brating their rediscovered contact as people from nearby villages were drawn by rumours of the festivities and enjoy-ing the noise and heat of a sun-blushed crowded pub night. With one of Tressa's grandchildren and another boy from the village, Janet worked tirelessly behind the bar – she met Alice's eye and gave her a friendly nod, while serving a pint with one hand and cashing up the order with another.

'Usual?' she called, and Alice nodded back, warmed again by the recognition. The atmosphere was infectious here, giddy and jubilant, and after Ena's sourness it felt like something filling Alice's head so she couldn't think or feel any more. She saw Clemmo and Bert, albeit at either end of the pub, and Sally, customers from the shop, and even the taxi driver who had brought her to Polperran those weeks ago. The driver gave her a nod of acknowledgement, and Alice smiled back.

She noticed Santo further along the bar, talking to a man with a dark beard and blue eyes. They were roaring with laughter, Santo slapping the blue-eyed man on the back, noise absorbed by the sheer volume of this new crowd. Alice felt embarrassed about the hostility Luke had shown him last time she had seen him, and headed straight over.

'Can I buy you a drink?' she said, gently tapping his forearm. He turned around with what looked almost like a leer, but which changed instantly into a sunny smile.

'Hello, stranger!' he said. His friend gave him a nod and disappeared into the busy pub.

'I feel I owe you one, since our last encounter wasn't the most pleasant.'

His face dimmed. 'Ah, Mr Penrose. He's not my biggest fan. Not a lot of good things to say about me, and you know how he gets around the place. A word in everyone's ear.'

'Really?' Alice said.

Santo shrugged awkwardly. 'I've got used to it,' he said. 'That's the price you pay for living in a village, I suppose.'

'Well, I'll be escaping out of it again soon, I'm sure,' Alice replied. 'So the next one's definitely on me.'

She took her gin and tonic and he shouted his order over the noise, and once she'd paid they were carrying their drinks to the only empty table when someone in the crowd stumbled, knocking a wave of people backwards and against Alice. Santo grabbed Alice and as she started falling, her arm flew up and grabbed around Santo's neck. They steadied themselves and stood together only for a moment, before a woman in the crowd stopped in front of them.

'Oh, aren't you the most gorgeous couple!' she cooed.

214

Alice and Santo stared at her, then at each other, before they both laughed – Alice self-consciously, gently removing her arm, Santo merrily, keeping hold of Alice just a little bit longer. He let her go but put his hand on her back, half-guiding her to the table, half-shielding her from any more crowd movement. At the table, Alice had no idea what she would say to him now. When he had been laughing with his friend at the bar he had seemed separate, so distinct from her, but now she could smell his scent on her from where they had stood so close only a moment ago.

When was the last time she had socialised with anyone who wasn't from her college or her department? The wedding of a college roommate, three years ago? She had been offered a plus-one, but had no one she wanted to ask. A friend of a colleague had asked her out for a drink around her last birthday, but she hadn't known whether it was a pity-date – poor Alice alone on her birthday again – and anyway, when the time came, she had preferred a bath with a new book and some egg fried rice, the height of treat-ness when it had been just her and Maurice. There were college dinners and drinks, departmental conferences, meetings with other historians and lecturers, but nothing like standing in a noisy pub feeling the strong arms of a handsome fisherman around her. *Ridiculous*, she thought, *a handsome fisherman*, and rolled her eyes at her own imagination, so cloying and clichéd.

'Something wrong?' Santo said, close to her over the small table. She realised she had actually rolled her eyes, and laughed.

'No, sorry.' She looked around. 'When was the last time it was this busy?'

He turned to gaze round the pub. 'A while ago. I don't know. When the early emmets come, they flood the place like they owned it.' He glanced at Alice. 'No offence,' he said, and grinned.

Alice remembered that was the worst of all slurs against the tourists who came to the area. 'Do I still count as an emmet?' Alice asked, starting to smile back.

'Ooh, I don't know,' he replied. 'Takes marrying into a local family to really stop counting.'

She looked down at the table, embarrassed but also flattered. *Obviously he's not asking you to marry him,* she thought, but knew he was trying to tell her how he felt, the only way he could – lines and looks. Would a little liaison be so bad? If she was only here for a short while, why not have a little fun? Something to tell Morag, at least, something to show she wasn't always exactly the same person day after day, year after year, frozen in place and terrified that something, anything, might come along and touch her. Morag might even count that as progress.

Alice downed her drink in one, and slammed her glass down on the table. 'Your round,' she said, and smiled broadly at Santo. He looked taken aback for a moment, then knocked his own back and stood up.

'Right you are. You: stay.'

She felt a warm glow as he went to order again, already slightly tipsy and allowing her decision-making worries to dull. And if it was a mistake, it was a mistake. Not a disaster. People made mistakes all the time and lived to tell the tale.

Back with the drinks, Santo sat even closer.

'Why don't you tell me something about yourself? I don't know much about the mysterious Alice.'

She sipped her second drink. 'I'm a historian.'

He pulled a face. 'Not my favourite subject at school.'

'Lucky we're not in school.' She had meant it as a come-back, but he took it as a come-on.

'Lucky we're not,' he said, and put his hand on her knee under the table.

She drew in breath, and crossed her legs so his hand fell off. 'Tell me something about you,' she asked. 'Besides the fact that you don't get on with Luke Penrose.'

He looked cross. 'It's not me that has the problem,' he insisted. 'I'm a live-and-let-live kind of man. It's that whole family that's got issues. All of them Penroses are mental.' He looked at Alice. 'Let's talk about something else. My boat? I'll take you out on that one night. A beautiful clear night, stars everywhere, no one else about. Fancy that?' For a second, Alice remembered the evening spent stargazing with Luke and Melder, and wondered if being on Santo's boat could possibly improve on it. He spoke lower. 'Or is it only books you spend the night with?'

Again, she could feel the pulse of his words. 'It's a bit loud in here,' she said. 'Do you want to get some air?' For a moment, he looked confused, then his eyes widened in stunned delight. Alice didn't know what had possessed her. She didn't care.

They made their way through the throng of people, now louder than ever, and out of the back door, where one woman was resting against the wall of the pub, smoking, watching them both standing awkwardly in the half-light of the pub kitchen; eventually she stubbed her cigarette out with one toe, and staggered back inside. As soon as the door closed, Alice stepped forwards and Santo tipped her face up to his.

217

Close up, she could see the grime on one cheek that he hadn't managed to wipe off from work, and some black pores above each nostril. What was she feeling now – she tried to think for a moment, to discover what this feeling was in the pit of her stomach, desire or repulsion, with his eyes so hungry, his fingers hard on her upper arm and the back of her neck. And if they kissed – that was next, wasn't it? Then what? Did she want to do this . . . in the car park of the Dolphin? . . . In her mother's house? . . . – she didn't want this, she felt sick, as if she might die if he kissed her or tried to touch her – at once she wanted to run away, to not be here at all, because being here meant that she was going to die –

Her breathing was getting harder, her throat tighter. Santo had taken his hands off her, was backing away, looking around to see who might be witnessing this. 'What's happening? What's wrong with you?' Alice backed against the pub wall, struggling to breathe.

'It's . . . my heart . . .' she panted. 'It's not – my heart – I –' She gripped her chest, terrified, sliding down the wall and into the dirt of the pub car park, the cigarette butts and bottle caps, balancing on her heels, then on her knees, then on all fours, wheezing, her fingertips lifting to dig into her chest as if she could pull her heart out and protect it in the cage of her hands.

She could feel Santo over her, feel his looming shape silhouetted in the kitchen lights, but she couldn't see him, see what his face was doing. She heard, '. . . get someone . . .' and then, he was gone. Sick and dizzy, retching, she waited in the noise of the empty car park until she could stand up, before eventually walking home.

Chapter Twenty

Alice didn't want to see anybody in the morning. She stayed in bed until lunchtime, unthinkingly flicking the pages of some of Bea's art books, stewing in her attic sheets, knowing she wanted to be alone for the rest of the day at the very least. She got up to wash her bed linen and hang it in the garden, promising herself that if anyone came in, including Luke, she would walk straight inside and lock the door. But when Luke did come, she didn't rush inside, but sat in silence beneath her billowing bedsheets as they dried in the baking sun, Belle curled in the shadow beside her, and Luke working wordlessly around the beds. When he left, she ate her lunch inside, drew all the curtains tighter, and took herself to bed in a miserable fury. Even here, where nothing mattered and no one counted, the rotten anxiety knitted into her blood and bones was still waiting to bloom and remind Alice who was truly in control.

Alice couldn't understand her reaction to Santo. But when she closed her eyes and pictured him again, so close, against her, her gorge rose and she pulled at an imagined tightening collar. Not that. Not him. She would go to Peter Blandford tomorrow and tell him that it was over, done with. She was leaving Polperran and going home, and she wouldn't have to see them again. She would drive back to

Cambridge, however long it took, and deal with what was waiting for her there, and that would be the end.

Of course, few ever sleep well on such a furious resolution. The day after, Alice was in the sea again as the sun rose, salt water stinging the grazes still on her hands and knees from the car park behind the Dolphin, so tired she could barely remember that she wanted to finish this project and get home as soon as possible.

At Blandford & Sons, Peter was delighted to see Alice, as always. He had barely even let her speak when he'd guided her into his office, requested a pot of tea from his secretary, and rummaged around in the drawers before coming up with another envelope.

'Well,' said Peter. 'This is it! Your final task for the project!'

Alice's swim had calmed her racing mind but her ribs still ached. She felt her muscles tense. 'What?' The end of the project meant she had no reason to stay now. Which meant she would have to tell Morag that she wanted to come back. Or not *wanted to*. But would be. And that meant – 'It's . . . the last one?'

'The last task! You've done so well with these. Your mother would be so proud.' He beamed at her.

Alice was momentarily dumbstruck. She had thought there would be hundreds of them, all the things that could possibly need fixing in the village, that they would keep her here for months. She realised that until yesterday, somewhere in her mind she had begun rehearsing why she couldn't return to Cambridge in September. It wouldn't be because of grief, of course, but a project from her dead mother that she *had* to do. That's what she would say to colleagues. She was a historian, and her job was to take documents from Bea, interpret them, and fit them into a narrative with logic and a human understanding. And here, in Polperran, she was taking these handwritten documents, and interpreting them with the skills she had always lacked – with Bea's urge to try to not fix, but *improve* people. Or what was around them. But Alice had forgotten that even a historian does not remain unchanged by their work: documents might contain the exact same information day after day for centuries, but no person ever remains unchanged.

And now Peter was saying that this was all over. Which meant that it was back to Cambridge, and the cottage would need to be packed up and sold on. She had no more excuses. She couldn't justify keeping it as a holiday home: not least because she would be another emmet, ruining the village; but also because she simply couldn't afford it. Her salary wasn't large, and on top of her tiny Cambridge house, the bills and maintenance on a cottage like this, not to mention upkeep of the garden . . .

So that was it. She would complete this final task, ensure the house was closed for the last time, and it would be time to deal with Cambridge. She knew she wouldn't return here again.

'Sorry, I – thought there would be more.' She forgot that this project was supposed to be about her defeating Bea, or being defeated, or that she had wanted to quit only days ago. She was only disappointed to discover that she hadn't had a real choice anyway.

'Your mother was very ill towards the end of her life; it was much quicker than anyone expected.'

'So do you think she meant to write more? Do you think there was more of this project she would have wanted me to do?'

Peter gave her a sad smile. 'We have no way of knowing, Alice. But I do know she would be so pleased with everything you've already done.' He handed over the envelope. 'That's the final task. Think of all the people you've met through this! I hope you will take away fond memories of your visit here. We've so enjoyed having you among us, even for this brief time.'

Alice let the envelope sit on the desk for a moment: To Alice, number four.

This is an intolerable sadness, Alice thought. *I won't be manipulated by a dead woman who gave up her rights to my feelings a long time ago. She can't leave me in Cambridge and leave me in Polperran, then keep making me miss her. Or miss what she offered me. Or miss what she's taking away. Oh, I don't know!*

She was furious and panicky, disappointed and hurt, relieved and frightened. She had nothing to lean on any more. It was almost over.

Outside, Alice didn't wait to read the contents. Standing in the shaded doorway of Blandford & Sons, she tore open the envelope.

To my darling daughter,

This might sound like a strange task, considering the other jobs I've asked of you.

If I know anything of Polperran, you'll have met Ena Penhaligon. And if I know anything of Ena, she will have greeted you with her usual warmth, comfort and easy familiarity. I'm sorry, Alice, but I'm laughing as I write this. I hope so much that you've got to know her a little.

For your final task, I wonder if you might put together a scrapbook for Ena. She is the oldest resident of Polperran – which doubtless has come up in one conversation or another – and has so many memories of the village. She has very few photos of her life, and I think she would treasure greatly the memories that other people hold: of her, of the time when she was younger, of people she knew that have gone, pictures, anecdotes, clippings. It's something I started to do, once upon a time, and then I ran out of time and must instead pass it on to you, my legacy, to turn into your own.

There's a photo album in my studio which I had intended to use – I've painted the front, you'll know it when you see it – but this is your project now, so if it doesn't feel right then please don't feel obliged to use it.

Do you keep any photos of your father and me with you? I find it's become so hard to remember the house I grew up in; I have only vague snatches of feeling, echoes of echoes of what those voices sounded like. I tried to paint them once, the feelings, but of course it was an unmitigated disaster. Someone saw the painting and congratulated me on capturing so successfully the lichen-covered postbox on the High Street. Oh, hubris.

This last project will mean involving others in Polperran, but I'm making the assumption that they will know you by now, and you them: you'll need to ask for help, which might be hard, but is almost always worth it when we need it. I think you will do a wonderful job.

Always,
Your mother, Bea x

Alice was baffled by this. Not a village party or some great finale, but a craft project. For Ena, of all people, who seemed most embittered by the life she'd suffered in this village, and who barely had a kind word for anybody. Not Tressa, with her descendants basically propping up the population of Polperran. Or Frances, with a lifetime given over to her garden, a thing of beauty which might last for generations with the right caretaker. Or Clemmo and Bert, who had witnessed and played through so many happy moments in the village. (She had failed there, Alice thought guiltily.) But for Ena, the one person who had tried so hard to make Alice feel unwelcome.

She read the letter again, puzzling so much over why this should be her final task that it took her a third reading to notice something else: Bea's handwriting, usually so neat and looping, was jagged here and there towards the end of the letter. How close had she written this to her final days?

It took a few shouts for Alice to realise someone was calling her. Luke, emerging from Gwen's café, was calling her name and waving. He stopped Belle in the doorway, checked the traffic and ran across the road to her, saying, 'Alice! Just who I was looking for!' Then he saw what she was holding, where she had just come from, and said, 'Oh, is that . . . ? Sorry, we can talk later.'

'It's fine,' Alice said, a little more sharply than she intended. 'What is it?' She tried to soften her tone and paste on a smile. 'What were you after me for? Something good?' She winced slightly even as she said it.

'Well,' Luke said, frowning momentarily before continuing, 'it's two things, actually. Firstly, it's Mel's birthday in a couple of weeks and I thought she could do with some-

224

thing nice, after the year she's had. Would you come? It's nothing big,' he added hastily. 'At the pub, whoever's about, maybe some food, or something? Two weeks tomorrow? And it's a surprise. Not a word to Mel!'

Alice smiled with real feeling. 'Of course, that sounds lovely. Let me know if I can help.' He nodded at her for a while, smiling back. 'But you said it was two things?'

'Yes! Right.' Luke tipped his head back over his shoulder. 'Do you want to come and see the finished job?'

Alice blinked where he was indicating, back at Belle, then said, 'Oh, the paint! Yes! Definitely!' They crossed the road in silence, and he held the door open for her to step inside.

It felt like a different place – or the same place, but better. The walls glowed white, and green plants of all sizes were layered around the café. The tables and chairs had been repaired, the curtains and nets had been washed and rehung differently, so light now flooded the room, and there was a pile of clipboards on the counter that made Alice raise a querying eyebrow.

'Menus,' Luke confirmed. 'Mum's suspicious, but she's coming around.'

'Cheeky,' Gwen called from the kitchen.

'It's so different!' Alice called back.

'No offence,' Luke continued.

'No! I mean – I liked it before, but this is . . .'

Gwen came out of the kitchen, and she and Luke looked around. 'It's not bad, is it?' Gwen said, reaching up to put an arm around Luke's shoulders. 'Thanks to you lot.'

Luke smiled at Alice, and stage-whispered, 'Wait until she sees our bill.'

Gwen nudged him with her hip, and said, 'I owe you, Alice, so next time you're hungry, come and have a feast here: on me, all right?'

Alice reached up to the bag on her shoulder, twisting the handle in both hands, feeling a strange sensation in her stomach that she realised she hadn't felt for a long time. She'd achieved so little while she was here, at least of anything that wasn't Plague-related, but her small part in this transformation of Gwen's café and the happiness it obviously brought to her – and also, Alice had to notice, to her children – was perhaps responsible for the happiness Alice also appeared to be feeling. 'That's so kind, Gwen,' she said, 'but – I'm not sure how much longer I'll be around.' She held up the envelope from Peter Blandford. 'Last one,' she said. 'Time's up!'

Gwen looked at Alice and said, 'Oh, love,' and gave her a hug, and Alice responded with a weak hug back and tried to list in her mind the documents she still needed to work on for her next chapter to stop herself from crying. Then Gwen pulled away and said in a choked voice, 'Well, it's been lovely having you here,' and turned back into the kitchen without looking at either of them.

Luke looked at the envelope, trying to find the right words. He nodded and smiled back at her, and finally said, 'Last one? You must be pleased!' and they both nodded and smiled at one another with strange uncomfortable faces, until Alice said she'd better go, and would he just let her know when he had specific plans for Melder's party, and she'd do anything she could.

On the way home, Alice passed the Dolphin. The combination of the evening with Santo, Bea's final task and now

Luke – Luke's what? His invitation to Melder's? Or his face when she'd said it was over? – made her swerve in. She wanted somewhere to put the feelings that were roiling inside her; she wanted somewhere public, and possibly supervised.

Janet wasn't at the bar, just the young lad from the night of the cake competition, and Alice almost snarled her order. *Channelling my inner Ena*, she thought peevishly.

As she turned around with her drink, she saw again: Bert one end of the pub, Clemmo the other.

'Bert!' she shouted. Thin as the custom was at lunchtime on a weekday, everyone in the pub looked up. 'Bert! Do you remember me? Bea's daughter? Alice?'

Bert stood and started walking over to her. Everyone had seen this before, a drunk in the middle of the day, and turned to their silent pints again. When he got to her, he tried to put his arm on Alice's, to lead her gently to his table, but she jerked away. She hadn't even tasted a drink yet, she was stone-cold sober, and the stoniness ran fully through her. She no longer cared what the fine folk of the Dolphin thought of her. This felt like she was back at college, with troublesome bloody students.

'Why won't *you* talk to *him*?' she shouted, pointing with both hands at Clemmo, who lifted a hand and flapped it, as if to bat away this nonsense. 'It's been *years*. Don't you know you could be dead soon?'

There was a small gasp and a slightly bigger chuckle at this, but Bert turned his back and sat down again. She faced Clemmo and called out to him, 'My mother thought a great deal of you two. She said you'd made her feel welcome here. So are you happy that's the last you'll get from him? That's you and Bert done, is it?'

227

Clemmo opened his mouth to say something, then closed it with a snap, looking more turtle-ish than ever. '*Bah*,' he scoffed. 'Nothing that man ever said made the least bit of sense anyway, I'm not missing out.' Some of the drinkers laughed at this; others looked stunned at Clemmo acknowledging Bert at all.

'You'd be the one to know about not talking sense, Clemmo Carter!' Bert called across.

Alice watched, frozen, one hand still up in the air from gesturing at Clemmo.

Clemmo put down his drink and stood. 'You're an ignorant man and you've no business peddling your . . .' He seemed lost for words for a moment. 'Lies!' he said triumphantly. 'Your lies about anything, whether it's who my son ought to marry or what apples to pick for my cider.'

'My lies! *My* lies!' Bert roared. 'You were born with a forked tongue, and everyone in this village knows it. You've always been at your best when you've been sitting in your little 'ole over there, not disturbing anyone. Why don't you *crawl back there*?' This was said with such venom that no one chuckled, and the tension became greasy and electric in the air.

'Hold on,' Alice said. 'Hold on. This is about Bert not approving of your son's partner?'

There was a brief silence. Bert said in almost a mumble, 'O' course I approve o' her, she's my daughter . . .'

'*Your* son is married to his *daughter*?'

'Oh aye,' Clemmo said. 'Been sweet on each other since they were tiny tots, the pair of them. 'Cept Bert there said they were too young to marry, and it were a mistake for them both.'

Alice looked between them. 'And *have* they broken up? *Was* it a mistake?'

Both men looked shocked. 'Oh no!' Bert said.

'No, not at all, they just had their . . .' Clemmo thought for a moment '. . . twelfth wedding anniversary last month or so.'

'They've been married twelve years and you've stayed fallen out this long?' Alice cried.

They both looked at her as if she was mad. 'No, I said, of course I approved of them both, although they did seem young at the time, but they've had a good few years . . .'

'Then *what*?!'

The pub was silent again, watching her.

Eventually, Clemmo cleared his throat. 'As I said,' he explained carefully, but not quite meeting Alice's eye, 'Bert there thinks he knows best which apples make the best cider. I told him it were Lord of the Isles, but he said it were Plymton Pippin!' He shook his head in amazement, chortling. 'Plymton Pippin!'

Bert stood up too. 'You know perfectly well that Plymton Pippins age better than Lords, and they last better in the bottle! You cannot argue with that!'

Clemmo walked closer. 'I don't *need* to argue with that, because any toddling baby knows that if you make the cider well enough, you don't *need* to rely on –'

Alice stepped between them, her hands held up. She spoke softly, so both men were forced to lean forwards to hear. 'You haven't spoken. For over a decade. Because you can't agree . . .' she breathed in, then out, 'on *cider apples*.' She felt the same bubbling up as before, that disconnected feeling of leaving her body and watching everything from above, just like that day at college. She looked between them, old men with aching old squabbles, keeping the village in silence for twelve years.

Then she laughed. Bert and Clemmo almost joined in too after a moment, but Alice's laughter went on growing, past the point of reunion and all the way back out into chaos, laughter she couldn't control and had nowhere to put. She shook her head and wiped her eyes, but every time she caught sight of their stunned faces again – everything they had missed out on! for the sake of holding tight to nothing! – it set her off again until she had to walk out of the pub, still shaking her head, holding her hands up in an almost-apology, her miserable laughter echoing in the statue-still pub and out along the edge of the green.

Chapter Twenty-One

Sally had laughed at Alice's final piece of business in Polperran, but not unkindly. 'That'll be good fun, collecting those,' she added. Alice noticed that Sally laughed more now, and was dressing ever-so-slightly differently, her clothes choices displaying more colour and shape, and the bowl-cut hair which had seemed so ageing and strange when Alice first saw her now seemed creative and modern. She agreed to spread the word to her customers and would ask Radka to do the same, now she was offically working at the shop three days a week.

Janet said the same for the clientele of the Dolphin, and if anything came in, she would pass it on to Alice. (Janet had been extremely kind to her, and waved away her apology for her behaviour with Bert and Clemmo. 'The things I've seen people do in this pub, Alice,' Janet said, 'I won't even remember your little outburst tomorrow. And to be fair,' she added, 'which of us haven't wanted to box the ears of those two?' Alice had a sudden moment of *Is that it? Is that how easy it could be?* but then stopped herself.)

As the days passed, Alice found people still sought her out to ask her things: was this all right? Would she mind black and white pictures? What about objects? They weren't photographs, obviously, but Ena was involved with their story. Could Alice use those in some way? She wondered if anyone would provide any of these things, or if it was only nosiness posing as enquiry.

Now, Alice went into Bea's studio, looking for the album mentioned in the letter. It was only the third time Alice had been in there since she'd come to Polperran, although since it sometimes seemed years and sometimes only days since her arrival, she didn't know if three was a reasonable number or if she was avoiding it almost as much as Bea's bedroom.

The studio today had a different light; not a golden whiteness but something a little thinner, paler, clouds hanging in front of the sun, possible signs of an afternoon shower. Everything looked a little different, as perhaps was the point of this room, changing each moment along with the weather and seasons.

She first looked among the canvases, wondering if the album had been tidied up with them and fallen between them, but no, it wasn't there. Nor was it among the paints and palettes on the table top. Alice finally found it in a dresser drawer, pushed right to the back, covered with a handful of leaflets advertising takeaways and local walks. As she pulled it out, she could see that even in this thin light the cover was beautiful, a view from the garden over the sea, with the headland on the left hand side curving gracefully down to the water, hiding the small harbour from view. It looked like a turbulent sea, perhaps a winter storm, the sky heavy with brown-grey massed clouds like a smothering blanket; but also with a distant shaft of sunlight breaking through and hitting a cresting wave. It reminded Alice of a Caspar David Friedrich painting she'd once seen, but with less precision and details, more love and nerve. It struck her too that the view wasn't possible, or at least wouldn't have been for a long time. To get that view the artist would have had to stand on Bea's terrace, a terrace that had been bramble-clogged for many years, it seemed.

The album was thick, and when she opened it a note slipped out, in Bea's handwriting, that just said *Good luck! xxx.* Alice swallowed hard to get rid of the lump that had suddenly appeared in her throat. She worried that she would never receive enough to fill all of the pages.

But the next time Alice went into the shop, Radka handed her a large brown envelope. 'Four more people come in today. They give me pictures and paper, all in here.' Alice peeked in, and there were photographs and several different pieces of writing, typed out and printed, scrawled in haste on torn-out notepaper.

Alice frowned as she tried to see each piece.

'Is this bad thing?' Radka asked.

'No, it's . . . good. It's just surprising. I thought we'd have to go to the local paper and copy a few articles from their back issues, pad them with some village photos I'd take . . . Look at this –' she held out one of the photos from the envelope, 'this looks like it was from the . . . seventies?'

'Oh no love, that's earlier than that.'

Alice turned around to see that Tressa had joined them and was peering over her shoulder.

'Let me have a look at that – that's around, what . . . '62? '63? It was a blistering hot summer, and I was pregnant with Michael. Look, there she is.' She pointed at a figure in the photo, a woman in a black dress holding a silver whistle between her lips as children raced away from her towards the finishing line.

'That's Ena?' Alice said.

'Aye. You'd be hard pressed to find a photo of any village event that she's not elbow-deep in. Until her stroke a few years ago, she kept as busy as me.'

'But – I thought she didn't have much to do with the village. I thought – After the war, I'd heard after her parents died that she cut herself off from everything.'

Tressa slid the photo back into the envelope. 'Cut herself off? Don't believe everything you hear, Alice. Anyway, you just wait and see – If you don't believe me now, have a look at what people bring in, and then tell me she cut herself off.'

And Tressa was rapidly proven right. Over the next week, envelopes and small packages turned up at the shop so quickly that Alice could go twice a day to pick up a new pile and start sifting through them. There were menus that Ena had written for local fundraising dinners, kept for decades until they were yellowed and faded, funny thank you notes she had written to people for gifts they had given her, small things: eggs and jam, then as people began to travel, ceramics and foreign chocolate bars and soaps. People had stored scraps and cuttings mentioning Ena for years and years for no reason other than they marked an important moment in their lives. And the photographs: christenings, weddings and funerals, pub dances, dances on the green, Christmas parties, New Year parties, Easter egg hunts and birthday after birthday after birthday, Ena always in black but always present, carrying a cake, arranging flowers, hanging balloons, offering trays, a dark peg from which everything in these photographs seemed to hang.

Alice searched through Bea's drawers, and found scissors, tape and paperclips, and started arranging the submissions – photographing the clippings, photos and notes, keeping meticulous records of who gave what and with what explanation, and taking pictures too of the objects, the dried posies, the milk-bottle-top medals, the champagne corks, so she could return everything to the generous contributors.

Tressa, surprisingly, was one of the last people to give Alice something for the book. She brought an envelope to Bea's cottage, and said, 'Are you able to copy it straight away, love? It's just a bit precious and I'd rather get it straight home if it's all the same to you.'

Alice opened the stiff brown envelope and pulled out a single black and white photograph, of two children laughing together on a low stone wall. It was the wall she recognised first; the slate wall which connected the green with the cemetery, just at the start of the path. Looking closer she realised two things: they weren't children – perhaps around sixteen, although the boy was in uniform; also that the girl was Ena.

'Tressa, this is wonderful.'

Tressa was looking at the photograph too. 'It's a good picture, aye. Sheer luck it turned out so well – we didn't take very many of these back in the day.'

'Who's the boy?' she asked.

Tressa smiled. 'One of those GI lot. Came over from America for D-Day, only here a few months. They were awful good fun, though,' she laughed wickedly. 'Gum for days, cigarettes too – although I was a bit young for those. They'd let you sit in the Jeep and if there were none of the big brass around, they'd drive us around and get us screaming as they tore round the back roads. They were so smart-looking.' As Tressa spoke her accent changed, became broader and softer. 'So many of the boys from round here'd already gone, it were so quiet, and this lot turned up and it were all music and dancing again.' She smiled. 'We were all so *young*.'

Alice looked at the photo again, to let Tressa enjoy her memories. She heard Tressa give a little sniff, then clear her throat a few times.

'Right then, that's all copied, is it?' Tressa asked.

'Oh, no, let me photograph it and you can take it away again.'

While Alice lined up the shot, Tressa said, 'How long do you think it'll be until you've –' she nodded at the scrapbook on the table, 'done with it? Much longer, do you think?'

Alice pulled out the box and flipped through the copied items, ready to paste in. 'I think I've got as much as we'll get,' she said. 'Now I've just got to organise it all.'

'That's where your history training'll pay off,' Tressa said.

Alice looked at her. 'I keep thinking the same thing – all this evidence, all these sources, and I've got to shape it all together into . . . *something*. How can I make the life of someone I don't even know . . . coherent?'

'All lives are coherent,' Tressa replied. 'You've just got to look at them from the right angle.'

'I know, I know. And that's the other thing: lots of these things have dates on, in the notes people gave with them, but lots of them don't. I don't know when half these events were, let alone what they were.'

'Listen, love: if you put in order the things you *do* know, I'm happy to come over one afternoon and have a look at the things you don't. I doubt there's much Ena's ever been to that I've not. And my memory'll be sharper than any of those old fools in the pub or the shop.'

'Are you sure?' Alice said. 'I mean, it might be hours of work. Even if you remember when something happened –'

'I beg your pardon, young lady, *if* I remember?'

'*When* you remember, sorry, we'll still have to fit it in with all the other clippings. I mean, I've started ordering the things I can – that's if the dates they've given me are even the right ones – but once we think we know all the dates we'll still have to check the whole thing makes sense!'

'Makes sense?' Tressa closed the lid of the box, and rested her knuckles on top. 'Alice. You can do this. You've been training to do this your whole career.'

'Maybe not exactly this.'

'But you're more than capable of putting a few bits of paper into the right order, especially with a first-hand witness helping you.' She gestured to herself.

Alice sighed. 'I know. All right. It just seems so *huge.*' Tressa looked sceptical, so Alice tried to explain. 'When I'm doing my own work, even if it's about a whole country, or a plague, or a . . . trading route, I can pretend that no one will ever see it. Mostly because no one *will* ever see it. But this, with the whole village watching – it's partly professional pride, Tressa, that I want to show Ena I can do justice to it, but . . . she's ninety-two! That's so much life to make sure I do justice to!'

Tressa knocked on the top of the box. 'I've got faith, love. If anyone will do it justice, it's you.' She carefully picked up her envelope. 'Right. Tuesday suit? I'll bring the biscuits, you make sure that big pot of tea is ready.'

After Tressa had gone, Alice started making piles of the pictures: those that came with useful information in the notes, those that appeared to have the date included (Alice's favourite was a photo of a New Year's party with 'Happy 1982' painted on a banner behind a black-clad Ena, who was sporting a very fetching gold party hat and waving a tiny flag), and those she had no clear information on. Making the piles made her feel better, that order was gradually being introduced to the fathomless well of a life's evidence. Then she divided up each pile again, into decades, all the way back to the 1940s, where she put a piece of notepaper in as a holding spot for the photo Tressa had just brought, until she could have that printed too. She made herself a cup of tea and started putting the piles into month order, as best she could. There was so much. She worked backwards from the present day, sorting events from recent years back through the nineties: Ena looking younger, auburn still visible in her salt and pepper hair, through the seventies, her hair darker, her face softer, back, back, younger and younger, notes and photos, Ena's handwriting sharp and controlled, until finally the piece of paper standing in for Tressa's photo.

Alice looked over the piles, from now to then, and decided she would keep them this way around when she pasted the whole book together. Did they need the notes with them, too? Some would, she thought, as the notes themselves were sometimes funny, sometimes moving, sometimes just packed with context. Other times the images were enough, and would tell an interesting story of Ena's life. She hoped.

Chapter Twenty-Two

Besides Ena's book, Alice remembered she was also supposed to be helping with Melder's party. Luke had given her two particular jobs: the cake, and inviting Ena.

'I'm so sorry, Alice,' he'd said, 'I've been snowed under with work recently. But I've organised the food, the drinks, the music, the decorations – it's all going to be round the back of the Dolphin, now – and Mum's taking Mel out for the day so she won't see anything.'

'Wow. This is growing into quite a party,' Alice had said, delighted.

'Oh, no, most of this is other people doing it, I'm delegating everything, and people really want to help. I just want to make it nice for her. But: Ena and the cake – do you mind?'

Alice didn't mind at all, in fact was glad to be doing something to show her gratitude to the Penrose family, who had fed her and taken her stargazing and looked after her garden, and befriended her and told her the truth when she had asked for it.

If it had been a long time since Alice had been invited anywhere, it was even longer since she'd been involved in the planning of a party, and that feeling of crafting something for someone, building something just to make them happy, allowed Alice to put down Bea's project and her latest notes on witch hunts (both metaphorical and literal), and happily take on these two new tasks of her own.

Joy had at least opened the door when Alice went over, but had then become increasingly rude because Alice didn't know exactly what cake she was asking Joy to make. 'Carrot cake? Walnut and coffee? Chocolate? Fruit? Do you want a genoise? A sponge? A lemon cake. An angel cake. A honey cake –'

'Oh! Yes. A honey cake, please.'

'Right. Honey,' Joy said, and seemed rather disappointed to have had her question answered. 'How many?'

'How many?' Alice replied. 'Um . . . big? I think Luke's invited . . . everyone.'

'Has he now?' said Joy. 'That'll be *interesting*.' She waved her hands at Alice, shooing her out. 'Go on, let me think. I've got to try and work out how to make a cake suitable for guests numbering somewhere between three and a whole village.'

'And will you come?' Alice said.

Joy just made a scoffing noise and chased her out of the door.

At Ena's cottage, the sun was hot in the garden and two chaffinches chased each other excitedly around the lawn, but inside the cottage was cool, and Ena looked small in her chair by the fire.

'I've got an invitation for you, Ena,' Alice said.

'If it's another cake competition, they can forget it,' Ena replied. 'They had their chance.'

Alice laughed. 'It's Melder's birthday shortly, and Luke's organising a surprise party for her. Will you come?'

Ena scoffed with a remarkably similar tone to Joy's, but didn't refuse and didn't ask Alice to go. 'Not necessary, is it? All this fuss?' she grunted. 'Has anyone asked her if she wants all this?'

'No one says they *want* fuss, Ena,' Alice replied. 'And this was all Luke's idea. He'd know what his sister wanted, wouldn't he?'

Ena made a noise of disagreement, doubtful eyes narrowing at Alice. 'Fine!' she snapped. 'I'll make a couple of tarts for it. But that's it. And I want a table near the front, to keep an eye on everyone. Otherwise I'm not involving myself. And why are you so involved? Shouldn't Luke be here asking me himself?'

Alice shrugged. 'I'm just helping out.'

'Just like your mother,' Ena said, crossly.

Alice sat down on the other chair. 'I thought you got on with my mother,' she said.

Ena sat watching the fire for a long time. Eventually, she croaked, 'Go on, off you go. You've done what you had to.' When it was clear she wouldn't say anything else, Alice left.

Over the next few days, Alice made sure she'd taken photographs of everything she'd been given, and drove to Falrigg to have the last batch of her photos turned into fresh prints. But just when she thought she had everything, she'd been stunned when Clemmo had whistled her down from the doorway of the Dolphin one night, and handed her a foxed white envelope. Inside, Alice found a sepia print of a young girl with dark plaits, smiling sweetly at the camera.

'This is Ena?' Alice said.

Clemmo took the photo back and looked at it in the light from the pub. 'Aye,' he said. 'Our mothers were cousins, and Ena didn't want any of the family photographs, so my wife made me hold on to them. Never knew anyone else would want to see 'em.'

She took particular care of that one, its edges warping from age, and showed it to Tressa when she visited on Tuesday, arriving promptly at four. Alice had a teapot ready as requested, the kettle having been repeatedly boiled since quarter-to in readiness. As soon as Tressa took a seat, Alice filled up the pot and covered it with Bea's crocheted tea cosy, adding a milk jug and bringing the teacups and saucers down from where she had found them on Bea's top shelves. Tressa was looking through the pile of unknowns Alice had made, and when Alice put down the tray she looked up with delight.

'Ooh, you make me feel like a visiting queen, Alice,' she said.

'Is that a good thing?' Alice asked.

Tressa reached down and pulled a tin of homemade flapjacks from her enormous handbag. 'Get these on a plate and we'll decide later.'

She recognised almost all of the pictures immediately, even if some of them required her to hold them at arm's length, squinting, or tilt them towards the kitchen light to better see details.

'That's old Bert's place – Bert's father, that is – when he still had the farm towards Ferrow, and that'll be Bert's elder daughter's wedding, so that must have been . . . 1997, that was, in the May. Beautiful day, it was, even though the wedding car broke down on the lane and Tilly had to be taken to the church by tractor. Quite the fashionable thing, now, I've heard. Oh, this one – this is from a party Janet had –'

Tressa remembered everything, every birthday, every funeral, who was and wasn't present, what rows it caused, what flowers were arranged. They worked through the pile rapidly, Alice carefully pencilling in dates and names on the back of each print while Tressa took the next one and began her remembering again.

Then she started on the pile Alice needed more details on. Those were easier; Alice often had some information already, so it was just a matter of giving Tressa a prompt and she would fill in an immense number of other facts.

While Alice was writing in the last notes, Tressa paused. Alice looked up, and saw that she was holding the reprinted photo of Ena and the GI, laughing together on the low wall. 'Do you know much more about that one? The year? I don't suppose you remember his name, do you?'

Tressa gave her a *don't be silly* look, and turned her eyes back to the picture. '1944, I said. June. And his name was Teddy.' She sighed. 'We'd spent years forgetting what normal was like, sweets and dancing and all that. Our fun then was watching the planes going over to and from the airfield along the way, and avoiding anything the enemy planes might drop in the fields. It wasn't fun, Alice.

'But it was amazing how different it felt when they came. They took the big children's playground that was behind the church, and filled it with tents – huge things, full of all

243

sorts of luxuries, and all the soldiers looked so *smart*. We'd stand watching them for hours, all those young men, so different to the fathers and brothers who'd gone off to war, or the ones that had been left behind, too ill or old. They'd give us gum and ice cream, if we asked nicely, and they'd mimic our accents and laugh at us, and we'd do the same back. They were the centre of our lives for just a brief moment, before they all headed off to Polgwidden and the boats.'

Tressa's face grew sorrowful as she regarded the photo. 'Oh Alice, I thought he was the most handsome man I had ever seen in my life, but he was just a boy. I was ten. He'd told the army he was eighteen, but he was really only sixteen. His mother must have been terrified. And furious.' She looked up. 'I cried for two days when I found out he'd died. It was really only luck that we even found out – the whole camp up and disappeared almost overnight, off to the Normandy beaches – and we chased around for so long trying to discover if he'd come back, where he was. Of course, everything was top secret in those days, but Clemmo's cousin worked in a field hospital at Tregarne, and weeks after Teddy'd gone she told us someone from his regiment was there. I cycled over with a few friends – it was blistering hot, I still remember the sunburn we got – and I managed to sneak past a doctor. A nurse let me in who knew Clemmo.' She stopped.

Alice waited. 'Tressa?'

Tressa looked up, her eyes wet. She sniffed. 'Oh, it's so silly, isn't it? It's such a long time ago. We were just children.' She brought a tissue from her pocket and wiped her eyes. 'He was such a sweet boy. For some reason, among all of it, his death was one of the hardest.'

She took one more look at the picture, and handed it over to Alice. On the back, Alice carefully wrote *Teddy & Ena, June 1944*.

Tressa picked up the next picture, sniffed again, and cleared her throat. 'Oh yes, *now* we're talking. This was Sports Day in . . . '75? No, '76, and Ena got stung by the biggest wasp you've ever seen . . .'

Every evening Alice sat at the kitchen table with a low lamp and the piles Tressa had helped her arrange, and rough-tacked them into place on the pages. This evening she was sticking them all in, and was hot, and tired, and she'd grown stiff from sitting for so long, remaining almost motionless as she ensured every item was lined up perfectly with the page-edge before being glued. On her last run to the nearby town for prints of her photographs, she had noticed a small path heading towards the sea, and suddenly she wanted to stop smelling Bea's paints and thinking of the years of Polperran behind her. Instead she wanted to swim, far from all the walls and windows and eyes of the village.

It was late when she drove there, and in the moonlight she missed the path, then parked Bea's car flush against a hedge so she had to climb out of the passenger door. At first she could hear the sea but not work out how to get to it. There were thick hedges between her and the dark water, so she decided to walk along systematically until she found a gap, and a sandy path beyond. She half-slid, half-stumbled down the sandy path to the bay, where she could see a distant boat, far enough off-shore that she'd run no risk of being interrupted.

The water here looked strangely smooth in parts, and she wondered if that was something to do with the just-past-full moon above her, bright and heavy in the sky, blenching out most of the stars that weren't hiding near the surrounding clifftops. She pulled her dress over her head, folded it loosely on top of her shoes and car keys, and headed out to the sea in her swimming costume.

It was comfortable on her feet, and she stepped forwards into cooler waters, the top waves still temperate from thousands of sun-warmed miles. She walked deeper then dropped, tucking her knees up, so she could bob her shoulders under and let the waves carry her for a moment, noticing the silence of the night – it seemed even the birds had turned in. Rolling onto her stomach, Alice did some gentle breast-stroke away from the beach, swimming until she could feel the sandy floor only when she reached her feet straight down. Then she began swimming parallel to the shore, the gentle motion calming her, soothing the voices in her head, her To Do lists, her plans – the scrapbook, the cottage, the college, her life – until her blood was the same temperature as the ocean, or the ocean as her blood, and she was merely being carried along, flotsam in an infinite space.

Then, suddenly, she was.

She hit a bump in the water, somehow, something solid and liquid at the same time, and was yanked hard to one side – the wake of a boat, she thought – no boats – then she kicked against the pull as she realised it was dragging her away from the shore but it was so strong – she was kicking harder, kicking and pulling with all her swimming strength, lashing out against this force because it was so quick, and she did not want to be carried off dead like her mother – not yet, not finished the bloody project yet – she was still kicking and pulling, harder and faster than she had ever swum before, but the water pulled her under, washed her below and above the surface, even faster than she could think, and the more she kicked the harder she would go under, the shore disappearing impossibly fast, and the water was pulling her under again as she pulled up – she needed air – she couldn't kick like this for much longer, the pain now – there were sounds – the moon was bright – a flash of oil paint – salt in her mouth – and then nothing.

Chapter Twenty-Three

There was rain on the roof of the house, rain on the tiles and in the gutters, filling the butts and the concave leaves and the garden beds. It washed the cars and bicycles that came to the house and left again, and rained on the washing that Alice had left in the garden and not had the chance to bring in. It was a limp kind of rain, half-hearted and hypocritical, dampening but not soaking, and it made Alice feel sick.

She lay in bed, a notepad and pen beside her, another full mug of cold tea on the bedside table next to a small brass bell. She watched the grey nothing through the skylight, view skewed by the blotting drizzle, and wondered why she was alive.

She'd had half the village at the cottage, either in Bea's kitchen or, occasionally, making it all the way to Alice's bedroom, where Gwen would quickly explain that Alice shouldn't be disturbed, and maybe they'd just better say a quick hello and not hang around until she was well. Sometimes Alice pretended to be asleep, and other times she'd raised the pad and pen – *can't talk right now*, as if she was on an important phone call – and they'd signalled back to her, not talking either, as if her partially collapsed voice box was contagious. Mostly she'd been left alone. No one had actually asked her what had happened. But the whispers through the house had made her suspicious, and when even Melder had been bustled from the room she'd heard them outside, *she's under so much stress, she's still grieving, she shouldn't have all this responsibility, it's too much for anyone*, and she had wanted to scream until she remembered she shouldn't be talking for days, if not weeks. So she waited, curious to see whether anyone would want to see what she could tell them with the pad and pen they'd left for her to order food and drinks and medication. No one asked.

She remembered snippets of the hospital, grey-yellow walls and a print of a boat at sea. Funny, she thought, and tried to speak but her throat was on fire. A nurse saw she was awake and came over, explained she'd need to keep to her bed for a while. The doctor was called, and she talked to Alice about where she was, what had happened; Alice couldn't remember much, but she was seemingly up to her eyeballs on painkillers. Sally visited, told her that she'd been fished out by Santo, out at night on his boat. Alice wasn't sure about the precise order of anything – it was all woolly, and out of joint, like a jigsaw left in the rain.

She remembered Luke coming in, his face pale.

'Alice?'

She'd nodded, lifted a hand in greeting. Touched her throat. 'Sore,' she mouthed.

'Of course. How are you?'

There was a pause as they both thought about the question, then she tried to laugh, but it caught in her throat and she winced, her eyes pricking with tears.

'Sorry, don't, Mum'll kill me if I make you feel any worse.'

She gave him a pained smile as he took the plastic seat beside her bed.

'Alice, why would you do something so bloody stupid?'

She closed her eyes.

'Please. Alice. Listen to me. Why did you do that? Why would you go swimming on your own, at night, on a beach you don't even know? Do you understand how stupid that is? Do you know how many bodies we pull out of the sea –'

'Santo?' she whispered. *Are you angry that Santo saved me?*

She heard Luke gasp. 'Santo! Are you – Alice, saving your life is probably the one good thing that man has ever done in his entire life. I don't care that it was him – I'm just glad *someone* found you. Do you understand? You could have *died*. You could have died, Alice.'

Alice opened her eyes, and she saw with shock that he looked red-eyed, and terrified.

Santo had apparently come to the cottage. It was his boat she had seen in the distance when she'd got in the water, it turned out, in the one bay most notorious for its rip currents. He hadn't seen her on the beach, Tressa told her, but she'd come up for a moment near his boat and he'd got her aboard, diving in and lifting her out with his crewman's help. He'd given her mouth-to-mouth – Alice had burned at that, the shame of that unknowing closeness overwhelming the gratitude that she had been saved – and called the coastguard, and she had been taken to the hospital and kept overnight, when Sally and Luke had visited her. After that, Alice had woken up again at home to find Melder by her bedside, tried to ask what was going on and been told again that she wasn't to speak. That's when she'd been given the pad and pen.

He hadn't come to the hospital; something about the Polperran people kept Santo away from places like that, Alice thought, places where other people gathered together to whisper and decide things. But he had come to Bea's cottage. He didn't try to come up; Tressa told Alice that he'd asked after her, asked whether she remembered much about her swim, said he was glad she was all right, and that he hoped she'd learnt her lesson about swimming wherever she damn well fancied. Alice was glad she didn't have to see him. She enjoyed the floating sensation of the last of her painkillers. This was a feeling she could live with.

Radka came in to see her, sitting on the end of her bed, and sipping her own hot drink while Alice's sat cooling with the growing collection of full cups on her bedside table.

'Are you all right?' she asked.

Alice rolled her eyes away from the wall, and looked at Radka wearily.

Radka shrugged. '*I* do not nearly drown. You nearly drown. So I ask: are *you* all right?'

Alice gave her a thumbs up. Radka laughed, and patted Alice's knee through the blanket, and said, 'We are all downstairs, if you need, you have bell.'

When Radka had cleared the cups and gone back to the kitchen, from which faint voices emanated, Alice sat up and swung her legs around, sitting on the edge of the bed. She was still dizzy, but she opened her top drawer. It was there, somehow: her swimming costume, dry and ready.

On the shelves, she found Bea's old sewing kit, and fished out the tiny scissors, sharp and pointed.

It took her a long time; her fingers grew sore and the handles wore lines into her thumb, but slowly she dismantled the swimming costume into ragged flaps, *shnick shnick shnick* across the black fabric. Her whole body ached when she had finished. She threw the scraps into the bin, and covered them with a scrunched-up page from a magazine someone had left out for her.

How stupid she had been to believe she could take anything from the sea that it wouldn't willingly offer. Her happiness meant nothing to the great mass of water. She was just another heartbeat waiting to be consumed by it, and she felt humiliated at her stupidity. Everyone in Polperran knew – how arrogant she was, what an emmet, coming here and nearly dying. As if the boundless sea was a municipal swimming pool, that she could splash about in for the good of her health and climb out when the whistle blew.

It was several days before anyone let Alice go out alone again. There still seemed to be some kind of understanding that Alice had tragically flung herself out to sea with the intention of ending her life, which was never how Alice planned it. But if she was out of eye- or earshot for more than a minute or two, they worried she was Up To Something. In Bea's cottage, once no longer bed-bound, she was constantly being called upon to look at something or being brought something to taste, check-ups on her status in the guise of interested housemates.

Melder was there the most, sleeping on the sofa despite

Alice's scrawled entreaties, if she was insistent on staying, to take Bea's room. Otherwise there was Gwen, and Radka, Sally coming by, Tressa bringing biscuits and news, and even Ena, surprisingly. She always seemed to be there, hovering in the background in black, perhaps checking that Alice hadn't been selling off the silver since Bea's death.

She shuffled about from room to room, and Alice sometimes caught Ena watching her, narrow-eyed, and was desperate to ask why she was there. One of the only things Ena had said to her since her return from hospital was, 'I was a swimmer.' Alice hadn't known how to reply, but Tressa had joined in as they recalled that Ena was the strongest swimmer of any of them, could go out the farthest and dive the deepest and brave the water where none of the other children would. Then Alice understood. *Ena* wouldn't have been so incompetent and fool-headed as to be caught in a rip tide and nearly drowned.

Luke didn't visit Bea's. Alice tried not to notice. Sometimes she heard his voice in the garden, but he didn't come to see her. Once Gwen brought a note up, after Alice had heard him outside, but all it said was *Less than a week to go – I'll postpone Melder's party until later.* Alice had flagged Gwen's eye and mouthed, *No, it's fine, let's carry on* and Gwen had looked puzzled before taking the note and reading it, and rolling her eyes. 'Fine, love, I'll let him know. You rest, now.'

When she finally convinced her wardens that she could be allowed out for a few hours to work in the sun, that it would be beneficial, if anything, and no she wouldn't go near the sea, and no, she wouldn't talk, Alice took her books and notes and went straight to the cemetery. She didn't want to work in the garden. She didn't want to be around anybody. The cemetery looked completely empty, and Alice relished the prospect of a few hours' real silence, uninterrupted by people checking on her. Pushing aside the willow leaves, however, she found Santo on the bench.

He was as surprised as she, and they both looked at one another for a long time, uncertain what the etiquette is in greeting someone who has saved your life, or who has almost died on you. Eventually he simply moved to one side and smiled at her, leaving room for her to sit.

They remained in silence for a moment, on Alice's part more from necessity than choice, until she turned to him, and mouthed, *Thank you*. Santo mouthed back, *You're welcome*, and they both laughed at how infectious not-talking could be, Alice silently, then he said aloud, 'You're welcome. Sore throat?'

Alice touched her throat and swallowed, wincing. The doctor had said it would be a few weeks at least before it felt anywhere near back to normal, with all the sea water it had suffered. She took out her pad.

How are you? she wrote.

He shrugged. 'All right. Ena was pleased I found you.'

Ena?

He laughed. 'Oh yeah. Ena's always got her eye on me. She almost raised me.'

Alice paused, then wrote: *?*

Santo looked around the branches of the willow for a moment. 'My mam left when I was little, and my dad wasn't the nicest man in the world. Ena found me in her garden once, eating all her fruit. She looked like she was going to hit me with her walking stick, but she ended up looking after me. Lived with her for a bit. She kept everyone off my back.'

Alice didn't know what to write. *Ena* had raised *Santo*? Was that why she was at the house all the time, to check her boy's life-saving effort wasn't going to waste?

She kept the pen on the paper for a long time.

??

Santo laughed again. 'I know we're an unlikely pair. But she stuck up for me when no one else would. I owe her a lot, I suppose. Maybe we're the only sensible people in Polperran. Got to stick together.'

Alice shook her head again. Ena and Santo. She would see if Tressa or Gwen could explain more of this, sometime.

She wrote, *Coming to the party?*

'Melder's?' Santo asked. 'Not sure how welcome I'll be. You know what they think about me round here.'

Come! There's live music, food, drink.

'Music?' Santo looked almost bashful. 'Is anyone allowed to play?'

Alice didn't write this time, just pointed at him and raised questioning eyebrows.

'Mmm, yeah. Me. I played guitar when I was younger and didn't have better things to do. I mean, if you want, I can find something. It can be my present to Melder. But you won't tell anyone, will you? I get terrible nerves.'

Alice smiled at him, and he looked charmingly bashful. He stood suddenly, and said, 'Better get practising!' and left Alice to lay out her work for the afternoon, slightly relieved, and lose herself in the pleasant white noise of focused study.

By the next night, Alice was deemed healthy enough to be permitted one drink at the Dolphin, closely supervised by Radka. As she walked in, she recognised at once the muddy concoction being mixed at the bar, and sure enough, there was Bert, who saw her and almost backed into the customer behind him. That was noticeable too, Alice realised: there were certainly more people in here than when she had first visited, and they were talking too. It would have been a battle to make her current voice heard about the chatter, but Janet nodded to Alice and Radka, and said, 'I'll bring them over.'

Alice watched as Bert hurried away. He settled himself into his usual chair and table, craggily regarding everything in the pub but his old friend. And at the other corner, of course, sat Clemmo, who blinked around as if he was slowly retracting into his shell. Radka took a seat at a spare table, pulling out a seat for Alice, who had instead gone to Bert's table.

'Come with me,' croaked Alice, before turning and walking to Clemmo's end. She turned back to check Bert was coming. Radka watched, amused, but looking uncertain about whether or not to stop Alice speaking. Bert shuffled across the pub and stood by Clemmo's table, where Alice had now joined him.

'Stand,' she croaked. Clemmo stood. The two men still wouldn't look at one another.

'I nearly died last week,' Alice said. 'Which was,' she paused, to swallow carefully, 'my own fault, but still. Can you imagine: wasting your precious life,' she swallowed again, and her voice came out as a painful hiss, 'on an *apple argument*?' After a moment, she added, 'Ow.'

She rasped to Clemmo, 'Hand,' and waited for him to put out his hand, confused. She turned his wrist so it was in the correct position, then repeated, 'Hand?' to Bert and did the same. They were now inches away from shaking hands, the tension between them thickening the air. They stood silent, facing one another, unable to look away. 'Now you say, "I'm sorry",' she instructed Bert, but before she could finish both men were saying it, chuckling and standing up and banging each other on the back, laughing again, as if amused at this silly woman coming and making such a fuss of such a small thing. Janet brought over a drink for each of them, then put down Radka and Alice's as Alice sat down at her own table.

'Banging their heads together. I told your mother that's all they needed,' Janet said.

'Old men are very silly,' Radka suggested.

'Not just old men,' Alice croaked, thinking of how most of the history she'd ever studied was shaped by stubbornness, personal feuds and pride. She was suddenly exhausted, and didn't want to be anywhere near anyone at all.

Chapter Twenty-Four

'Luke!' Alice called from the gate, the word disappearing half-way through as her voice gave up and she clutched her throat.

She could see, for the briefest of moments, Luke debating whether to pretend he hadn't heard, poised by the side of his van, but Belle betrayed him and came bounding over. Luke followed, squinting at the late afternoon sun and shielding his eyes.

'Luke!' she whispered. 'It's been a while – it used to feel like every time I opened the door you were in the garden. And . . . you came to the hospital. Thank you.'

He squinted tighter, then dropped his face. 'Been busy, recently, summer houses getting ready . . .'

'Oh, right. Yes. Sorry.' They stood silently for a moment.

'Was there anything you wanted?' Luke asked.

Alice looked at the tan line on his biceps, white edges peeking just below his sleeve when he moved. She swallowed. 'No, I mean –' she touched her throat, sore still each time she swallowed, 'I was thinking about getting started on the terrace, but if you're busy, we can . . . do it . . .' This wasn't what she had meant to say. She didn't know what she had wanted to say, only that she had a sudden need to keep Luke from leaving, and this was the first thing she could think of. After all, they had talked about it before. It was something Bea had wanted doing. This was an OK thing to ask. It *was*.

Luke finally looked at her. 'No . . . let's . . .' He sighed. 'I can take a look, while I'm here.'

He walked into the garden, almost dragging his feet, but when he got to the tangle of brambles Alice could see his gardening eye take over.

He looked at his watch. 'There's nothing urgent on for the rest of the afternoon – I was just clearing up.' He sniffed. 'We could get started on that section there, nearest the back?'

'We?'

Luke smiled. 'Don't worry. I've got another pair of gloves.'

It turned out that not only were there spare gloves, but shears and clippers too, all from Bea's shed. Between them, they moved quietly but surprisingly fast through the brambles, chopping them up and piling them behind them on the lawn, only stopping for a cup of tea, and later some chicken sandwiches Alice brought out for them, and some sausage for Belle.

The light was still clear but softening when Luke started talking. 'Do you think things are ready for the party tomorrow?' he asked. 'I mean, if it's not, we can cancel. The good thing about surprise parties is that the guest of honour will never know if you do.'

Alice turned her gaze on Luke. 'That ship has sailed,' she croaked. 'Tressa's family are putting up the gazebo, Clemmo and Bert are on music –'

'At last,' Luke observed. 'Great work.'

' – Janet's got the barrels, Joy's on cake, and Tressa's granddaughter has got her whole Primary class making the decorations.'

'Child labour,' Luke said. 'Only the best for my sister.' Then he added, 'Really, though, Alice. I just want this party to be the best it can for Melder. I don't think any of us can – I'm sure we don't know the half of it.'

'I know,' Alice replied. 'I'm sure she'll love it.' She smiled as they bent back to the brambles, but as she began snipping, Luke spoke again.

'So.' He cleared his throat. 'Do you think you'll go back soon?'

Alice dropped her batch of brambles onto the pile, then straightened up, stretching out her back and lifting her hands to the high air, and thought for a moment. 'Um.' She stopped. 'I'm not completely sure if I'm allowed to go back yet.'

She could feel Luke watching her, but he didn't say anything.

'There was . . . a problem, before I left.'

He still waited.

'I . . .' She took deep breath. 'I had a breakdown. In front of my students.'

Luke eventually said, 'I'm really sorry. That sounds . . . awful.'

Alice gave a soft groan. 'It was horrible.' Her voice was a rasp now, raw in her throat. 'Worse than when Dad died, I think. Like I was . . . losing my mind. Just . . . shut down inside my body, and I couldn't stop anything –' Whispering this helped, but still her heart began racing again. 'A whole room of people, all of them just watching me – disintegrate –'

Luke came to stand next to her. 'Alice, you don't have to talk about this now if you're not ready.'

She breathed through her nose, blew out through her pursed lips, over and again, nodding at him. She closed her eyes for a count of four long breaths.

'No. I want to,' she said, in a calmer whisper. She picked up the shears and chopped vaguely at the remaining brambles. 'I'd had a rough couple of months, with funding issues, and someone trying to take credit for my work,' she swallowed the pain. 'The department trying to promote someone over me . . . Ridiculous back-stabbing academia. So *tedious*. And I was feeling bad all the time – too weak for sleep, too tired to cook, and at night I was *wired*.' She threw the fallen brambles onto the pile. 'I think Morag noticed – she'd come into my office to check on me a few times, which she hadn't done for years. I was behind in my marking, but too exhausted in the evenings –' She shrugged. 'And then I'd brought my post to read before my first seminar. The first thing I opened was from Peter Blandford, telling me my mother had died.'

Luke breathed out softly. 'Oh, Alice.'

'I didn't even know she was ill! I didn't visit when my mother was dying because I didn't even know she was *ill*.' Alice squared her shoulders up and swallowed carefully, her voice almost disappearing, her throat raw again. 'So I read it twice, and called Peter Blandford, then got my books and papers ready for the seminar – and this student was late, always late.' She waved her hand, gesturing a story she couldn't speak now, with more important words to get out

261

while she still could. 'When he got there, he was interrupting me, chatting, distracting.' She flipped the shears upwards, resting the sharp tip against the soft flesh beneath her chin, swallowing again. 'I asked him why he was there if he wasn't going to do any of the work. And he said, "No offence – "' She laughed strangely. '"No offence, but why would I want to do the work if I'll end up with a life like yours?"'

She looked quickly at Luke, saw he was still watching her, his eyes steady.

'I was OK at first, just calmly asked him to get out. He laughed. Sniggered. Looked around at the others. And I snapped.' Her voice had completely gone now, was just a whisper. 'I remember this sense of drowning, of being completely smothered and crushed and not being able to breathe, and I started shouting, then screaming, *Get out get out get out get out get out* over and over again, and throwing my books at him. I think the only reason I didn't actually hit him with them is because he'd started running – literally *running* – the second I opened my mouth.'

Luke stood completely still. When she looked up, he said again, 'I'm sorry.'

She thought for a moment, and snorted, thought of that awful young man's face, his shock at someone answering back for once, and she laughed out loud, a sharp rasp of sudden strange amusement that made her drop the shears and hold her throat. Her amusement was instantly replaced by a sick, deep remorse.

She put her head in her hands, and rubbed her forehead with her fingers, up and down, up and down. 'After that – I didn't stay in the seminar. I went straight to my office and . . . I tore it apart. I remember it so clearly, but it was like it was happening to someone else,' she said, whispering faster and faster. 'The notes and pictures on my notice-board, the papers on my desk, the plant in the corner, shredded. I picked up the chair and started smashing it into my computer, into my desk, and then I was tackled. Someone down the corridor had heard the noise and called Security; someone else had called Morag. Fortunately for me,' Alice paused, slowing, 'Morag got there first. She took me straight to her office and gave someone my keys to lock up my office. I was sitting on her sofa, with a blanket around me, and I started . . . coming back to myself. I didn't know how to explain that I knew what had just hap-pened, but it wasn't me.'

Luke stood watching Alice, stroking Belle's head.

'She was great, of course. She checked the student was OK, that the class was OK. No one wanted to complain, thank god, so maybe they were as sick of him as I was. And she gave me leave, as long as I needed. It was only when I asked her about lectures for the next day, that she began saying something . . . else.' She sighed. 'I don't think I'm supposed to go back there. I strongly suspect that I don't have a job to go back to.'

'Can they do that?'

'I'm not sure it matters what they can or can't do. I think it's more about whether I've got the time, money and energy to fight it if that's what they *want*. And whether fighting it will damage any chance I have of a career afterwards.'

Luke was quiet again. 'I think you'll be OK.'

Alice was suddenly furious, everything spiking in her at once in a terrible wave so her hands were shaking and her head pounding, bile in her throat. 'Do you? Do you think I'll be fine?' she hissed. 'Because that night I went home and toyed for quite a serious amount of time about how to kill myself. Obviously it wasn't my first ever ride – I've had anxiety on and off for most of my life and when I say off I mean constant. Do you know how that feels? Do you think I'll be fine? When I am constantly, constantly worrying that I'm going to die, and it'll be my own fault?'

She finished, her chest bursting, and wiped her mouth, feeling the adrenaline coursing around her body.

'Do you still feel like that now?' he asked.

She crossed her arms tightly across her chest and shrugged. 'Sometimes. Yes.'

'I . . .' Luke's voice disappeared, and he cleared his throat. 'I thought Melder was going to die, the last time she was in hospital,' he said. 'And Mum's brilliant, she's always been brilliant, but when Dad died it was Mel and me, the two of us looking out for each other, and the thought that – I just don't know what I'd have done if something had happened to her. I felt like I was losing my mind watching it –' He toyed with his shears. 'I can understand a tiny, tiny bit of that feeling.'

Luke was now looking down at the ground.

'Luke. I –'

He looked up at her.

'I want to swim,' she said.

'I know you do, and you will again.'

Alice took a deep breath, then before she could stop herself let out a cracked moan.

'Alice, you don't have to –'

Belle trotted over to her, nosing her hand, and Alice collapsed down to bury her face in the dog's ears. 'I do,' she insisted. 'I'm so sick of this controlling me. I'm *so tired* of being frightened of everything, all the time. It's so ridiculous, and embarrassing, and I can't do anything, *ever*, because it's new and it might pitch me into this . . . mortal terror that I'm about to die.' She looked at him. 'Do you know what that's like? It's so. *Fucking. Boring.*'

Luke's face was a mixture of alarm and amusement. 'If it helps, I'll go for a swim with you. Tomorrow morning?'

Alice started to shake her head, still feeling Belle's soft fur on her face. Then she stopped. 'No,' she said, 'now.'

She ran up to her room, pounding past Bea's, which still remained untouched and unexplored, and changed into shorts and a t-shirt – her swimming costume was snipped to pieces – grabbing a towel and her mother's yellow raincoat. Luke was now standing in the kitchen, tucking Belle into the armchair and holding up another coat from the rack, a red woollen coat that had also been Bea's. 'Can I borrow this?'

Alice nodded, not wanting to lose any momentum. This frustration and fury could be useful, she knew, and she had to ride it all the way to the beach if she was to have any chance at all of getting in the water.

She marched from the house, out, down, all the way to the steps, Luke just behind her, letting his stride match hers but not getting in her way. At the edge of the water, Alice shook off the raincoat and dropped the towel. She saw Luke carefully fold the red coat out of reach of the waves.

She stepped in.

The water was warm, but she could feel her muscles freezing up. Still, she forced herself to take another step. Luke stood back, on the beach, watching.

Another step in, and she started shaking. All the muscles in her body were twitching, her breath was growing ragged, her heart pounding. She was knee-deep and her feet kept moving, and she couldn't breathe any more. The water was splashing her thighs, and her muscles gave way, plunging her into the water.

Before her head touched the surface, Luke had caught her, his arms coming under hers, carrying and pulling her to the beach, laying her on her towel on the pebbles. She couldn't breathe; the sea was coming up; it was too close; this was it, this time; her heart, exploding, her breath, impossible, too thick and syrupy to pass through the tiny pinprick her throat now was. She curled up on the beach, pebbles under her head, t-shirt cold on her skin, fists tightly clenched and pushing harder and harder against her forehead, the knuckles of her thumbs painful against her eyebrows.

'Alice,' she heard. 'Alice, I'm right next to you.' She thought that if she was sick, she would choke and die from that too. Luke's voice again, gentle, complementing the waves. 'My phone is in my hand, and I can call an ambulance whenever you need, just lift up your hand if you need it.' He shifted beside her. 'I'm going to lie next to you, if you need me, I'm right here.' His voice matched the waves, slow and steady. 'It's such a clear night, they'll find you no problem. A nice bright moon like this.' It was his normal voice, but slower, lower, softer. She could hear his breath next to her, the air going in, and out, long deliberate breaths with sea air reaching far down into his lungs. 'There's a skylark over there. I haven't heard one of those all year. It's beautiful, Alice, can you hear it? It sings while it's flying – we might not see it but we can still hear its song.'

She couldn't open her eyes, but she reached a hand up, and felt Luke's alertness and the *wrackle* of moving pebbles as he lifted his phone. But she just felt for his other hand, and held it, and squeezed it.

She didn't know how long they lay there.

Chapter Twenty-Five

'Alice? Do you want a coffee?'

Melder was at her bedroom door, holding a mug of steaming coffee, heading to the foot of her bed. The scent of the coffee had woken Alice before Melder had, she realised, but when she tried to sit up her muscles yawped.

'How are you feeling? I heard you went in last night,' Melder added.

'How did you –'

'Luke – he had to go, but he called me before he left this morning.'

Alice clutched her throat, still sore, and rubbed her face with both hands, tasting last night's panic still at the back of her tongue. 'Luke was here all night?'

When she'd eventually stood up from the beach every muscle had screamed, and she knew the panicked, twitching muscles would be screaming even worse tomorrow – she remembered that familiar ache each time. Luke had wrapped both coats around her, and offered his forearm to her to grip, if she wanted, just like when he had taken her stargazing. She did want. They'd walked home slowly to the cottage, and she leant on Luke's arm all the way to the attic. He'd pulled the bedding back and let her fall in, covered her up, turned off the light, and left.

Melder passed her the coffee. 'He slept on the sofa, just in case you weren't well. Gave me a call to check on how you were feeling as I passed by. So? Can I report that you're in one piece?'

Alice looked at Melder to see what Luke had told her about her college meltdown – so public, so humiliating – but her face was the same as always, warm and friendly.

'I'm fine. Thank you. I've just . . . got some work to do.' She heard the distance in her raw voice, and as Melder said she'd leave her to it, she was off out with Gwen for the day, Alice remembered and added hoarsely, 'Melder? Happy birthday.'

It was only the last few pages of Ena's book that needed completing now, pages that Alice had counted carefully: Bea's album had fitted everything perfectly, and with Bea's own painting on the front, it had sometimes felt like Alice and Bea had been working on it together, just not at the same time.

As Alice planned it, the childhood photos would fall on the very last double-page spread. She glued in the photos of Ena in her thirties, and her twenties, and then on that last double-page she decided at the last moment to swap as the very final image Ena's toddler photo for the photo of her as a teen with the GI, Teddy. The toddler photo was smaller, and could be paired up with a picture of Polperran in the 1930s, but the other picture Alice had had printed larger, and was now her favourite. She wondered how Tressa had felt when she'd taken it, and what Ena and Teddy had been saying to one another. She wondered if Ena would remember this boy, who had clearly had such an effect on Tressa.

She pasted both photographs in, smoothing down the corners, looking at the eyes of Ena in each one and wondered if she could ever have guessed at all the things those eyes would see, how long they would go on looking, longer than so many others Ena would know.

She turned to the last single page, blank and empty, and decided to ask Tressa if she would write a note to Ena to paste there. Some message about the highlights of her life, as her oldest friend. And that was it, thought Alice. Done.

By the time she got to the Dolphin, feeling fragile but determined to manage, there was already activity everywhere, whole groups of people Alice felt like she was beginning to recognise from the cake competition, from the pub, and from more frequent glimpses on the green or the streets, all helping build and move and decorate. They called out to Alice and to each other to help with this table, to take the other side of this light, and Frances called her over to bring some of the plants with her and Sally, and people Alice had seen from the café window included Alice in their jokes. Bea's gazebo was up again, covering the same trestle tables, which would tonight be laden with food brought by the guests.

Despite Luke's earlier intention to make this a simple affair, in the end everyone in Polperran had been invited, more or less, which made it even more of a miracle that Melder hadn't caught wind of the grand plans. She was being taken out by Gwen for a birthday lunch and film in Falrigg, and wasn't due back until early evening, when Gwen would bring her straight home to get ready for a night at the pub with Luke.

Luke, when Alice saw him, seemed distracted and hurried. She knew that for him, this evening wasn't just to give Melder a good birthday, but to celebrate communally his sister's gradual recovery, both physical and mental. And Alice didn't know how to thank him for the previous night, especially with all these people around them. Eventually she remembered her own jobs, and decided to check that Joy had finished the cake. Down at Pilot's Cottage, the house smelt of honey and vanilla, and Joy invited Alice in to see the final moments of piping before the cake was complete.

'Why are you moping about down here then, anyway?' said Joy, with her characteristic discomfiting insight and usual bland tone.

'I'm not *moping*,' Alice rasped.

'That means you are. Trouble in paradise, is it?' Joy asked.

'What does that mean?'

'Heard about things between you and Luke Penrose.' Alice dipped her finger in the bowl of icing and ate the fingertip of sugar angrily. Joy chuckled. 'And *that* means it's true. What's the problem? Don't want to get involved with some local when you've got big Cambridge plans?' Joy snickered. *How does she know just how to push my buttons?* Alice thought.

Eventually she shrugged. 'I don't know. I'll be off soon, back home, and the house will . . . sell, and . . . I don't know if I'll ever be back in Polperran . . .'

'Alice,' Joy said, her voice suddenly softer than Alice had ever heard. 'If Marco had spent half as much time mooning around after me as Luke Penrose apparently has after you – more fool him – then I'd have tried a lot harder a lot sooner . . .' It was obviously difficult for her to admit this.

'That's . . .' Alice didn't know how to finish the sentence.

'I'm saying, you idiot –'

'Excuse me?'

'– that if you have feelings for someone, and they have feelings for you, why are you putting obstacles in the way?' Joy sighed, and began beating something vigorously in a bowl. Her voice deadened again as she furiously whisked. 'Oh, I know. The great intellectual thinks that if something feels simple, it's not worth it. That if something's uncomplicated, it means it's unexceptional.'

'No!' she croaked. 'Of course not –'

'You've tried it your way, Alice Kimbrel,' Joy said, pointing a dripping balloon whisk at her. 'And how happy has that made you? Maybe it's time for a different approach.'

Back up at the Dolphin, without the cake – Joy had said she was perfectly capable of bringing it up herself, wouldn't trust Alice with it – there was more to do, but still no looks from or conversation with Luke, who appeared almost panicked by the size to which the party had grown. He seemed well-surrounded by helpers, so she stopped trying to catch him.

She hoped this would be a good party; after the kindnesses she'd been shown over the last weeks, she wanted to remember Polperran fondly. And she wanted to do something for Melder, who had always been so kind to her, a new kind of friend Alice hadn't had before. Alice had always been so convenient before – the easiest student to teach, the best daughter to have when your wife left, the best researcher for getting the work done with no excuses like having a personal life. Melder had shown Alice how to begin seeing that just being herself could be enough for some people, and Alice wanted to repay her.

She had checked Ena's chair was positioned near the front at the party, and was meant to be collecting the tarts from Ena's cottage. But when she knocked on the door, it wasn't Ena who answered, but Sally.

'Oh, hello love, come on in, the tarts are just here on the worktop. Ena said to wait until they've cooled to cut them.'

'Is she out?' Alice croaked.

'Out? No, love, she's just upstairs. Not feeling too good today – said she might have a little cold? In the middle of June, I ask you, but she's gone for a lie down before the party.'

By the time Alice had got back to the Dolphin with the tarts, everything else was set up, and guests were heading home to change, or staying for some pre-party drinks. On the way back to Bea's cottage, however, Alice was drawn again to the peace of the sea before the noise of the pub, and followed the path down to the water. Advancing, she saw someone sitting on the steps.

'Luke?'

He turned around, and moved over so she could sit beside him.

'Hello, stranger,' he said softly.

She sat down, welcoming the noticeable warmth and shelter he brought this close to the sea, with the cooling breeze coming in.

'Busy day?' she whispered, her throat all but giving up.

'Just going over everything for the party.' He turned to her, and she looked at his face lit by the salmon-pink sky. 'Do you really think she'll like it?'

Alice smiled, and nudged against him. 'I think she'll love it.'

He relaxed beside her. 'And we've got everything on the list – food, music, decorations . . . are you sure there's nothing I've forgotten?'

'*You* might have forgotten something, but I doubt Tressa, or Sally, or Clemmo and Bert, or Janet, or any of the hundred other villagers we've got involved will have,' she replied dryly.

He chuckled. 'Right, right. Yes. But . . . no. I'll stop. It's going to be OK.' They listened to the waves for a minute. 'Are *you* OK?'

Alice sat for a long while. Eventually she said, 'They gave me a prescription. After . . . the stuff at college. Morag said I had to go to my GP, and the doctor gave me a prescription. It's not the first one I've been given.'

'And you didn't take those other ones?'

'No,' Alice said, lifting her shoulders to her ears before dropping them with a sharp breath out. 'But . . . I did start taking these. Last week. Not drinking. Trying to sleep a bit better.'

Luke looked out at the sea with her. 'And is it helping?'

She laughed softly. 'It's a bit too soon for that. And these ones are only beta blockers. I just . . . can't keep feeling awful and waiting for something to magically make me feel un-awful. I'm a grown woman, for god's sake.' She kept her eyes on the sea, lit an extraordinary pink by the fleece sky. 'And she said I needed to think about therapy too, once I felt more secure. I think by "more secure" she meant "not terrifying my students and the general public" . . .'

'And have you been particularly terrifying the last week?'

'You tell me,' she replied, looking at him, and both of them laughed.

'Good,' he said. 'Can't have you missing out on the party of the year.'

'Come on,' Alice said. 'Some of us need to make ourselves look presentable.'

They stood from the steps at the same time; Luke stumbled at the top step and was about to slip back down before Alice instinctively caught his arm, giving him enough stability to catch the railing with the other.

'Thanks,' he whispered.

'You're welcome.' She didn't take her hand off his arm, even as they both looked down at it. He bent the arm, and Alice tucked her hand around it a little further, and without a word they were again walking arm in arm back to the cottage.

Back by her door, Alice looked inside. She only needed to change into her dress, then they could walk together to the pub. Right now, she didn't want to let go of Luke's arm. 'Are you –'

He leant towards her, and she drew closer. She lifted her face to his. They breathed together for a moment.

Then Luke muttered quickly, 'I'd better go', looked at his watch and peeled his other arm from Alice's without looking at her. 'I'll . . . see you at the party.'

Chapter Twenty-Six

Alice saw even more of Frances's plants than she and Sally had carried over that afternoon, potted up and brought to the former car park, along with chairs and tables from all the gardens of Polperran. Luke had fitted lights around the walls, and hung the edge of the roof with more plants, while Sally and Radka had, with some extra help, built the stage at one end, laden with mikes and speakers and kit. At the other end, Janet and the young barman were managing a hog roast, and villagers were filling the space, depositing dishes and bowls on the trestle tables as they came. Ena was there with two walking sticks, edging her own tarts front and centre, eyeing everything else on the table with a dismissive sneer, before taking her reserved seat. Someone offered Alice a drink and she explained she wasn't drinking tonight, so was handed a lemonade instead to toast Melder on her arrival.

After only a few minutes, there was the sound of Luke's frantic whistle from the front of the pub, and the lights went off. Everyone grew still, half-crouching behind tables and hay bales. They listened to nothing, for a moment, then heard Luke's muffled voice saying, 'Can you give us a hand out back – I'll buy the first round?' and Melder's vague protestations, before the pub's back door swung open and everyone could make out two silhouettes. The lights went on with a flash, and the crowd called out, '*Surprise!*'

Melder gasped, genuinely staggered, looking stunned at the transformation and decoration, and more than anything the people, all those people gathered there for her birthday. She burst into tears, and Luke immediately gathered her into his arms and Alice could see him wipe away a tear too, talking into her hair, and then Gwen was hugging them both from behind.

After a moment Melder composed herself, and was able to look up and start laughing, filled with happiness, her red hair pinned up on her head and a pink dress making her look like a wonderful snapdragon. It was clear, too, that Luke had spent some time getting ready: instead of the standard mossy tangle his beard was sleek and groomed, his hair to match, and he wore a soft checked shirt that Alice had never seen before. Someone came over with a plate charged with food, and someone else brought her a glass of something, and then there was a tapping on stage and the music started up as the spotlights were turned on. There were Clemmo and Bert, accordion and fiddle in hand, singing and playing like there had never been a day's break since their last performance. The crowd went wild, even those who might have been too young to hear them play together last time, and by the second song the food had been momentarily abandoned and almost everyone was dancing.

Everyone but cantankerous Ena, Alice saw, who sat on her high-backed pub armchair as if under great sufferance. *Why am I so uncharitable?* Alice thought. *She's old and unwell and deserves an armchair.* Ena sat still, her hands clutching the top of her walking sticks, watching everything, looking truly old and weak for the first time since Alice had met her. Alice went over.

'Ena? I got your tarts. Thank you.'

Ena *tsk*-ed at her. 'Not for you. For Melder.' She looked over Alice's shoulder, peering about.

'Are you all right? Ena? Can I get you anything?'

Ena scowled at Alice. 'I don't need anything. Just – go on, get off with you.' She seemed to be getting more upset, though Alice didn't know what she'd done. She weakly banged one of her sticks on the floor. 'Go and enjoy the party.' Ena turned her face away until Alice finally left her.

At the buffet, Frances came over to her. 'It's a splendid job, isn't it?' she said.

'You've done wonders with the place,' Alice replied in her hoarse voice. 'I'd never know where we were with all this greenery.'

Frances looked pleased. 'It *is* good, isn't it? And, really, we all did it together. You should be proud of yourself.'

Alice was touched, but a little puzzled. 'It was Joy who made the cake, not me. And otherwise all I did was invite Ena.'

'Alice!' Frances gave her a hard look. 'I hope you know that Joy hasn't made a cake for anyone else for years. Not for anyone. And look at those two!' They both watched Bert and Clemmo on the stage at the front, instruments paused for a moment to trade music-hall barbs. 'You should be very pleased with what you've done, Alice.'

A moment later Luke was suddenly there, pulling Alice for a dance as Bert and Clemmo restarted, and they managed two whole dances before Alice was winded and asked for a rest, and at the drink table someone told Luke what a good party it was, and someone else told Alice how much her mum would have loved it, and asked how long she was staying; Alice gestured at her throat, mouthing *Can't talk*, and as she and Luke stayed listening to the music, standing closer and closer until their whole sides leant against each other. Alice realised she hadn't seen Santo yet, but she did see one of Tressa's children walk Ena out, offering his arm for her to cling to as he carried her other stick in his other hand: Alice was impressed that Ena had lasted even that long at the age of ninety-two. The crowd danced until Clemmo and Bert needed a break, a staggeringly long time considering their age; though Alice thought surely the years of rest they'd had before tonight's performance were enough.

While the party-goers headed to the trestle tables to fill – or refill – their plates, Alice finally saw Santo, saw him nod at her, and she excused herself from Luke and headed to the stage, and took the microphone.

She tapped it, and saw the faces turn to her expectantly, laughing and high-spirited in the gentle lights of the decorations.

'One more performer tonight,' she croaked. 'Just for you, Melder, in honour of this very special occasion . . .' Her voice was almost gone. She saw Luke whisper something to Melder, and Melder start laughing, clutching the arm of her younger brother. 'Here's . . . Santo Hammett!'

Even before she'd been able to put the microphone back in the stand, there was a gasp from where Melder was standing, frozen. As Santo strode on stage, guitar to his chest, Melder gave a horrifying cry and ran, and Luke looked up at the stage with something close to pure loathing. Gwen was being held back by two men to stop her getting to the stage. Even Tressa was looking at Alice with horror.

Suddenly, everything slid into place.

That was why Santo was so unwelcome in the village. Why no one had wanted Alice involved with him. Why Luke had been so cold when he'd seen Santo about. And why Santo had been so insistent about his performance being a surprise tonight.

Santo had started strumming, now, utterly delighted by the chaos he was causing. Alice staggered off stage, dizzy and sick. To this crowd of people who had only known her this brief time, who had seen her with Santo countless times, this must look like the sickest of jokes. She pushed through the crowd. She couldn't forget Gwen's fury, Melder's cry, Tressa's look of disappointment. But most of all, as she ran from the car park through the darkness to Bea's cottage, as she frantically packed a bag and started the car and drove as fast as she could from Polperran, she couldn't forget Luke's face, and his expression of pure, furious, hatred.

Chapter Twenty-Seven

She didn't leave the house for the first few days. It was disorientating. She had been away only two months, but it felt like years; yet laundry she had left drying was still lying stiff on the rack, and the dust she'd left on every surface had barely altered in her absence. She spent those first days tidying everything, cleaning the whole house, emptying out the attic and piling things up by the door to take to charity shops or the recycling tip. She spent a full day cleaning door frames and skirting boards, unscrewing light fittings and carefully washing and drying them before reattaching them. She went through years and years of paperwork, binning almost everything, and she contacted an estate agent in Falrigg to start arrangements for putting Bea's cottage up for sale.

Alice avoided going out into her tiny garden, though in previous years meals in the little courtyard had been a point of pleasure: now the sky seemed so small, a rectangle directly above her like a trapdoor that hovered between pale-blue and blue-grey. The traffic was loud, too, something Alice had grown up with and never even heard before, let alone been bothered by. It was just as Ena said: Cambridge was just noise and pollution compared to Polperran.

Although she still didn't sleep, when she opened her eyes

in the mornings it was always in the wrong direction. She turned them towards an attic window which wasn't there, before dragging herself down for a coffee in her small, dim kitchen.

She lay on the floor for hours at a time, just staring at the ceiling. Her house smelt of nothing, no paints and linseed oil, no fresh loaves, no cut branches, no salt air. If she opened a window it smelt of petrol and next door's bins. At the corner shop, she was able to conduct a whole transaction without speaking to anyone or anyone speaking to her, and no one even made eye contact with her when she went to order a latte at her old café. Just took her money, turned away and passed her the cup while saying *Next* and sneaking a look at their phone half-hidden under the counter. She took her coffee home and let it grow cold on the table, as she lay on the floor and stared up at the ceiling again. She stayed in the house without leaving for four days, and the only time anyone knocked on her door was her neighbour, checking if she'd taken a parcel for him.

'No,' she said, her voice grown croaky again. 'Sorry, I –' but he had already turned away, moved back onto the pavement and along the road to try the other side.

She ate from cans in her cupboard, opening them and eating straight from the can with a fork or a spoon, standing up in the kitchen. She started drinking her coffee black, so she didn't have to go to the corner shop again. She forced herself to have a shower every morning, a short, scrubbing, hurried shower, but wouldn't let herself run a bath. She felt the crystallising that had started in her teens spread through her body. She had warmed up only to let the damage invade her entire system.

Polperran started to feel like it had been a dream. After a while, it had that same disorientating quality in Alice's mind: somewhere impossibly beautiful where everyone had seemed to know her, but something wasn't quite right, and she had done something, *something*, unspeakably bad. She drew all the curtains, and stayed on the floor.

Eventually Morag got in touch with her. She said she'd called the house phone number Alice had given her and someone else had answered, a woman, and told Morag that Alice wasn't there any more.

'I'd rather hoped you'd taken yourself off on a relaxing tour of the south of France or something, but from the ringtone you're still in the UK.'

'Still here,' Alice said dully.

'Will you come into the department?' Morag asked. 'I'm happy to clear up your office if you don't want to, and I've kept everyone out, but . . .'

Alice heard the unspoken end of the sentence. *But your time is up.*

Morag signed Alice into the building the next morning, wheeling her empty suitcase through the corridors. Alice didn't know what looked worse: Alice sadly trudging along alone with the suitcase, or the Head of History escorting her through the building with it. Either way, she felt people watching her, whispering. *What fun to have a Senior Lecturer thrown out right in front of everyone!* She knew that some of her students would dine out on the whole sorry tale for years.

Her office was indeed untouched. Morag – Alice imagined it had been Morag, or one of the few colleagues Alice had been passingly civil to – had carefully stacked up the paper torn down from the noticeboard, and made a neat pile beside the battered sofa of the broken chair, lamp and plant pot.

'I didn't know what you wanted doing with those,' Morag said. 'God, it looks horrible now, looking at it, but I just wasn't sure. Sorry.'

'It's fine, Morag, thank you. I'll . . . get some bin bags and sort it out.' She started slowly picking up some of the pins which had fallen from the noticeboard, unnoticed.

'Alice.' Morag's voice was gentle. 'How was Cornwall? Did something happen? With your mum's stuff?' She paused. 'With the gardener?'

Alice groaned, and covered her face. 'Luke. His name is Luke. And no, nothing happened.' She rubbed her face with both hands. 'It's fine.'

Morag took hold of Alice's wrists and lowered them, looking at her directly. 'You're going to have to talk about this at some point, you know.'

'Talk about what?' Morag raised an eyebrow. 'I mean, what in *particular*.'

'We need to know if you're ready to come back. Not just willing,' Morag held up a hand to stop her. 'But really ready. Have you had any counselling? Did you see your GP?'

'Yes,' Alice said heavily. 'I mean, yes to the GP, no to the counselling. When have I had time?'

'No one has time, Alice,' Morag said. 'But sometimes we have to make time. I mean, you had the horrible shock of your mother dying, and between one thing and another, you had – minor or otherwise – a breakdown.'

'So you're saying I need to leave.'

'No!' Morag laughed. 'Alice! You've been here long

enough – do you think you're the first person to have a breakdown? Do you think you're the first person in this department – in this corridor, this *room*! – to have had mental health issues? You know there's help if you want it. But you need to *ask*.'

'But . . . I still have a job?'

Morag looked deadpan. 'Alice. Do you *know* how much *paperwork* is involved in getting *rid* of someone? And that's someone I *don't* like.' She looked around the office, then at a stunned Alice. 'Look. Just tidy up in here. Have a think. Take your time. This academic year is all taken care of, and I can hold on a wee bit longer for next year. But you really need to make sure that *you* are taken care of. Because you can't do any job unless you're really, truly ready.'

Alice frowned at her. 'And then I can come back?'

'If you *want* to. Of course you can. But . . . let's get this lot sorted, first.'

There was little in the office to sort, thank goodness. Alice had always been ordered, at least until that day, so it was a simple matter to move the things she needed for her book-work into her suitcase, and the rubbish into the bags and boxes Morag provided. She left the broken pile for last, and began cleaning the general office debris.

'Hello?'

Alice was on her knees beneath the desk, untangling wires to bring her own chargers and cables with her. 'Give me a second, Morag, I'm nearly done.'

'Alice?'

That wasn't Morag's voice. She crawled backwards and poked her head above the edge of the desk. She stared. '*Melder?*'

Chapter Twenty-Eight

'Oh thank god,' Melder said. 'I asked where to find you, and one person said you'd left and another person just laughed, but one woman gave me this office number but I couldn't find the right floor –'

'Melder! What are you doing here? I mean – it's so nice to see you! What are you doing here?' Alice went to hug Melder, but as she stepped forwards remembered Melder's face the last time she had seen her. 'Melder. Are you OK? Your mother? Is Luke?'

Melder gave a slight smile. 'We're fine, Alice.'

'But what are you doing here? How did you get here? What are – what are you doing? Here? What are you doing *here*? Are you here to see *me*?'

She gave a soft laugh and held her hands up. 'Slow down – yes, to see you, and we drove. Well, not me, Luke.'

'Luke is here.' It was a statement, not a question, because Alice didn't want Melder to say that he wasn't. Luke had driven up to Cambridge.

'Alice, can we sit down for a second?'

Worried, elated, shocked, confused, Alice pushed the broken pile to one side, took the threadbare armchair and offered Melder the cleared space on the more comfortable tiny sofa. She realised her hands were shaking.

'Alice, Ena died. I'm so sorry.' Melder watched her. 'We wanted you to come back for her funeral.'

Alice looked at Melder for a moment. That didn't make sense. 'No, she didn't,' Alice insisted. 'She was alive at your –' she stopped, didn't want to say *your party*. 'She was alive.'

Melder winced. 'She died the day before yesterday. She wasn't well the last couple of weeks. Hardly anyone knew, though, just Ena and Tressa and Ena's doctor. She didn't want anybody fussing, Tressa said.'

Alice slumped back in her chair. She looked at Melder. 'Are you OK, though? Since – since – Melder, I'm so sorry about –'

Melder waved her hand. 'Don't. It wasn't your fault, Alice. They got it out of Santo, not that he ever needs much persuading to tell everyone how clever he is. He was bragging how he'd got one over on you, to get right up on stage –' Melder's voice caught.

'I'm so sorry, I never caught on that *he* was . . . your ex, I just thought he wasn't popular in the village because . . . Luke had bad-mouthed him.' She realised as soon as she said it what puerile nonsense it was, how pathetically foolish she had been to not see through him the moment he had said it.

'Is that what he told you? Sounds like him. Never done a thing wrong in his life, that man. And yet everyone's out to get him! Poor thing.' Melder chuckled, but her face was pale and sickly.

Alice couldn't look at her. The things she had done with Santo – had nearly done with him. She looked at her notice-board, paper still clinging to staples and pins where she had ripped them out, months ago.

287

'Ena's dead, though?' Alice said, still uncertain.

'I'm sorry, Alice. Will you come back?'

'For the funeral?' she asked.

'Tressa wants you there. And all of us.' Melder spoke so softly. 'We all want you there.'

Outside in the van, Luke greeted her with a cool, distant smile, as if she was merely a friend of Melder's. As they drove from her college towards Maurice's house, he paused at a junction, and said, 'It's much more beautiful here than I expected.'

Alice knew he was trying to be kind. Perhaps it was the unexpected kindness causing the heavy lump in her throat, and her inability to reply.

At the house, she packed quickly. The black dress from her father's funeral, unworn since then, toiletries, her notes, just in case. Her keys to the cottage, which were already in an envelope to send to the estate agent. Black shoes, medication. She filled her bag swiftly. She locked up and returned to Luke's van within fifteen minutes, but when Melder held the door open for her, Alice held up Bea's car keys in her free hand. 'Shall I follow behind you?'

Luke looked away, nodding. Melder said, 'Will you be OK to drive?'

Alice didn't know. She couldn't remember the drive back from Polperran, only that it had been fast and numb, that she hadn't stopped the whole way, except on the outskirts of Cambridge when she realised she didn't know the driving route back to her house. She nodded and smiled back at Melder.

'We'll stop on the way for some food and a break – we'll stay together?' Melder asked.

Alice nodded again and went to the car.

By the time they stopped at the services near Salisbury, Alice's fingers and wrists had grown numb again from her grip on the steering wheel. She was dry-mouthed and her head was aching. When Melder and Luke got out of the van she rubbed her lips together to try and bring some feeling back into them, and climbed out too.

'Food?' Melder said. 'Don't tell Mum, though, she'll disown us if she knows we've bought service station pasties.'

They all bought coffee straight away, which Luke and Melder drank steaming hot but Alice kept for the onward journey. Sandwiches, crisps, and Melder picked up a bag of sticky buns to share too. Alice felt her appetite disappearing, and excused herself to the toilets.

Inside a cubicle, she put her head in her hands and did some deep breathing in the plasticky stagnant air. She tried to slow her heart rate – *just get there, and it's one more night, one more day* – but the thought of Luke and Melder, driving all that way to collect her, made her retch over the bowl. She wanted to be left alone. She didn't want to face the rest of Polperran, not with this tight hard ball in her stomach which grew with every mile. It was growing higher, pressing against her lungs, and by the time they got to the village it would be impossible to breathe at all. Her medication might be packed safely in her bags in the car, but she hadn't actually taken any since she'd left Polperran.

She ran her hands under the tap, and then stuck as much

of her face under as would fit. When it was completely numb, she rubbed it dry with the hem of her jumper, and found Melder and Luke finishing their sandwich in a sad little seating area outside.

'We'll wait for you to eat,' Melder said.

She shook her head. 'If you're done here, I'd rather just get back on the road.'

'Do you want me to come in your car? Keep you company?'

Alice watched Luke finish the last of his coffee, and throw the cup in the bin.

'No, that's OK,' Alice said. 'I'm not much company right now, anyway.'

Melder looked at Luke, then at Alice, then shrugged. 'Sorry, Luke. I might stick with Alice anyway, if that's all right with you.'

Alice was surprised that Melder had insisted on coming with her, but not surprised enough to have any further anxiety attacks. She felt like her emotions had been completely exhausted over the last week, and she had no more feelings to feel, whatever happened.

Melder sat quietly for a long time, but eventually said, 'Can I tell you what happened? At the party? After you left, I mean.'

Alice glanced over at her for a split second. 'Of course. Do you want to?'

Melder sat quietly again, thinking. 'Yeah. I think so.' She breathed in and out slowly, a premeditated pattern all too familiar to Alice. 'Right. I ran off, and apparently you ran off too. But I only ran to the pub toilets. And I got there, and I saw myself in the mirror, in my favourite out-fit, on my birthday, with all the effort that everyone had put in, and I was crying. *Again*. I looked like someone had punched me in the face, which reminded me that – not recently, but recent enough – that *fucker*,' Melder paused, 'sorry, Alice – *had* punched me in the face. On several occasions.' She stopped again, did some more slow breathing.

'Melder, you don't have to tell me.'

'Listen. I saw myself in the mirror and was so . . . *angry*. I was *so* angry. I was just so furious that yet again, *again*, he'd come along and consciously, purposefully, tried to ruin something. Just because he could. Because he was allowed to. It made me so, so angry.' She laughed, a hard, short laugh. 'So I washed my face, and I went back to the party. And I realised that I hadn't been gone that long, because he was still being wrestled off stage. And I also realised that he'd only got onto that stage because almost everyone in Polperran thought we'd just had a rocky rela-tionship, and a bad break-up. That this might even look romantic to some people. The only ones who knew what he'd done were Mum and Luke, and Tressa. Tressa found out because Tressa always finds out, and she . . . well, she agreed to keep it quiet, because I didn't want anyone to know. I was so humiliated by what he'd done to me, by how weak I'd been, what a terrible girlfriend, that I just wanted it to be our secret. That's why none of us told you. I had this . . . messed-up idea still that it must have been my fault, and if you saw something good in him then who was I to interfere and tell you anything different? You'd just think I was his crazy ex.'

'Melder, no,' Alice said.

'Wouldn't you? We didn't know each other all that well when you met him, did we? Why would you take my word over his? And I *know* how charming he can be, believe me. No one has ever been loved like someone loved by him. All the promises, all the romance, all that raw appeal, and you can't *believe* he's picked you. Which is fine, until you say the wrong thing, or wear the wrong thing, or look the wrong way when he's speaking to you. But no one else knew. I hid at Mum's until the bruising went down each time, and meanwhile *he* got loads of sympathy. He told everyone the doctors thought I had some kind of blood disorder or something, because I kept waking up with loads of bruises. He said he was so worried about me.'

'Christ.'

'I know. Such a catch, right? And while people didn't know, there were plenty of people who just had a bad feeling about him. Sally wouldn't stay in the same room as him, I noticed, and Bert would make his excuses not to drink with him at the Dolphin. Some people just listen to their gut. Like I should have.'

'But that's the point of people like that, isn't it? That so few people do pay attention to their gut reaction.'

Melder pointed to Alice's coffee. 'I'm sorry – can I have this? I'm crashing a bit.'

'Yes, drink, drink. If you want to talk later, we can do this later.'

'No, no. If you can bear to keep listening to me ramble on –'

'Mel, you can tell me whatever you want. Or not.'

They drove in silence for a few minutes. Then Melder

said, 'The bruises weren't even the worst. I mean, I know how worried Mum and Luke were, I know how serious it was the last time I went into hospital, but it wasn't the worst bit.' She took another gulp of the lukewarm coffee, tipping it up to get the last of it. 'It was the constant feeling that I was a failure, that every part of me was pathetic, and stupid, and incapable. And I just absorbed it as true. He had total control.' She turned the coffee cup in her hands. 'I wasn't able to talk to Mum about that. I just couldn't . . . I couldn't make her suffer too.'

She blew the fringe out of her face and rubbed at her forearms, and went on. 'So the police and the nurses and a few other agencies hadn't been able to make me leave, until the last time I was in and I woke up to see the doctor talking to Luke and Mum, and I heard her say, "We just have to pray that she wakes up," and Mum was crying so hard. And Luke's face . . . Honestly, Alice. Moments like that don't go away.' She sighed. 'So I started accepting all the help I'd been offered – counselling and therapy and groups – and I started getting free of him, bit by bit. And when he saw that happening, he didn't like it. At all. So he started following me, turning up outside my therapist's building, or if I was meeting someone he'd suddenly be there too, watching me. And of course it's so hard to prove he was up to anything, I had no evidence and he always had an excuse. But I promised myself I wouldn't let him win, that I wouldn't let him make me small again. So I kept going to those things, and kept meeting people, and kept walking around Polperran without letting myself be frightened. And then you came.'

Alice waited.

'I'm so sorry, Alice.' Melder's voice fell. 'When you arrived he just . . . backed off a bit. Not completely, but I saw him so much less. I don't know if he was seeing you or just didn't want to get caught following me around when you might be an option – and I know that sounds like I threw you to the wolves, but –'

'But it meant he left you alone a bit?'

'Alice, please, I'm so sorry.' Melder buried her face in her hands, crying.

Alice looked over at her, astonished.

'I don't mind! You don't have to apologise! My god – I feel terrible for getting involved with him at all – if you can even call it that. But if it gave you a *moment* of peace then it was worth it and I'd do it all again. Melder! Stop! Please – you haven't done anything wrong.'

Melder's crying changed, and she laughed despite her tear-soaked face. 'Well. Wait until you hear about the rest of the party.'

Alice found a pack of tissues in the door pocket, and passed them to Melder.

'When I came back, I walked up to the stage, and I took the microphone. And I told the whole party what he'd done to me, why I'd been in the hospital those times, that I hadn't had accidents or a blood disorder, that it was him. And he suddenly realised that just because we'd all grown up together, didn't mean that the big boys of Polperran would let him off for what he'd done.'

'The big boys . . . ?'

'Oh, and, someone at the party tipped someone else off, and the next morning his boat was raided, and they found a lot of things that means it looks like he'll be spending a lot of time somewhere he won't be able to bother either of us. Like, a very long time.'

'And . . . Melder, did they plant that stuff?'

'What? No!' She wiped her face. 'I always knew he was up to some shady stuff. Illegal fishing my eye. He did a lot more out there on his boat, but he'd only ever drop hints.'

'Bert said that too,' Alice said. 'Or at least it felt like he knew something was going on.'

She felt Melder watching her. Then Melder said thoughtfully, 'And who'd have believed him, either? Some old fisherman making trouble.'

Alice reached over and put her hand on Melder's, and Melder put her other hand on top for a moment, before Alice took the steering wheel again. They sat in silence, Polperran drawing nearer, companionable in the growing dusk.

Chapter Twenty-Nine

They'd hit rush-hour traffic when they were still some miles from Polperran. It had taken over eight hours altogether, and Alice was almost asleep behind the wheel by the time she got home to Bea's cottage. Luke pulled up just ahead of her on the road, and Melder stretched in her seat and turned to Alice.

'If it's all right, I'll walk with you to Tressa's – she asked if you'd come by hers when we got back.' She waved Luke off.

'Tressa's?' Alice said.

Melder nodded. 'I'll wait, don't worry.'

Alice took her bags from the car, opened the front door and felt unsure what to do. Knowing Tressa was waiting, she wasn't going to shower or change or stop for a meal. She left her things in the hall, washed her face and hands in the kitchen sink, and went back outside where Melder waited.

They walked in silence, Melder taking her arm with easy calm as they crossed the green. They turned into a large, low cottage, thatched and painted, with an immaculate front garden of cosmos and agapanthus. Gwen opened the door before they could knock, and gathered Alice into a large embrace.

'Alice, love. Come on in.' She released her and hugged her daughter. 'You all right, Mel?'

Melder nodded. 'Can I do anything here?'

Gwen looked Alice over. 'No, I think we've got it.' She kissed her daughter's forehead, and Alice thought of all the times Gwen had seemed worried about Melder, and how she had managed to keep going when everything had been happening to her daughter. 'You get home, I'll see you tomorrow.'

Melder waved to Alice, before Gwen closed the door and led her into the house.

'Come on through, love. I know it's warm out there, but Tressa feels the cold a bit in these old houses, so we've got a fire on. Can I get you anything to eat?' Alice remembered Gwen asking that same question on her very first day here, at her café. In the kitchen, several of Tressa's daughters and granddaughters were preparing food, along with Radka; Alice lifted a tired hand in greeting, which they returned with smiles as Gwen bustled Alice further through the house, down a corridor.

'Don't worry, we'll bring something in,' Gwen said to Alice, opening the door and gesturing her through.

Inside, a small fire lit the room, two armchairs in front of it, a similar arrangement to Ena's kitchen. Here, however, every flat surface was filled with picture frames, every member of Tressa's enormous family featuring repeatedly. The hundreds of tiny eyes watched as Tressa beckoned Alice over to the other armchair and Gwen waited by the door.

Alice didn't know what to say. 'Tressa, I'm sorry. About

Ena. I can't believe she's gone. She was alive at Melder's party . . .'

'That's generally how it works,' Tressa retorted from her chair, but when Alice looked at her she saw her eyes were full of tears. 'Ooh, don't fuss at me, you two.'

'We're not fussing at you, Tressa – Alice just got back –'

'Alice is perfectly capable of sitting down with me and having the tea you're about to bring us.'

There was a moment's silence.

'Now?' Gwen asked.

Alice felt both of them watching her.

Tressa sighed. 'Yes, now.' She caught Gwen's eye as she turned back towards the kitchen. 'Thank you, Gwen.'

Gwen nodded at her, mouth clamped shut, and gave Alice one more look before hurrying out. Tressa indicated the chair again. As Alice took it, she realised how old Tressa suddenly looked.

'And I'm a good six years younger than Ena, you know,' she said, making Alice jump. She smiled. 'I don't imagine I look my best right now. And it might not seem it, but I'm lucky to get to looking like it. Plenty don't.'

Alice gave her a polite smile. 'I'm sorry I let Ena down. Everyone down. I really wanted to finish that album for her. I know she wasn't always the fondest of me –'

'Coo!' Tressa blew air from her mouth, shaking her head. 'You think she was bad? You should have met her mother. Seventy-four years ago, in particular.'

They looked into the fire for a little while, as Alice waited for Tressa to explain, or for Gwen to return with some tea. Instead, Tressa said, 'Hang on a minute,' and reached beside her for two glasses on a side table, then into her handbag for a little bottle. She sloshed something brown into each glass, and handed one to Alice. 'To Ena,' she said.

Alice raised her own. 'Ena.'

The silence continued a little longer. Tressa shifted position, turned a little more towards the fire. Without looking away from the flames, she said, 'Did you know that Ena was short for Lowena?'

Alice shook her head. After a moment, she said, 'It's a good name. That's my middle name, actually.'

'I know, dear.' Tressa kept her eyes on the fire.

'Did you?' Alice looked at Tressa, her face lit a flickering orange.

'It was me that suggested it to your mother.'

In the sleepy heat of the drink and the fire, it took Alice a moment. 'You? To my mother?' She stopped again. 'To Bea? How did you suggest *my* name to Bea?'

Tressa lifted Ena's scrapbook up from the table beside her chair, moved her feet closer to the fire, and looked directly at Alice. 'Seventy-five years ago, do you remember that the GIs moved in down the road? Operation Overlord, they were here for. All the houses and pubs and fields and playground full of them.'

'I know, you gave me the photograph –'

'Let me say it. It's been years and none of us ever say it out loud. Now, this bit, I'm a bit hazy on; like I say, I was six years younger than Ena. I remember the chocolate, and I remember the records, and I remember our mothers warning us off the fields where anything had landed. Their uniforms felt so soft, compared to our soldiers'.' She sighed.

299

'They all looked so good – so healthy, so full of life. I can't tell you, Alice, it was like Technicolor had come to our villages.' Tressa took another sip of her drink.

'And Ena, she was a pretty girl. Quiet, but pretty. Her parents worked her hard, but we all worked hard then, and when she went out with her friends she wanted to dance and laugh and flirt with those pretty young men just like all of us did. And one night she and one of those young men caught each other's eye, and after that they were inseparable.' Tressa chuckled. 'Or as inseparable as you can be when one of you is a sixteen-year-old working on your parents' farm and the other is an American soldier on his way to war. She and Teddy were out every night, first with everyone, then just the two of them, and as things went,' she shrugged, 'things went, if you know what I mean. Teddy had already proposed, it turns out, and he'd written to his parents to tell them. Once he got back from France, he'd get permission from his officer to marry Ena, and her parents would give their permission, Ena thought. After the war they'd go back to Virginia together, and that would be that.' Tressa sighed again, softer, and spoke wearily. 'Only, as we know, Teddy was killed on Omaha Beach a few days later, while Ena remained pregnant, and her parents were getting too old to be pretending it was theirs, so when the baby was born the little girl was given away.'

Alice swallowed, her mouth dry.

'It seemed like a nice couple that the baby went to – I remember playing in their car while they were inside Ena's house collecting her – and they took her off and never bothered Ena's family again. All that evening Ena howled, like an animal it was, terrifying and awful. But the next

300

morning she got up and worked on the farm and never spoke about it again.'

The fire crackled in the grate.

'Until?' Alice said.

Tressa gave her a sideways smile. 'You're as sharp as she is. Was.' She lifted the glass to her mouth to take the last mouthful. 'Until your mother turned up, pregnant with you, years later. Her mother had given her Ena's details, bless her. She didn't look much like Ena but those that could remember saw she looked like him. You've got both of them, of course. Ena took one look at her and shut herself in the house for as long as Bea stayed, that time. I gave her a cup of tea and some name suggestions. Didn't know she'd come back again for good one day.'

Alice swigged the last of her glass too. 'And Ena didn't want me turning up, either, is that right? Couldn't think how to get rid of me?'

Tressa chuckled again. 'Not quite. I think by that time she'd spent so long building up that protection, she didn't know how to take it down again. If she'd ignored you, shut herself away like when your mam came first time, that'd be one thing – but she didn't, did she? She tried as hard as she could to get in your way, under your feet, under your skin, didn't she? Always there, in the corner of your eye. I watched her try to make something of your time together, but there was never any telling Ena.' She smiled at Alice. 'She liked your name, though.'

Alice watched the fire again. 'What about Santo? He said Ena raised him, that they were close. Did he know?'

A long, sucked-in breath. 'Santo. Ena really tried with him. She had such faith, took the longest time for her to

301

believe he was what everyone said. Only when she saw Melder with her own two eyes did she finally understand. Furious, she was, and I think it was that heartbreak that caused her first stroke. She thought she'd found a child to raise and he turned out to be a brute.'

'So he didn't know about Bea?'

'Oh no, love, plenty knew but we were all very careful to keep him in the dark about her, and about you. Ena tried her best to keep him away from you too, but a man like Santo has a sixth sense for going where he shouldn't.' Tressa's face turned angry. 'She looked after him for years and years, gave him a roof over his head away from that terrible father of his, fed him and loved him – and what did he become? Well, I'm glad he's in prison. And I'm glad the news never reached Ena,' and she dusted off her hands, shaking Santo from Polperran for good.

Alice paused a moment, then reached over to take the scrapbook from Tressa's lap.

She turned to the last double page, hurrying to see the picture again.

'So this is . . . ?'

Tressa's face softened. 'That's your grandparents. Look at his smile.'

'And you kept that photo all these years?'

'Not exactly.' Tressa looked momentarily shifty, then took off her glasses to polish them, and grinned. 'That night I brought it to you – do you remember? I was in a hurry? I'd pinched it from Ena's house, had my eldest there keeping her distracted.' Her smile softened again. 'But I *had* kept it for years. I gave it to her, when it was developed. She had it in her bedroom, hidden from her parents – and

302

if I know her mother, it must have been very well hidden. But when Bea was taken that first time, she threw it away. It was sheer luck that I saw it before it got damaged. I kept it safe; I loved him too, of course, but not like Ena. And when Bea moved here, I gave it to her.'

'So she knew about her father?'

Tressa nodded. 'She did. And when Bea came back the second time, came for good, Ena didn't want to know, for years and years, would cut her dead if she saw her in the street. Then suddenly one day she invited herself into Bea's cottage, nosiness probably, now that Bea was so welcomed by the village, and she saw that photo of her and Teddy sitting framed in Bea's studio –'

'Wait – I remember that! Dark wood frame,' Alice said.

'That's the one.'

Alice shook her head in wonder. 'I only went in there once, and it was on a shelf near the window. I thought it was for some painting. Did Ena take it back?'

'Far from it,' Tressa said. 'After she saw it framed like that, she couldn't get enough of your mother. I'd never seen anything like it. And when Bea got ill, it was Ena who was there every day, giving her her medicine and bringing her fresh spring flowers. She was with her at the end, you know. She finally got to mother her, just for those last few years.'

Alice stared down at the face of her grandfather, his gentle smile, wide-set eyes, dark brow, slick of dark hair, and Ena's beaming face beside him. They were so young.

'But she never got to see it. Any of it. Ena never got to see any of this book.' Alice's heart felt heavy.

There was a bump and clatter at the door, as Radka

came in with a laden tray. She lowered it onto the side table, and poured out two cups of tea for Alice and Tressa. As she passed Alice her cup, she saw the scrapbook in her lap. She looked worried.

Tressa saw her look. 'What's wrong, my dear?'

'I don't want you to be upset,' Radka said. Tressa looked at Alice with raised eyebrows.

'Radka, love, what is it?'

Radka was looking more and more distressed. 'I know that she didn't like me very much – Ena – but I thought it was an all right thing to do, everyone so busy, and away,' she said, gesturing to Alice.

Tressa breathed in and out slowly through her nose. 'Radka?'

'I thought it best – when Ena was so very ill, I thought perhaps that the book was finished, Alice gone, all that work . . .' She stopped again, and Alice saw Tressa's fingers tighten on her clattering saucer.

Alice touched Radka's arm, and Radka finally tore her eyes off the book. 'What is it?'

'I showed her the book. I took it to her, her last afternoon.'

Alice blinked at her.

'I thought it would be nice for her, even if it was me bringing it. I didn't want to break your surprise, but – I think she liked it very much. She couldn't speak so well, but she –' Radka mimed a weak hand banging on a chest, a heart, ' – and she cried a little, but I think she liked it very much. The photo of the two children near the end – that was her, yes? She goes back and again to that one, again again again, but then she sees the last page and she takes

304

my hand, and looks at the page for such a long time that I sit down with her, until she falls asleep with her hand on that page.' Radka swallowed, and added quietly, 'I think she liked the book very much.'

The last page? Alice had put the photos of toddler Ena, and Ena and Teddy on the last double spread and left the final page for Tressa's note.

But when she opened the book at the very final page, she saw that Tressa had instead pasted two other pictures there. One of young Bea, in a long flowery dress with a huge bulging stomach on what must be the visit where Alice was given her middle name; and one of Alice, taken at the cake competition, laughing at someone off camera. And Tressa was right: Alice's eyes were like Ena's, but her smile was just like Teddy's.

Chapter Thirty

It was a blisteringly hot day. But Alice woke not in her golden crow's nest attic room, but in Bea's bed. She remembered: when she had returned home from Tressa's, she was shivering, her teeth chattering, shock staggering her with its blunt force. She had climbed one set of stairs and collapsed onto all fours on the landing, right in front of Bea's bedroom, and she had found herself opening Bea's door, and crawling into Bea's bed, wrapping tightly around herself the patchwork bedspread, and sobbing into the pillows that still carried Bea's scent. Her cries were animal, and she had no thoughts at all. Alice didn't remember falling asleep, only waking up now in this agonisingly familiar bed, in this room with a photo of her young self on the bedside table, Bea's satins and soft wool clothes still impossibly undimmed on the clothes rail, while the heat was already so great that she had to run a cold bath and sit in it until her head hurt.

She ignored the ringing phone, and the knocks on the door, and at two p.m. she dressed in her plain black dress and black lace-up shoes, brushed her hair into a bun, put on her dark glasses, and packed a handbag with her keys and her wallet. She walked down to the church, and didn't look at anyone.

But someone took Alice's arm and guided her through the church door. These people, whom she had pushed away at every turn, judged and dismissed, who had cared for her mother and her grandmother; they all looked at her, and offered her gentle smiles. *They all know*, Alice thought. She was led to the front pew, where she sat with Tressa, and someone passed her an Order of Service.

Through the prayers, Alice was dizzy, discombobulated. During the welcome, she felt like she was choking, and Tressa felt it and took her hand, squeezed it tight. They kept holding hands, locked together, an old friend left behind and a hidden granddaughter, until the first speaker got up. Clemmo, reading John 14:1-3; he didn't sit back down when he finished, but stood for a moment longer.

'Not everyone understood Ena, because not everyone was lucky enough to get the chance,' he said. 'I count it amongst one of my life's greatest blessings that I was able to have that chance.' He paused. 'Even if we fought like cats and dogs as children.' The congregation gave a soft laugh. 'But she fought against every instinct to give up, to turn away, to become acid and angry, and she never gave up. She never did. I know it was hard for her, some days, but she never stopped trying to be the person she believed she ought to be. And I hope I'll never forget her.'

Alice had that same feeling again, the same as that day in the seminar room, in her office. She was leaving her body, feeling everything that was happening but completely detached, as if watching it from another room. Her eyes went first, like taps, running – not crying, but simply gushing water, and for a moment it was almost comical. Then the tide changed: she was rushed back into her body, slammed into the feelings, the wall of grief that swept towards her, too quick for her to turn away, crushing her and sweeping her away in a ten-tonne wave of pain and loss, for Maurice, for Bea, for Ena, for the little girls Alice and Bea and Ena could have been, the lives they might have lived, *all of us living so fast that we never understand how to get to where we need to be.* She thought of Bea when she was younger than Alice was now, bright and hopeful, battling constantly all her own feelings of rejection and difference and responsibilities. How Bea had found Ena, found the village where she was born, and how it had called to her, this buried history that she hadn't been able to share with Alice; how she must have tried, year after year, hoping this long chain of women in Polperran was something Alice could join, even if only for the summer holidays, and how Alice had shut her off again and again, clamping her eyes and closing her ears and hating, *hating* Bea for how much Alice still loved her when she thought Bea had chosen to desert her.

She could see in her mind's eye how much Bea looked like Teddy, and how Teddy was so young – Alice could have a son that age! – and how much optimism he and Ena must have had, how much youthful naivety and hope in a time and a place of violence and death. How Ena had worn black her whole life, grieving the husband and child she had lost, but how she had tried, always, to fight the grief that made her want to blame the world. She had been a mother and grandmother to any that wanted her, even Santo whom she had still hoped for, until it was too clear to ignore. How she had been waiting for Alice; perhaps had seen her each childhood visit, just a glimpse; she had watched and waited and connected the only way she knew how, with hooks and spears because she had already lost a daughter, and hated the thought of losing another person she could love that much.

Alice cried with gratitude that Radka had shown Ena the book, and that Tressa had given her the photo of Teddy. She cried for Tressa's loss, for the years lost when Alice and Maurice and Bea could still have been a family, spread across miles but still together, and for all the people of Polperran who had known who she was but had let Alice come to it when the time was right, because it was the only way anyone learnt anything. All of those people who had known Ena their whole lives, who had seen her example and never given up on seeing the best in her, even if they'd never known the whole battle she was fighting, just to do things better.

Tressa wept too, and held her hand tightly in her grip, leaning against Alice as Alice leant against her.

The vicar, when he stood up, cleared his throat several times before he could speak, more prayers, heads bowed. The tears didn't stop; Alice watched them drop onto the stone floor, pooling around her shoes. She thought of Alice lost in her Wonderland, swimming in tears, then cried more for Bea who had read the book to her so many times when they were both younger.

Prayers, another reading, then a hymn, on their feet singing together. The few times Alice had been in church in recent years, the congregational singing had been a lacklustre affair, a mutter beneath the wheeze and squeak of the church organ. But here, suddenly, another wave, a swell of togetherness and joy, a celebration expressed through breath and body, lifting up Ena and the gap she left.

Lord of all kindliness, Lord of all grace,
Your hands swift to welcome,
Your arms to embrace,
Be there at our homing

And Alice could see, hear and smell everything: the wood of the pew under her thighs, the weave of her dress, the scent of snuffed candle at the end of her pew. Everything was clear. But she still didn't know what to do.

The service closed, and an invitation was extended for everyone to join together at the Dolphin to share some recollections of the deceased, and Alice said to anyone who tried to talk to her, 'Yes, I'll be there shortly, I'm just going to change my shoes – I'll just change my shoes – yes, I'll be with you in a short while.'

She walked away from the church and back to the house, where she took out the car keys and loaded up the bag she'd left in the hall. Nothing was left in the house this time – it was a clean escape, no getting trapped here again. This grief was hers and she would pack it up and take it with her and deal with it alone in Cambridge. She looked around the hall of the cottage one more time, then pulled the door to and locked it.

Only as she was walking towards the car did she remember the paintings of Bea's that she had wanted to keep, but she didn't want to stop, couldn't stop, would sort it out with the house clearance company. Then she was loading the bags into the back, starting the car, and driving away, the cottage disappearing in her rear-view mirror. The village slowly floated by as she drove, past the green, the church, and towards the road out of Polperran where none of the mourners could spot her. But just as she was stopped at the junction, about to turn, a shape appeared at the passenger side, and the door opened.

'Hang on.' Luke slid into the passenger seat, out of breath, Belle leaping into the seat behind, and did up his seatbelt.

Alice stared at him, the engine chugging beneath her. Belle licked her ear.

Luke looked from the road to Alice, then back to the road. 'Come on then,' he said.

Alice glanced at the empty road ahead, then at Luke. 'Get out of my car.'

'Oh,' said Luke, 'that does make things difficult. I thought you'd say, *What are you doing?* and I was going to say, *Going with you*, but you're being a bit more direct than I'd planned, and it doesn't seem very ... gentlemanly to stay now.' He reached to unclip his seatbelt.

'What are you doing?' Alice said. She let the car stall, and put her hands in her lap.

Luke stopped trying to leave and turned to face her. 'Alice.'

She sat still, staring ahead once more.

'Alice. You've had a rough time lately –'

Alice made a short humming noise.

'Alice, no one can make any decisions about your life except you. But that's the point – you're the only one who can make those decisions. I can't, Morag can't, your students can't, no one here can. But if you want your life to be different, to feel different –'

'It's too hard,' she cut in.

'It's not easy,' he said. 'All the greatest things are at least a bit difficult, or they wouldn't be valuable. So maybe you need to try something different.' He paused, but Alice hadn't moved. 'Like staying at your grandmother's wake.'

He settled back into his seat and looked ahead with Alice.

'Or we can absolutely floor it and see how far we get before they track us down.'

Alice hiccupped.

Luke looked at her. 'It's not easy, and it's not always fun. Funerals generally aren't. But we're all with you, Alice. If you'll stay.'

When they got to the Dolphin, Alice realised she was exhausted, but with a new kind of exhaustion. It wasn't a tiredness, but a lightness, as if she had climbed a hill and breathed in a new kind of air; not a draining, but a scooping-out of something heavy. The exhaustion she had known for years always left her unable to speak, bed-bound for days, but now she felt lightened, calm, like she had released something that she thought would never go.

She didn't want to drink anything stronger than tea, so Alice found she was offered, at five-minute intervals, cup after cup of it. Luke would occasionally come past to sweep away the stagnating cups and saucers on the table beside her, while others came over to talk about Ena.

Peter Blandford took her hand, shaking it with both of his. 'Alice, my poor girl, to lose your grandmother as well when you have been with us for such a brief time –' He paused, and shook his head. 'I'm sorry, this is so tactless of me –'

'Two is carelessness?' Alice asked, with a small smile.

He chuckled. 'Well, indeed. More fool me. But there

was something else, a final document I intended to give you – but you left so suddenly, and I wasn't sure whether to forward it to your Cambridge address . . .' He pulled from an inner pocket an envelope: a cream, long envelope, identical to those previous four she had been given, even to the curling writing on the front.

'Is this . . . another task?' Alice asked, unsure whether to weep or laugh.

'No, my dear. I think it's something rather more . . . personal. Your mother asked me to give this to you whether or not you completed her project. I think she would have been most remarkably proud of how you have acquitted yourself over these last months, don't you?' Peter looked at her. 'She really was a remarkable woman, Alice. But I think you might surpass even her.' Alice suddenly understood that, even while Peter was still mourning his beloved deceased wife, he had also been in love with Bea, quietly, from the other side of his desk. He squeezed her hand again as she took the envelope, then muttered, 'Now, I must get you a cup of tea from somewhere . . .' as he wandered away across the room.

'Another one?' Luke said, appearing at her side.

She turned the envelope over. No number on this one.

'Peter said it's not. I don't know whether to open it now.'

Luke looked around the pub. 'If you want some privacy, you can go in the corner? I'll intercept the teas for as long as you need.'

She smiled at him, then leant forwards and kissed him on the cheek. She didn't know what his face did, because her eyes were closed, and stayed closed for a few seconds, the cool glow of his skin beneath her lips so overwhelming that she didn't want to open them and feel it disappear.

Eventually she bowed her head, opened her eyes and took the armchair in the furthest corner, without looking back at him.

Dearest Alice,

Whatever choices you make, wherever your life may take you, I hope that you will one day understand that you are the greatest thing that has ever been in my life. I am proud of my paintings, of my friends, of my marriage, of my work, but you are the single most shining joy that I ever experienced.

I left you too fast, and travelled too far, and regretted leaving you every day after that. I couldn't undo what I had done, the devastating error of abandonment; only try to offer you something I would otherwise not have been able to offer, had I stayed.

So: I don't know what you have made of my project, whether the tasks were unnecessary or utterly impossible, but you were the only person who could even have attempted them. I do know that as much as I loved the people of Polperran, they will love you more. And I know that now I am no longer able to take care of you, even from a distance, even only through school reports and academic papers and crossed fingers, these people will take care of you for as long as you are alive. This is your family, my dearest mermaid girl. And my final wish will always be that you can find every possible happiness, wherever you go.

Forever, always, and above all,

Your mother
x x x

Alice tried to help clear up after the wake, but no one would let her. Eventually she found herself outside, sitting alone at one of the pub tables, everyone else in the noisy companionship of the main bar. As she stared up at the Plough through filling eyes – so many years of not crying, and now she couldn't stop – she heard a noise behind her.

'Can I sit down?'

Alice nodded, and Luke sat opposite her, squeezing his legs between bench and table. 'So. How've you been?'

It was such a large question: did he mean through the wake, or the funeral, or today, or since Cambridge, or since she'd left here? She could go on and on, and none of the answers were 'Fine'. She gave a short, desperate laugh, and wiped her eyes.

Luke smiled.

She watched him.

'I don't know if you see it,' he went on. 'But you remind me a lot of Ena.' She opened her mouth to refute this, but he went on. 'She kept going. Even when things were hard, or seemed impossible, she kept trying. She tried to look after Santo, wasted mission that it was, tried to look after your mother, and you. Worried about everything, all the time, but she never gave up.'

Alice scratched at Belle's head beneath the table.

'And neither have you. You came down here, knowing no one, and moved into the house of your mother who you had a . . . difficult relationship with, and you accepted her project – who would do that? Who would just agree?' he laughed. 'And you took yourself swimming in the sea, and even when you nearly killed yourself doing it, you went back in again. And you let me pretend to garden for *weeks*

315

even though there was absolutely nothing that needed doing. I was almost reduced to taking nail scissors to those brambles, just to spend time with you.'

Alice laughed properly, surprised.

'And at Cambridge, I bet you would have gone back to your classes the day after your . . . incident –'

'It was a breakdown. And I wasn't allowed to.'

'But you would have tried, though. You wouldn't have just run off.'

She dabbed her eyes again. 'I ran off from Melder's party.'

'And you came back for Ena's funeral.'

They sat in silence for a moment. Then Luke said, 'I don't know how long you're back, but I'm so glad to see you.'

Alice took a deep, shuddering breath. She said, 'Do you feel like a swim?'

In the moonlight, the sea was bright and smooth, rippling into the beach. The water was warm, Luke beside her, as they swam together out beyond the shallows. She swirled onto her back, and let Luke slip his arms under hers and lie beneath her in the deep water.

Alice turned to look at him, his eyebrows pearled with droplets and sand. 'I'm glad to see you too,' she said.

Chapter Thirty-One

The next morning, the house phone rang. It hadn't rung for so long that Alice didn't recognise what the sound was to begin with, but through layers of sleep rushed down to the hallway, where the phone sat in its cradle.

'Hello?'

'Alice? Christ, woman, are you all right?'

'Morag, I'm fine. I'm back in Polperran.'

'I know, I've just called you there. Oh thank God. I thought you'd done something stupid.'

'Again?'

'You just disappeared from the department! You didn't say goodbye and someone said you left without half your things, and I've been trying to call you for the last forty-eight hours –'

'Oh Morag, I'm so sorry. I came back for a funeral. Melder and Luke came to get me –'

'Luke? Ah, Gardening Luke! I'm beginning to understand why you left in such a hurry.' She paused. 'Listen, everything is all boxed up, ready to be delivered whenever you want, just let me know when you're home. Wherever that might be.'

'Morag?'

'Yes?'

'The funeral was for my grandmother.'

'I thought your mum's mum died when you were little.'

'No – well, yes. For her biological mother.' There was a long silence.

'Is that why your mum ended up there?' Morag asked.

'I think so. She was given up for adoption by a woman here. A girl, really – she was only a teen when she had her.'

'And did you get to know her? Your grandmother, I mean?'

'A bit.' Alice thought for a moment. 'No, quite a lot, actually. Mum had left me a task to get to know her, researching her life. And she got to see it before she died.'

'I'm glad, Alice. It sounds like you might have made a difference in her last months.'

Alice made a non-committal noise down the phone.

'Do you think you'll come back?'

She made another noise, slightly less non-committal.

'Do you think you'll stay there a bit longer?'

Alice paused. 'Will you come and visit if I do?'

Morag laughed. 'Try and stop me. And listen, whatever you decide to do, you'll always get amazing references from me, and whatever reading and advice you need.'

'Thank you,' Alice said.

'And don't forget your book.'

'I won't!' Alice insisted.

There was a noise from upstairs, a crashing. Luke's muffled voice called, 'Alice?'

Morag started giggling. 'Of *course* you won't, Alice,' she laughed.

'Stop,' said Alice, laughing too.

'Me?' Morag said. 'Now get off this phone, and go and do something better with your morning.'

And Alice didn't argue.

318

Six Months Later

The cottage was warm in the winter, even the attic, heat rising from the busy kitchen below. But Alice no longer slept in the attic, which was kept for guests: this was Alice's home now, so she slept in Bea's old room. She had thought it would take a while to settle there, to shift any psychological ghosts, but once the painting from the attic was on the wall and she'd got into bed with a book, Alice discovered this room gave her better sleep than any other. Not perfect – there were still nights where she would work until dawn at the kitchen table – but good, more than enough to keep her on an even keel.

Gwen and Melder were in the kitchen now, working on a festive meal for them all; Melder doing the starters, and Gwen the main course. Gwen had brought a pudding from the café for dessert, as who could do it better than Joy? While still working from her tiny kitchen in Pilot's Cottage, Joy now sold all her cakes at Gwen's café: sweet buns and herbed rolls in the summer, spiced tarts and rich puddings in the winter. She'd spent the last few weeks making Christmas puddings to sell to the upcoming tourists, although she'd said crossly to Alice, 'I don't really like to put my name on a Christmas pudding that's been made less than six months before the day, though.' (She had refused tonight's invitation on the grounds that she had a new recipe to try, and Alice had known better now than to push her.) But the summer goods had sold amazingly, both with the tourists and with the villagers, and when she had time, Joy also made boxes of biscuits for the village shop.

Radka now ran the shop; Sally had signed the whole thing over to her once her own floristry business with Frances had taken off. When Radka moved in upstairs, Sally and the children moved into Ena's old house, paying a peppercorn rent to Alice, who'd been the beneficiary of Ena's will and told Sally that she'd sell it to her the moment Sally wanted it. Sally had laughed, one day, 'I don't know how I lived for so long with all of us in one bedroom,' and Alice had felt awful for not understanding why Sally might have looked so unhappy when they had first met.

Radka, meanwhile, had turned the whole shop around: after redecorating, with help from several kind volunteers, she had set up a suggestion box of what the shop might do differently, and followed those suggestions sensibly. She had fewer choices of dishwasher tablets, but more of Joy's bread – she had arranged that before Gwen could take everything Joy made – and now Joy also had an apprentice, the nervous young barman from the pub who wanted instead to be a baker. After only a few months, her apprentice was making most of the shop's loaves, and everyone was satisfied.

Radka's shop was bright and welcoming, full of wonderful treats and useful things that people didn't know they needed until they went in: matches and candles, hot chocolate and tinfoil, and țuică, a plum brandy that almost every tourist appeared to leave the shop clutching. Local, very fresh fruits and vegetables, local cheeses and milk, honey from a beekeeper in the next village, even coffee from a roaster just up the coast and meat on order from a nearby butcher. She'd also introduced a delivery service for villagers who might finding reaching the shop difficult, and for tourists who wanted local food literally on their doorstep when they turned up in their crowded cars. There was a book-swap corner where customers exchanged their old reads, and a wine-tasting night once a month that Janet hadn't minded losing from the pub, since really the Wine Club wanted somewhere warm with cheese and crackers where they could hear themselves over Bert and Clemmo's music.

Bert and Clemmo now played at the pub most week-ends, and often in the week too, as if making up for lost time. Alice could frequently hear them if she went into the garden in the evenings, and in recent weeks they had begun playing carols too. They'd even taken a few younger members of Polperran under their wing, teaching them fiddle and accordion, so on frosty evenings you could hear wheezing and scraping carried across the whole village, with the more able players joining them at the Dolphin for full musical nights.

It was warm in the house this evening, and particularly warm in the kitchen, where the Penrose women were working in perfect choreography around each another. Alice felt the slight sweat of claustrophobia and too much glühwein from the night before, and rugging up in a coat and scarf from Bea's branch, now by the front door, she stepped out into the garden.

Frost was already tipping the plants and the sleeping beds, and the air caught in front of her in great wolf breaths. She crossed the garden to the terrace, which she and Luke had cleared over the rest of the summer. When it was finished, with paving straightened and ironwork fixed, Alice had come home one day to find Luke unloading a large wrapped object from his van.

'Give me a hand?' he asked.

They had staggered with it to the terrace, and placed it with its back to the hedge, its front to the sea before them. Alice went to tear off the heavy cover, but Luke held her hand back for a moment.

'It's going to seem like I don't mean this once you've opened it, but if you don't like it, you *really* don't have to keep it.'

'That sounds promising.'

'I'm serious, we can . . . burn it, or something. Send it off to sea aflame like a Viking boat.'

'Now you're definitely making me not want to like it.'

Luke went to say something else, but instead handed Alice shears to tear open the cover, revealing an iron bench, worked beautifully with a pattern of leaves across the seat back.

'It's lovely!' she said.

Luke nodded at the seat back.

Alice saw there was a small plaque among the leaves, which appeared to be almost growing over it. On the plaque, she read:

BEATRICE ANN KIMBREL
&
ENA CHARLOTTE PENHALIGON
YOU DID GOOD THINGS

She sat on the bench now, in the cold. They were remembered, and Alice was grateful to them both. What would she have without them? No life to begin with, no ends to grieve, and not all the other good things in the middle: swimming, and Polperran, and all that came with them. Bea and Ena's ashes were now in the sea, and this bench watching over it was the perfect memorial for them both.

Alice was glad they'd arranged a swim for the morning, now she thought of it: she suspected tonight would be late, and loud, and a dawn sea-swim would be exactly what her mind and body would need tomorrow. There was a group of them who met three times a week, rain or shine, Radka, Melder and Joy among them, heading to the shore as dawn rose, whatever time that was. At the moment they splashed into the winter water in neoprene suits and gloves and socks, watching out for one another and swimming against the cold, cold waves. Alice loved it. She knew it would be pleasant too in the spring and summer, as the dawns got earlier and they were watching the world wake, seeing everything before it happened, but for now the raw roughness of the swims scoured all the anxiety from Alice's mind.

And when the swims were too far apart, or her brain was too far ahead, there was medication, better medication, which Alice had tried and stuck with until something worked, and there was counselling which hadn't clicked yet but had given a few small suggestions that it could, that it would, in the future.

The garden gate opened and disclosed Frances, carrying a huge wreath.

'Am I very late?' she called apologetically, as Alice rose from the bench.

'No, let's go in,' Alice called. 'Not at all late. Is that for the front door?'

'It's for wherever you want it, my dear,' Frances said. 'It

was our demonstration model for the class today, and it turned out so nicely I thought I'd bring it along for you. Do you mind having the demo?' she smiled.

Alice took it from her, and admired it in the honey-coloured light flowing from the house. 'The reviews your courses get, I'm flattered by a demo,' she said. 'Will Sally come later for a drink?'

'No, dear,' Frances said, in a thoughtful tone. 'She said the children wanted to go to church this evening –'

'Christingle sweets,' Alice said immediately, remembering her own childhood Christmases.

'Ah, yes, that makes more sense,' Frances said. 'Anyway, she thanked you for the kind invitation, and sends her love to us all.'

Inside, Frances greeted the others and immediately found something useful to do in a way Alice hadn't quite mastered – instead, she just straightened all the cutlery on the table for the fortieth time until the door went again.

'Radka!' Alice cried as she opened it. Radka gave her an enormous hug and a basket of cheese from the shop, explaining that actually this cheese should have sold but Radka had thought to put it aside for tonight before any of the Christmas emmets could get it. Alice knew she shouldn't feel this way, but she loved the way Radka said emmets now.

When they headed into the kitchen, Frances came to give Radka a hug too, and Radka was so pleased to tell Frances that several tourists down for the festive holidays had asked whether Frances's garden was open for Christmas tours, and if not, when it opened again next year.

'My gosh,' said Frances, genuinely stunned. Though Alice would have been able to tell her that nothing had been more predictable than the success of Frances's garden as an attraction, not just to tourists but to locals across the wider area. And while the summer cream teas might not have been up to Joy's perfect standards, they were excellent enough for Polperran to have been put very firmly on a particular kind of map.

Alice watched Melder now, how happy she was with these people who loved her. She'd been seeing a new therapist that one of Tressa's children had recommended, and had come on in leaps and bounds. It had helped, of course, that Santo was gone for good.

Pieces of Santo came to her over the months, from different people. She discovered from Janet that the night she was with Santo in the car park, having a terrible panic attack, he hadn't gone for help, but had pelted through the pub and disappeared out the front, unwilling to be associated with further difficulties. She'd heard from a very reluctant, although increasingly furious Radka that he had tried to make something happen between him and Radka, and only Radka's violent willingness to use her knees and her fists had stopped anything from occurring.

Luke had apologised to her for not being clearer about Santo: beside it being Melder's story to tell, it had been his vanity, he said, that had initially stopped him saying anything, not wanting this beautiful new woman to see him as anything other than completely easy-going, that as an outsider she'd be safe from him, and then when that hadn't worked he began to believe there was something between Alice and Santo, so he didn't want to come across as jealously trying to sabotage that. And then Santo had saved her life and he was so torn between the man he hated so much, saving the woman he cared for so much, he didn't know how to tell her then, either. At the party he had felt particularly terrible, because he was doubly furious at Santo, partly for trying to ruin Melder, and partly for trying to ruin Alice. On top of all that he felt guilty that he felt as strongly about protecting Alice from Santo as he did about protecting Melder from Santo. He knew that Alice didn't feel the same about him, Luke, as he did about her, so he just tried to stay out of her way, all this guilt and frustration bubbling up in him.

'So you can imagine how much fun I was, those days between you leaving and Ena's funeral,' he'd said to Alice, and she had rested her head against him and he'd scooped her hair over her shoulder and put his arms around her.

Now, Alice heard the door go, and it was Luke, taking the last place at the table. He greeted everyone individually before gathering Alice up and kissing her forehead, and her cheek, before she said, 'Ooh, you're cold,' but neither of them moved until Gwen said, 'Hm-*hem*.' Then they sat at their places and held hands beneath the table as much as they could, without even realising, Belle's tail wagging against Alice's feet.

At the table, Gwen said a very brief and possibly very rude grace in Cornish, but as Frances choked on her wine and Radka said, 'What is this?' the others, including Alice, leapt for the serving spoons and dishes. When they were all served, and much of a first portion had been eaten, they began talking about ideas for the upcoming year.

Luke had got a new trainee, one who loved both the physical and social parts of the work, and was doing so well that Luke was considering asking him about partnerships this time next year. Alice's research had been given the rubber stamp by Morag, and she had even found an agent who talked of this book – with a few slight tweaks – being submitted to real-life, non-academic publishers.

Alice didn't worry what *a few tweaks* might mean, because she was so happy to have her own office, Bea's old studio, to work from uninterrupted: no students, no marking, no departmental infighting. Officially, she was on a two-year sabbatical, but she and Morag both knew it was unlikely she'd return. She could do writing and distance marking here, if she chose, and this way of working, so far from what she would have chosen even a year ago, suited her abundantly more.

She'd kept several of Bea's paintings on the wall where she worked, beside the re-framed photo of Teddy and Ena and a photo of Alice and Maurice building sandcastles; the other paintings had gone out on loan to various galleries along the coast. She would happily give the paintings away – in fact, Gwen had one in her café, given by Alice to adorn her still-gleaming walls, and she'd given Sally another when she and the children moved into Ena's house – but Alice couldn't imagine a figure she would ever sell one for. She loved to look up from her work and see her mother there.

'So, Radka,' Frances asked, 'do you have any grand plans for the shop next year?'

And Radka described the things she would like to do, and Gwen offered advice, and Sally suggested how that could work together with the school, and Alice said she'd be happy to join in.

Under the table, Luke took her hand again. She could begin to see how this was done.

She squeezed back.

Acknowledgements

For help with the world of academia, my enormous thanks to Dr Charlotte Riley and Jessie Price, and for Operation Overlord and history pointers, Sarah Knowlden. For coast-guarding information, I am very grateful to Marc Thomas at the Falmouth Maritime & Coastguard agency. Any playing fast and loose with facts is my fault, not theirs.

Boundless gratitude to Hannah Duncan for her infinite patience, reading, thoughts, and time, and to the Great Gardens of Cornwall for existing. Finally, thank you to the Society of Authors and their grants, without which I would have been unable to work on this book.